BLAST FROM THE PAST

Lindsey handed Thomas a three-by-five black and white print. It showed three Mayans in robes, laughing and smoking dark conical cigars. They were Lacondones, from Nahá. A fourth man, with equally long hair and the same kind of cotton robe, looked like he was trying to get out of the picture.

The fourth man was his brother Eddie.

"Where did you get the picture?" Thomas asked.

"A kid reporter named Carmichael took it. He's trying to get an interview with the rebels for *Rolling Stone*. His editor knew Eddie in the seventies and recognized him."

"So now what happens?"

"So now I go up there and look for him. What else?" Thomas shrugged.

"What's wrong with you?" Lindsey said. "Eddie's your *brother* for Christ's sake! Don't you care?"

"I care," Thomas said. "Maybe I care more than you do. I care enough to leave him the hell alone if he wants. This entire country is coming down around our ears. Those mountains are full of rebels and the guardia is going nuts trying to find them. If you get caught up in that, you're going to need somebody to rescue *you*."

"That's why I want you to come with me."

Bantam Spectra Books
Ask your bookseller for the titles you have missed

Deserted Cities of the Heart

LEWIS SHINER

BANTAM BOOKS

TORONTO • NEW YORK • LONDON • SYDNEY • AUCKLAND

Portions of this book have been previously published in substantially different
form, as follows: "Americans" in *The Fiction Magazine* (U.K.), "Rebels" and
"Deserted Cities of the Heart" in *Omni*, and "Cabracan" in *Isaac Asimov's Science Fiction Magazine*.

The designs on the title page and part titles are from a clay stamp found in
Texcoco, Mexico. It represents flowers. From *Design Motifs of Ancient Mexico*,
published by Dover Publications. © 1947 by Jorge Enciso, © 1953 by Dover
Publications, Inc.

This edition contains the complete text
of the original hardcover edition.
NOT ONE WORD HAS BEEN OMITTED.

DESERTED CITIES OF THE HEART

A BANTAM SPECTRA BOOK / PUBLISHED BY ARRANGEMENT WITH
DOUBLEDAY

PRINTING HISTORY
Doubleday edition published August 1988
Bantam edition / March 1989

Bantam Books are published by Bantam Books, a division of Bantam Doubleday
Dell Publishing Group, Inc. Its trademark, consisting of the words "Bantam
Books" and the portrayal of a rooster, is Registered in U.S. Patent and
Trademark Office and in other countries. Marca Registrada. Bantam Books, 666
Fifth Avenue, New York, New York 10103.

PRINTED IN THE UNITED STATES OF AMERICA

KR   0 9 8 7 6 5 4 3 2 1

For Neal Barrett, Jr.,
friend and guru

MY THANKS to the following: to my father, Joel L. Shiner, for advice and Mayan materials; to Ed Jones of Austin Helicopter Training for the flying lesson, the tour of the UH-1, and the benefit of his materials and experience; to my agent, Martha Millard, and my editor, Shawna McCarthy, who believed in this book from the beginning; and to the many others who contributed ideas and encouragement, including Ellen Datlow, Gardner Dozois, Pat Murphy, Chris Priest, Rick Shannon, Edith Shiner, Bud Simons, and Bruce and Nancy Sterling.

MANY OF THE EVENTS in this novel are factual—the Mexico City earthquake, the border riots of 1986, the looting of the forest at Nahá, and so on. In some cases, for dramatic purposes, the dates of these events and even their locations have been changed.

ONE

SUDDENLY THE PATH opened up and Carmichael walked out of the jungle. The perpetual green twilight turned into bright afternoon. The ragged kid who'd been guiding him got excited and ran on ahead, leaving Carmichael to stand blinking at the edge of the rebel camp. He waved at the cloud of white flies around his head and tried to look harmless.

They didn't seem to be expecting him. A teenager in orange pants and a plaid shirt was pissing against a tree. When he saw Carmichael he zipped himself up and made nervous little half-bows, grinning in embarrassment. Somebody else slapped at a jam box and cut off a scratchy, distorted dub tape in mid-echo.

The silence made the others turn and look. Carmichael smiled and held his hands away from his sides. *"Periodista,"* he said. For Christ's sake don't shoot, I might be the New York *Times.*

From where he was he could see maybe thirty or forty guerrillas. Most of them wore a uniform of blue jeans and a khaki shirt. There were a lot of straw cowboy hats and billed caps. A few of them had leather lace-up combat boots, a lot more had Converse All-Stars or Nikes. The rest got by with rubber beach sandals or bare feet.

The clearing was a chaos of green canvas tents, sleeping bags, yellow army blankets thrown over poles, and tin cans. The cans were stacked empty around the tents or filled with water or beans or corn soaking for supper. A collie with matted yellow fur and a cut over one eye came up to sniff his ankles.

"Carla said she would do an interview," he told them. His Spanish wasn't great, strictly California high school, but he'd been in Mexico over a month now and he knew they could understand him if they wanted. A woman in a striped shift stared at him from the shade of a tree, both straps of the dress down, a baby at each breast. Finally a middle-aged guy in a flat Fidelista cap and graying beard took a couple of steps toward him.

"Cómo te llamas?"

"Carmichael. John Carmichael. I work for *Rolling Stone.* The magazine." He took a card out of the front pocket of his hiking shorts.

"I know of them."

"Listen, Carla sent word she'd talk to me. She sent a *correo.*" He looked around for the kid but there was no sign of him. The kid was a case. He'd seen his mother raped by the *guardia* a few months back. At least that was how Carmichael read it. The kid was only eight and didn't really understand what was going on. But they killed her when they were done and now all the kid wanted was to be old enough that they'd let him have a rifle. Which would be another year or maybe less, depending on how desperate they got.

The man chewed on the inside of his cheek for a couple of seconds. He didn't seem so much reluctant as nervous. He had a hunted kind of look about him that was making Carmichael nervous, too. "Okay, I'll talk to her. My name is Faustino."

Carmichael shook hands with him, fingers up, movement style. *"Cubano?"* he asked.

Faustino thought again. "Yes," he said finally.

Carmichael nodded to show it was okay with him. Maybe it was a test. The rebels liked to pretend there weren't any Cubans or Nicaraguans in Mexico, but then

Reagan liked to pretend there weren't any U.S. troops here either.

Carmichael just wanted the interview. He hadn't believed he would really get this far, and now if it went sour it was going to break his heart.

"Come with me," Faustino said. They walked uphill around the edge of the clearing. Through a stand of trees Carmichael watched an instructor in jeans and khaki with six teenage girls. The instructor was trying to get them to run up to a line, drop prone, and fire. They had to pantomime the rifles and they kept giggling.

Faustino took him to the top of the hill and Carmichael could see the next valley and the mountains to the south, just over the border into Guatemala. The mountains were the violet-brown of old, faded photographs, the color of unreal, untouchable things. It was almost noon but there were shreds of cloud still trailing off the highest peaks.

"Beautiful, no?" Faustino said.

Carmichael nodded. He wanted to take a picture but it was too early to risk pulling out a camera. Later, maybe, if Carla was willing.

Carla sat by herself a few yards away, reading. Carmichael recognized her from the few pictures that had found their way to the States. She was short, a little heavy and round-faced by Hollywood standards, but not unattractive. She had the long nose and high forehead and reddish skin of Mayan ancestry. He squinted and made out that she was reading ex-president Portillo's novel *Quetzalcoatl.*

"Wait here," Faustino said, and went over to her. Carmichael couldn't hear what they said. Faustino gave her the card and she stood up and dusted off the seat of her jeans. Then they both looked up to check the sky and Carmichael's nervousness came back.

They shook hands and Carmichael introduced himself again. "I don't understand," she said. "You are with a rock and roll band?"

"A magazine," Faustino said. "Very prominent. They have it in all the supermarkets in the United States."

"Is this what is to become of the revolution? We are to be sold in the supermarkets?"

Apparently Faustino couldn't tell she was kidding. Before he could break in again Carmichael said, *"Rolling Stone* sells only the finest revolutions. Nicaraguan, South African, Argentinian . . ."

"You did an article on my husband," she said. At least she wasn't frowning anymore.

"That wasn't me personally, but yes, we did." Her husband, Acuario, had been murdered in Mexico City back in December, during a kind of rebel summit conference. She'd taken over his guerrilla band in the wave of outrage that followed.

Carmichael took off his backpack and got out a cassette recorder. "I was afraid I was going to be too late. There's been nothing on the radio for days but reports of you being killed."

"No," she said gently. "You're still in time. Can we sit down? This is going to be painful enough."

She was a great interview. Carmichael wanted to hug her. During the bus rides and the long walk that brought him up here, he had held on to an image of the story in his mind. Not just the printed article, a headline bled across a two-page spread, the photos here, lots of white space. The story itself. It would explain not only what was happening in Mexico, but the rest of the world too, would make sense of the entire decade. Mexico as microcosm for the struggle of third-world visionaries against an outmoded industrial system. They couldn't lose. As she talked it filled out in his mind, perfect, spherical.

Faustino handled the party line in his crisp, Cuban Spanish that was as easy to understand as English. Comrades in a common struggle, destiny of Latin America, that kind of thing.

Carla wanted to kick ass. Carmichael had to keep stopping her, getting her to repeat a word or phrase that got past him. She spoke Veracruzano, the Mexican equivalent of a Southern accent, slurred and full of Caribbean slang.

She'd grown up in the village of Boca del Río, just south of Veracruz, where the water in the bay had a permanent oily sheen. By the time school got interesting she had to drop out, going to the fish market in the city with her father, waiting outside the pool hall across the street where he pissed away what little they'd made that morning.

Sometimes she would wander over to *las portales,* the rows of open cafes on the Plaza de Armas where the tourists from the U.S. and Germany and Mexico City sat and drank beer and watched the marimba trios, one man on each end of the wooden xylophone, the third with his fish-shaped *guiro* and book of songs and prices, all of them in their white or yellow or pale blue guayabera shirts, two or three songs and then down to the next cafe, the tourists pale and drunken and talking loudly to each other in languages she never wanted to learn.

Acuario was a medical student at the Universidad Veracruzana. He drank at las portales too, but he did it to observe the enemy. Acuario was in a study group with a priest named Father Antonio who had introduced him to both Teilhard de Chardin and Karl Marx. Once he started talking to Carla he saw it as his sacred duty to raise her consciousness.

He explained to her why she instinctively hated the Northamericans, taught her Marxism-Leninism, and, Carmichael gathered, screwed her brains out in a ninety-peso room in the Hotel Santillana across from the fish market.

When Acuario got kicked out of college he took Carla on the road with him. For a while the action was in Villahermosa, trying to run off the gringo oil companies. Then one of Acuario's med school friends shot a cop with a stolen handgun and they had to move up into the hills.

Carmichael really liked her. He could see Acuario's clay feet between the lines of her story, but Carla herself seemed like the real thing. A working class hero, a perennial victim, and best of all a crackpot idealist.

"Acuario believed all that hippie stuff," she said. "You know? That we are the start of a new age. A turning point, and all that. He wanted a new world where everybody could have enough to eat and clothes to wear and schools to go to and everybody could believe whatever they wanted. He was a lot better than me. I just grew up poor and mean, watching politicians getting fat off people like my father and me. I just wanted to shoot somebody. But Acuario, when he talked about all this stuff, he made me believe it too."

"That's great," Carmichael said. "What about pictures? Can I take your picture?"

"I don't know," she said. "I'm no Somoza, I don't want my picture all over the place. I don't want a personality cult. What do you think, Faustino?"

Faustino shrugged. "I don't think it would hurt. Let the Northamericans see us as we are, simple people caught up in a great struggle."

"Okay, but ask everybody before you take their picture. Some of them have families, where the guardia can get to them, you understand?"

"Sure, that's great," Carmichael said. He got the Nikon out of the backpack and posed her with the purple mountains behind her.

He got a great shot of the correo, the messenger kid who'd brought him up. The kid said Carmichael should call him El Tigre, the jaguar. They all had this passion for the nom de guerre, that affordable little touch of glamor. Somebody loaned the kid an M16 for the picture and just before Carmichael pushed the button he puffed up his chest and scowled. The Nikon was motor-driven, so Carmichael also got him cracking up afterward.

There was a teenaged kid who called himself Rigoberto after the guy that killed Tacho Samoza, Sr. He had a paper bag full of Pepsi bottles that he took with him everywhere, hoping to find enough gasoline to make Molotov cocktails.

There was a woman in her mid-thirties that they called La Pequeña, the Little One. She was short and thin, but

Carmichael sensed a certain irony in the name. She'd gotten married in high school and she had dry, cracked hands from her years at the sink. When her husband didn't come home from work one day she started asking questions. She kept asking them for two years, all the way to President de la Madrid. "The next time I see him," she told Carmichael, "I will have this." She pointed to the rifle she was cleaning, the parts spread out over a black plastic bag.

There was a kid in his twenties with a lot of African blood in him. He had deep brown skin and peppercorn hair that he was trying to tease into dreadlocks. They called him Righteous. He was the one with the jam box and the dub tape. His Veracruzano was impenetrable and Carmichael could only smile and nod and take his picture and move on.

There was a sixty-eight-year-old man with little islands of whiskers on his wrinkled face. They called him Abuelo, Grandfather. He'd joined after his granddaughter was murdered by the Army.

"How old was she?" Carmichael asked. He had the recorder going again.

"Seventeen. Now what happens to her children? Three girls and two boys, and now they have no mother?"

Carmichael nodded, thinking, Jesus Christ. Five kids at seventeen. Just when he thought he had a handle something else came along and slapped him in the face. It was the kind of thing that went beyond political solutions. What were you going to do when there were seventeen-year-olds all over the country with five kids? How were you going to feed them all? Where were you going to put them?

Easy, he thought. Have a war and kill them all off.

Two men came running out of the jungle. They had three or four rifles apiece slung over their shoulders and they carried a bundled army blanket between them like a stretcher. They spread the blanket out in the middle of the camp. Inside were another half dozen rifles and zip-lock bags full of bullets.

The rifles were Belgian-made FALs. They were clean

and efficient-looking, with flared pistol grips and short,
straight magazines just in front of the trigger guard. On
full automatic they could put out about ten rounds a
second. Carmichael had spent a couple of days in the
library back in L.A. just reading up on weapons, from
small arms to the Mi-24 Hind helicopter gunships. Supposedly Castro inherited thousands of FALs from Batista
in 1959. Then he started getting Kalishnikovs from Rus-
sia and didn't need them anymore. They tended to show
up all over Latin America, wherever there was trouble.

It was like Christmas. Carmichael took a couple of
quick pictures and then got out of the way as the whole
camp converged on the guns. A short, heavyset man
pushed his way through the crowd and started calling the
names of the chosen. He did it from memory.

"Who is that?" Carmichael asked the old man.

"Lieutenant Ramos."

"Yeah? Who's he?"

The old man stared off at the mountains for a while.
"He's from Mexico." Meaning Mexico City. "He's with
the FPML. *'Enlace' con este Raul Venceremos.'"* Liaison.
The old man sneered when he said it. The FPML, the
Popular Front for a Free Mexico, was the most vocal of
the dozen or more rebel groups. Their leader called himself Raul Venceremos. The last name meant "we shall be
victorious." It was something Ché used to say a lot.
Venceremos had brought his love of uniforms with him
when he defected from the guardia.

"There is a radio station," the old man said. "Radio
Venceremos."

"Sí," Carmichael nodded. *"Lo conozco."* It was still the
only reliable information anybody could get out of El
Salvador.

The old man shrugged. "He calls himself for a radio
station. What kind of man is that?"

"Abuelo!" Ramos shouted.

"Excuse me."

Carmichael watched the old man trade a single-shot
.22 for an FAL so new the barrel was still sticky with oil.
When he came back he was smiling wide enough that

Carmichael could see all five of his teeth. "Here is my 'liaison.'" The old man shook the rifle happily.

When the FALs were gone Ramos handed out the trade-ins. The kid in the orange pants got the old man's .22. The barrel was held on with silver duct tape, but the kid strutted up proudly to take it. A gun, any gun, was what made you a real soldier.

Carmichael shot another roll of film and went to tell Carla goodbye. He shook her hand and said, "I need to get back with the story." If he hurried, he could make it back to the farm where he and El Tigre had spent the night before. He didn't want to get caught in the jungle after dark.

"I understand," Carla said. She was restless again, and Carmichael could tell she was just as happy to see him go. "We want to get the revolution into all the supermarkets while it's still fresh. I'll send a correo with you."

"You don't have to," Carmichael said. "I'll be okay."

He waved from the edge of the camp and Carla and the old man and some of the others waved back. Faustino stood with his arms folded, like he was posing for a memorial statue in downtown Havana.

About ten minutes out of camp Carmichael couldn't stand it anymore and sat down to take some notes. There was a fine, rapid trembling in his hands. He dug a joint out of his backpack and lit up. With the joint hanging out of the corner of his mouth he covered three pages of yellow legal paper with rough impressions.

"Goddamn," he said. It was good stuff. It was career stuff. It was the kind of stuff that got picked up by AP and UPI and the goddamn New York *Times*. When he got back to Villahermosa he was going to buy himself a couple of drinks.

He didn't hear the planes until they were right overhead.

They filled a whole spectrum of sound, from the high whine of their turbines to the roar of their exhaust, the rattling of machine guns somewhere in the middle of it.

The sound came in waves, pounding at him until it made his ears ring. Orange tracers cut dotted lines from the sky to the rebel camp.

Between the joint and the suddenness of it his brain had fogged. It took long seconds for the message to get through. The planes were attacking Carla's army.

He jumped up and looked around frantically. A ragged white contrail blossomed out of one of the planes. There was a flash on the horizon and a couple of seconds later the ground shook. Finally the sound got to him, a long, shrill scream and then thunder.

Carmichael's best guess was four planes. They moved in spurts across the sky, like toys in the hands of a giant, invisible child, and it was hard to focus on them. He knew what they were, though, Italian SF-260 "Warriors." The Mexican government had bought a dozen of them with borrowed U.S. money specifically to use against the guerrillas.

The ground shook and Carmichael realized he was still standing, exposed, in the middle of the trail. He ducked into the forest, unable to hear the crashing of leaves and branches for the noise of the planes. He huddled behind something that looked like an oak just as a squad of rebels came running down the trail, their faces vacant with terror.

Somebody screamed. A bullet hit just over Carmichael's head, spattering him with bark. The exposed white flesh of the tree was a ragged arrow, pointing at him. Tracers lit the forest like demonic fireflies. He had never realized how powerful a .50-caliber bullet was. They were like small meteors. The ground exploded where they hit.

He curled into a ball against the tree trunk, knees bumping his forehead, staring upside down at the shower of twigs and leaves sifting slowly out of the trees. The dope or the fear turned a switch in his head and time went out of whack.

The bullets fell around him like slow metal rain. The air turned milky white. A thick fog of dust and humus and wood chips and green, shredded leaves hung motionless around him. The planes and the gunfire had all tangled together and sounded like a waterfall.

Then the bullets turned to water and ran down his back and pooled in his hair.

He sat up. The planes were gone and the pattering in the trees was rain. His legal pad was in one hand, his knapsack in the other. He put the pad away and scrambled to his feet, his bladder suddenly aching so badly that he didn't care if the planes were coming back.

He had to go back to the clearing. There wasn't really any choice. The story had changed under him and he had to see it through.

At first he didn't think anybody was left alive. The ground smoked from WPs, white phosphorus rockets, and the trees were shattered and blackened. The rain turned to steam on the bodies, and the steam had the sharp, acetic-acid smell of Carmichael's darkroom back in L.A., but mixed with the smells of cordite and burned meat and wet ash.

He didn't realize how lightheaded he was until he staggered and nearly went down. He grabbed at a tree and the bark was still hot to the touch. He breathed through his mouth and swallowed the bile that was trying to come up and got out his camera. His fingers were so stiff it took him two minutes to load a fresh roll of film.

He started taking pictures. Most of it was too ugly to be printed, limbs without bodies, jeans soaked purple with blood, faces burnt through to the skull. He shot some of the burns because he knew the government was going to deny using phosphorus and he wanted proof.

He got long shots without a lot of gruesome detail. Then he started on the faces, getting the ones that were relatively intact. He was looking for Carla or Faustino and instead he found Abuelo, the old man. He focused and was about to trip the shutter when the old man opened one eye.

Carmichael lowered the camera. The old man was gutshot. There was blood everywhere. His skin had the same dark, waxy look the corpses had. The rain ran like tears off his face. The two of them stared at each other for about ten years, and then the old man shut his eye again.

Carmichael put the camera away. Somebody started moaning and then the moan turned into a scream. An entire stack of bodies twitched and shook.

I'm in hell, Carmichael thought. One of those bullets hit me and I didn't even know it, and now I'm dead and in hell.

Something crawled out from under the moving stack of bodies. It was Carla. The bodies on top of her had saved her from the rockets, but she'd been shot up pretty badly. Her left foot was such a bloody mess that it hurt Carmichael to look at it. How much of the rest of the blood was actually hers he couldn't say.

He took her under the arms and pulled her free. It couldn't do her any more harm than she was already doing by struggling. She went limp in his hands and he stretched her out on some scraps of tent canvas.

"You came back."

Carmichael stood up too fast and nearly passed out again. Faustino was staring at him, pale and shaking, holding himself up by the barrel of his rifle.

"Yeah," Carmichael said. "Are you all right?"

"Some scratches," Faustino said. The right hip of his jeans was charred through and his shirt was in rags. He was losing his hair, Carmichael noticed. It made him look less intimidating, now that his cap was gone. He knelt next to Carla and started doing professional-looking things, rolling back one eyelid, taking the pulse in her neck.

"Did anybody else make it?" Carmichael asked.

"Some ran away in the forest. We have a rendezvous, in case of something like this. I'll find them tonight." He sat up on his heels. "We have to get her out of here. There is a doctor in Usumacinta who is with us. You have to help me carry her there."

"Me?" Carmichael said.

The rain trailed off while they improvised a stretcher out of one of the cots. Carmichael wanted to look away while Faustino cut off Carla's jeans and shirt but he couldn't seem to do it. She wore stained cotton panties and a heavy-duty 1950s-style brassiere. There were bullet holes in her right arm and her left foot and thigh. Faustino rinsed them and squirted in some Betadine and wrapped them in bandages.

There were three others still alive, but none of them could walk. Faustino gave them morphine. "I'll call the Red Cross when we get to Usumacinta," he said. "Maybe they'll get here before the guardia."

Faustino cached most of the undamaged weapons in a tree well away from the clearing. He slung three FALs on his back and filled a knapsack with cartridges. Carmichael saw him wince when the butt of one of the rifles touched his hip.

"Unless you want to carry one . . . ?" Faustino offered.

Carmichael shook his head.

All the way down the mountain Carmichael asked himself what the hell he was doing. He wanted to believe it was for the story. His nice, spherical, perfect story that had suddenly exploded over the countryside. If he stayed with Carla maybe he could make sense of it again.

The truth, he suspected, was that he really hadn't had a choice. There was simply no way to walk away from Faustino and still be able to feel like a human being.

By the time the sun went down he was beyond thinking about anything. He couldn't see and he kept stumbling over rocks and branches in the trail. But none of it bothered Faustino, who kept leading him on by the stretcher handles.

They took a rest break a little after dark. Carmichael got two bags of trail mix out of his pack and gave one to Faustino.

"What is this?"

"Dried fruit and nuts. It's good."

In a few seconds the bag came back. "Animal food," Faustino said.

Animal? Carmichael thought. Who the fuck are *you* to

call me an animal? He felt his face getting hot. He would have shouted at Faustino but he didn't have the energy.

Carla started to make noises. Her head was right next to where Carmichael sat. "Oil them," she was saying. "Keep them oiled. You have to . . ." Carmichael brushed the hair off her forehead, working by touch in the darkness. He couldn't see her eyes until she opened them and they glistened faintly.

"Planes . . . ?" she said.

"Gone," Carmichael told her.

"How many . . . left . . . ?"

"We don't know yet. Faustino's here. Go back to sleep."

Her breathing changed and her eyes disappeared again. Carmichael said, "Is there any morphine?"

"No," Faustino said.

"Looked like moonlight," Carla said. "After the bullets hit."

"Don't talk," Faustino told her.

"Saw men in the jungle. Mayas. Three of them, looking at me. Only the one in the middle wasn't Maya. He was Northamerican. Kukulcán. It was Kukulcán. They were burning something in a pot, something sour-smelling. They had feathers, green feathers, in their hair . . ."

Right, Carmichael thought. Kukulcán was the Mayan name for Quetzalcoatl, the great white god. He had news for her. There weren't any more great white gods. They wouldn't be coming to save her, not this year, not this century.

"I was there," Faustino said. "There weren't any Indians. It was a dream. Some kind of vision or something." Carla didn't answer. "She's asleep," Faustino said finally.

Carmichael said, "I think she's dying."

"She's not dying. She meets with Raul Venceremos next week. She will not die."

Carmichael nodded, then realized Faustino couldn't see him. "Okay," he said. The trail mix had helped the pain in his stomach, but not the ones in his shoulders and neck. His feet were swollen tight against the sides of his boots and his bare legs and arms itched with mosquito bites. Faustino gave him a drink of water and he felt better for a few seconds. Then he remembered the water would probably give him dysentery and he felt very tired.

"Come on," Faustino said, and he bent to pick up his end of the stretcher.

At the bottom of the hill lights came out of nowhere and pinned them where they stood. "Please," Carmichael said, squinting. He couldn't cover his face without letting go of the stretcher. "Don't shoot." He couldn't believe he'd come this far, survived so much, only to die this way. "I'm an American."

"Somos todos Americanos," a voice said.

"Northamerican," Carmichael corrected himself. "Journalist."

"Cálmate," Faustino said. "They are *compas, compañeros,* you understand? They are with us."

"Oh." Somebody took the end of the stretcher out of his hands and his arms cramped immediately, snapping the lines of pain all the way back to his shoulder blades.

"They will find you a place to sleep," Faustino said. There was an awkward silence. "We are grateful for your help."

"It was nothing," Carmichael said.

"This is true," Faustino said. "But if you had not helped, it would have been less than nothing."

A kid led him to a shack on the edge of town. It could have been El Tigre but he never said anything and it was too dark and Carmichael was too tired to be sure.

They gave him a hammock. He was pretty sure somebody would be sleeping on the floor so he could use it. At the moment he didn't care.

He woke up once in the middle of the night, sure he'd just heard a gunshot. He listened but there was only the sound of a stranger's snoring from across the room.

Not for you, he told himself. It may have been for somebody, but it wasn't for you.

GUNFIRE AGAIN. Thomas' office was in the back of the old hotel complex, a good half mile from the street, and the rifles sounded like firecrackers. It was the third time this week the guardia had opened up on demonstrators. They were nothing but warning shots so far, but the thought of it still made Thomas a little sick. Two days ago one of the kids, running away, had tried to climb the project fence and gotten hung up in the barbed wire on top.

His concentration was gone. He rolled his chair away from the computer and picked up the letter again. It was on lined notebook paper and it said, "Coming to look for you. Where are you hiding out? Love, Lindsey." The envelope had been addressed to him care of the Anthro Department at UT Austin, Please Forward. It had arrived with the morning mail. He put it back in the envelope and put the envelope in his shirt pocket.

The shooting stopped and now there was another noise, a roar that kept climbing and dropping in pitch. Heavy machinery.

Oh Christ, Thomas thought. A tank.

His intercom hummed. "Wake up, Thomas," Sarah said. "The sixties are over. Big Brother is here. They're coming in."

"What the hell are we supposed to do?"

"I don't know about you, but I'm going to lie down behind my desk and chant some mantras."

Sarah was overweight and pushing fifty. "That's really funny," Thomas said.

"I wasn't kidding. Look, don't do anything stupid, okay? It looks like the entire Mexican National Guard out there. They *will* kill you, okay?"

Thomas kicked the screen out of his window and crawled outside, holding on to his glasses with one hand. Straight ahead was the crumbling orchestra pavilion, its wall of solar cells glistening in the afternoon sunlight. The smell of manure and damp earth drifted off the gardens in front of it. To his left, running for hundreds of yards back along the hillside, were experimental permiculture and agriculture plots, animal compounds, ponds, and stables.

To his right were the front gates and the guardia.

Thomas watched the tank come right over the fence. It had been a hell of a fence, eight feet high and topped with barbed wire, cutting them off from the hungry and the poor and the desperate. Now the poles snapped like toothpicks and metal treads ground the chain links into the lawn.

The tank crawled past the ruins of the casino and parked up against the fountain. The casino had been the social center of Cuernavaca back in the twenties and thirties, when this was still the Hotel Casino de la Selva. The project had put a geodesic dome over it, made out of aluminum framework and triangular insulating plastic pillows. Next to it the tank looked like a bloody-jawed Tyrannosaur.

Thomas estimated fifty soldiers. They would outnumber the project staff two to one. He sprinted around the back of the main building, toward the swimming pool. The humidity glued his shirt to his back and bunched up his underwear between his legs. Beyond the dark, algal green of the swimming pool were the jai alai courts. The perpetually stoned Texas A&M botanists had lost them to a new gene-spliced kudzu a year ago and been fighting to get them back ever since.

"Thomas!" It was one of the summer kids, out in the middle of the enormous pool on one of the ocean arks. He had his shirt open and was leaning off the boom. "What the hell is going on?"

"We're busted," Thomas yelled. "Head for the fucking hills."

Between the pool and the back guest houses was a stretch of imported sand, with umbrellas and folding beach chairs. Weeds were slowly taking over, but the footing was still bad. Before Thomas could get across it

he heard the slap of running feet on concrete and the
unmistakable rattle that rifles make when they get lifted
to the shoulder and cocked.

"Alto!"

Thomas stopped and slowly put up his arms.

The soldiers took him into the mural room. Most of
the others were already milling around in the middle of
the floor, dwarfed by the fifty-foot ceilings and the alle-
gorical figures on the walls. The project had been using it
for their main dining room. The soldiers had pushed the
tables and chairs off to one side so they could herd everyone together. Every so often the doors would open and
another two or three people would straggle in from the
backwoods, soldiers behind them to shove them if they
slowed down.

Thomas found Judy Shapiro, the project director. She
and Bill Geisler were the center of attention, but they
didn't have any answers either. Geisler was Shapiro's
roommate and lover. He was also the only person on the
project who didn't seem to know about her penchant for
graduate students of either sex, the younger the better.

They were both in their early thirties, five years
younger than Thomas, both veterans of the New Alchemy Institute on Cape Cod and the Lindisfarne Ham-
let in Colorado. They were sunburned, earnest, and wore
odd clothes. Geisler was project secretary, which meant
he greased palms and got permits and generally tried to
maintain Shapiro's supply lines to reality.

Thomas had his own title. He was project anthropologist. It didn't mean much, except that Margaret Mead
used to hang out at New Alchemy so Shapiro had wanted
an anthropologist of her own. He was supposed to pro-
vide expertise on native shelters. The fact that he could
fly a helicopter and save them having to hire an outside
pilot was also a consideration. In practice, when he
wasn't doing the shitwork that was expected of all of
them, he had plenty of computer time to work on whatever he wanted.

That being the application of Ilya Prigogine's dissipative structures to the Mayan collapse, circa 900 A.D. He'd run out of funding at UT, the project had made him an offer, and now he'd been here two years and there was a tank in the yard.

"I don't suppose *you* know anything," Shapiro asked Thomas. He shook his head. "Stay close. We have to put up a united front on this thing."

Thomas wandered off, found a chair, and sat down. A guardia officer came in and stood for a while with his hands behind his back. He was bareheaded and his uniform hung loosely off his shoulders. He looked about sixty. His hair was dark black, a stigma of Indian blood. He was a captain and Thomas suspected he wouldn't go much further. European ancestry was still the thing in Mexico. Thomas had seen him out here before, asking questions, pounding his fist into his left hand. His name was Espinosa.

"This is everyone?" he asked. Sarah, out of breath, came over to stand next to Thomas' chair. Everybody else got more or less into a line facing Espinosa.

"I thought you were cowering behind your desk," Thomas said.

"They dragged me out," she said. "The fascists."

Espinosa walked slowly down the line. He pointed to Shapiro and Geisler and finally to Thomas. "You three will stay here." His English was accented but plain enough. "The rest of you will go back to the United States, to your homes and families. You will be searched and your belongings will be searched but you will not be harmed. We will bring a bus to take you back to Mexico City where you will take an airplane."

"Why you?" Sarah asked.

"Seniority, I guess." Shapiro and Geisler had been here three years, since the beginning. Outside of Thomas and the clerical staff, like Sarah, everybody else was pretty recent.

Thomas stood up and Sarah put her arms around him. She was crying. "I don't want to go," she said. "There's going to be concrete everywhere and chlorine in the water. The food's going to taste wrong and I'll get cancer."

"It's just temporary. Got to be. We'll get this straightened out and send for everybody again."

"Goddammit, Thomas, don't patronize me. It's over. The world's not ready for us, and so they're going to destroy us."

"Sarah . . ."

"G'bye, Thomas," she said, backing away. "Peace, love, and all that maudlin crap." She wiggled her fingers at him, and then turned and let one of the soldiers lead her out.

It took half an hour to get the room cleared. Thomas was amazed to see how hard some of them fought to stay. Who was going to take care of the compost, who was going to check the pH in the fish tanks? What about aphids, what about nitrogen shortfalls?

One of the grad students, a thin girl from UCLA, tried to get loose. Espinosa signaled to one of his men, who slapped her hard across the face, jerked her arms behind her back, and marched her out.

Espinosa kept three soldiers behind with him. They were just kids, Thomas thought. The older ones would be fighting in the eastern jungles or the streets of Juárez and Zihuatenejo.

"I want you to show me the weapons," Espinosa said.

Shapiro let out a theatrical sigh. "Is that all? The weapons business again? We haven't got any. How many times do we have to tell you?"

"It is known that you are supporting the rebels. We know this, you see. The rebels line up outside the gate. We don't look for the guns or the mortars. We look for the nerve gas. The virus."

"For God's sake," Shapiro said. "Those kids outside were protesters. They want us out of here as much as you do. In *spite* of the fact that your government asked us here in the first place."

"I am not playing with games, here," Espinosa said. "The rebels must be stopped. They are fighting against legal elected candidates. They are breaking the law."

It was a bad year for the Institutional Revolution. The

PRI had been continuously in power now since 1946, and counting a few name changes they went all the way back to 1929. Parties didn't last that long by losing elections. Sometimes they just had to keep recounting the votes until they came out the way they were supposed to.

The PRI had tried that in Zihuatenejo and Juárez after the July 6th elections and people had started turning over cars and lighting matches. Half of Zihua had burned to the ground before the guardia shot enough people to quiet things down. There were still crowds of people holding the main bridge between Juárez and El Paso.

"Okay, we hear you making all the right noises," Shapiro said. "What is it you want? *La mordida?*"

Thomas flinched. There was plenty of corruption in Mexico, but a certain style was expected. One didn't haggle over bribes in public.

"No, lady, I don't want you money. I want to see the things you have keep hidden from me. Everything, you understand? Everything."

A couple dozen of the soldiers searched the staff cottages. Thomas could hear drawers slamming and furniture being pushed around. They even dragged a couple of mattresses out onto the lawn and ripped them up with bayonets to make their position clear.

Thomas felt sorry for Espinosa. What was the old man supposed to make of windmills that looked like toy rocket ships on top of miniature oil rigs? Five- and six-foot-high columnar fish tanks with giant water lillies floating on top? The glass walls and aquaria on the south sides of all the bungalows?

The worst was the solar wall, troughs of hyacinths inside a long, louvered greenhouse. It ran straight out from the main building to the fountain where the guardia had parked their tank. The project's sewage ran through the troughs to get rid of organics, then out to the fountain and a series of sand filters to clean and aerate it. But the greenhouse itself stank of shit.

Espinosa hesitated at the door, wrinkling his face.

"I'm with you," Thomas said. "But these folks don't

seem to mind the smell of their own shit. All part of living in harmony with the planet."

"Fuck you, Thomas," Shapiro said.

" 'These people?' " Espinosa said. "Are you not one of them?"

"That's something Thomas was never good at," Shapiro said. "Making up his mind. Committing himself."

"Could we maybe have a little less dissension in the ranks?" Geisler asked.

"I want to see inside," Espinosa said.

"What in hell for?" Shapiro asked.

"What better place to hide weapons?"

"Oh Christ. Go ahead. Make yourself at home."

"You," Espinosa said, looking at Thomas. "You come with."

They went in. Thomas breathed through his mouth. He felt like he was getting shit on his tongue and gums. Espinosa made out that it didn't bother him, poking at the rubbery plants, bending over to check the bracing under the troughs.

"There aren't any weapons," Thomas said. His glasses had misted from the humidity and he wiped them on his shirttail.

"I want to believe you," Espinosa said. He rolled up one sleeve and felt around in the murky water. "Maybe I do believe you. But I don't trust you." There was a certain dry humor in the slant of his eyebrows. "You understand?"

"Los requisitos," Thomas said. Formalities.

"Claro que sí." Espinosa dried his arm thoroughly with a handkerchief and then dropped the handkerchief on the floor. It was like they had sealed some kind of bargain, though Thomas wasn't sure what it involved.

They went back outside. A soldier came running up with a three-foot marijuana plant, dirt still crumbling off its roots. *"Mira, Capitán! Marijuana!"*

"It's not ours," Shapiro said. "Goddammit, I told everybody no dope!" Thomas found her histrionics nearly convincing.

Espinosa told the soldier in Spanish, "Go talk to the

sergeant. See if he's found any drugs in the rooms." Then he looked at Shapiro. "You could go to jail for this, all of you. Smuggling the drugs and helping the rebels."

"I already told you—"

Geisler put a hand on her arm. "Judy, take it easy . . ."

Espinosa wasn't bluffing. The plant was more than enough to get them into jail. And if their paperwork got lost and they spent months or years there, even died there, well, it had happened before.

Thomas' skin felt clammy. "Look," he said. "We're trying to cooperate. We didn't know about the marijuana." He was lying, of course. The A&M gang was famous for their killer hybrid pot. If Espinosa tried to burn the plants he would stone all of Cuernavaca.

"Sargento!" Espinosa shouted. The sergeant came running back, knees high, British army style. "Lock them up," he said in English, then repeated it in Spanish.

The sergeant looked confused. "Where, sir?" he asked in Spanish. "Everything is glass."

"Think of something," Espinosa said.

The sergeant shut them in the kitchen and posted guards at the doors. "It was time for supper anyway," Thomas said. He made himself an avocado sandwich and sat down at the long, grease-soaked table.

Shapiro ranted for ten or fifteen minutes about how none of this could be happening. Finally she got hungry too and Thomas made some more sandwiches.

Thomas hadn't worn a watch in over a year, but he was sensitive to the cycles of daylight. Close to sunset the goats and chickens and parrots got restless and let out more than their usual amount of noise. He made it to be about eight o'clock when they heard the tank start up and drive away. A few minutes later Espinosa came in. He was slumping a bit, looking his age.

"You can sleep in you same places tonight. There will be guards at the doors."

"You want something to eat?" Thomas said. "We'll just have to throw it out if you don't."

Espinosa looked uncomfortable. "We meet here tomorrow morning. Seven o'clock." He turned and walked out again.

None of the cottages had locks. Thomas waited until dark to open his door and look outside. There were two guards, neither one over eighteen. They started to raise their guns, then saw the bottles in his hands. He gave them each a beer and asked in Spanish if he could sit by the pool for a couple of minutes. It was only a few yards away.

"If you try to run," one of them apologized, "we'll have to shoot you."

"Claro," Thomas said.

When they saw he just wanted to sit by the water they faded into the darkness and left him alone.

The pool was gigantic, the largest Thomas had ever seen. It was the center of the project, not just physically but metaphorically. The project was a model of the world, and the pool was its ocean. It was stocked with mirror carp, who made imitation tides when they thrashed their tails. It had tilapia instead of whales to eat the algae and clean the water. White amurs ate the bigger plants and the project ate the amurs and the talapia.

Thomas was far enough into the metaphor that listening to the patter of the murky water against the tiles had become like listening to real waves. It cleared his head, relaxed him.

Eventually he noticed an orange glow off to his right, on the hotel side of the shallow end. About the same time he smelled the smoke from the cigarette. It had been so long since Thomas had actually seen anybody smoking tobacco that he was a little horrified.

"I think," Espinosa said at last, "my men have not much discipline."

"They trusted me," Thomas said. "Don't blame them for that."

"You are believers in trust, you Northamericans. True?"

"What do you mean?"

"Tell me about you boats."

"You mean the ocean arks?" One of them was anchored in the deep end. Thomas could hear it scraping gently against the edge of the pool. It was a revolutionary design, strong, light, simple, made of balsa wood and epoxy. It was twice as fast as the gasoline-powered boats it replaced, silent, needed no fuel or engine repairs.

"They use them on the south coast now, true?"

"There's two of them in Zihuatenejo. The people down there love them. They're catching twice the fish they used to."

"No," Espinosa said. "The rebels have you boats now. One is sunk. The other they sail around in the bay. It is a weapon now, you see?"

Stupid bastards, Thomas thought. They'd sunk a boat that could have fed hundreds of people for the rest of their lives. For politics.

"You trust too much," Espinosa said. "You trust the money and the tools and you think people are stupid that don't speak English as good as you."

"No," Thomas said. "Maybe I used to think like that, before I came here. But people can change. People can learn. That's what this place is all about."

"I would like to believe you." The orange light of the cigarette flew out over the pool and sizzled into the water. Thomas heard a second splash as a carp struck at it. "But I don't trust you."

Thomas went back to his room. The guards, who must have heard Espinosa complaining, looked nervous as he shut them out. He stuck a doorstop in the frame to wedge the door closed.

He didn't want to think about Espinosa anymore. He spread out Lindsey's letter on the bed next to him and tried to decipher it. She had signed it "love"—that had to count for something. What he wanted to believe was that she'd developed, after all these years, a physical passion for him that she could no longer deny. None of the other men she'd had, and God knew there had been enough of them, had worked out. Now Thomas would get his shot.

She was his brother's wife, which had always been a problem. Even though his brother was legally dead, had disappeared from the Timberlawn Psychiatric Hospital in Dallas back in 1978 and hadn't been heard from since. In those eight years he'd seen Lindsey maybe twice, written to her a couple of times a year.

But he hadn't forgotten her. The first time he'd ever seen her was backstage after one of Eddie's concerts. It would have been in the early seventies sometime. She was hanging all over Eddie. She had on a thin white tank top and no bra, leather jeans, eyeliner all the way around her eyes, boots with three-inch heels and zippers. A cigarette hung out of her mouth, the smoke not as strong as her perfume. Her hands rattled with too many rings and her hair was brittle from bleach.

He was still used to thinking of Eddie as a little kid, but seeing Lindsey changed all that. Her image was primal. A little kid wouldn't have been able to live up to her.

It was bullshit, of course. Under the blatant sexual propaganda she was like anybody else. She watched soap operas and read *Cosmo* and ate canned peach halves wrapped in a slice of Wonder Bread. But Thomas had imprinted her as some kind of bush-league sex goddess, the way ducks imprint their mothers, and his left-brain logic had no power over her.

He remembered the letter she'd written him back in the spring of '77. Eddie had just checked into Timberlawn, and she'd come to Dallas to sign the papers. There was perfume on the letter and it said how much she appreciated the way Thomas had always been there for her. So he drove the two hundred miles to Dallas in a white heat and ended up sleeping on the couch. She couldn't bring herself, she said, to do that to Eddie. Not yet. She hugged him but wouldn't kiss him. He'd woken up again and again, all night long, thinking every noise was Lindsey coming to him to tell him she'd changed her mind, to lead him back to her fragrant bed.

Thinking about her, even now, made his dick hard as a piece of lumber. He took his glasses off and pulled musty-smelling drapes over the fish tanks built into the south wall. "This could get ugly," he told the fish. "You wouldn't want to see it." He masturbated, picturing Lindsey stretched out on her back, arms reaching up for him, breasts flattened a little toward the sides, eyes a little crossed. Kid stuff. Then he drank a bottle of *agua mineral* and took a shower and went to sleep.

Espinosa met them in the kitchen for breakfast, *huevos rancheros.* "This is good food," he said. "Very rich."

"Thanks," Shapiro said. "Since you sent our dishwashers home yesterday, you can do your own dishes."

"Forget the dishes," Espinosa said. He looked at Thomas. "Today I want to see what you do with the computer."

"Today," Shapiro said, "is Thomas' day in the gardens. There's nobody to trade out with him."

"Tomorrow," Espinosa said, "maybe there *are* no gardens. Today I look at the computer."

"Suit yourself," Thomas said. He put his dishes and Espinosa's in a sink full of water. They went to his office and Thomas turned on his PC. "You want to see my stuff or the project stuff?" He was networked to the project database and could call in any of the monitor programs.

"You," Espinosa said.

Thomas logged on and called up his mapping program. He was suddenly conscious of his open window, of the screen lying out on the lawn where he'd kicked it. Espinosa didn't say anything about it so neither did he. But the memory of the tank, the rifles, the men pawing through the cottages, was a physical presence in the room.

A graph scrolled down the CRT. It looked a little like a topographic map, the various regions shaded with dots, brackets, plus signs, asterisks, and rectangles. "This is a trend surface analysis of Mayan sites," Thomas said. It came out fast and harsh. "It's a kind of regression analysis, using the region as a response surface."

"Trend . . . surface . . . analysis," Espinosa said. He looked like someone was explaining to him why his children were dead. Sad, frightened, unable to understand. Thomas suddenly saw the deliberate sadism in what he was doing, slapping Espinosa around with words and machines that were as alien as he could make them. He swiveled around in his chair.

"Look," he said. "I understand your position. You don't want to be here. The government's scared, you're scared, you're grabbing at straws. *Es decir, asirse a un bledo, OK?*"

"Just talk English. I understand you."

"Maybe you're afraid of this place. Because you don't understand what's going on here. But there's no big mystery. I can show you how to use a computer this afternoon."

"My son, he uses the computers at the University City. We don't afraid of computers."

"Okay, fine. But what I'm saying is, this isn't what you're looking for. This is ancient history. This is about the Mayan collapse, a thousand years ago. It shows when the cities died out. We're still trying to figure out why it happened."

"Maybe they had rebels," Espinosa said.

"Maybe they did." It was, in fact, one of the models he was testing, and consistent with Prigogine's work.

"The dark areas, they are the most recent?"

"Kind of," Thomas said. "It's showing a lot of different things at once. Population, economy, what the land is like, government."

Espinosa was nodding. "My son is study the, what you call it? Science of politics."

"Probably a real good idea," Thomas said.

"Why are you so interest in the Maya? For something that happens a thousand years ago?"

"There's a Mayan ruin called Na Chan. I did my dissertation there. It was a book, *The Lords of the Forest.*"

"Ah yes. The mushroom book. Last night I read you, what you call, file folder."

Wonderful, Thomas thought. Here we go again. The book was a serious attempt to reconstruct the culture of the area. Part of that culture was a mushroom that allowed a shaman to see backward in time. At least that was what they seemed to believe. Thomas had taken endless shit from his professors for even mentioning it. The people at Mentor books loved it and wanted him to beef it up. He could be the next Casteneda, they said.

Espinosa, to his relief, let it go. "You fly the helicopter," he said.

"That's right."

"Where you learn to do this? Vietnam?"

"No," Thomas said. "I didn't go."

"Why not?"

"I was in school."

"But you learn anyway."

"We used a helicopter to get in and out of Na Chan. The pilot taught me."

"This is not something you learn in two–three days. You must have want to learn very bad."

Newsreel footage of the fall of Saigon came back to him, the helicopters taking off from the roofs of the buildings, refugees clinging to the skids like insects, the weird sense of loss it had given him to watch it. "It's hard to explain," he said. "It's like . . . I know we shouldn't have been in Vietnam. But I still feel like I missed something. Something important."

"Maybe now you have a Vietnam here, no? Maybe you still get you chance."

One of the soldiers knocked on the open door and came in. "There is a woman," he said to Espinosa in Spanish. "A gringa, blonde. Looking for him." He tilted his head toward Thomas.

"Lindsey," Thomas said, his throat closing up on him. *"Se llama* Lindsey."

The soldier looked at him. *"Sí, verdad."*

"OK," Espinosa said. "Search her. But be careful with your hands, you understand me? And bring her to me."

Thomas got up, sat back down again. Espinosa watched him. It's the first weakness any of us have let him see, Thomas thought. We've been holed up here like some kind of pale foreign gods, doling out favors and expecting to be loved in return. No wonder they resent us.

"She is you girlfriend?" Espinosa asked gently.

"No," Thomas said. "Just . . . she's just a friend."

"*Sí, claro,*" Espinosa said. "Of course." It was the way he might have smiled at his son, at the university in Mexico City.

The guard brought her in and Thomas stood up again.

"Nothing, sir," the guard said in Spanish and Espinosa nodded him away.

Her hair was darker, not quite brown, and some of the long strands had gone white. She still wore eye makeup but the eyes looked softer, set in a web of fine lines like the ones that had come up at the corners of her mouth. No other makeup except a little pale lipstick. Nothing to hide anymore. She wore a simple knit dress, navy blue, loose enough to fit local standards of modesty. Flat shoes, no jewelry.

Except her wedding ring.

"You look wonderful," Thomas said. "I can't believe how good you look."

"You too," Lindsey said. She had trouble meeting his eyes. She held on to her bare upper arms, forearms crossed over her chest. Thomas saw she wasn't going to hug him. The rest of his fantasies crumbled and blew away like fairy dust.

He offered her his chair and she settled cautiously, tugging on the hem of her dress, fiddling with her purse. Finally she looked at Espinosa and then at Thomas. "What in God's name is going on here?"

Thomas shrugged. "Up until yesterday we were trying to save the world. New energy sources, new food supplies, new shelters, the whole bit. Now it looks like the world is not interested in being saved." He wanted a reaction from Espinosa but he didn't get one.

"Are you like under arrest or something?"

"I don't know. *Dígame, Capitán* Espinosa, am I under arrest?"

"Not officially. Not right now."

"Can I talk to him?" Lindsey asked Espinosa. "I mean, in private? It's . . . it's a personal matter."

"Ah," Espinosa said. He put his hand around his chin

and looked away. After a few seconds he said, "We go outside. You sit and talk, far enough away we don't hear you, but we can see everything."

"So I don't give her any microfilm."

"No film, no virus, no nerve gas." Thomas could no longer tell whether he was kidding or not.

"I have to show him a picture," Lindsey said. "Is that okay?"

"Show to me."

Lindsey passed him a three by five black and white print. Espinosa looked at it very hard for a few seconds, then turned it over a couple of times. He shrugged and handed it to Thomas.

It showed three Mayans in robes, laughing and smoking dark conical cigars. They were Lacondones, from Nahá. Thomas recognized them from the research he'd done for his book. A fourth man, with equally long hair and the same kind of cotton robe, looked like he was trying to get out of the picture.

The fourth man was his brother Eddie.

They sat on folding chairs by the pool. Thomas shifted from side to side, listening to the sand crunch under the runners of the chair. "Do you want to talk about it or not?" Lindsey asked.

"Sure," Thomas said. "Where did you get the picture?"

"A kid reporter named Carmichael took it. He's on assignment for *Rolling Stone,* trying to get an interview with the rebels. He did a feature on the Lacondones while he was waiting. His editor knew Eddie in the seventies and recognized him."

"So now what happens?"

"So now I go up there and look for him. What else?" Thomas shrugged.

"What's wrong with you?" Lindsey said. "If this *is* Eddie then it means he's okay! He's alive! He's your *brother* for Christ's sake! Don't you care?"

"I care," Thomas said. "Maybe I care more than you do. I care enough to leave him the hell alone if he wants.

Look, even if I could get away from here, even if we could talk Espinosa into letting me go, who says Eddie even *wants* to be found?"

"Maybe he has amnesia."

"Amnesia. Shit. Maybe it's not Eddie at all, maybe it's his evil twin. You watch too much TV."

"What do you want me to do, just forget about him?"

"That's *exactly* what you should do. The entire country is coming down around our ears. Those mountains are full of rebels and the guardia is going nuts trying to find them. If you get caught up in that you're going to need somebody to rescue *you.*"

"That's why I want you to come with me."

"You're chasing the past. Eddie chucked it all ten years ago. He cut his records and said what he had to say and got out. He's finished. He's retired. If he wants to play Indian for the rest of his life, he's entitled."

"What about you? Are you retired, too?"

"No," he said. "Maybe I've been standing around for a couple of years with my thumb up my ass, but I don't think I've given up. Not yet. There's still work to be done. Changing people's heads, people like Espinosa. Maybe stopping the next Chernobyl or Bhopal before we kill off the whole planet."

She shook her head. "You tell me I'm living in the past, and then you start up with all this Woodstock Generation crap. You're not going to change anything hiding out down here."

"Who's hiding out?" Thomas said. "They're right up against the future every day here. They've got close to a thousand sensors all over the complex, feeding a central computer. They've got plans to retrofit entire cities with solar technology, to teach poor villages how to build boats like that one there—"

"Listen to you. You keep saying 'they.' I hear everything you're saying but I don't buy it. I think you're kidding yourself. People aren't going to tear down all their beautiful ranch-style homes and start living in greenhouses. Things are just going to go on the way they always have."

Thomas looked down at his sneakers, tapping the sides together. "You know what they say about me here? They say I'm *sanpaku*. It's Japanese or something. It means I show too much white along the bottoms of my eyes. It's supposed to mean I'm out of balance or something. Well maybe I am. I'm thirty-eight years old. I'm divorced, no kids, no house, no car, no pension. It's time for me to start believing in something."

"Thomas . . ."

"No," he said. "Maybe we can't change everything overnight. But we can get started. A little at a time. Retrofitting, rebuilding. When the ranch houses fall down we can put up something better. Even just getting the information *out* there would be something. It would be *something.*"

They both got up. She put out her hand and Thomas took it, wanting to wrap her up in his arms, knowing he could do it if he wanted, knowing he wasn't strong enough to deal with it if he did.

"I'm at the Hotel Capitol," she said. "Calle Uruguay, near the Alameda. If you change your mind."

She stopped once by the far side of the pool and looked back. Thomas sat down and stared into the water. Finally she went away.

Espinosa sat in the chair next to him, the one where Lindsey had been sitting. "She want you to leave with her?"

"Yeah," Thomas said. "That's what she wanted."

"She is a very beautiful woman. Very handsome."

Thomas nodded. He picked up a thumb-sized chunk of cement and tossed it at the nearest carp. The water killed its momentum. It drifted slowly past the nose of the fish, who had backed up two inches to watch it. Fuck you too, Thomas thought.

"I could let you go," Espinosa said. "To go with her. You don't need to be here."

"That's not the point," Thomas said. He saw that Espinosa meant it, and the kindness made him uncomfortable.

"Then what is the point?"

"I don't know," Thomas said.

"We close you down," Espinosa said. They were in the mural room again. Espinosa had brought two of his men along, but their rifles were slung over their shoulders, out of the way. "For two weeks. Then you open again."

"Two *weeks?*" Shapiro said.

"What about our people," Geisler asked. "Do we get our people back?"

Espinosa shook his head. "The Republic will be you partner now. We bring in people to help you."

"Great," Shapiro said. "We've been fucking nationalized."

"What people?" Geisler asked. "The Army?"

"No. I think maybe my son like to work here. He can bring others from the University City to help him."

"Your *son?*" Shapiro said. "What kind of bullshit stunt—"

"Judy," Thomas said, "just shut up for once." He nodded to Espinosa. "I think it's a good idea. I think we'll have a lot to learn from each other."

"Thomas . . ." Shapiro said.

"That is all," Espinosa said. "You may stay here in Cuernavaca or go back to Mexico City." He walked over to where Thomas was sprawled in one of the plastic chairs.

"Two weeks," he said quietly. "Long enough to do what you have to and come back."

"And if I don't want to go?" Thomas said.

"Then, my friend, you are more stupid than I think." Espinosa smiled and took his guards away with him.

WHEN EDDIE got to the godhouse he still had to wait outside for the old man to notice him. Chan Ma'ax sat and mashed yellow pine gum into *pom* for the incense pots and pretended Eddie wasn't there. Eddie was sweating and his nerves were bad, but the old man demanded patience.

In their time the Mayans had worked out the cycles of the planets and built stone temples so graceful they made Eddie's eyes burn. And nothing survived but a dozen wood poles and a thatched roof and a wrinkled old man sitting crosslegged on a mat.

A tractor coughed in the distance, then crashed screaming into the underbrush. Behind the godhouse the logging road split the dense green of the jungle, two orange ruts filmed over with standing water. To either side the pale ovals of mahogany stumps stared back like frightened eyes.

The air was thick and smelled of cookfires and diesel. It congealed on Eddie's face and neck; if he tried to rub his hands together they would stick, just from the humidity.

"Oken," the old man said at last. "Come in, Eddie."

Eddie hiked up his tunic and sat on a low mahogany stool. After a couple of minutes the old man said, "Ma'ax García spent two days in the forest, looking for copal to burn in the godpots. Nothing." He spread his hands, palms down, then turned them over and pretended to search them for copal. He spoke in Maya, but slowly, so Eddie could follow. Eddie smiled and nodded to show he understood.

The Ma'ax García he was talking about was Eddie's age, mid-thirties. He was Chan Ma'ax's oldest son by his second wife. He loved the old man and wore himself out trying to help him.

"They took all the mahogany," Chan Ma'ax said. "So now we can't even make new canoes. I guess now we have to take that one and start using it on the lake." He pointed to the ceremonial canoe full of sugar cane pulp, white bark, and water. It had been fermenting under a covering of palm leaves since the day before. "So what then? No more *balché?* Then it will truly be the end of the world. My sons will all turn into *evangelistas,* no?"

He laughed, showing brown stubs of teeth. His name meant "little monkey" after his clan, and over the years he'd started to look like one: flat nose, hunched back, matted black hair. The first time Eddie had been introduced to him as the *t'o'ohil,* the "great one," he'd assumed it was just another joke.

That had been a long time ago. Now, even when the old man was clowning around, it scared the living daylights out of him.

In his more lucid moments Eddie saw himself as a victim of a fashionable malaise, the leading edge of a fin-de-millennium craziness that would peak in another fifteen years. The rest of the time it seemed like some kind of short circuit in his talent that had made him walk out on a career that was just getting started. But it had gotten to the point where everything sounded stale, where he'd go blank on stage and play obvious shit with no energy or heart. And then late at night he'd hear things in his head that were more feeling than music, things he could never find on the neck of a guitar.

So he'd done a stretch in a private sanitarium, and when he decided it wasn't helping he walked away. He bummed around Europe, where the massive, colorless buildings all seemed to want to crawl on top of him. He tried to work up the nerve for Asia or North Africa but when the time came he got on a plane for Mexico City instead. And it was there, pissing away the last of his money, that he found *The Lords of the Forest* by Thomas Yates in the rack of English books at Sanborn's. It was about his brother's excavations at the Mayan ruins of Na

Chan. He started reading it on the Metro and stayed up that night to finish it.

There was a postage stamp photo of Thomas on the back cover. He looked tanned and academic in short hair and black framed glasses; he had a tattersall shirt and a tie and a wall of books behind him. The picture didn't account for all the weird shit in the book, the digressions about Chan Ma'ax at Nahá, about the student that had gone crazy from the hallucinogenic mushrooms at Na Chan, the reconstructions of rituals that read like something out of Tarzan.

It was the mushrooms that really got Eddie's attention. Thomas said the shamans, like Chan Ma'ax, used them to get visions of other times. There was a wistful quality when he talked about them that Eddie recognized. Thomas, who hardly used to smoke grass, who had only dropped acid a couple of times, wanted to take them himself. Eddie could see it, even if Thomas never came out and admitted it.

Eddie's brain caught fire and he got on the next bus east.

He came the last leg in an oil company pickup. The oilmen were lining up right behind the loggers to take their turn in the gang rape of the Mexican rain forest, and Eddie saw he'd made it just in time.

That had been three years ago. He hadn't expected the Lacondones to make him a better guitarist. All he knew was acid and yoga and macrobiotics hadn't done it for him and he was running out of things to try.

And the Lacondones had opened up to let him in and then quietly closed up behind him. It was like they already knew him from somewhere. They helped him build a hut and gave him black beans and balché and their sour hand-rolled cigars and otherwise left him alone. He felt like somebody's retarded brother that they'd agreed to put up with.

In three years he'd lived a couple of months with Nuk, one of Chan Ma'ax's daughters, who'd gotten more and more distant every day; he'd had a week or so with an

evangelista girl from the Christian side of the lake who
was having a crisis of faith and had put deep scratches in
his back; and in the last year or so he'd had a kind of
clinical sex with the English doctor who passed through
every couple of months, who'd lived her whole life in
Mexico and never listened to rock and roll.

And beyond the sudden widening of the doctor's eyes
when she came, the quick "oh" of her indrawn breath,
he'd had no effect on any of them.

"Listen," Eddie said to Chan Ma'ax in halting Maya.
"Something's up. Not just the balché. Something's going
on."

The smile died on the old man's face and his eyes went
distant and glassy.

Shit, Eddie thought. He's not going to talk about it.

They were like the Japanese. They had a mental curtain they dropped over themselves that cut them off from
somebody who offended them. "Those bags over there
are full of clay. That's why you're keeping them wet.
They're for new godpots. You're going to break the old
pots, aren't you?"

Chan Ma'ax looked down at the pine sap. Eddie wasn't
there anymore.

He'd been through this before. Once, pretty badly
smashed on *aguardiente* he'd brought back from San
Cristóbal, a kid named Chan Zapata had said something
about Chan Ma'ax and the *Haawo'*, the Raccoon Clan.
Eddie had read about them in his brother's book. They
were supposed to be the last ones with a working knowledge of the Mayan calendar and ceremonies, could even,
some said, talk to the gods. They knew where the sacred
mushrooms grew and how to use them to call up visions
of the past.

As soon as the word came out of his mouth Chan
Zapata shut up, too embarrassed even to change the subject. After that Eddie had gone to Chan Ma'ax and then
to the rest of the village, but even a mention of the
Haawo' turned him invisible on the spot.

Finally young Ma'ax García had taken him aside and

said, "It's bad luck to talk about . . . you know. The thing you were asking about. Okay? It's bad luck even to say the name. I'll probably get bit by a *nauyaca* just for talking to you about it, but I like you. I don't want you to get in trouble."

Eddie could take a hint, then as well as now.

He stood up and said, "Okay, Max. I'm sorry. *No estoy aquí por pendejo.* I'll shut up."

He was walking away when Chan Ma'ax said, "Eddie?"

"Yeah?"

"You will be back for the balché later, no?"

"I wouldn't miss it."

"Groovy," Chan Ma'ax said. It was his favorite English word. It meant Eddie's wrist had been slapped and now they were friends again. In Maya he said, "Bring your guitar. You can sing for us."

For a second Eddie wanted to tell the old man who he was, that he wasn't just some clown who happened to know a lot of songs on the guitar. But the old man wouldn't care. It had no bearing on whether or not Eddie was a *hach winik,* a real person.

He walked out into the center of the clearing and let the stupifying July heat wash over him. He shut his eyes and concentrated on the pores of his skin and felt his sweat break all at once, on the backs of his knees and between his shoulders. It made him feel less poisonous.

When he opened his eyes the mountains were in front of him, pristine, sharp-edged, nearly the same color as the pale sky behind them. A few thin clouds floated over them, motionless.

Fuck it, he thought. Time to move on.

Everything snapped into focus. He tasted the dust in the air, smelled the jungle broiling in the sunlight, heard the high-pitched drone of the cicadas like dueling synthesizers and, over them, the faint voices of women on the far side of the clearing.

Nepal, maybe. Why not? He thought about ragged, ice-covered mountains, impossibly green terraces set into the sides of valleys, whitewashed monasteries growing out of cliffs. For a second he saw them superimposed on the drab browns and tans of the village.

It would be complicated. He didn't know the politics anymore, didn't know if he could even get into Nepal. He would have to spend a while in the real world, long enough to get his bearings and put some money together.

He went on to his hut feeling lightheaded, precarious. The hut was the same general shape as the godhouse, longer than it was wide, rounded on the ends, and thatched with sweet palm leaves. Unlike the godhouse it had walls of a sort, vertical strips of yellow bamboo, braided with string and baling wire.

He opened the door and a woman's voice from inside said, *"Tal in wilech."* I have come to see you.

"Nuk?"

"Yes," she said, switching to Spanish. "I need to talk to you."

He made her out in the dimness. She was barrel-chested and thick-waisted, not even as tall as Eddie's shoulders, but she was a beauty by local standards. His eyes found the red of the tattered plastic anthurium she always wore in her hair.

Eddie shut the door and sat in the hammock. He smelled the dry, spicy odor of her skin and thought about the nights they'd spent together. *"Cómo no?"* he said.

"It's about my father."

"I just saw him. He's getting ready to drink balché."

"Yes," she said. "They will drink balché and in the morning they will go on a pilgrimage to Na Chan."

"Pilgrimage," Eddie said, stunned. Na Chan wasn't just a ruin that his brother had tried to excavate. It was where Chan Ma'ax's gods lived. Chan Ma'ax would never talk about what went on there. It was hach winik stuff, for real people only.

"He must not go. He's old, almost eighty. The government has told him to stay away from there. If he goes I don't think he'll come back. You have to talk to him."

"I don't know why you're asking me," Eddie said. He

didn't want it to sound bitter, but it came out that way just the same.

"He trusts you. He thinks you are a good man. He listens to you."

"He'd listen better to Ma'ax García."

"Ma'ax García is too much a part of the old ways. He doesn't care about the danger."

The old ways. Nuk was awed by cars and planes and portable stereos. She still talked about the TV she'd seen in San Cristóbal five years ago. That's what I am to her, Eddie thought. Just one more new thing.

"If he talks to me," Eddie said, "I'll do what I can. I'll tell him I think it's dangerous. Okay?"

"Thank you, Eddie." She leaned over him, kissed him quickly, and ran out the door. Her lips were soft and he felt the kiss a long time after she was gone.

He stood in front of his shaving mirror, hating the way he looked. It made him nervous, impatient. He got out his straight razor and cut his shoulder-length hair to within an inch or so of his skull. He had to do the back by feel. When he was finished he washed himself with the last of his hard pink shaving soap and water from the clay jug in the corner.

There was a bamboo shelf above the hammock and he reached to the back of it and took down his shoulder bag. The zipper was stiff from disuse. He got out a pair of jeans and a T-shirt and put them on. The jeans were loose, but he punched a new hole in the belt.

The longest journey begins with a single step, he thought. Already he felt different, cut off from the heartbeat of the village, his genitals armored in heavy denim.

He rolled the mirror and razor up in the blue and orange strings of the hammock and put them in the bag. There wasn't anything else to pack.

He left the bag sitting in the dust of the floor and picked up his guitar. It was a gut-string accoustic he'd bought for twenty dollars in the *mercado* in Mexico City. The action was brutal and the octaves were about a quarter tone off, but he'd been trying to wean himself from material objects and it had seemed like a good idea at the time. He carried it back outside and saw Chan Zapata headed for the godhouse.

"Hey," Eddie said. "Chan Zapata."

The kid turned around and smiled nervously at Eddie. He was one of Chan Ma'ax's youngest sons, only in his twenties. Everybody seemed to assume he would take Chan Ma'ax's place when the time came. He had a smooth face and penetrating eyes and he worked hard for Chan Ma'ax when he wasn't on a binge in San Cristóbal. He made souvenir bows and arrows that he traded for aguardiente and whores, and every time he came home his wife had moved out. She would stay gone a week or so and then he'd convince her he'd never do it again.

He would be going to Na Chan if anyone did.

"How's the balché?" Eddie asked him.

"Good," Chan Zapata said. "Heavy." It was Chan Zapata's job to carry the balché from the ceremonial canoe to the godhouse. He had to use a huge clay pot, the size of an old-fashioned kettle.

"So," Eddie said. "Tomorrow you go to Na Chan, no?"

Eddie assumed Chan Zapata would just ignore the question, the way his father ignored anything he didn't want to hear. Instead he looked angry. "No," Chan Zapata said. "Not me."

"Why not?"

"You don't know?" Chan Zapata said. "Truly?"

"Truly," Eddie said. "I don't."

"Then it's not for me to tell you." Chan Zapata smiled again, sadly this time, and walked away.

Everybody else was back from the *milpa,* the cornfield on the far side of the lake. Maybe fifteen men sat or squatted in a loose hierarchy on the floor of the godhouse. Eddie nodded to them and sat next to Ma'ax García. Nobody said anything about his clothes. Ma'ax García handed him a bowl of the deep brown balché and Eddie took it in both hands. It tasted a little like weak stout, a little like strong *pulque.* Eddie drank it off and

Ma'ax García passed it forward to be filled again. When the bowl came back Eddie set it at his feet and wrapped both hands around the neck of his guitar.

Chan Zapata served the balché from a big clay pot at the front of the godhouse. He didn't meet Eddie's eyes. The others sat in twos and threes, drinking, complaining about the Christian converts on the north end of the lake who'd sold off the mahogany and kept all the money for themselves. One old man asked Chan Zapata if he'd saved up enough "arrows" for a trip to San Cristóbal and everybody laughed.

If I painted myself purple, Eddie thought, would anybody say anything?

Chan Zapata took the pot back out to the canoe to refill it. The full pot had to weigh close to a hundred pounds and he staggered back with his knees bent and his arms all the way around it. His face was agonized. If he dropped it the gods would never forgive him. Just past the edge of the roof Eddie could see towering black clouds blowing in from the Gulf, erasing Chan Zapata's shadow and turning the jungle behind him into a wall of foggy green.

The rain started just as suddenly, falling in handfuls that cratered the dust outside and filled the air with the rusty smell of ozone. The sky cracked into a web of white lines and the thunder came after it fast and loud enough to make one of the old men jump.

"It's only lightning," Chan Ma'ax said. His monkey face wrinkled with silent laughter. "Nuxi' is afraid Cabracan is waking up." The others laughed and Chan Ma'ax said to Eddie, "Cabracan is what they call in Spanish the *temblor*."

"Earthquake," Eddie said in English. The old man's smile terrified him. There had been earthquakes in California all week, in the Sierra Nevadas, just like they'd been predicting for years. He'd heard it on the radio yesterday, in between garbled reports that Carla had been killed and the last of her guerrillas wiped out.

"Urt quack," Chan Ma'ax said. *"Urt quack."* He finished his balché and tucked his legs up under him. "You

know the story of Hunahpu and Xbalanque and Cabracan?"

"No," Eddie said. The godhouse went quiet and Chan Ma'ax started to talk.

"Heart of Heaven sends Hunahpu and Xbalanque, the twins, to kill Cabracan. Cabracan, you know, he has been saying, 'I am greater than the sun. I shake the earth and sky and everyone bows down before me.' Heart of Heaven, of course, he can't just let this go.

"Cabracan is walking across the land, shaking the mountains flat, and the work is making him hungry. He sees Hunahpu and Xbalanque and says, 'Who are you?'

" 'Nobody,' says Hunahpu. 'We are only hunters.'

" 'What do you have to eat, then?' says Cabracan.

"Now Hunahpu and Xbalanque have the idea that they must bind Cabracan to the earth. They shoot quetzal birds from the branches with their blowguns and the giant thinks it is really wonderful because they only use air instead of darts. They cook the birds and they smear some of them with white lime from the lime pits and cook them until they are golden brown and dripping with juices.

"The giant eats the birds that have the lime on them and then he starts walking toward the west again, smashing the mountains. But the lime is making him heavy and it is harder and harder for him to lift his arms or his feet.

"He begins to stumble and fall. Soon he can't get up again and he falls asleep under the mountains. Hunahpu and Xbalanque dance on the ground that covers him, but they are so noisy that they anger Heart of Heaven. Heart of Heaven wanted to see a good contest. He is disappointed that the twins beat Cabracan by trickery.

"So every year, while Cabracan sleeps, Heart of Heaven lets him get stronger. You can hear him sometimes turning in his sleep, making the mountains shake the way he used to. Making the *urt quack.*"

Chan Ma'ax refilled his bowl, drank it all, smacked his lips. No one moved. They knew when there was more coming, like the audience at a symphony that knew when not to clap.

Finally Chan Ma'ax said, "If you go east, toward the old cities of Chichén Itzá or Tulúm, you can see the land where Cabracan knocked the mountains down. Cabracan is very restless now and soon he will wake up and shake these mountains to pieces."

He looked at Eddie. "Wearing the clothes of a hach winik will not save you." Eddie thought there was approval in the old man's voice and it caught him off guard. "Hunahpu and Xbalanque will not save you. They are a part of the old ways. After Cabracan wakes up, there will be only new ways."

The balché made another round. The old man had always told sports stories before, Hunahpu and Xbalanque playing soccer with the king of the underworld. Nothing like this.

And then Eddie remembered Thomas' book. According to the Mayan calendar a five-thousand-year cycle was just now ending. It was supposed to wind up with some kind of disaster that would wipe everything out. The book figured it to be earthquakes.

Jesus Christ, Eddie thought. He's talking about the end of the world.

"Play something, Eddie," Chan Ma'ax said.

"Yes, for God's sake," Nuxi' said. "Something cheerful."

Eddie picked up the guitar. What they liked best were the *rancheras,* the traditional crap like "Cielito Lindo" that they could sing along with, but they liked old rock and roll too. He tried "Twist and Shout" and then "La Bamba" to the same chords but the lyrics depressed him savagely. He stopped singing and just hammered the chords, hard enough to split his cuticles and to pull the strings out of tune.

They had all been singing along, slapping their hands in the dust to keep time, but now they stopped and stared at him. The chords disintegrated into two- and three-string grips, and then out of it somehow came a melody line, taking Eddie by surprise.

His fingers ground into the neck, slurring and smearing the notes, the cheap strings rasping skin from his fingertips, the music pouring out of him uncontrolled. He didn't have any idea how long it went on. Finally his hands slowed on their own and the notes trailed off into silence.

He got up. He was breathing hard, like he'd been running. He walked out into the rain and let the cool water run down his face.

After a few seconds he felt the pressure of the balché in his bladder. He walked a little farther into the jungle and loosed a strong, clear stream into the undergrowth. He was already high, not fuzzily drunk but tight and focused as a laser. It took a long time to piss.

When he turned back he saw Chan Ma'ax with the front of his robe tucked under his chin, using a neighboring bush. He took a breath and let it go. "Listen, Max," he said. "It's over. It's time for me to move on."

"Okay," Chan Ma'ax said, smiling.

A vague guilt nagged at him, like he'd left the water running somewhere. He wondered if he was being an idiot. Too late, he told himself. He took another step toward the godhouse.

"Eddie," the old man said. Eddie stopped. The old man looked over his shoulder and grinned like he was brain damaged. "I have a goodbye song to sing for you." He straightened out his tunic and faced Eddie and started to sing. The words were meaningless warbling noises but they approximated the lyrics and melody to "Whatcha Gonna Do," the only hit Eddie ever had, peaking just under the top 40 in 1971.

Eddie's teeth started to chatter. This isn't happening, he thought.

"I have that little radio, you know," Chan Ma'ax said. "I listen to it all the time. I hear crazy things on there sometimes." He waited a few seconds and then he said,

"I don't have answers, Eddie. All I have are the old ways, and the old ways are finished. You understand?"

Eddie nodded. He didn't seem to be able to talk.

"We go on a pilgrimage to Na Chan tomorrow. The last one. To say goodbye. You understand?"

Eddie nodded again.

"You want to come?"

Na Chan, Eddie thought. Na Chan and the mushrooms and gods that talk. "Yes," Eddie said, shaken, scared, suddenly aware of the rain running down his back, soaking his jeans. "Yes, I want to come."

"Groovy," Chan Ma'ax said and walked away.

And then, so gently that afterward he couldn't be sure it had really happened, he felt the ground tilt and settle under him, like a boat taking a wave. Enough to turn fear to terror, just for a second. To turn solid earth to eggshells, to betray everything he'd ever taken for granted.

He wanted to fall down and cling to the rain-soaked grass, but it wasn't the kind of thing a hach winik would do. He stood and watched the raindrops cluster on a stalk of bamboo. The last time, he thought. To say goodbye.

Each drop shone with a fierce and crystalline light. For the moment it was enough.

THE JUÁREZ MONUMENT was a notch cut out of the southern edge of the park. There were three tiers of white marble seats and columns along the back. In the middle was a pedestal taller than the columns with Benito himself and a couple of angels on top. It was the only monument Lindsey knew of that was built to be sat on. Even Benito was sitting down, as if to show how it was done.

She was on the top level, her back against a column, a half-finished postcard to her parents in her lap. The city's high altitude kept the morning cool, though she could feel the strength of the sun on her face and hands. She was waiting for Thomas. Even though he'd told her yesterday that he wasn't coming. Sometimes it seemed like she'd been waiting for one thing or another all her life.

Across the street was the Hotel Del Prado with its million-dollar Diego Rivera mural and its uniformed doormen and its polished pink granite steps. A couple of blocks to her left, facing the eastern edge of the park, was the Bellas Artes palace, the massive neoclassical opera house that was slowly sinking under its own weight.

Most of Mexico City was sinking. In Aztec times this had been a lake with a little island in the middle. The Spaniards had filled it in to give themselves more room for their cathedrals and palaces and pawnshops.

Just beyond the Bellas Artes was the Latin American Tower, forty-four stories high, with the time in lights just below the observation deck. Last week, on her first day in the city, Lindsey had bought a ticket to ride to the top. When she got there she couldn't see anything but an endless gray-white blanket of smog.

Even now, on a Wednesday morning in the middle of the city, there was no way to tell that it was the biggest in the world. Nobody even knew how big it was anymore. Estimates ran from twenty to twenty-five million. She had a guidebook she'd bought along with the postcards, something to help kill time after she finished her pastry and milk for breakfast. The guidebook told her the population of the entire country was only twenty million back in 1940. Every day another three thousand refugees staggered into the city, every day another two thousand children were born here.

A man in a brown corduroy jacket was climbing the steps toward her. Oh no, she thought, not another one. "Good morning," he said in English, and sat next to her. He left a couple inches of neutral ground between them. She nodded at him and looked down at her postcard. She held the pen over it like she was about to write something.

"You are from United States?"

He was maybe forty, dark hair combed straight back, wearing a thin yellow polyester shirt under the jacket. "Yes," she said, and went back to the postcard.

"I am bother you. I am sorry."

She gave up and put the pen back in her purse. "It's okay," she said.

"I study English in night classes. I like very much to practice. Where you from in United States?"

"California," she said. "San Diego." Where her parents were, probably worried sick about her. She wondered if she should just forget the postcard and try to call them tonight.

"Is that where they have the earthquakes?"

"No," Lindsey said. "That's way to the north." Still the thought made her uncomfortable. She'd lived so many years listening to prophecies of doom that she didn't like to hear about them coming true.

"That is good. My name is Ignatio."

"Lindsey." It was her cue to offer her hand but she just nodded and he let it pass.

"Please to meet you."

"I'm sure," she said. She wanted to get up and walk away but if she did Thomas wouldn't know where to find her. She had left word at her hotel that there would be an American looking for her, to tell him she would be at the Juárez statue.

He had to come. He was a Capricorn and she was a Scorpio. It was strong sexual magic and it would bring him to her.

"What is it you read?" Ignatio asked. "May I see?" Lindsey gave him the thin yellow book, Bloomgarden's *Easy Guide to Mexico City.*

Please, Thomas, she thought. Come and get me out of this.

He would come, she told herself. He wanted her. He had always wanted her. She'd known it since that winter in Austin, back in '72. Back when Eddie had just split from Maya and he and Lindsey were living in a three-room apartment near the UT campus, huddled all winter in front of their one open gas heater, the air warped and fiercely dry as it boiled off the glowing ceramic tiles. The three of them sitting around it after dinner, two or three times a week, their backs freezing, their feet too hot, Thomas with his quart bottles of Old Milwaukee, Eddie with his beat-up cream-colored Telecaster, not even plugged in, his hands moving restlessly up and down the neck, like they were checking to make sure all the notes were still there where they were supposed to be.

She remembered the warm flannel smell of hugging Thomas goodnight, the way he held on so tightly. And the way she'd led him on a little because he was Eddie's brother and so he was safe. She had to flirt with somebody or go out of her mind. She'd turned twenty in October and it was already starting to feel like her life was over. She'd wasted it waiting for something, and she didn't even know what she was waiting for.

Watching Eddie play guitar through headphones, unable to hear any of the music, just the dry rattle of the strings. Or watching him sit there, on the cheap tube-steel kitchen chair with the slick green vinyl back and seat, the guitar just hanging off him, his forehead resting on his hands, his eyes closed but his sock feet nervously beating out rhythms on the floor. Or watching him walk around and around the apartment, looking out the fogged windows, staring at the TV with the sound turned off, shutting off the radio anytime she put it on because he couldn't stand to hear other guitar players.

He was working on the *Sunsets* album, she knew that, even though he wouldn't go into the studio for months yet, even though the record wouldn't be finished for another year and a half. That much was okay because playing the guitar was what he did. He was worried about the record because he'd always leaned on the band and Stew's vocals and he was obsessed with making this one better than anything Maya had ever done.

All of that would have been all right if there was something left over from it, but there wasn't. He wasn't just making an album in his head, he was off again, chasing all that mystical shit he could never seem to let go of. All his passion and humor and energy were going into this goddamned album and even when they made love it was like he was grabbing a sandwich, just taking the edge off an appetite so he could concentrate better.

So she'd flirted with Thomas because she could get his undivided attention, at least, and with Eddie right there all the time it had never gone beyond that. And in the spring the new contract with Epic had come through and they'd gone to New York and there broken up for the first time, a couple of weeks only, but still the beginning of the end.

If he comes, she asked herself. When he comes. Will you do it? Will you go to bed with him because you know it's the way to get him to do what you want? And because it's been so long since the last man that you're starting to wonder what the big deal ever was?

Will you?

"You have seen all these things?" Ignatio asked, holding up the Bloomgarden guide.

"A few," she said. The man was harmless, really. In the last week there had been at least two other middle-aged men just like him who simply came up and started talking to her. She understood that talking to strangers was something that was still done in Mexico. He probably wouldn't have done it with a local girl, but it was known that women from the States had no morals. And if she wanted to come up to his place and screw his brains out she was sure it would be okay with him. And if not he would settle for conversation.

Maybe he was just waiting too.

She could tell him how much she loved the city and how wonderful the anthropology museum was and how friendly everybody was and he would smile and go away happy. For a second she wanted to take the guidebook away and make him tell her about the reality, about the colonies of *jacales,* the shacks made out of cardboard and flattened cans that surrounded the cities. She'd read all about them in the library back in San Diego. *"Ciudades perdidas"* they were called, lost cities. Or the suburb

called Santa Fe, a few miles to the west, an island nation
of garbage, run by a garbage king who sent his peons out
through square miles of stinking refuse looking for
spoiled food to eat and scraps of metal to sell to him.

And what about the elections, and the riots? she
wanted to ask him. What about the colonel down in
Cuernavaca who had taken Thomas' project away?

But none of that was Ignatio's fault. She was about to
make the expected noises when she saw she'd lost his
attention. He was staring down at a crippled old man,
limping up the steps toward them. Lindsey looked away,
embarrassed and a little annoyed at the same time. There
were beggars everywhere in the city, even right downtown here, and they never gave up. They waited for you
in the subway entrances, wrapped in shawls, with pathetic, fly-covered children. They chased you through the
park with their shine kits, yelling insults about the condi-
tion of your shoes.

This old man was almost completely devoid of color.
He wore loose khaki pants, stained to the color of pavement, and a dark gray zipped jacket. His skin had the
same asphalt color. She'd sent him away at least once
every time she'd been in the park. She was raising her
hand to wave him off again when Ignatio called him over.
I really don't need this, she thought.

"Cómo va?" Ignatio asked him, and the two of them
started talking in slurred Spanish. Lindsey couldn't make
out a single word. For the hundredth time she promised
herself she would learn the language. She could start that
afternoon. She even had a copy of *Spanish Made Simple*
and a Spanish-English dictionary back in her room. They
were the relic of a night-school course, from back when
night school had seemed like a good idea. She hadn't
gotten past the third week.

The old man squatted on the step below hers, holding a
cigar box in his lap. There were coins and a few dirty bills
in the box, and carefully ordered rows of cellophane-
wrapped gum, four pieces to the package. They were
Chiclets, the little white candy-covered squares of gum
that Lindsey hadn't seen since she was a kid. Her mother

used to give her Chiclets to keep her from getting carsick and they only seemed to make it worse. She didn't know the stuff was still being made. The sight of it brought back memories of a stuffy backseat and Walt Disney's *Comics and Stories* and the dry taste of vomit in the back of her throat.

Ignatio gestured and pulled a money clip out of his front pants pocket. The old man gave him one of the packets and Ignatio dropped a 500-peso note in the old man's box. It was worth a little less than a dollar now. Lindsey could remember trips into Tijuana only a few years ago when it had been worth forty.

"Everybody has a story to tell," Ignatio said. "Remember this. I was afraid of men like this, but then I learn. Everyone has a story, and if you ask, they tell it to you."

"So what did he tell you?"

"He used to be a *chiclero*. You know what that is?"

"It means he sells gum?"

"It means he was a criminal. Not a bad man, just a little criminal. But they put him loose in the forest with a machete. If he comes back each month with the chicle, the juice from a kind of tree, they give him food and whiskey. Then they sell the chicle to the United States to make this things." He held up the packet of gum.

She risked another look at the old man. There was a long scar across the top of his nose that curved around under his eye and across to his ear. The wrists that came out of his jacket sleeves were thin as chicken drumsticks.

"How horrible," she said.

"He says is not so bad. After thirty years you get a, *cómo*, a *promoción*." He held up the wrapped gum again.

"Promotion," Lindsey said.

"*Sí*, promotion." Ignatio and the old man were laughing now. The old man had two teeth, both uppers, one in front and one off to the side. His laughter was nearly soundless, though he opened his mouth wide for it. Lindsey felt like all of Mexico was laughing at her, laughing because she was so ignorant and foreign and spoiled. She took her guidebook out of Ignatio's hands and got up.

Her cheeks felt sunburned. She ran down the steps and into the crowd lined up for the bus on Avenida Juárez.

The crowd slowed her to a walk and she looked down at her feet and pushed her way through. Someone grabbed her by the arm and she jerked it loose.

"Lindsey!"

She turned back. It was Thomas. An old woman wrapped in layers of black cotton had squeezed between them. Thomas looked hurt and confused, like she'd bitten him. A bus hissed to a stop at the curb and the old woman finally inched out of the way. Lindsey ran to him and put her arms around him. The bus gasped and rattled away. Thomas smelled clean and comfortable, like an old bed with fresh sheets on it.

"Are you okay?" he said.

"Yeah, I'm fine, it just . . . it's been a weird morning. It's like . . ." She stopped and listened, her head still against his blue oxford shirt. "There aren't any birds. You always hear birds in the morning."

"Maybe the smog killed them all. Jesus, it's bad here."

"I'm glad you came." His hands were loose and awkward on her back. She didn't want to let go of him. Finally she counted to three in her head and stepped away.

"I got thrown out," he said. "For a couple of weeks, anyway."

"Long enough. I don't see how it could take more than a few days, just to fly up there and back."

"You never know."

"I'm really glad you're here. Thank you, Thomas. I mean it."

"It's okay. Can we get something to eat? I've been on buses and trains all morning."

"Sure," she said.

There was a thrashing sound in the dark green hedge that ran along the sidewalk. Something brushed against her leg. A few feet away somebody screamed. She started to look down, then looked at the screaming woman instead. It was a middle-aged woman in a blouse with a little bow at the throat. Her eyes seemed to be coming out of her head.

Lindsey looked back at the sidewalk, turned, saw a gray rat the size of a shoe scuttling out into the street. "Oh my god," she said, inhaling the words. Another rat lurched out from under a park bench, and then, twenty feet away, another.

There were screams coming from everywhere now. Some kind of bizarre suicidal impulse was driving the rats into the street, dozens of them, thudding into the tires of the cars, scrabbling frantically at the pavement, going crazy from the howling of car horns and brakes. The stench of blood and burning rubber hung in the dead, humid air. Her stomach began to quiver.

A shoulder slammed into the middle of her back and she huddled against Thomas again. People ran in circles, or ran back and forth along the edges of the street, all of them yelling or moaning or calling out to God. Some of them stood in one place and swung umbrellas like clubs. Men and women both had climbed up on the park benches and had their arms around each other.

"Are they gone?" she whispered.

"Mostly," Thomas said. Lindsey looked up again and saw two more rats circling the Juárez monument, flashing between legs, their eyes wide and black with terror.

"Where did they come from?"

"They live in the park. They're everywhere, you just never saw them before. Come on, let's get out of here." Thomas was looking a little queasy himself. He grabbed her hand and pulled at her. She shut her eyes and breathed through her mouth but her stomach wouldn't settle. She felt dizzy, seasick. Maybe it was the pastries, she thought. The air was thick, motionless, unbreathable.

There was a noise like a jet overhead, or like air being let out of a tire. The sidewalk turned to jelly. Thomas was jerked away from her and there was no place to stand. She couldn't figure out what was going on.

Thunder rumbled in the distance. She looked up at the clear morning sky in confusion. Then she started shaking and it was a couple of seconds before she realized the

ground was shaking *her*, like hands had grabbed her by
the shoulders and were jerking her back and forth. She
staggered half a step toward the street and then lurched
backward, her arms flailing. Overhead the power lines
cracked like whips and broke loose from their poles, spitting sparks and snaking through the air.

Finally she understood and she said the word out loud:
"Earthquake."

Cars were thrown sideways into each other as the
street humped up like a shaken rug. Lindsey's teeth
banged against each other. The noise was unbelievable:
the hissing, the rumbling, cars crashing, bricks and tiles
smashing into the sidewalks. She dropped to her knees,
then all fours, saw that she'd been turned completely
around, back toward the Juárez monument.

And then the columns started to move.

They flexed and wobbled like they were pieces of string
somebody was shaking instead of twenty-foot columns of
solid marble. She blinked and stared as waves rolled
through the plaza, lifting marble blocks five feet into the
air, crashing like heavy surf against the shore of the monument.

Less than ten feet away a tree split with a crack that
hurt her ears and tilted slowly across the sidewalk, groaning as if in pain. She could hear Thomas shouting her
name but she couldn't see him. Already the quake had
seemed to last an hour, two hours, all her life.

The worst of the noise eased off and she thought she
heard gunfire, and tiny bells ringing after each shot. She
glanced up long enough to see windows exploding out of
the hotel across the street, glittering and weightless as
soap bubbles, floating toward her. She ducked as the glass
hit the curb with a faint tinkling noise, felt splinters prick
her left arm and the side of her neck.

If it would stop, she thought. If it would only stop.

The Hotel Alameda, just down from the Del Prado,
came apart with a noise like shuffling cards, amplified a
thousand times. The collapse sent its own shock waves
through the park and for a second the two forces fought
each other like angry gods. Lindsey knew then that it was

the end of the world, that it would go on this way forever, and the tears ran down her face and spattered the dust and broken glass on the sidewalk.

It ended with a single long, convulsive shudder. In the silence that came after, Lindsey heard a stuck car horn somewhere in the distance, voices crying softly, a whisper of wind in the bushes. Then there were sirens everywhere.

She turned her head. Thomas was sitting up on his heels a few feet away. He wiped his glasses with a corner of his shirt and put them back on. There didn't seem to be anything wrong with him beyond a few scrapes and cuts. She tried standing up and Thomas got up to try to steady her.

The ground felt wrong. It wasn't moving anymore but it didn't seem exactly solid, either. It was only her willpower that was keeping it together. If she ever relaxed, she thought, it would start again. It was a terrible responsibility. She didn't know how she would ever be able to get any sleep.

"You okay?" Thomas asked.

"Uh huh. You?"

He nodded. She moved her head so she could see the Alameda Hotel. The front wall was gone. The floors had all settled on top of each other, leaving a sandwich of mattresses, flowered dresses, and red plastic wastebaskets between the slices of concrete. Twisted rods of rebar stuck out everywhere. People were climbing the mound of rubble, throwing chunks of debris to one side, digging into the ruins with their bare hands.

"We can't stay here," Thomas said. "We'll only be in the way."

"Shouldn't we . . . I mean, aren't there, like aftershocks or something?"

"I don't know," Thomas said. "I know I could use a drink."

"I've got a bottle in my room." She glanced back at the hotel. "But I don't know if I want to go inside anywhere. Like ever again."

"It's all right," Thomas said. "It's over."

The first aftershock came then, mocking him. Lindsey felt like she was trying to walk across a trampoline. It was so slow and gentle compared to the quake itself that she wanted to laugh hysterically and never ever stop.

Thomas put his arm around her waist and pulled her close and they leaned into each other as they walked, like teenagers. Lindsey had always heard that coming close to death was a major turn-on. It was true; she could feel it happening. There was a hollow kind of ache between her legs and she could feel her nipples pushing out against her bra.

Everything around her lost its focus. They crossed Avenida Juárez, chunks of broken safety glass sliding under her feet like marbles. She looked up and saw that the clock on the Latin American Tower was still running. It was only eleven in the morning. People sat on the sidewalk weeping. The air smelled of concrete dust. Bright spots of color kept snatching at her attention but they would turn out to be a child's T-shirt or a magazine cover and not blood after all.

The front doors of the Hotel Capitol were laced with spiderweb cracks. They didn't close quite right anymore. Inside everything seemed all right. The lobby was a tiled patio, circled by four tiers of rooms and roofed over by a dusty skylight. A maid looked up from a broken clay pot and the ruins of a corn plant and smiled sadly.

In the corner was the landscape artist that she watched every morning. He did a canvas a day, always starting with a horizon line across the middle of the painting, drawn with a pencil and a metal ruler. Then he would paint the top half with a three-inch brush. She could see the long streaks on the canvas where it had slid facedown across the tiles. He was methodically painting out the damage.

They took the stairs to the third floor. The stucco walls were aqua, the doors brownish-red. Her room was tiny, with a cracked bentwood chair and a double bed with a thin mattress. The bathroom door hung crookedly in its frame. Lindsey turned the key behind them and the movement of the lock was graphic, intimate, erotic.

Her suitcase had been knocked to the floor. She stuffed the clothes carelessly back into it and came up with an unbroken fifth of Canadian Club. She held it up to show Thomas. "I wanted Jack Daniel's," she said. "But I couldn't believe how much it cost down here."

He nodded. "Some kind of tariff or something." They were both awkward, afraid of wrong moves. There was a lot of history between them, a lot of tension, a lot of possibility. She twisted the cap off the bottle and took a swallow and then passed it to Thomas.

He drank without looking away from her. She couldn't have said exactly what he looked like just then. The details went away, what kind of glasses he was wearing, the length of his hair. She was waiting again, but it was okay because something was about to happen. She didn't have to do anything except not get out of the way. Thomas lowered the bottle and handed it to her. She put the cap back on and tossed it into the suitcase.

When she turned back Thomas had taken his glasses off and put them in his shirt pocket. She looked at the floor and crossed her arms, holding herself by the shoulders. She didn't resist when Thomas came to her and took her by the wrists and put her arms around his neck.

He kissed her and she kissed him back, and then she felt his breath get short and he kissed her eyelids and throat and ears, and the stubble on his chin burned the underside of her lip. "Easy," she whispered, but even though it was a little scary to see him want her so badly, still her hands were moving through his hair, kneading his scalp like a cat's claws.

He tugged at her sweater and she moved away far enough to pull it over her head. She reached behind her to unhook her bra. He pulled it down her shoulders and ran his hands over her breasts. She felt her nipples tighten and reach out to him. A warm weakness spread out from them and down into her legs.

He took off his shirt and held her against his skin. She could taste the sweetness of his need in the sweat on his neck. He tugged at the snap on her jeans and she twisted away, putting both hands on his chest.

"Just a second," she said.

"Why?"

"Listen, I'm just getting over some herpes. It's no big deal or anything, but you need to like use a condom, okay?"

"Yeah, okay, sure, but I don't—"

"That's okay," she said. "I'm prepared." She unzipped the side pocket of her suitcase and tore a condom off the end of a strip.

"Jesus," Thomas said. "What have you got, a regular sex boutique in there?"

"I'm just careful, that's all. Men don't think to buy the lubricated kind anyway." She sat on the edge of the bed and reached for the zipper of his trousers.

He took the condom away from her and backed up, kicking out of his shoes and pants. Lindsey started to work her own jeans off and then Thomas lifted her under the arms and tossed her back onto the bed. He pulled her jeans off by the rolled cuffs. Lindsey got out of her panties, leaving them dangling around one ankle.

Thomas ripped open the little square of plastic and clumsily unrolled the condom onto his penis. The smell of latex mixed with the smells of sweat and sex and whiskey. Lindsey lay on her back, one hand brushing at her forehead, the other touching herself lightly on the stomach.

Thomas knelt over her and said, "Now." Lindsey lifted her hips toward him. His weight came down onto her. His tongue slid into her mouth and his penis went deep inside her and she came instantly, a hot, paralyzing flash that shut down the crazed aching inside her but left her unsatisfied.

Thomas' eyes had rolled back into his head and he was gasping for breath. She put both arms around his neck and kissed him hard, grinding her pelvis into him. Sweat pooled between her breasts and soaked the sheet under her. Thomas had gone rigid all over and she leaned into him, finding her pressure point, coming just as he did, long and slow this time. She held his buttocks and kept the spasms going through her even after he was finished, until she was exhausted.

She passed out for a few seconds. When she came back Thomas was still on top of her. She stroked his back absently. She was glad he hadn't just pulled out and rolled over, but he was starting to get heavy. Finally he got up and went into the bathroom, holding the condom on with one finger and a thumb.

He shut the door and she rolled onto her left side, pulling up her knees to ease that small sense of emptiness she always had after sex. The toilet flushed and she heard Thomas pad back into the room, hesitate for a few seconds, then climb into the space she'd left him in the bed.

She felt his arm go around her breasts, his knees touching the back of hers, his slack penis against her thighs. He kissed her on the neck but she was too tired to respond. She sniffed once and settled deeper into the pillow.

"Are you okay?" he asked quietly.

"Sure," she said. "It was nice."

"Okay. I just thought . . ."

"What?"

"I don't know. It sounded like you were crying there for a second."

"No. I'm fine."

"Okay," he said.

She felt totally burned out. Karma, she thought, closing her eyes. Sleeping with some guys was like saving their lives. Like it made you responsible for them. Maybe this was a bad idea, she thought. It was a question she'd had more than once after going to bed with somebody for the first time. And, she thought, she was usually right.

Not to mention that Thomas wasn't just some guy she'd let pick her up in a bar. He was Eddie's brother, for Christ's sake.

I'm not going to think about this, she told herself. Not now. She covered Thomas' hand with her own, pressing it into the softness of her breast.

It was still light, barely, when the second aftershock woke her up. The bed shook slightly, squeaking an inch or two across the floor. Thomas groaned and rolled over and went back to sleep. Lindsey felt her heart pounding in panic.

She sat up in bed. There weren't any windows in the room, just a transom over the door that looked down into the lobby. It doesn't matter, she thought. You don't need to see it. She had a sense of everything crumbling behind her, California and now Mexico City.

Her brain burned with half-finished thoughts. Her parents would hear about the quake on the news and panic. She had to call them. She needed plane reservations—could she and Thomas even fly out with everything in ruins this way?

Finally she calmed herself. She imagined the room was moving, accelerating on rails into the darkness. She closed her eyes and let the thrust push her back into her pillow.

O UTSIDE, the house was sky-blue stucco. Inside it had screens behind the louvered windows and black-and-white tile on the floors. The tile was set right over hardpacked dirt, with no slab underneath, so it had settled a bit in the middle. But it was tile just the same.

Carmichael sat on a metal folding chair. Once it had been the same color as the house, but most of the paint had flaked off. He was watching the closed door of the nearest bedroom.

It was Wednesday morning. Ten minutes ago, when he'd first gotten here, the bedroom door was open and he walked right in. He stopped when he saw Carla. She was sprawled across a hammock on her stomach, biting down on a wad of saliva-soaked denim. The room smelled like raw hamburger. A woman in loose white pants and a white T-shirt stood over her. She was digging in the back of Carla's thigh with hands that looked like they were smeared with melted chocolate.

They had both stared at him and he'd quietly backed out of the room and shut the door. There was nobody else in the house. Faustino and the others were out trying to scare up food and money. The people who owned the place, whoever they were, had apparently decided to stay with relatives. Carmichael knew the feeling. He saw it in the faces of the people the rebels had put him with. That look of dread and guilt and impatience, the look of somebody that had just been swindled and then found out they could go to jail for it.

The bedroom door finally opened. The doctor stood drying her hands on a stolen hotel towel. "You can come in now," she said. She had the vestiges of some kind of British accent.

"Thanks," Carmichael said.

Carla nodded to him as he came in. She sat high in the hammock, fresh bandages on her shoulder and foot. Carmichael couldn't see the bandages on her leg because of her jeans. She looked a bit stunned, but that was better than she looked ten minutes ago.

The doctor had a deep tan and blonde hair that curved to just below her ears. The hair put parentheses around her pale eyes and jutting nose. Her oversized T-shirt, barely dented by her small, pointed breasts, was now lightly dotted with drying blood.

It had been weeks since Carmichael had seen a woman from his own culture, which was to say, tall and blonde and English-speaking, not bound up in brassieres and long skirts and centuries of Catholicism. Despite the bloodstains he expected her to smell of perfume; in fact she didn't smell of anything at all.

"I've heard of you," Carmichael said to her in English. "You're the one that comes through Nahá every few months, takes care of the Lacondones. They all talked about you."

"Yes, that's me. I just came from there, in fact."

"I was there about three weeks ago." He tried to make

eye contact with her but she was looking at her instruments, washing them in orange-stained water, and laying them out on a stack of the hotel hand towels. "I did a story on Chan Ma'ax."

"Mmmm," she said.

"One of the compas comes from Nahá," Carla said in Spanish. Carmichael didn't know she'd been paying attention, let alone that her English was good enough to keep up. "He talks all the time about this old *brujo,* this Chan Ma'ax. Is he still alive?"

"As far as I know," the doctor said, switching now to Spanish too. "I'm here two days early because Chan Ma'ax and half his village are off on a pilgrimage. Nahá is practically deserted."

"Where did they go?" Carmichael asked. "Na Chan?"

The doctor nodded. She put the towels and the instruments into an expensive-looking leather and canvas backpack.

"Na Chan," Carla said.

"It's a beautiful place," the doctor said. "I've been through there two or three times. The Americans got the place mostly dug up and then went off and left it again. It looks like the Mayans just left or something. Very eerie, sort of decayed-looking." She buckled the pack and hefted it. "Well. I have to go. The arm and the thigh are not so bad, I think. The foot is serious. If you don't take care of it, it may have to come off. It may have to come off anyway."

"Thank you for what you've done," Carla said. "The revolution could use your skills."

"Your revolution is already giving me more patients than I can deal with."

"You don't approve," Carla said.

"I don't take sides. Yours *or* the government's." She got into the pack and adjusted the padding on the straps. "But I should warn you. There's a big convoy of American soldiers just outside town. They're coming this way."

"Northamericans?" Carla asked. *"Yanquis?"* The way she came down on the "y" it sounded like "junkies."

"Yes," the doctor said.

"You're sure?" Carmichael said.

"Why should you expect to know about it?" Carla asked. "Your government doesn't tell you these things."

"But where did they come from?" Carmichael had lapsed into English.

"The sky, I should think," the doctor said. "Like great white gods. Descending from heaven on the wings of an airlift. Now if you'll excuse me I really must be going."

"Wait," Carmichael said. "Ever since I've been down here everybody's just sort of taken for granted that there were U.S. troops here. But nobody had actually seen them with their own eyes."

The doctor was smiling to herself. "I expect you'll have that privilege before much longer."

He didn't want her to leave. "I don't even know your name," he said.

"You won't be needing it," she said, and shut the door behind her.

Carla sat up in the hammock. There was a pile of old woman's clothes on the floor next to her and she started trying to fit her bandaged arm into the sleeve of the dress.

"I thought you would be gone by now," she said to Carmichael. "What happened to your story?"

"I have a little portable computer in my pack. I wrote the story on the computer, and then sent it over the phone."

"Fantastic," Carla said. "But aren't you afraid to stay here?"

"You have a meeting with Raul Venceremos. I want to see it. If I could just get some pictures, the two of you together, that would do it. I could feel like I was finished. Then I could go home."

"You're crazy. You can't come."

"Why not?"

"Do you know what you're asking? Do you know what would happen if the guardia caught the two of us together?"

"You can trust me. You know you can. Faustino trusts me." In fact Faustino had sent a correo to tell him where

Carla was. "Don't tell me Venceremos isn't looking for publicity."

"All right, all right." Even sitting up seemed to exhaust her. "You can come. But if Venceremos says no, you have to go away. You promise?"

"Sure, okay, I promise."

"Good. Now get out of here and let me get dressed."

She wouldn't let Carmichael walk with her. She told him she looked suspicious enough hobbling around on the crutch Faustino had made her. It was a forked branch, and the crosspiece was tied on with twine. Folded newspaper was scotch-taped into the fork for padding.

Carmichael gave her a two-minute head start and then went after her.

The streets were empty except for little clouds of dust that flared up in front of the wind. This was the upper-class part of town, separated from the jungle by a few acres of cornfields. It was high enough on the hillside that Carmichael could look down on the village church and the *zócalo* in front of it, half a mile away. As he moved downhill the blues and pinks and yellows of the houses gave way to whitewash and plain adobe or cinderblock.

The doors and windows were shut. Word had obviously gotten out that the U.S. soldiers were coming. There was a bonfire burning two streets away, and another at the foot of the hill. The air was full of sour smoke. The Sandinistas had used bonfires to lure people to their rallies. Now they were a symbol of revolution all across Latin America.

Carmichael turned a corner and saw Carla a block and a half ahead of him, limping painfully. Her disguise was good. In the shawls and the rosary, the black dress padded out with dirty clothes, the red and green mesh plastic shopping bag, she was perfect. She was virtually invisible.

She stopped in a doorway and talked to someone for a few seconds, then went inside. Carmichael counted to a hundred and walked up to the house.

There were two kids in jeans and T-shirts on the doorstep. They had bandanas on, ready to pull up over their faces Sandanista-style. The older one was maybe fifteen. In the shadow of the doorway Carmichael could see a .22 single-shot rifle. The younger boy had a Saturday night special tucked into his pants.

"*Qué queres, gabacho?*" the older one asked.

"I'm invited," Carmichael said.

"Invited to what?"

"The meeting. Carla and Venceremos."

"You got the password?" the younger one said.

"*Cállate, pendejo!*" said the older one, slapping him hard on top of the head. "There isn't no fucking password."

"Quit hitting me!" The younger one's eyes were red and his voice had turned shrill.

"Shit, you're such a baby."

Suddenly the younger one was standing up and his hand was on the cheap revolver. "I'm not a fucking baby."

Carmichael took a step back.

"Okay, okay," the older one said. "You're not a baby. You're a fucking pendejo, but you're not a baby. Now sit down and watch this asshole while I go ask." He looked at Carmichael. "What's your name?"

"Carmichael. John Carmichael."

"Okay. You stay here while I go in. Or Rafael, he'll shoot your ass."

"That's right," the young one said.

The older one went inside with the rifle.

"How old are you?" Carmichael asked.

"None of your fucking business," Rafael said.

Carmichael raised his hands. "Yeah, okay," he said. "Relax." He stood in the heat and silence for a minute or so. Off in the distance he thought he heard the low hum of machinery. The U.S. convoy, Carmichael thought.

Then the older kid was back, motioning him in with his rifle barrel.

"Raul Venceremos," the man said. He got up and shook Carmichael's hand. Just a few seconds before, Carmichael had taken him for a posturing clown. Now the smile and the body language were saying that Carmichael had no choice but to take him seriously.

Venceremos wore neatly pressed green fatigues. He was short and heavyset, with a thick mustache. He wore a black beret at an angle and had a single gold stud in his right ear. His handshake left cheap cologne on Carmichael's fingers.

Across the table from him, Carla had pulled her shawls down around her shoulders. The shopping bag was on the floor next to her, in easy reach. Carmichael knew there was a .45 automatic buried in the rags inside it.

Two young soldiers with M16s leaned against the wall behind Venceremos, acting like they weren't paying attention. Otherwise the house was empty. The young soldiers had clean fatigues, just like Venceremos. Carla was staring hard at their boots. They were black, high-top combat boots that laced all the way up, probably Vietnam surplus. Informant's boots, the compas called them, because none of the real guerrillas could afford them.

"Did you want pictures?" Venceremos asked.

"Sure," Carmichael said. "Can I get you two together?"

"Not dressed like this," Carla said. "I look like an idiot." She waited for Carmichael to let her off the hook, but he didn't say anything. He really wanted the pictures. Finally she unbuttoned the top of the heavy black dress and pulled it down over her shoulders. She had an olive-drab T-shirt on underneath. It obviously hurt like hell for her to get her arms out of the dress, but nobody offered to help.

Carmichael posed them shaking hands across the table. They both looked appropriately grim. "Okay," he said. "That should do it for now." If they loosened up he would try to shoot some more later.

"There isn't much time," Carla said. "While we sit here talking the Northamericans are moving into town."

"I know this." Venceremos scratched one nostril and

then smoothed his mustache. "I'm willing to get right to business if you are."

"Please."

"We both know what the problem is," Venceremos said. "The problem is there are at least two dozen leftist parties and revolutionary movements in this country. There is no common leadership, no coordination."

Carla's face was blank. "Like you say, we all know what the problem is."

"And we both know the answer. All of us do. We need to have some kind of umbrella organization, like the FSLN in Nicaragua. We have to do what the PSUM tried to do and failed. We have to all agree on someone to lead a united front, and we have to all dedicate our soldiers to the common leadership. Until then we are only a lot of different fleas annoying the same dog."

"Yes, we know this. We all know this. Does this mean you're offering me the job?"

Venceremos leaned back in his chair, rubbing nervously at his mustache. "Your name was of course mentioned."

"Shit. Who mentioned it? What did they say? When did you have all these discussions? Why wasn't I there to mention some names for myself?"

"You were needed with your soldiers. Lieutenant Ramos was there to represent you."

"Mother of God!" Carla leaned across the table. "Ramos does not represent me! He represents *you!* He doesn't speak for me, he just says whatever you tell him to say!"

Venceremos looked at Carmichael for sympathy. Carmichael held completely still. Venceremos turned back to Carla. *"Cálmate,"* he said gently. "Nothing is settled yet." Carla sat down. "Just answer one question," he said. "Would you want the job if we offered it to you? Honestly?"

"No," Carla said. "But that's not the point."

"It *is* the point. Be realistic. Your strengths are as a soldier, a fighter. You belong in the mountains. To unite all these factions will take a diplomat, a politician. Let each of us serve according to our abilities."

"I'm sick of politicians. Fuck all politicians. The politicians gave us the world we have now."

"I admire your idealism. But what happens after the revolution is successful? Who will lead us then?"

"Let the people decide that."

For the first time Venceremos dropped his watery smile.

"Don't be an idiot! Even a totally free election must have candidates. You know as well as I do the people will vote for whoever they think they're *supposed* to vote for."

"What's the use in arguing? Why am I even here? You've already decided. You've elected yourself. So what do you want from me? You want me to sprinkle you with holy water?"

Venceremos turned to one of the guards. "Get me the paper," he said. More cheap theater, Carmichael thought. The kid made a big deal out of getting a cardboard tube out of a knapsack at his feet and presenting it to Venceremos.

Venceremos took a sheet of onionskin paper out of the tube, rolled it in the opposite direction to flatten it, and laid it on the table in front of Carla.

"You want to see this?" she asked Carmichael.

He read over her shoulder. The top of the page said, "Manifesto of the Popular Front for Free Mexico." In Spanish the acronymn came out FPML. Underneath were six numbered paragraphs calling for the resignations of President de la Madrid and eight other key PRI members, free elections, land reform, a new oil policy. The paper promised "acts of terrorism and violence" if the demands were not met. It was typed on a cheap machine; the "a" and "g" keys needed cleaning.

It was signed by "Raul Venceremos, FPML," and half a dozen others. Most of the bottom of the page was filled with the names of the movements they represented: the Socialist Worker's Party, the Nationalist Revolutionary Civic Association, the Party of the Poor, the Communist

League 23rd of September, the Armed Revolutionary Movement.

"Let's just say I didn't want to sign it," Carla said. "What would happen then?"

"Why would you not want to sign?" Venceremos said.

"Let's not talk about reasons. Let's just say for the sake of argument that I didn't. What then?"

"Then you would be left behind. Your efforts would be wasted because they would not be coordinated with the rest of our work. We would not be able to include you in the provisional government we will set up after our victory."

"And, of course, you would no longer be able to guarantee my safety. True?"

Venceremos shrugged.

Carla read the manifesto again, rubbing the palm of her right hand with the thumb of her left. It looked to Carmichael like she was doing it to keep from wadding the paper up and throwing it at Venceremos.

Finally she said, "The language . . . is very . . . nice." She would not look at Venceremos. "You have to understand. I can't make a decision like this on my own. I have to put it to a vote. That's the way Acuario would have wanted it."

If he were alive, Carmichael thought. If Acuario were alive there would be no question as to who would lead the united front. For just a second, Carmichael wondered if Venceremos could have been behind Acuario's murder. With one shot the movement got a martyr and Venceremos moved into the top slot.

"I understand," Venceremos said. His head moved in stiff little increments, like a lizard's or a bird's. He looked like it caused him physical pain not to shout at her.

Carla stood up. "I'll be in touch in a day or two. I'll send a correo."

Venceremos nodded. His face was red with rage. He pulled the paper back toward him with the ends of his fingers, as if Carla had pissed on it. Carmichael kept thinking of the .45 in her shopping bag. Carla turned her back on Venceremos. Nothing happened. She opened the door and Carmichael followed her into the street.

Rafael, the little boy with the pistol, waved to her. *"Ten cuidado, vieja,"* he said. Take care, old woman. Carla stared at him in amazement.

"Come on," Carmichael said.

"The little prick," Carla said, walking away. "He could be shot by the guardia, just for having that gun. But it means nothing to him. It's just a game. Like with the bigger prick inside, that he works for. *Piricuaca!* I don't believe that shit he was handing me."

"What are you going to do?"

"Go back to the mountains. Fight. At least that's something I can understand. Fuck politics. Fuck this Venceremos and his manifesto."

"What about all that business he was telling you? About you getting left behind?"

"Oh, I believe it. It's politicians that make the revolutions. Venceremos will probably get to write the history of this one. The people really don't come into it at all, not till the end. I mean, they sympathize, and eventually, when they can see it's safe, they all join in. But mostly they're afraid."

She stopped in the middle of the street, leaning all her weight into the crutch. Carmichael reached out to steady her. "No, don't," she said. "You have to leave. In just a second."

"Okay," he said.

"You know what happened this morning? The safe-house I'm staying in belongs to this man Hernández. He comes over this morning with his little boy to get some things. The boy is maybe six or seven. Hernández is in the other bedroom and I'm showing the boy my pistol. Unloaded, you understand. This is something I got out of your CIA book, to show the people your weapons, let them not be afraid of them. So I'm letting him handle the pistol and you know what he says?"

Carmichael shook his head.

"He's pointing the gun and playing like he's shooting and he says *'cowboy'* just like that, in English. *'Cowboy.'*

He knows nothing, you see? Nothing. Just television. And his father comes in and sees him with the gun, and I'm thinking he's going to be angry, or maybe even he's going to be proud and happy, but all he is is sad. He just stands there, watching, looking like he's going to cry he's so sad."

Carla looked away from him, down the street. "It makes you wonder. You wonder why you keep on."

"Are you going to be all right?" Carmichael asked.

"*Claro que sí.* I'll be fine. I'm just tired, very tired." She took a tentative step. "I have to go. Don't follow me anymore. It's too dangerous."

He stood there in the street and watched her until she turned the corner and disappeared.

He had to walk almost to the zócalo before he found a cafe where he could sit down. The waiter brought him a Tres Equis and he squeezed a pool of lime juice on top of the can and knocked half of it back. It was only eleven in the morning, for Christ's sake. The restaurant was deserted and he could hear the creaking of the overhead fans as they threatened to rip themselves loose from the ceiling.

Everything seemed to be coming loose.

Time to get the hell out of Dodge, Carmichael thought. Cobble something together on the computer, get the pictures developed before the film got accidentally X-rayed, and catch the next anything back to L.A. It wasn't going to be the story he wanted. It was going to have a lot of loose ends, and not much opinion in it. It would end just where things got interesting, with Carla's fate left hanging. Too bad, he thought.

A jeep bounced down the street, past the open front of the cafe.

Carmichael took his beer over to watch. Before the dust of the first jeep settled, a second one shot by. Carmichael figured they were doing at least forty, twice what the narrow, bumpy streets were built for. A third jeep squealed to a stop just a few yards away and this time Carmichael got a decent look at the insignia on the side.

It was a shield shape with the word "FIGHTING" above it and the letters "666TH," done comic-book style, breaking out of the edges. Ram's horns came off the top corners and there was a laughing mouth under the letters, where the shield came to a point. The overall effect was of a three-eyed Satanic face that made Carmichael very uncomfortable.

The men in the jeep didn't make him feel any better. The sunlight was bright and the bar was dark and he could watch them without being seen. He'd expected them to be a bunch of green kids with shaved heads. Instead they looked like construction workers. Only one of the six looked to be younger than late twenties or early thirties. They wore T-shirts, gimme caps, long hair, and various cutoff and tie-dyed variations of fatigues. They had mustaches, sideburns, and in one case a full beard. There were three anglos, two blacks, and one somewhere in between who could have been Chicano, Indian, or Iranian as far as Carmichael could tell.

The jeep lurched forward again and the rest of the convoy rattled after it. By this time the dust was so thick that Carmichael couldn't see any more faces. He counted another seven jeeps and then it was over.

"So what do you think?" he asked the bartender.

"About what?"

"The Northamericans. The soldiers. Coming to your town."

"Good for them. I hope they kick the rebels' asses." But he wouldn't look at Carmichael while he talked.

Is it the truth? Carmichael wondered. Or are you telling me what you think I want to hear?

He took another swallow of beer but it had gotten too much dust in it. He left it sitting on a table by the door with a handful of nearly worthless hundred-peso notes.

He could barely hear the phone ringing but Pam's voice was clear enough. "Wilshire Bureau."

"This is Carmichael."

"Carmichael. Jesus Christ, where are you?"

"Usumacinta. It's a little town in Chiapas."

"So what are you doing? I thought you were coming back."

"I was. I just saw something weird. A whole company of U.S. soldiers. They had a thing on their jeeps that said Fighting 666th."

"What? Did you say 666th?"

"Yeah, do you know who they are?"

"Don't you get the papers down there? Jesus Christ, hold on a second."

Carmichael looked out through fogged plastic at the long-distance office. It was a wide linoleum hallway with booths along one side, cheap plastic chairs along the other. The operator had dialed Carmichael's call and assigned him a booth when it went through. He would pay the collect-call charge at the desk on his way out.

Pam came back on the line. "You really haven't heard any of this?"

"Any of what?"

"*Sixty Minutes* did an interview Sunday with a so-called retired major general named Singlaub. He's head of something called the United States Council for World Freedom."

"That sounds ominous."

"They're part of the World Anti-Communist League. They finance private armies all over the world. The Nicaraguans just shot down a plane of theirs carrying arms and stuff to the contras."

"So you're saying this 666th . . ."

"It's one of theirs. We're talking an entire private army here. This '666th' is commanded by a Colonel Marsalis. We started a file on him Monday. Just a sec." Carmichael listened to the dry rattle of computer keys. "Listen to this. Vietnam vet, court-martialed and acquitted for a My Lai type deal. Took early retirement three years ago. At which time he recruited a bunch of his old unit from Nam for this guy Singlaub."

"Can he do that?"

"Legally, you mean? There's no law against American citizens fighting in foreign wars. It's illegal to recruit inside the U.S. for a military strike against a country we're not at war with. But how are you going to prove it? And if you mean realistically can he do it, let me mention that the pilot of that plane in Nicaragua worked for Southern Air Transport. Does that ring any bells?"

"CIA," Carmichael said.

"Bingo. Singlaub as much as admitted in the interview that Reagan was personally giving him Company money. Now the shit's hit the fan and everybody is denying everything. We figured this 666th was in Nicaragua. Have you got pictures?"

"Not yet."

"If you can get them, do it. If you can prove they're in Mexico, we could be talking Pulitzer here. But be careful, okay? No kidding. They are not going to want this getting out."

The long-distance office was a block off the zócalo. From the doorway Carmichael watched the jeeps circle like Indians attacking a wagon train.

There was a fresh roll of Tri-X in the camera. He stood and held it for a little while, feeling the strap cutting into the back of his neck. He stopped down to f/5.6. That would at least give him a little depth of field.

He lifted the camera and started shooting. He shot the entire roll as fast as the motor could wind the film. Once he started he was afraid to keep going, afraid to stop. When he was finished he wrapped the strap around the camera and put it in his shirt. They hadn't seen him yet, or somebody would have come after him. Now all he had to do was get away.

It was about five steps to the corner. After that they wouldn't be able to see him. What are you worried about? he asked himself. They're your fellow Americans. Ha ha ha.

All he could think about were the guns. It wasn't going to get easier. He opened the door and stepped out in the street. He didn't want to turn his back to the jeeps in the square, but he did it anyway.

He couldn't remember how to walk normally. It was like sometimes when he was trying to get to sleep and he forgot how to swallow. Once he started thinking about it it wasn't automatic anymore and it got very awkward and his mouth filled up with spit. Walking now felt like there were strings going from his hands to the ends of his hiking boots, like he was some kind of clumsy, self-propelled marionette. A marionette in a shooting gallery.

The corner was a lifetime away, and then suddenly, finally, he was around it.

He broke into a shuffling run. The streets all looked the same. Their names, set in tiles on the corners of the buildings, changed every few blocks. But he oriented himself by the bonfires and worked out where he had to go.

Three blocks uphill he cut to his right. He was going to have to cross one of the parallel streets that led back to the zócalo. Either they would see him, he thought, or they wouldn't. There wasn't much he could do about it.

He slowed to a walk and started across. He couldn't hear the roaring of the jeeps anymore. It made him nervous but he didn't want to look, superstitiously afraid that they would be able to feel him watching. If only there had been somebody else on the streets. If only he had dark hair and a suntan. If only he didn't have the goddamn camera pushing out the front of his shirt.

Somebody shouted. He heard an engine kick over. I'm dead, he thought. He glanced down the hill. The jeeps were all stopped and in one of them a ragged blond soldier in a headband stood up, staring at him. "Hey!" the soldier yelled. "Hey, wait up!"

Carmichael smiled and nodded like he hadn't quite heard and kept walking. When he got past the edge of the first building he bolted, then saw there was nowhere to go.

He ran to a door in the middle of the block and pounded on it. "Help me!" he shouted in Spanish. "For God's sake! Let me in!" He tried the flimsy latch on the door and it opened.

Inside was a tiny dirt patio. There were pots all around it, full of purple flowers. Beyond it was a screen door with clouded plastic stapled over where the screen should have been. He shut the gate behind him but didn't see any way to bolt it. "Hello?" he said. He could hear jeeps in the street outside.

He tried the door. It led into a kitchen, with a family sitting around a scarred wooden table. The mother was a short, thick *campesina,* the father not much taller, with a mustache and oiled hair. Four kids from puberty on down. A grandmother, dressed the same as Carla had been that morning, all in black, an ersatz nun, the last stage of evolution of the Mexican female. Her eyes were filmy and she was still eating, probably didn't even know Carmichael was standing there.

"Lo siento," Carmichael said. "I'm sorry. I have to hide myself. American . . . Northamerican soldiers are coming. Can you help me? Please?" His hands were shaking. He put them in his pockets.

The kids just stared at him. The mother looked at the floor. The grandmother was still eating. Finally the father stood up. He didn't say anything. He curled his hand at Carmichael and took him back into a bedroom. There was a shelf in the top of the closet, over a wooden dowel loaded with women's dresses. The man pulled down an old green army blanket and then laced his hands together to make a step for Carmichael's foot.

It was the posture of the conquered, and it made Carmichael feel petty and soiled. It made him feel almost as bad as the idea of getting in that closet.

"Par allá?" he said. He didn't believe there was room, let alone that the ancient boards would hold him. The man didn't move or change his expression. Carmichael put his hands on the shelves and let the man boost him up.

His shoulders hit the walls and ceiling, and it took three tries to get his legs to bend far enough to squeeze them through the doorway. He clutched the camera, afraid it would fall and smash on the floor. He couldn't seem to get his breath and sweat crawled out of his pores. The boards creaked and bent under him and he struggled to get his weight as close to the ends of the shelf as possible.

Somebody was pounding at the door of the house. Carmichael heard shouting in Northamerican accents. The man threw the blanket back over him and shut the closet. Carmichael fought with the blanket until he could see stripes of light leaking between the boards of the door.

The blanket was frayed and motheaten and had a sweet, musky odor that nearly gagged him. It felt like sandpaper on his bare legs. His clothes were soaked in sweat and he thought he was going to black out. He forced himself to suck in huge lungfuls of air.

He could hear plates and knives in the dining room, badly accented Spanish and the husband answering. What if he set me up? Carmichael thought. What if he chickens out? Or if he's a lousy actor? What, for God's sake, if they start lining up his kids and shooting them until he tells where I am? Would our guys do that?

His left leg started to go numb. The muscles in his right leg were hard as steel cables. Claustrophobia. He'd never had it before. He just needed to be able to kick his legs and stretch his shoulders and he would be all right. Knowing he couldn't, feeling the pressure of the gritty mud walls around him, gave him fierce muscle spasms.

He turned enough that blood could get to his left leg, then braced against the walls and pushed. Pushed and relaxed. It was starting to help when he heard something outside the closet.

He could see somebody moving in the bedroom, making shadows through the cracks in the door. He heard the mattress come off the flimsy metal springs and hit the floor. "Closet," a voice said in English.

The door opened. Carmichael saw a white kid with a mohawk, not a punk mohawk but a wide strip of short-cut hair down the center of his head. He wore fatigue pants and a Def Leopard T-shirt. The black man behind him was bare-chested, with camo pants and a rolled bandana around his forehead. They both had bullpups, plastic infantry rifles that looked like toys, the trigger guards and handle too far forward and the magazine coming out of the buttstock.

The white kid poked his gun around in the clothes. "Ain't shit in here," he said. "Bunch a fuckin' dresses."

"Let's move," the black man said.

They left the closet door open and the mattress on the floor. Slowly Carmichael let the air out of his lungs. He heard them crashing through the rest of the house and then everything went quiet.

He waited another half hour before he finally staggered back onto the street, drenched in sour sweat, muscles cramped and aching, heartsick and afraid.

A correo came for him that night in the safehouse. It was a ten-year-old girl he'd never seen before. She took him to the edge of the jungle where Carla and Faustino were sitting a few yards off the trail, waiting for him.

"The soldiers didn't find you," Carmichael said, sitting down next to them. He could barely hear his own whisper over the grinding of the insects.

"No," Carla said. "But we can't stay any longer."

"Where can you go?"

"Back in the mountains. To Na Chan, I think."

"Is this . . . because of that vision you had? That Kukulcán business?"

"No," Carla said. "It's just good sense. The ruins give us plenty of cover. The government wouldn't think to look for us there. If they did, they wouldn't attack for fear of hurting the temples."

Faustino watched her while she talked and then looked at Carmichael. "It's because of the goddamned vision," he said.

"You think I'm crazy," Carla said.

"Yes."

"Are we going to have a mutiny? A coup?"

"Not yet," Faustino said. "You're still too weak. It would be no contest."

"A joke," Carla said. "My God, he made a joke. Don't forget to tell this in your story. The night Faustino made a joke."

They all stood up. "I had to hide from the soldiers,"

Carmichael said. "My own people, my own countrymen. I had to hide in this little closet. I was lying there, thinking, this is crazy, you can just talk to them, explain everything. But I couldn't. If I'd had a gun I think I would have killed them, I was so afraid."

"Where do you go now?" Carla asked.

"I'm going to find out about this Colonel Marsalis, find out what these soldiers are doing here. That's where the story is now."

"Good luck," Carla said.

"You too," Carmichael told her. He couldn't help thinking, as he watched her limp off down the trail, that she was going to need it more than he would.

The next morning Carmichael woke up to the sound of starters cranking. It was just after dawn. He borrowed a pair of ragged pants and a beat-up straw cowboy hat from a pile of clothes in the corner. Standing in the open doorway he could see the soldiers all the way down at the end of the street, driving uphill toward him.

And then, without any kind of signal, things began to fly out of the doors and windows that faced the street. Bottles, cans, broken furniture, sacks of garbage, old tires. Nothing hit the jeeps, or even came close. It just piled up in the road in front of them.

Carmichael stepped back into the shadows. The lead jeep crawled by, the driver hunched over the wheel, swerving around the worst of the glass and nails and piles of trash. The men in the back of the jeep were standing up, facing the houses with rifles up and ready. But they didn't have anything to shoot at.

Carmichael remembered the way they'd come into town, racing their engines and laughing and shouting. They weren't shouting now. The thought made him feel tight and congested, like he had a chest cold. "Adiós, motherfuckers," he whispered, and then he started laughing.

It was a long time before he could stop. By then the sun was up and the jeeps were gone and the streets were full of broken glass.

TWO

EDDIE'S SENSE OF TIME got turned around in the moonlight. He was in a hammock off to himself, about fifty feet from the Temple of the Inscriptions. A stucco serpent god stared down at him from one corner of the pyramid. The moonlight made it look like it had been carved that afternoon. The pits and scars faded away, the low, flat forehead tilted toward him, the cheeks bulged into spheres, and the fangs arched in a hideous smile.

The god was young again and the city was his.

As an exercise, Eddie made himself work out the date. Wednesday, July the sixteenth, 1986. The numbers didn't mean anything to him.

He'd expected to find the lost city of Na Chan buried under jungle and tons of earth. Instead the half-dozen temples Thomas had restored were still pretty clear. He could see their shapes, even in the daytime when his imagination was at low ebb. The clearings had filled in with skinny fruit trees and low palm thickets, but the sense of the place, of its geography, was still there.

So were its ghosts. Eddie heard them in the long, narrow rooms on top of the pyramids. He thought about the power that a physical place could have, to be able to

warp time. He'd felt it from the start, from the first time
he saw the serpent god.

It had taken them three days to walk from Nahá. At
least a dozen times during the first day Eddie was sure
they were going to have to leave him behind. He was out
of shape, hung over from the balché, and he still didn't
know why Chan Ma'ax had decided to let him come. He
was wearing socks and tennis shoes, but the socks were
worn through at the heel and just behind the big toe.

When the afternoon rain hit they just kept walking.
Eddie couldn't believe it. The rain came down so hard it
bent his head and shoulders over, so hard that he could
barely see Ma'ax García right in front of him.

There were twelve Lacondones, making thirteen of
them altogether. Thirteen men on July 13th. Eddie didn't
much like the omens. Half the men in the village had
come; Chan Zapata was one of the ones that hadn't.
When Eddie asked Chan Ma'ax for a reason all he got
was the silent routine.

Eddie's breath steamed out in the rain. Everything had
gone gray. The dirt of the logging road turned instantly
to fine-grained mud that clung like cement. He heard a
kissing noise behind him, the Mexican equivalent of a
whistle or a "hey, you." He looked back. Nuxi' was waving at him to get out of the road. The others had already
climbed down out of the way.

There was a logging truck coming at them, just head-
lights and a black shape in the rain. Eddie stepped down
and watched the long empty bed of the truck rattle past.
We could all ride there, he thought. We're using their
road. What's the difference if we sell out just a little
more?

It was like Chan Ma'ax heard what he was thinking.
They suddenly turned off onto a trail that was so narrow
Eddie could hardly be sure it was there. They were completely under the trees now. The rain hit them in trickles
and sprays, making clicking noises as it worked down
through the network of leaves. The tops of the trees were

forty or fifty feet above them and there was plenty of room between the trunks for them to walk.

Eventually the rain stopped and the sun came out. The light seemed to thicken the air, like flour stirred into a sauce. It was hard to breathe. Eddie's wet socks ground into the blisters on his feet and he had stitches in both sides.

They walked until all the light was gone and then built a fire. One of the men had killed a peccary while Eddie wasn't paying attention. The roasting meat smelled wonderful but Eddie had been a vegetarian so long he knew he couldn't digest it.

He woke up shivering at dawn, his clothes and hammock and mosquito net soaked completely through with dew. Within fifteen minutes they were moving again.

By the third day Eddie was strong enough to notice more of what was going on around him. Nuxi' explained to him how the jungle had changed in the last fifty years. Most of the big animals were gone. The migrant Tzeltal Indians had moved deeper into the jungle, cutting and burning vast acres of trees for their milpas and leaving only grasslands behind. Now there were logging roads everywhere and the smell of diesel never quite went away.

On the afternoon of the third day Eddie saw his first limestone block, just off the trail, etched in green moss and covered with decaying leaves. Nuxi' stopped next to him. Eddie said, "It's from . . ." He didn't know the word in Mayan. ". . . *un templo*. Yes?"

Nuxi' nodded. "It gets better," he said. "You don't have to stop here." The Lacondones all seemed excited. They were talking to each other for the first time, moving faster down the trail.

They walked downhill, deeper into a valley. The single stones became mounds of rock, the exposed surfaces got more ornate. Through veils of branches Eddie could see a stucco hand or a carved helmet, like scattered pieces of a jigsaw puzzle.

The path bent around a hill of broken stone and the valley opened out in front of him.

He recognized the landmarks from his brother's book. Straight ahead were the long, low ruins of the Palace. It could have been a collapsed twentieth-century court-house, except for the mansard-style corbeled roofs and the four-story observatory that came out of the middle like a bell tower. To Eddie's right was the Temple of the Inscriptions, a stepped pyramid jutting out of the hillside. It was seventy-five feet high and almost free of vegetation. Right at eye level a hideous face stared back at him from the corner of the steps.

The enormous empty eyes held him. Nothing he'd seen before could compare. The concrete and asphalt of Teo-tihaucán, the arid plains of Chichén Itzá—they were all silent, dead, obsolete. Something at Na Chan was still alive. He could feel the vibration through his tortured feet, through the skin of his wrists.

Chan Ma'ax said, "The last time we were here, it was fifteen years ago. All this was still buried. They really did a job, no?"

"It was my brother," Eddie said.

"Yes, I know. I know your brother. Tomás."

"You never said anything."

The old man shrugged.

Thomas' camp had been in the square between the temples. Ma'ax García had brought plastic trash bags and now the men moved through the area, cleaning up ten-year-old shreds of plastic and empty cans.

"Does it bother you?" Eddie asked. "To see it this way, I mean? Put back like it was?"

"No," Chan Ma'ax said. "No, this is the way it should be. It's almost ready now. Ready for the end."

The Lacondones spent their first full day at Na Chan building two *ramadas,* thatched huts without walls, one to sleep in, one for a godhouse. They smiled and shook their heads whenever Eddie offered to help. Ma'ax Gar-cía had finally let him know how it was going to be.

"So," he said, as Eddie watched them trim the poles and set them in the ground. "Where do *you* want to sleep?"

Yeah, okay, Eddie thought. It's back to being the dumb white man again. "Where do you think?"

"Maybe over here someplace?" Ma'ax García took him off to a stand of trees in a corner of the courtyard between the Temple of the Inscriptions and the Palace.

"Sure," Eddie said. He had a good view of the serpent god, at least. "This'll be great." He would do what he was told and maybe eventually somebody would give him a clue to what was going on.

That afternoon Chan Ma'ax found him while he was working on one of Thomas' abandoned tents. It was a green nylon hemisphere with exterior aluminum poles and a couple of major rips in the side. But there were other tents in various stages of decay and he thought he might be able to cobble something together that would at least keep out the rain and the mosquitos.

"Come," was all Chan Ma'ax said.

Eddie got up and followed him. They took a path that cut between the two big temples. It led uphill for a while and then leveled off. On the right was a small pile of rocks that had once been some kind of structure. He couldn't imagine putting it back together with anything less than a full set of blueprints.

Chan Ma'ax kept turning off the path and cutting across through the trees to another one. It didn't take Eddie more than a couple of minutes of this to understand that the old man was deliberately turning him around. It gave him the idea that this was about the mushrooms. His palms started to sweat.

Finally Chan Ma'ax led him down the side of a hill and through a narrow ravine full of weeds. And then Eddie saw them.

Some of them were no bigger than the back of his hand, others nearly two feet tall, colored in reds and browns and golds. "They're beautiful," Eddie whispered.

They didn't look like anything he'd ever seen. The caps weren't as pointed as the psilocybin mushrooms in Texas, but they weren't the perfect spheres of an agaric, either. The skins were rough and knobby and the color reminded him more than anything of the sunburst finish on his old Fender Stratocaster.

"These are the only ones," Chan Ma'ax said. "They don't grow anywhere else. It's because of the ground, you see? Sacred ground."

Eddie nodded. It was all in his brother's book. Thomas had tried to transplant them and they'd all died. He'd tried to grow them from spores and nothing had ever sprouted. Eddie reached out to touch the nearest plant.

Chan Ma'ax snatched his wrist, hard enough to hurt. "No. These are not for you. The gringos and the *ladinos* that eat them go crazy. You understand? Very dangerous for you."

The old man was still holding on to him. "Why did you bring me here?" Eddie asked.

"Because I don't want you looking for them on your own. You see them now, okay? Now you know. Now you leave them alone."

Eddie stared at him. It didn't make sense. It sounded more like a challenge than a warning. "Okay," Eddie said. "Whatever you say." Chan Ma'ax let go of his wrist. Eddie rubbed it with his left hand. Jesus, the old bastard was strong. Eddie thought he was going to say something else, but he just stood up and waited for Eddie to follow him.

But Eddie paid attention on the way back, making a map in his mind, and he knew he could find the mushrooms again.

Eddie flipped the mosquito net up and got out of the hammock. He'd been sleeping in his socks because of the mosquitos; even with the net they bit him through the bottom of the hammock. If he could get one of the tents put together it would have to help.

He took the socks off and started for the trees. The Lacondones' ramada was only a dozen yards away. Eddie wondered if Chan Ma'ax was really asleep, or if he was lying awake, waiting for Eddie to make his move.

If he is, Eddie thought, let him stop me.

His bare feet didn't make any noise on the path. Once

he passed the threshold of the trees he lost most of the moonlight. What light there was seemed to come out of the rocks and trees themselves. Mushroom light, hallucination light.

He was trembling, a little. It had been a long time since he'd done any psychedelics. Balché was no substitute. He would, he thought, just go have another look at the things. They were beautiful. They would be something to see in the moonlight.

He took the left-hand path and skipped a couple of the detours that Chan Ma'ax had made. There were noises in the distance, high up in the trees. The *Yumil Qax-ob,* the Lords of the Forest. Most of them were dead now, Chan Ma'ax said, or sleeping. Waiting for Cabracan to wake them for the end.

He found the ravine with the mushrooms and sat down in front of them. If I eat some of this, he thought, not that I really would or anything, but if I did, I'd never find my way back.

One of the kids on his brother's crew had eaten a piece. He was down for the summer from Arizona State, a classic early seventies freak, wouldn't cut his hair even to save himself endless hassles in Mexico. Somebody found him in the mushroom grove with red blotches all over his face and neck and chest. He was sweating like crazy and his temperature went up to 105 and stayed there, even after they packed him in ice. Thomas knew enough to give him Thorazine, but it might as well have been Rolaids. The kid couldn't verbalize at all, just stared and clicked his jaws together.

They got a helicopter to fly him out and after a week his parents came and took him back to the States. At the time Thomas wrote the book, which would have been '75, the kid was still catatonic.

Okay, Eddie thought. I'm just going to look.

He leaned back with his elbows in the dirt. The caps of the mushrooms glistened in the moonlight and Eddie could smell the damp earth they grew out of. The wind cooled the left side of his face and moved the plants from side to side. They looked like cartoon Orientals in conical hats, swaying to some inaudible music.

The wind died out but the mushrooms kept moving. Hypnotic, sensual. Beckoning to him.

He reached out and broke a thumbnail-sized piece off the nearest plant. The others stopped moving as soon as he touched its flesh.

I'll take it back to the camp, he thought. I'll get up now and take it back.

He put the sliver of mushroom in his mouth. He chewed it cautiously with his front teeth and swallowed. It was crunchy, in a damp sort of way, and tasted like boiled celery.

I've done it now, he thought, oddly calm. He moved up the hill a little and settled his back against the furred bark of a ramón tree. He shut his eyes and listened to the true lords of the forest, the insects and the tree frogs and the distant, hooting monkeys.

Fifteen minutes later the drug took him with a kick that nearly lifted him off the ground. His heart pounded and he felt the dizzy, roller-coaster rush of the alkaloids going after his nervous system. Christ, he thought, all this from one sliver?

The night pulsed with incandescent purple highlights. The mushrooms in the grove snapped into high relief, as if lightning had hit right behind them. They seemed to go on to infinity in all directions. Eddie tried to stand up, to head back toward camp. Just moving his shoulders made him so dizzy that he collapsed back against the tree. Holy shit, he thought. Holy shit.

His eyes turned up. He couldn't stop them. The lids came down and he fell into graphite-colored darkness. A double spiral made of bits of red and green and yellow neon spun toward him. He had just enough sense of his body left to know that he wasn't moving, not physically. Still he felt himself reaching out, being sucked into the spiral.

Colored images shot past him like speeding cars. He could feel the roar of their passing in his stomach. Each image was a tiny window, and there was a world beyond each of them. This is where he lost it, Eddie thought, remembering the kid from his brother's dig.

He forced his eyes open. His face ran with sweat. He could feel tiny salt crystals burning the flushed, fevered skin. He tried to focus on the infinite regression of plants. His eyes would not stay open.

He told himself he was all right. He'd managed to pull himself out of it, at least for a few seconds. He was in control. He shut his eyes.

This time when he fell into the spiral, when the neon bullets shot past him, he managed to slow them down. It was like falling into a well, a well hundreds of miles deep. At the end was a point source of white light that was pulling him, hard. Where the kid ended up, Eddie thought. If he fell that far he wouldn't be able to crawl back up.

He looked at the blobs of colored light. They leaked images, sounds, emotions. There were pieces of himself inside. The harder he looked, the more disoriented he got. It was like one of those brain teasers, the pyramid of blocks that would turn upside down if he blinked. Suddenly the blobs of neon were under him instead of beside him, the concave pattern warping in the center, pulling him down.

He stopped fighting and one of them puffed out like a golden fireball and took him in.

He stood in a room with pale mustard walls. Through the window he could see trees and a white two-story building with columns. He knew instantly what he was seeing. Timberlawn Psychiatric Hospital, Dallas, Texas.

Christ, he thought. He'd hallucinated plants growing up through the floor before, alien landscapes through the window. But he'd never hallucinated anything this *real* before. This ordinary. The weirdest part was how solid and boring everything seemed. No squiggles, no halos of soft golden light.

Somebody was talking. He realized it was his own voice, and the next second he couldn't remember what he'd been saying. He looked down and saw his hands. He wasn't supposed to be able to see his hands if he was dreaming. He told the fingers to move and they moved.

"Yates has lost it again," somebody said. It was a thin-faced young guy in a lab coat. Bergen, Eddie thought. His name was Bergen.

"Sit down, Eddie." Now it was Ryker talking, an LSD burnout case with long hair falling diagonally across his left eye.

"Yeah, Eddie," said Meyers, the fat retarded kid. "Yeah, Eddie. Yeah, Eddie."

He felt cold all over. He looked down, saw he was standing on his bed. He sat in the middle of the mattress and put his legs over the side and wrapped his arms around his chest.

"Okay, show's over," Bergen said. "Meyers, come on. You've got PT now."

It's not happening, Eddie thought. It can't be. I'm not back here in the looney bin. I'm in Mexico, I'm lying in the jungle. There's this bunch of mushrooms right in front of me. All I have to do is open my eyes and they'll be there.

But his eyes were already open. And Mexico was receding from him, like a half-remembered dream.

"Hey, Eddie, man, what happened?" Ryker said. Eddie was staring at the knees of Ryker's striped bell bottoms. "You were really going good, and then, blammo, nothing."

"What was I saying?"

"You were doing Stein, man. Don't you even remember? Oh, hey, man, sorry, I didn't mean to bum you."

Eddie shook his head. "It's okay." Stein was the deputy administrator. He wore Western-cut leisure suits with lots of topstitching. He screamed at patients when their families got behind on bills and was irrational on the subject of psychedelics, even marijuana.

Eddie remembered it all. The wards that smelled of farts and sour piss. Patients that acted like nobody could hear them, always crying or laughing or screaming. Bergen speed-rapping about God at four in the morning when all Eddie wanted to do was sleep. The slack eyes of the 11 to 7 nurse in the Women's Building who numbed out with tabs of Demerol from the pharmacy. Once she'd pulled Eddie into a janitor's closet and propped herself on the edge of the sink and hiked up her skirt. She wasn't wearing any panties. "Do it," she said, "hurry." But Eddie was dizzy from Stelazine and the tiny room smelled so much like Pine Sol that he couldn't breathe. He said he was sorry and she acted like it was about what she'd expected.

Eddie was here because he was temporarily unable to look at a guitar. Instead he made chords against the palm of his left hand. The C7, with the tucked little finger, was the best. The chords had become *mudras*, gestures of power. It felt good to put his fingers into the shapes, as long as he didn't have to get up in front of an audience or make any noise.

It had started in London, when he collapsed right before going on stage at the Palladium. The doctors told him to cancel the rest of the European tour, but said he would be all right for North America in September if he rested up. The week before the American tour he lost seventeen pounds and then put his hand into the bathroom mirror.

It was just that he wanted to hear something he hadn't heard before, to make the sounds in his head come out of his guitar. Right before he hit the mirror he'd been playing, watching his left hand. The worthless left hand. He knew everything it was going to do, all the pentatonic minor bullshit, and he hated the notes before they came out of the amp.

He'd been in Timberlawn almost a year now. Whenever he thought about going home he stopped sleeping. If he did get to sleep he woke up at 5 A.M. and thought about every bad thing he'd ever done. The time he slapped Susan Bishop in sixth grade. Sophomore year in high school, when he threw up Old Grand-Dad on the Minzers' Persian rug.

It was the bottom of his life. He had rolled back into it like a pinball falling between the flippers and dropping out of play.

"You sure you feel all right?" Ryker said.

"No," Eddie said. "I feel like shit."

"You want to talk about it?"

"You wouldn't believe me."

"So what have you got to lose?"

"I must have been dreaming," Eddie said. "I dreamed like ten years of my life. I was out of here and in Mexico. I can't believe it didn't happen. It's like you woke up thinking you were rich but you can't find the money anywhere. Or even a checkbook or anything to prove you ever had it."

"Let's go outside, man," Ryker said. "I got a joint."

Ryker and Eddie were voluntaries, which meant they had the run of the place. They ate steak and lobster and Mexican food at the cafeteria right alongside the staff. They could talk to visitors. They had to keep out of Administration and Medical Records, and they had to be back in their rooms by eight at night. They had to stay at least a hundred yards away from Samuels Boulevard, far enough that they could barely hear the big diesel rigs just beyond it on I-30.

Ryker went behind a tree to light the joint and came back with it hidden behind his curled fingers. Eddie sat down in the grass. "Here," Ryker croaked, holding in the smoke.

Eddie took a long drag and then three quick hits to top off his lungs. "Jesus," he said. "That's good."

"You ever think about really doing it?" Ryker said.

"What?"

"Just walking out."

There were pecans all over the lawn, most of them still wrapped in fuzzy green casings. A squirrel came within a few feet of Eddie's hand to snatch one and then run away. He didn't like the way the squirrel moved, the hyper little twitches, the black, paranoid eyes. It's just the dope, he thought. The dope is really screwing me up.

"Come on, man," Eddie said. "You know better than that. I freak every time I think about going home." He spread his hand, palm up, in the cool grass. As he watched, a Day-Glo-green praying mantis walked down off the tree and onto his fingers. The touch of its legs was creepy but he couldn't pull his hand away.

"Not home, man," Ryker said. "Just away. Just walk. I mean, if your life was already a prison before you got here you don't want to just go back to it. I'm talking about getting right out of the whole system. Changing the paradigm."

"Is this some kind of est bullshit?"

"No, I'm serious, man. Personal transformation. Like rewiring your own head, you dig?"

"How would you eat?"

"You got money, right? You get out, you clean out your account. Then you just get on a plane. Maybe go to Hawaii. Would that be far out? And just get a job, man. Like anybody else."

"Doing what? Playing guitar?" The mantis seemed to be watching him. Like it's waiting to give me a message, Eddie thought. The harder he stared at it the more it seemed to glow. He was afraid to say anything to Ryker about it, afraid Ryker wouldn't be able to see it.

"That's up to you. You can be whatever you want to be, man. If you don't want to play the motherfucking guitar and you don't want to go back to your wife, you don't have to do it. Wash dishes. Work construction. Get an apartment and a stereo and a girlfriend. Get off these goddamn drugs so your dick can get hard again. So you can *think* again. You're a spiritual guy, Eddie, I can see that. You think about stuff."

"I think too much," Eddie said. He shook the mantis off his hand and took another hit. The dope was really powerful. It made him so dizzy the edges of his vision turned gray. The mantis was still staring at him, with those horrible little stalk eyes. Why did it seem like it meant something? "If you like the idea so much, why don't *you* do it?" It was getting hard to talk.

"Maybe I will," Ryker said. A few seconds later he said, "You gonna let that J go out, or what?"

"Unhhhh," Eddie said.

"Man, are you okay? You don't look so good."

Eddie rolled onto all fours. "Got to . . . get back inside. Really . . . fucked up." He couldn't get up. He lost his balance and slumped back into the tree. The mantis was still staring.

"Chrissake, Eddie," Ryker said. He took the last of the joint out of Eddie's hand, licked his fingers and pinched it out. He swallowed it and looked around. "I'll get Bergen, okay? Just don't tell him about the dope. He'll fucking kill me if he finds out."

Ryker sprinted for the Men's Building. The lawn seemed to curl up around him. Eddie closed his eyes. The neon spiral was back. He blinked. Timberlawn, the trees, the Administration Building. The mantis. He blinked again. Darkness. Colored bullets of light, shooting past him.

No, he thought. He stopped himself, kicking out with his mind. There was a thought in his head that he couldn't shake, something about going the direction the mantis was facing. The bullets of light slowed and started to fall away. He felt pressure letting off on his chest and throat and eyes.

And then, finally, he was lying in the dirt in the jungle.

His arms and legs shook feebly. He stank of sour sweat and his mouth was full of bile. He gasped and panted and finally got his heart to slow down a little. Suddenly he was freezing and had to roll into a ball to keep the chills from shaking him to pieces.

By the time that was over his stomach had started to cramp. He crawled off into the bushes and kicked off his jeans just before his bowels exploded with gas and diarrhea.

Finally he dragged himself back to the path. He could close his eyes now and not see anything but darkness. It was over. He rolled onto his back and spread his arms, laughing.

It had been the greatest trip of his life.

T HOMAS GOT THEM SEATS on a Mexicana flight to Tuxtla Gutiérrez. He had to go to the airport and stand in line all day Thursday to do it. Like a hundred other public buildings in the city, the airport could have passed for an abandoned Hollywood sound stage. Millions had been spent on high ceilings and exposed struts and modern wall angles and nothing had been left for maintenance. The huge glass windows were fogged by pollution, the lighted plastic signs were missing letters and filmed over with dust.

He and Lindsey left the hotel before six Friday morning. They ended up walking the last half mile to the terminal rather than sit in stalled traffic. The place was crammed with foreigners trying to get out of the country and journalists trying to get in.

Thomas slipped the gate attendant ten dollars U.S. to make sure they got on the plane. Ordinarily it would have been enough just to talk to him, but the mood of the whole city was paranoid since the quake and it had gotten to Thomas too.

Lindsey paid for the tickets with her VISA card. When Thomas offered to cover his half she shook her head. It was weird how sex had changed things between them. Before they went to bed there had been more intimacy than after. They'd had all those years of unfulfilled longing in common. Once that was out of the way Thomas didn't know anymore what she wanted or how she felt.

They'd made love Thursday morning and Thursday night. Lindsey seemed to like it well enough. She got on top and dug her fingernails into his chest and cried out when she came. But Thomas had been the one to start it both times and she'd been hesitant at first, distracted. Like it was something she hadn't really been thinking about.

They got into Tuxtla about noon. It was the capital of Chiapas state, a bottleneck of land just before the Yucatán peninsula curved up off the tail of Mexico. From there they could take a bus into the mountains to San Cristóbal de las Casas, the nearest big city to the Lacondones.

There wasn't much scenery between the airport and the Autobuses Cristóbal Colón terminal. Mostly Thomas saw oilmen in hardhats and khaki work clothes. Their taxi passed two tractors pulling work-over rigs and a lot of jeeps and pickups. He didn't notice many children. Everything seemed to be under construction, though nothing was actually happening at the moment. There were more soldiers hanging around than he was used to.

The bus got off a little after three-thirty. Lindsey fell asleep almost immediately. It was supposed to be a first-class bus, but the air conditioning didn't work and the windows were all stuck somewhere between open and shut. Thomas sweated through to the vinyl seat in the hot breeze.

The road climbed slowly through scrub brush to Chiapa de Corzo, where they stopped to take on a live pig. The pig's screaming woke Lindsey up. She leaned across Thomas to watch it being loaded. It was nearly four feet long and blue-gray in color. Its feet were tied front and rear and it thrashed its head in terror as the two Indians wrestled it toward the luggage compartment. Its eyes stuck out like baseballs.

"Oh my God," Lindsey said.

"There's nothing we can do about it," Thomas told her.

"They're just going to throw it in there with the baggage. Oh, that poor thing."

Thomas shrugged. He was just glad they'd kept their suitcases with them. He didn't need pig shit in his clothes. "Kindness to animals is a luxury," he said. "It's just not in those guys' income bracket." The bus driver stood to one side and looked on, twisting the metal band of his watch around and around his wrist.

After Chiapa de Corzo the highway started the five-thousand-foot climb to San Cristóbal. If it hadn't been for the switchbacks and detours it would only have been fifty miles long. While Lindsey dozed off again Thomas watched the bushes change to pine trees and the green mountains crawl out of the clouds.

Just outside of San Cristóbal the bus hit a bump and swerved to one side. Through the loosely riveted metal of the floor Thomas heard the pig squeal in pain and terror. Lindsey woke up and stared at him for a second in confusion. The right thing to do would have been to take her hand and tell her everything was okay.

Instead the sight of her weakness made Thomas irritable. He looked out the window. What the hell was she doing here? She could never have managed this on her own. She didn't even speak Spanish, for God's sake.

They crested the mountains that surrounded San Cristóbal. The jungle spread out behind them. The highest trees were caught in clouds, as if they'd been packed in cotton. The sunlight was intense, but in the shadows the air was cold. Thomas closed the window as far as it would go. The wind whistled through the quarter-inch crack. He could see his reflection in the glass, dark circles behind his glasses and lines around his mouth.

She's using you, he thought.

The bus turned down into the valley. The town was laid out in long parallel lines. At either end of the lines were hills with churches on them. The buildings were Spanish colonial, white with tile roofs, and Thomas could see at least a dozen with arched porticoes. The streets were crowded with Indians on their way out of town. The Chamula men wore white or black tunics with embroidery and peaked straw hats with ribbons on them. The ribbons of the married men were tied. The women all wore black. For a few seconds a Lacondon, wearing nothing but a loincloth and a pack tied from his forehead, jogged alongside the bus.

When they got to the station Lindsey said, "Can we get a hotel? And then maybe something to eat?"

Thomas nodded and waved to a cab. Lindsey's mood

seemed too fragile for walking. They got in and he asked
the driver if he knew the Hotel Esperanza.

"Claro," the driver said.

Lindsey dug in her bag for a sweater. "I can't believe
how cold it is."

"We're at seven thousand feet," Thomas said. "It's always cold here." At least, he thought, they hadn't had to
watch the pig being unloaded. They'd grabbed their stuff
and gotten into the terminal before the driver could open
the cargo doors.

The sun was hitting the top edge of the mountains. The
Indians were still trickling onto the streets and there was
a feeling of the city closing down for the night. There
were pigeons everywhere. Thomas had forgotten about
them. Pigeon racing was a local obsession and there were
cages of birds along all the streets, birds flying overhead,
birds roosting on all the buildings. Soldiers with M16s
stood on almost every corner, watching.

The hotel had lost their reservation. Thomas put
money on the counter and they found it again. San Cristóbal was close to where the government was shooting it
out with the rebels and it seemed to have affected everyone's self-interest.

Thomas carried the bags across the central courtyard
to their room. There were flowering plants everywhere.
The perfume shifted his mental gears. He unlocked the
door and Lindsey pushed past him and shut herself in the
bathroom. Thomas put on some deodorant, a clean long-
sleeved shirt and a brown corduroy jacket.

So she's using you, he thought. How often have you
ever gotten to live out a sexual fantasy? He might as well
enjoy whatever time he had left with her. They would
probably be in Nahá in another day or two. And if she
got Eddie back, all bets were off.

They ate in the hotel. There didn't seem to be any
other tourists around. Across the room a tableful of
soldiers drank beer and hardly talked to each other.

"The Aero Chiapas office may still be open," Thomas

said when the waiter took their plates. "I should go down and see about a plane."

"I'll come with you."

"You don't have to, you know."

"It's my party, Thomas."

He shrugged. "Okay."

The office was closed, but the old man inside unlocked the door for them. He told Thomas there would be a plane on Sunday, two days away. "One of the Lacondones is in town," he said. "Chan Zapata."

"Chan Ma'ax's son?"

"That's right. You know him?"

"A long time ago. When he was little."

"He comes up every couple of months to get away from his wife and drink a lot of cheap booze. He drank up all his money and he's ready to go back now. He's staying down at Trudi's, of course."

Thomas thanked him and went back into the street. "One of those Indians from Nahá is here," he told Lindsey. "He's staying at Na Bolom, Trudi Blom's place."

"Who's that?"

"She's an anthropologist. She and her husband pretty much discovered the Lacondones. Franz is dead, but she's still got a museum and library and puts up any of the Indians for free when they come to town."

"And this guy would know something about Eddie?"

"If that was really Eddie in the picture, yeah, he'd know something."

"Can we find him tonight?"

Thomas looked at his watch, strictly for show. Like she'd said, it was her party. "Sure," he said. "If that's what you want."

The mansion had a heavy mahogany door. The door was older than the Lacondones' current troubles, but it was still mahogany. And it was mahogany that had all but destroyed the Lacondones that Trudi was trying to save. Thomas knocked on it with the bottom of his fist.

Eventually a young woman opened it. She was heavy-set, with dark, greasy-looking hair to her waist. "The museum is closed," she said in English. "We'll be open at four tomorrow afternoon. The library is closed on Saturday."

"I'm Thomas Yates. I heard Chan Zapata was in town."

"Should I know you?"

"I doubt it. Chan Zapata might remember me."

"He's one of the Indians?"

"Yes, that's right." Thomas held on to his temper. "He's one of the Indians."

"Are you a friend of Trudi's?"

"We've met. I was part of the crew that excavated Na Chan, twelve years ago. I stayed here a few days then."

"Okay," she said, a little dubiously. "Trudi's in Switzerland, you know? I mean, I just work in the library. Why don't you come in and I'll look for . . . what was his name?"

"Chan Zapata," Thomas said.

The library looked like it belonged in some European castle. The walls were lined with books, some of them in cracked leather bindings, some with new dust jackets. Leather furniture was pulled up in a half circle around the fireplace. The fire burned so hard that the woman had to raise her voice to be heard over it. "I'll be right back," she said.

Lindsey collapsed on the sofa and shut her eyes. Thomas wandered over to the last shelf and found *The Lords of the Forest.* He touched the binding with one finger. When he turned back Chan Zapata was standing in the doorway. He wore a plain cotton robe with colored ribbons along the edges. The fabric had aged to a dull gray. He was barefoot. His hair hung down to the middle of his chest and he had the hatchet nose and sloping forehead of the ancient carvings.

"Utz-in puksiqual," Thomas said. It meant "my heart is good." Mayan greetings always seemed weirdly formal to Thomas because nobody touched each other, even to shake hands. "You probably don't remember me," he went on in halting Mayan. "I was in Nahá when you were just a boy. My name is Thomas Yates . . ."

"I remember you," Chan Zapata said in English. "But I practice my English these days. I will be a teacher in Nahá soon."

"Good, that's great," Thomas said. He moved onto the couch next to Lindsey. "Can you sit with us for a while? How is your father?"

Chan Zapata took one of the leather chairs. He leaned back and put both his arms on the arms of the chair, as if to prove he knew what they were meant for. "He is the same, always the same. Sad now the road is finished and the mahogany is gone. But he tries not to show it."

Lindsey shifted and opened her eyes. She actually fell asleep, Thomas thought in amazement. "This is my sister-in-law," Thomas said. "The wife of my brother. Lindsey . . . Taylor."

"Hello," Lindsey said.

She held out her hand and Chan Zapata, out of politeness, leaned forward to shake it quickly and let it go. "Nice to meet you," he said.

Lindsey reached for her purse and Chan Zapata leaned forward again. "You have a cigarette?"

"I'm sorry, no."

"Okay. The evangelistas say they are bad for me. 'I need to cut down.' That's what you say, no?"

He and Thomas laughed. Lindsey got the picture out of her purse. She handed it to Chan Zapata and said, "We're looking for Thomas' brother. We wanted to know if maybe you've seen him."

Chan Zapata glanced at the picture. "Ahhhh," he said. "Eddie."

Lindsey put the picture back in her purse, and then held the purse closed with both hands. "You know him."

"Oh yes. He is a good man, your brother." Something in his tone was a little off. "A hach winik. That means a real Maya, in here." He slapped his chest. "He is your husband? I would not leave such a beautiful woman as you if I was your husband."

"And how *is* your wife?" Thomas asked.

Lindsey shot him a nasty look but Chan Zapata sat

back in his chair and laughed. "She is fine, Tomás. Very pregnant."

"Is Eddie all right?" Lindsey asked. "I mean, does he seem . . . I don't know, crazy or anything?"

"He is different from the other *ts'ul,* the other white people. He feels things very strong, you know?"

"Intense," Lindsey said. "He's like that."

"Yes, intense. But not crazy, I don't think. Or maybe yes. He is with my father now at Na Chan."

"What?" Lindsey said.

"Na Chan?" Thomas said.

"They are on pil . . . pilmigra . . ."

"Pilgrimage," Thomas said.

"Yes, pilgrimage. Most of the men from Nahá. All the most holy ones."

The sarcasm wasn't obvious, but Thomas was pretty sure it was there. He wanted to hear the rest but it would be rude to ask. He waited to see if Chan Zapata was going to come out with it on his own.

"Your brother is in my place," Chan Zapata said finally. "Chan Ma'ax is very close with him. I think something is going to happen there. My father told me not to go. I think maybe now I was wrong to listen to him."

"So Eddie's not in Nahá," Lindsey said. "I should have known. How much farther is this place? How do you get there?"

"Helicopter," Thomas said. "Either by helicopter or on foot."

"Where do we get a helicopter?"

"We can charter one, probably. That was what we used to do. Maybe we can even find the guy who used to take us out there, when we were working."

"You are going?" Chan Zapata asked. "To Na Chan?"

"If that's where Eddie is," Lindsey said.

"I don't have any money," Chan Zapata said. "Not with me. But there is mahogany money that the town has. If you take me with you I could pay you back."

Lindsey shrugged. "It doesn't matter to me."

"Sure," Thomas said.

"Can we look for this pilot guy tonight?" Lindsey asked. "I really want to get on with this."

Thomas looked at her to get a sense of what she was really saying. There was nothing obvious that said she was tired of sex with Thomas. Still the implication was clear. "His name was Oscar. He leased a helicopter from PEMEX and worked free-lance. I'm not sure how to find him. I don't even know if he's still around here."

"Oscar?" Chan Zapata said. "I know him. He goes to the Olla Podrida. He uses the menses board there."

"Message board," Thomas said.

"Ah yes, sorry. But if he is not there we can leave him a, uh, message."

Thomas was worn out from all the miles and the strong emotion. The heat from the fireplace was putting him to sleep. He made himself stand up and smile. "Okay," he said. "Let's do it."

Chan Zapata led the way into the Olla Podrida. He was like an actor playing a Lacondon prince, Thomas thought. He projected a sort of innocent self-confidence. He made the tourists and students look out of place in their jeans and sweaters and running shoes.

It was a good-sized room, with lots of light. The walls were hung with baskets and straw hats and embroidered dresses. Near the front was a cork board with dozens of scraps of paper pinned to it.

"There he is," Chan Zapata said.

There was a lot of smoke in the air. Thomas saw Lindsey screwing up her face at it. They could hear conversations in four or five languages as they squeezed between the tables.

Oscar had tilted his chair back against the wall. A woman sat across from him, her back to Thomas. She was leaning forward, like she was trying to keep his attention. Oscar wore a khaki shirt, desert camo pants, and sneakers. A pair of mirrorshades hung out of his shirt pocket. He had curly black hair past his shoulders and a day's growth of beard. He'd put on weight in the last ten years, but then so had Thomas. He had a bottle of beer in

one hand and a glass in the other. He raised the glass to
Chan Zapata. Then he saw Thomas.

"An old friend of yours," Chan Zapata said in Spanish.

"Thomas Yates," Thomas said. "You used to—"

"I'll be goddamned," Oscar said in English. His accent
was more Texas than Mexican. He stood up and gave
Thomas an *abrazo* that knocked the air out of Thomas'
lungs. "What the hell are you doing back here, man?"

"That's what I want to talk to you about," Thomas
said. He introduced Lindsey and Oscar held her hand a
little too long, looking her over.

"I'd better go," said the woman at the table. She was
Northamerican and, Thomas noticed reflexively, nice-
looking. She had brown hair to her shoulders, done in no
particular style. Her eyes were hazel and serious.

"Hey," Oscar said to her. "This guy, this guy was my
first student. I taught him to fly a fucking helicopter and
lived to tell about it."

"We didn't mean to interrupt," Thomas said.

"No problem," Oscar said. It looked to Thomas like
the woman had wanted more from Oscar, had been trying to make some kind of play. It hadn't worked, and
now she was dismissed. She picked up her purse and
walked away.

Thomas watched her go. His hormone production was
way up and things seemed more dramatic to him lately.

"Sit down," Oscar told him. "Have a beer. You just
saved me from some really boring shit."

They all sat down. Thomas knew Oscar's macho act
was making Lindsey uncomfortable. Him too, for that
matter. As much as anything he felt embarrassed that
Oscar hadn't picked up on it. "We need to get to Na
Chan," he said.

"Hell of a time to do archeology, I'd say. Shit, it's
almost too dangerous to *fly* over that part of the world.
What do you want to be on the ground for?"

"This isn't about archeology," Lindsey said. "It's my
ex-husband. Thomas' brother. He's there with some of
Chan Ma'ax's people."

Ex-husband, Thomas thought. That was something.

Then he thought, cut it out. Quit mooning over every word and act like a grown-up.

Oscar looked back and forth between Thomas and Lindsey. "Okay," he said. "Sorry, I just thought there was something else going on here. I must of got it wrong. But what's the rush? Won't they be coming back in a couple days anyway?"

Chan Zapata said, "I don't know. My father is very strange these days. Ever since they cut all the trees. I don't think *he* thinks he is coming back."

"Besides," Thomas said. "Like you were saying, it's a war zone out there. They're not safe."

"And I've come a long way," Lindsey said. "I'm not just going to sit around and wait for him to show up again."

"Okay, okay," Oscar said. "I didn't say I *couldn't* do it, I just said things are bad. The guardia has Huey gunships up there, Italian fighter planes, all kinds of bad shit. You know why? 'Cause the fucking CIA told them the rebels had Mi-24 Hind helicopters, you know, those Russian platform things. Which is total bullshit, because if the compas had those, man, the PRI would be history. But the guardia, man, those are some paranoid motherfuckers right now. They'll shoot down anything, and the CIA will give them money for doing it."

"Are you saying we could get shot at?" Lindsey asked.

"That's exactly what I'm saying. Because once we're dead, they can say any shit they want. American citizens down here smuggling guns to the rebels. Believe it."

"Look," Thomas said. "How much of this is real and how much is just to jack the price up?"

Oscar shrugged. "It's bad, man, I'm telling you. We aren't just talking cost plus here, okay? We're talking insurance. Because I can't afford to do this too many times. And if the guardia shoots us down money isn't gonna matter to any of us anyhow. Right? You know?"

Thomas put his elbows on the table. He didn't like haggling, but it was part of life down here, and he knew how to go through the motions. "How much are you talking about, then? Two of you?"

"All three of us."

"Round trip, in and out, I'd say five hundred U.S. Cash, of course, no pesos."

Which meant they would end up at three-fifty to four hundred. Before Thomas could say anything Lindsey cut him off. "I'll pay it," she said. "Whatever it takes."

Thomas banged his knee into hers and stared at her in amazement. She looked back at him like he was a little kid pestering her for ice cream. "You'll have to take traveler's checks," she said.

Thomas watched Oscar think it over, wondering if he could get away with some kind of phony surcharge, deciding not to push his luck. "That's cool," he said. "When you want to do this?"

"As soon as possible," Lindsey said.

"First thing tomorrow, then. Come to the Aero Chiapas hangar out at the field. And we just hope the fog isn't too bad or we'll never find the son of a bitch. Six o'clock?"

"Good," Lindsey said.

"Well," Thomas said. "I for one need some sleep. I'm going back to the hotel." He looked at Lindsey. "Coming?"

"I guess I am, aren't I?" She stood up and nodded to Oscar and Chan Zapata. "I'll see you in the morning."

They passed the zócalo on the way back to the hotel. Couples were walking arm in arm around the square, all of them in the same direction. Lindsey slowed to watch them and Thomas waited for her.

"They should go the other way," Lindsey said.

"What?"

"They're all walking clockwise. They should go the other way. The clock is what's killing them. Time, you know. It's eating up their land and stealing their kids. It's turning Mexico into one big Burger King."

"You can't turn it back," Thomas said. "That doesn't solve anything. You have to go on, get through it, move on to something better. Trying to go back is stupid." He started off toward the hotel again.

"What's got you so pissy tonight?"

"You shouldn't have just agreed when Oscar quoted you a price. You could have talked him down at least a hundred bucks, maybe more."

"So what? It's my money."

"Are you rich now? See, I didn't know that. Because if you're rich we could have just chartered a plane in Mexico City and not spent all day getting here. Not to mention that Oscar now thinks you're a soft touch. He'll be hitting you up for money every time you turn around."

"Sorry," she said acidly. "I thought this Oscar was supposed to be a friend of yours."

"He is. But this is Mexico. Friendship only goes so far. If you're smart you don't let it get in the way of money."

"Goddammit," she said, "I'm getting sick and tired of hearing how bright you are and how stupid I am. I'm sure it's the truth and all, but I'm getting pretty tired of hearing about it."

"I'm sorry," Thomas said. "I didn't mean it like that. I'm just tired, that's all." We both are, he thought, but he didn't say it.

"Right," Lindsey said. She walked well away from him, arms folded, shoulders hunched against the chill.

Lindsey showered first, then Thomas took his turn. The whole bathroom was tiled and there was no shower stall, just a plastic curtain that would have divided the room in half if it had been a little longer. The soap was hard and green and odorless. If there had been any genuinely hot water, Lindsey had gotten it.

He came out wrapped in a towel and sat on the edge of the bed. Lindsey was in front of the mirror, working on her eyebrows with a pair of tweezers. She wore a flannel nightgown with tiny flowers on it and had her hair up in a towel.

The last two nights she'd slept naked. Thomas tried to tell himself it was the change in climate, fatigue, nerves. The infant in his backbrain wasn't listening. It couldn't see beyond the moment, and right now it saw everything slipping away.

He kissed her on the back of the neck. She shrugged him off. "Don't," she said.

He had this conviction that if they made love everything would be all right. If they didn't it meant something dire, something permanent. He couldn't tell anymore if he was in love with her or just crazy with testosterone. You're blowing it, he told himself. Why don't you lie down and shut up?

Instead he said, "It's Eddie, right?"

She sighed theatrically. "Eddie doesn't have anything to do with it. I'm tired, my stomach hurts, and we've been yelling at each other. That doesn't put me in much of a mood, okay?"

"Okay," he said. He hung his towel on the bathroom door and got under the covers. He set his alarm for five o'clock. Just over six hours away. It didn't seem long enough.

"I mean, Jesus," Lindsey said. "How can you be pissed off at me one minute and think I'm an idiot, and then want to screw me the next? It makes me feel like an inflatable love doll or something."

"I said okay. I'm sorry, all right? I'll keep my goddamn hands to myself."

Lindsey walked all the way around the bed and got in on the far side. She lay down with her back to him, crowding the edge of the mattress. Thomas got up and turned out the light and got back in bed again. He took his glasses off and put his hands behind his head. He wanted to kiss her goodnight or pat her on the ass or make some kind of affectionate gesture, just to cut the tension so he could get to sleep. To hell with it, he thought. It's her move.

Next to him Lindsey began to snore softly.

They were up before dawn, packing. They didn't talk to each other. Thomas got through it by writing scenarios in his head. Land at Na Chan by midmorning. Bundle Eddie up and be back in San Cristóbal by midafternoon. Spend the night in Tuxtla, Lindsey and Eddie in one room, him in another. Preferably not adjoining. He dwelt on that for a few seconds, just to see how much it was going to hurt. That early in the morning, as badly as he'd slept the night before, it sounded like something he could live with. Back in Mexico City Sunday morning, and home to Cuernavaca by afternoon.

He saw himself saying goodbye to Lindsey and Eddie at the airport. It was right out of *Casablanca,* very pure masochistic bullshit. But there were times that it took hard drugs or bullshit or movies just to get through.

The first words Lindsey said to him that morning were, "Are you really going to eat that garbage?"

The waiter had brought him *huevos motuleños,* a crisp tortilla covered with beans, a fried egg, sour white cheese, green peas, and a lethal brown sauce. Thomas smiled at her. She was one move behind; it was already over for him. "It's good," he said. "You ought to try it."

When the taxi came Thomas told the driver to stop by Na Bolom. Chan Zapata was waiting out front. He had a net bag with a towel and some magazines and fruit in it. His hair was tangled and his eyes were bloodshot, though he still moved with the same easy grace.

Nobody talked on the drive to the airfield. They were late and the sun was already coming up. The streets were full of mist that drenched the taxi's windshield and left gray streaks whenever the driver used the wipers. The Indians coming into town had plastic covers over their hats to keep them dry. Thomas tried to open his window. It rolled about halfway down and stuck. He could smell the damp and hear chickens waking up all over the city.

The airfield looked deserted. The taxi pulled up in front of the Aero Chiapas hangar and Thomas got out. The walls were corrugated steel, rusted through in a couple of places. Two olive-drab Hueys were pegged down just outside the front doors.

The inside of the hangar smelled like oil and metal filings. *"Hola?"* Thomas said. "Anybody here?" There was a door at the back of the place. Thomas knocked and then tried it.

Oscar lay inside on a rollaway bed. He was wearing his fatigue pants and nothing else. There were lines on his chest from the crumpled sheets. "Hey, man, what the fuck?" he said, sitting up and pushing the sides of his face together. "What time is it, anyway?"

"Six-thirty," Thomas said. "You okay?"

"Sure, man. It's just early, that's all." He padded out into the hangar and stuck his head into a fifty-five-gallon drum full of water. He came up shaking his head and spat a stream of water toward a drain in the concrete floor. "Everybody here?"

"Outside," Thomas said. "Did you need to eat anything, or . . ."

"No, man, after last night I may never use that stomach again. I'll be right out."

Thomas got the luggage out of the cab and told Lindsey how much to pay the driver. A couple of minutes later Oscar wandered out of the hangar. He'd put on a T-shirt, a leather jacket, and black motorcycle boots. "This one here," he said, patting the side of one of the Hueys.

"Is it safe?" Lindsey asked.

"Sure it's safe," Oscar said. "The aircraft is not what you need to worry about. Worry about the guardia if you want to worry. Did you bring the money?"

Lindsey signed five hundred-dollar traveler's checks and handed them over. Oscar stuffed them in his jacket pocket and opened the cargo door. "After you," he said.

"This is weird," Lindsey said. "This is like a Vietnam flashback or something." She and Chan Zapata climbed in and settled in the mesh passenger seats that folded down from the rear wall. Thomas handed her the bags and she stowed them under the seats. She reminded Thomas of somebody in an operating room, waiting for the anesthetic. She kept glancing around, but everything she saw seemed to frighten her more.

He didn't feel up to reassuring her. If she wants somebody to hold her hand, he thought, she'll have Eddie soon enough. "Better strap in," he said.

Oscar untied the ropes that held the copter down and then climbed up for a look at the Jesus nut. Sometimes they cracked, and if they did the rotor fell off. Usually in midair. When he was satisfied he got in the right-hand seat and got out a battered checklist. The lamination had almost entirely peeled off the paper.

He went through the preflight settings on the switches while Thomas shut the cargo door and got in next to him. There was a duplicate set of controls on his side. Thomas put on a pair of headphones and adjusted the mike.

"You want to take her up?" Oscar asked him.

"No thanks," Thomas said. "I'll pass."

"Ready to crank," Oscar said.

"It's all yours," Thomas said.

Oscar took the collective pitch lever in his left hand, twisted it, and pulled the ignition trigger. There was a shrill electric whine and the rotor slowly started to turn. As it picked up speed the turbine cut in with a sudden hiss. "You ever get to fly these days?"

"Some," Thomas said. "I've been in Cuernavaca, on a research deal. The people there have a little Robinson R22. I get to take it up sometimes."

Oscar nodded. He leaned forward for a look at the rotor disk and then pulled back on the collective. Thomas had forgotten the way the Huey always came up nose first. They hovered for a second while Oscar looked over the gauges, and then he shot them off into the sky.

From above, the hills looked like crumpled blue-green construction paper. Shreds of mist were still tangled in the trees. The grassy patches of abandoned milpas were like some kind of plant cancer eating the forest. The farther they got from San Cristóbal the fewer of them Thomas saw.

The hills got steeper as they flew toward the northeast. At first it was hard for Thomas not to watch the gauges instead of the scenery. As he got used to the noise and to the idea that he wasn't doing the flying, he slipped into a kind of trance state.

He wished he had music to go with it. Maybe one of the long instrumental tracks from Eddie's *Sunsets* album, with the layers of strings over the pulsing rhythm section.

He felt like he was sitting still in the air and the ground was being pulled under him from an endless roll.

The radio snapped him out of it. Somebody was telling Oscar to identify himself.

"Who is it?" Thomas asked.

"White Brigade, probably," Oscar said. The White Brigade was the antiguerrilla unit of the *Directorio del Seguridad Federal*, the Mexican FBI. Even Thomas had heard of them. They were the local equivalent of the Salvadorian death squads. "Maybe it's just a routine patrol."

Oscar told them he was carrying PEMEX engineers. It was, Thomas knew, his standard cover story. PEMEX let him moonlight in their helicopter for a small kickback. It kept Oscar from doing it on his own for free.

The answer came back garbled and full of static. "Did you get that?" Oscar asked. Thomas shook his head. "They say they killed Carla, that guerrilla leader. Monday. They're out looking for whatever's left of her people. They want us the hell out of here."

Lindsey had gotten out of her seat. "What's going on?" she shouted.

"Nothing," Oscar yelled back. "Sit down and strap in." He looked over his shoulder to make sure she did it. Then he worked the foot pedals hard and the copter dropped between the sides of a steep valley.

"*Bájale, ahorita,*" the radio said. "Set down, right now. This is an order."

"Maybe," Thomas said, "maybe we should turn back."

"No, fuck that." Oscar turned a switch on the pedestal between the seats and cut off the external radio, leaving them with just the intercom. "It's just a game, you know, a bunch of macho shit. They try to scare me off, we have a little chase." They hopped over a hill with a violent up-and-down motion that dislocated Thomas' stomach. "And then tonight I buy them a beer and everything is cool, you know? Just a kind of macho thing."

Sweat ran down Oscar's face. "Anyway, I think we lost—"

The government helicopter dropped in front of them.

It came out of nowhere, like it was just a color slide projected on the windscreen. Then it turned sideways and the cargo door opened and Thomas saw the perforated barrel of a .50-caliber machine gun tracking toward him.

"Ay chingado . . ." Oscar said. He wrenched the handle of the collective and shoved it all the way down. The engine throttled back to a whisper and Thomas' breath caught in his throat. The helicopter lurched downward toward the trees. Thomas could hear the wind screaming through the torn weatherstripping on the window next to him.

It was like being in a car wreck. He reached instinctively for the controls and Oscar shouted, "Don't!"

He pulled his hands away. They were virtually in free fall. The updraft was turning the rotor faster than the engine. Thomas listened for the sound of branches under the skids, the last sound he would ever hear. Instead he heard his own heart beating, twice, three times.

Oscar twisted the throttle back to full power and jerked the collective up again. The acceleration slammed Thomas into his seat and they were rocketing into the sky. Through his window Thomas saw the astonished faces of the guardsmen as their own machine fell nose down toward the valley floor.

When they leveled off again the government copter was gone.

Thomas looked into the back. Chan Zapata's eyes were closed. Lindsey looked more angry than frightened. They watched each other for a couple of seconds. There was too much noise to say anything. Finally Lindsey looked away.

Oscar rocked back and forth in his seat, completely wired. "Fucking guardia pilots, man, they're shit. They go to school in Mexico, they fly like old ladies."

"Did they go down?" Thomas asked.

"I don't know, man. I don't give a fuck."

They pulled out, Thomas told himself. We would have heard the crash if they didn't. He looked for a second at the radio and then told himself he didn't want to know.

* * *

Thomas knew they were close when he saw El Chichón, the dead volcano. It was twenty miles south of Na Chan. There was usually a faint plume of steam that came out of it in the mornings, making it a perfect landmark to steer by. The name meant lump or breast. It was a high, narrow cone, covered with trees right up to the diagonal slash of the old crater across its top.

"There she is," Thomas said.

Oscar nodded. "Soon now."

Five minutes later Thomas spotted a white triangle just at treetop level. "There," he said, pointing it out for Oscar. It was like seeing an old girlfriend. He was not prepared for the emotional impact. He remembered the smell of the dirt, the sound of the parrots and cicadas, the pleasure of the work. The morning light seemed transcendently beautiful.

Oscar brought them in right over the Temple of the Inscriptions. It looked better than he had any reason to hope. A few days' work could bring it back to what it had been.

Christ, what was he thinking about? They were there to pick up Eddie, and that was all.

There were two ramadas in the main clearing, their palm thatches still green. Off to one side was one of the expedition's old tents. Thomas couldn't see any humans, but that was no surprise. They wouldn't want to make targets of themselves for government gunships.

"I can't see any place to set down," Oscar said.

"Circle," Thomas said. "There has to be something."

He watched the ancient city move beneath his feet. The temples of the Lion, of the Cross, of the Sun, simple stone rectangles with high, elaborately decorated roofcombs. The Otolum River on the eastern edge that made a low falls where they'd gone swimming. The Northern Group, a single long base with three separate temples on top, where the summer kids had gone to smoke dope. The old landing strip, just north and west of the ruins.

"That looks as good as we're going to get," Oscar said.

"If those little trees are bigger than they look, we're fucked."

It wasn't much of a clearing. Grasses and saplings and cane plants covered the ground, but none of them were more than eight or ten feet tall. Oscar eased them down. Branches squealed against the fuselage, then shattered in the rotor blades. Pulp and chips of bark sprayed the windows. They bumped against the ground and Oscar killed the engine. It was quiet except for the fading chop of the rotors.

Lindsey was out of her seat immediately, struggling with the cargo door. Thomas got out and pulled it open. Nothing seemed real yet. A single cicada screamed in the distance and then another came in, off key. The air was hot and wet as a sauna.

Thomas held out a hand to help Lindsey down but she didn't see it. She was staring into the jungle. She climbed down out of the helicopter and brushed at her jeans. Her pupils were dilated, like a frightened cat's. Thomas supposed that he wasn't really there for her. If she was thinking of anything it was Eddie.

Chan Zapata got out after her and smiled. "It is beautiful, no?" he said in Mayan. Thomas nodded.

Oscar had climbed up to look at the rotors. "It's okay," he said. He got a machete out from behind his seat and said, "Let's get on with it."

Only the edges of the forest were overgrown. Once inside there was enough room between the trees for them to walk. Oscar went first, chopping pointlessly at a hanging vine or two. Lindsey had a little trouble keeping her balance on the flat, mossy stones of the jungle floor. Thomas didn't offer her any more help.

He wanted to tell her that she was walking on history, that every rock that was making her slip came from a Mayan temple. It wouldn't have mattered to her. Behind Thomas was Chan Zapata, who kept stopping to touch the leaves or look suddenly off to one side.

They came out into the central courtyard. Through the high grass and the thin trees and shrubs Thomas could see the Temple of the Inscriptions and the Palace. The snake god grinned at him. He felt like he was walking around on another planet, or in another century. It always hit him this way. He wanted to sit down in the dirt and look around him.

Not today. Today there wasn't time.

The ramadas were deserted but the Lacondones had left mats and pots and food behind. They couldn't have gone far.

Lindsey stopped and cupped her hands around her mouth. "Eddie!" she shouted. There was no echo. The jungle seemed to swallow the sound. She called again and something moved by the big pyramid, coming out of the shadows.

It was a Northamerican in jeans and a T-shirt. He walked up to within ten feet or so and then stopped. He couldn't have weighed more than 120 pounds. His hair looked like it had been cut with a lawn mower. He hadn't shaved in days and his eyes showed more red than white.

Well, Thomas thought, here we all are.

"Hello, Eddie," he said.

AFTER THAT FIRST TRIP Eddie slept all the way into the next afternoon. It was hard to finally wake up. He eased his legs off the side of the hammock and picked at the crud that had hardened in his eyes. The clouds overhead had already started to bunch up for the daily rain. Over at the godhouse Chan Ma'ax warbled some tuneless song. The words slurred together too badly for Eddie to make them out.

His muscles burned and his head ached and he had the sort of all-over poisoned feeling he used to get from playing too late in smoky, boozy clubs. He thought that if he could just ignore his stomach a little longer he might be able to keep from throwing up.

Somebody had left a clay pot of water for him while he slept the worst of it off. The pot was weird-looking. The ones at Nahá were rounded, with a handle that looked like a chicken head coming off one edge. This one had straight, thin walls, like a clay wastebasket.

He washed himself down and brushed his teeth and put on a clean T-shirt and jeans. Just that much wore him out. He sat down and got his breath and then walked over to the godhouse.

The Lacondones had unpacked the clay they brought from Nahá. The younger men, Ma'ax García and two others, worked it with their hands on slabs of wood and then wrapped it in leaves. Nuxi' and some of the older men worked up the basic shape, straight-sided pots like the one by Eddie's hammock. At the end of the line, Chan Ma'ax ground up white lime to coat them after they'd been fired.

The others had just about finished a kiln made from broken limestone blocks. They had a fire already going inside it and a stack of wood piled up close by.

Eddie sat on the bottom step of the pyramid, waiting for a sign from Chan Ma'ax. He felt guilty, not so much for taking the drug as for being so goddamn obvious about it. Zonked out all morning, filthy and pale and sweating. Everybody had to know.

Chan Ma'ax finally looked up. He glanced at Eddie for a second then went back to grinding the soft white rock. It didn't look like the old man even knew who he was.

Eddie heard the rain before he felt it or saw it, coming toward them through the trees with a noise like a press roll on a snare drum. He was obviously not welcome in the godhouse. If he stayed put he was going to get soaked.

He started up the face of the pyramid. It was about a sixty-degree angle, and some of the steps were missing. He had to use his hands to keep himself going. At the top there was a long, squared-off temple with five doors across the front. The rain was starting to really come down. Eddie ducked into the middle door.

The floor was covered in dirt that had leaked through the ceiling. The ceiling was a corbeled arch, built house-of-cards-style with each layer sticking out farther than the last until they met over the middle. Thomas had made a big deal about them in his book. It was supposed to be the only kind of arch the Mayans had.

The room smelled of animals, a musky, pissed-on kind of smell. Different kinds of grass and thistles grew out of the dirt on the floor. Eddie was a little worried about snakes but took another couple of steps inside anyway.

A rusty shovel leaned against the wall by the door. The handle was dry and splintery, but there was enough blade left to work with. He cleared off about five feet by four feet around the door. It made him dizzy again. He sat cross-legged on the damp stone and looked out at the city.

Even through the curtain of rain it was really something. He could see down into the Palace on his right, and past it the Northern Group, ghostly gray in the distance. The haze made the jungle look blue-green. Everything smelled clean, like water.

He didn't mean to fall asleep again but the hushing noises of the storm put him under. When he woke up the rain had fallen off to a slow ticking and Chan Ma'ax was squatting beside him. The old man's knees were inches away from Eddie's chest.

"Jesus," Eddie said, sitting up and scooting away. In Mayan he said, "You scared me."

Chan Ma'ax didn't say anything for a while, just squatted there staring at the floor. It was the kind of theatrical stunt that really got on Eddie's nerves. Finally the old man said, "So. Now you think you are ready to be one of the Haawo'."

Eddie started to freak. The old man wasn't even wet. "You showed me those mushrooms. What did you want me to do?"

"I told you not to touch them."

Eddie shook his head. "I didn't believe you. Since

when can you talk about this? About the Haawo'?" Even
now it scared him a little to say it out loud.

"Na Chan is a sacred place. Things are different here.
Like with the *onen,* the totem animals. It is forbidden to
eat them, except in ceremonies. Then you must *always*
eat them. You understand?"

"I guess."

"What did you see?"

Eddie knew he was talking about the mushroom again.
"Myself," Eddie said. "Younger. When I was very sick,
years ago."

"What else?"

"There was . . ." He realized he didn't know the
word for mantis. "An insect. Like a stick. With eyes that
come out like this and little hands that pray." He didn't
know why the mantis had stuck in his head.

"Xaman," Chan Ma'ax said. He seemed excited. His
face disappeared in wrinkles and he bounced a little on
his heels. "It is the same word as the direction." He
pointed north, out the door of the temple. "Because if
you ask the xaman he will tell you which way is north. It
is a good sign."

"Chan Ma'ax," Eddie said. "Tell me about the
Haáwo'."

"It is not a clan of the blood, an onen, like our Spider
Monkey clan. It is a clan of the heart, you understand?
Those who belong are those who are asked."

"Asked by who? By the mushroom?"

"The mushroom should have killed you. At least it
should have made you crazy. Maybe it was already too
late to make you crazy." The old man laughed like it was
really funny and the next second he was serious again.
"Maybe you were just lucky."

"My brother said they talked to the gods. The Haawo'.
I didn't see any."

"You saw the xaman. If you eat the mushroom again
maybe you will understand what he says to you. But you
will also make yourself very sick. Maybe crazy. Maybe
dead. You were lucky one time. Maybe not so lucky another time."

"I don't understand," Eddie said. "Do you want me to eat the mushroom or not? Are you trying to scare me? Or make me want it more?"

Chan Ma'ax stood up. He turned around and walked down the narrow steps like he hadn't heard Eddie at all.

The next morning Eddie felt better. He was still weak, but his head had stopped hurting and reality had lost its glittering edges.

East of the camp and downstream, Eddie found a swimming hole fed by a ten-foot waterfall. He could barely believe it was real. The bottom of the pool was white sand and it was deep enough to be over his head in the center. The water was clear and cold and the rocks behind the falls were dark greenish-gray and covered with moss. The trees met over the middle of the river and it was shady except for an hour or two around noon.

As he floated naked in the middle of the pool he found himself thinking, unexpectedly, about Lindsey. She would love this place. She would hate the jungle and the heat and not being able to stay as clean as she liked. But she would love this one little corner of it.

He couldn't remember her face anymore, not all at once. But he could find bits and pieces of her: the fine golden hairs in the middle of her back, the way her nipples seemed to reach out from the ends of her breasts when they were aroused, the smell of her neck. His penis slowly climbed out of the water. He left it alone, too tired even to masturbate.

After an hour or so he went back to the camp and spent the rest of the morning working on his tent. He'd turned up a repair kit and he used it to glue in triangular sections from two other tents that were too torn up for anything else. He lashed together a couple of narrow metal cots to make a decent-sized bed, and washed the mattresses in the river and left them in the sun to get rid of the mildew.

When he started putting the frame together Ma'ax García wandered over to help. The rest of the Lacondones were out looking for food and copal trees, except for Chan Ma'ax. Chan Ma'ax was smoking cigars and finishing the new godpots.

It took them half an hour to get the tent up. It was almost seven feet tall and twelve feet across. Ma'ax García smiled and nodded when they were finished but didn't want to go inside. Eddie moved in the double cot and his clothes and guitar. The guitar was still in the plastic garbage bag he'd used to bring it from Nahá.

He took it out and tuned it and tried to play some of his old songs. They only seemed to make him tired. Finally he put it down and stretched out on the bare springs of the cot. He had the window and door flaps open and there was a bit of a breeze. Civilization, he thought. Next he'd want a color TV.

No, he thought, not a color TV. The only thing he wanted was to take the mushroom again.

That afternoon one of the men came back with a *yuk,* a deer about the size of a wolfhound. Everybody got excited. It meant meat twice in one week.

Eddie had set up the tent so it faced east, away from the godhouse. After the sun went down the firelight came in through the screened windows and jumped around the walls. He'd brought the mattresses in and they were pretty comfortable. He could smell the meat cooking. He remembered that he hadn't eaten all day, and just then he heard Ma'ax García outside the tent.

"I brought you some beans and tortillas. We figured you wouldn't want any of the yuk, but you can have some if you want."

"No, this is good. Thanks."

Ma'ax García went back to the fire. They were really whooping it up out there. Somebody must have brought booze. Eddie ate some of the food. He felt like he was spending a boomtown Saturday night in the slammer.

He didn't remember sleeping, but the next thing he knew everything was quiet and the fire was down to a red glow.

He got up and ducked outside. He could smell woodsmoke and burned fat and the piny tang of copal. The copal always reminded him of the smell of rosin-core solder, like Stew had used when he worked on the band's amplifiers. Eddie's old Twin Reverb had smelled like that when he'd had it on 10 for a couple of hours and it got really hot.

The Lacondones were sacked out in the second ramada, just north of the godhouse. The drunken snoring drowned out the insects. Nobody looked up when he walked by, but he hadn't thought they would. He figured he was a sort of holy fool now, beyond reproach or help.

The moon was low in the sky and there wasn't much light. It didn't seem to matter. He found his way back to the mushrooms with no problem. He stood and looked at them for a little while then got undressed. A mosquito whined past one ear. The night air touched him all over like a damp cloth. He sat cross-legged in the dirt where he'd sat two nights before and reached out to the nearest plant.

New toy, he thought. When they were kids it was always Thomas in control, holding back, trying to be grown-up. Eddie was the one to fall obsessively in love. First with toys, then songs on the radio, then girls. He just kept after them until he burned out.

He could see the scar on the cap of the mushroom where he'd broken off his first piece. It had healed over, dry and wrinkled. He broke off another one right next to it. It was bigger than the first, though he hadn't meant it to be.

Lucky, Chan Ma'ax had said. Maybe not so lucky this time.

Eddie chewed the piece of mushroom and swallowed it. When he was finished he lay back and looked at the stars. Na Chan was high enough up and far enough from the cities that there were a lot of them. After a while they stopped twinkling and grew rippling auras.

It's starting, he thought. Oh boy.

It wasn't just the hallucinations, or whatever they were. It was the whole package, the feeling of being out of control. He loved it. He rode the rush until the stars began to jump and spin and shoot past him.

* * *

The bullets of colored light made flat, electronic popping noises as he fell into them. Behind the popping he could hear music, a guitar, the notes fast and guttural, played down close to the nut on the low strings. It took him a second to recognize it. It was himself, of course. The guitar solo from the last cut on *Sunsets,* an instrumental called "Roadwork."

The music leaked out of an oblong of red neon. It came toward him, afterimages streaking the darkness behind it. He could have pulled away but he didn't feel the need. The blob of light glowed like an electric coil, its edges smeared with brilliant red. It swelled until it filled his vision and then spun into tiny points of red, green, and blue light over his head. He made out the shapes of a darkened room through his closed eyelids. Then the eyelids themselves turned solid and he had to open them to see.

He looked at the circle of colored lights again and knew where he was. Studio A at Electric Lady, under the middle of Greenwich Village in New York. The lights were mounted on what looked like the bottom of a flying saucer, hovering just below the twenty-foot ceiling. Huge baffles cut the room in half. The engineers had put them there, Eddie remembered, to get rid of some weird echoes and some humps in the bottom end.

He felt the weight of the Strat against his left shoulder, the headphones over his ears, and, finally, the fretboard under his left hand. As soon as he realized what was happening he lost control of it. His little finger buzzed against the D-string and he let his hands fall to his sides.

The rhythm track went on without him, unrolling from the inch-wide Scotch mastering tape inside the booth. After a second it barked to a stop. Gregg came on over the hum in his headphones and said, "You want to try that again, Eddie?" The tape was already screeching and howling backward across the heads.

"Gimme a minute, okay?" He backed up until he found the stool he knew would be there. The Strat's maple neck felt cool and smooth against his left palm. The strings were like spider webs, barely resisting his fingers at all.

He pulled the headphones down around his neck and ran both hands through his hair. There was a lot of hair. For a second it felt strange, like he was a double-exposed photograph, one of him with short hair and the other long, one with a clunky steel-string acoustic, the other with the sunburst Strat.

He wiped both hands on his jeans and ripped through the opening lick. In his mind he could hear the way the violins would come in around it in the final mix. The guitar's sustain was sweet and strong, run through a Marshall head and a blown ten-inch JBL. The distortion gave it guts and heart, like the catch in a lover's voice.

"Yeah," he said. "Let's do it." The drums had the lead-in, a stuttering press roll. Eddie knocked off three quick harmonics that decayed into feedback then slid down to the third fret. He bungled the fifth bar, but he knew the notes, his fingers knew them, and he was sure he could get it.

"One more time," he said. "Quick now, give it to me as quick as you can." His head kept nodding 2 and 4 through the rewind. The drums came in. He had a second of nerves and then he was into it. This time he had it, letter perfect, right through to the end. He played on past where he knew the fade would come, letting the solo run down on its own. Both his hands were sweating and his right foot jerked spasmodically against the rung of the stool.

Finally he stopped and peeled off the guitar and leaned it against the amp. He was really jumped up. "You get that?" he asked. He felt like shouting. Man, that felt good.

"Yeah, we got it," Gregg said.

"And?"

"It's good, it's okay."

"Come on, man, don't bullshit me. What's the matter?"

"I don't know. Let's listen to it, okay?"

"Son of a bitch," Eddie said.

"You want to come up in the booth?"

"Yeah, I'm coming." He went into the hall and bought a Coke out of the machine. It seemed weird for a second that it only cost a quarter and came out in a squat throw-away bottle. His body felt wrong too. He was 190 pounds, the most he'd ever weighed. It came from Twinkies and Schlitz and White Castle hamburgers, too much sitting down and not enough all-nighters on the road.

He stood there under a pin spot and swigged half the Coke. The sugar sizzled through his veins like a lit fuse. His right foot was moving again, tapping out some inaudible rhythm against the orange carpet. This shit could make you nuts, he thought. But it tasted great.

He took the rest of the bottle into the control room. The walls were paneled in light wood and the carpet was gray. There were half a dozen people in there already. Gregg and an engineer who looked like a biker had rolling armchairs at the console. The console ran for fifteen feet along the window that looked out on the studio. It had faders and VU meters for twenty-four tracks, though it was still only wired for sixteen. Dick, Eddie's manager, sat along the back wall with a couple of girls and Anson, the drummer. Anson was hanging around hoping to get laid.

"Let's hear it," Eddie said.

The rough mix had the drums too high and the electric piano too far down. Eddie kept hearing the phantom strings that hadn't been dubbed in yet.

"I was thinking maybe some strings on this one," Gregg said.

"Sure," Eddie said.

"You okay?"

"I'm having some kind of déjà vu shit," Eddie said. "It's got me a little spooked." Gregg and Dick looked at each other. Eddie hated it when they did that. Hated it when people wouldn't tell you that you were nuts because they were afraid you really were. Then it hit him again, a memory of the future, five years away, sitting on the grass at Timberlawn.

"You aren't tripping, are you?" Dick asked. Dick was thirty-five, a former lawyer with Epic records. His lapels were too wide and his sideburns too long. He had cranberry-colored double-knit slacks and white shoes and a white belt.

"No," Eddie said. He made himself listen to the playback. Everything else could wait. "It sucks," he said finally. "The timing's off or something."

"No balls," Gregg said. "Nothing personal, you understand. But it's got no balls. It's not pissed off."

"Yeah," Eddie said. He drank the rest of the Coke and threw the bottle in the trash. The trashcan was full of bottles just like it and newspapers and pizza boxes. He could smell the oregano from the leftover pizza.

"I think maybe we should call it a night," Gregg said.

"No," Eddie said. Everybody looked at him. He was suddenly cold and sweating at the same time. It has to be tonight, he thought. That's when I *did* it. He felt like he was a train that had come off the rails.

"Eddie?"

He remembered the way it was supposed to be. He came in late. Lindsey was back at the hotel. They'd had another fight, a real barn-burner. He did the solo in two takes. The first was better but he'd hit the guitar so hard he actually tangled up his right hand in the strings.

He could remember the rage, but he couldn't make himself feel it. This is all real, he thought. I'm in my own past, and I'm fucking it up. Who's going to finish the goddamn album?

"Let's try it again tomorrow," Gregg said. "It's three o'clock now. We're not going to get anything else tonight."

Dick said, "Eddie was going to take tomorrow off."

Sure, he thought, the day off. He could make it up then, the *real* Eddie could. The rhythm of it was coming to him. "Yeah, wait, that's okay. I don't need a day off. But call me. In case I forget we decided to do it. Call me early, noon or something." He saw the two pasts linking up again, a puzzled Eddie in the middle, wondering what had happened to his perfectly good solo.

"I don't want to piss you off," Gregg said.

Was I really this much of an asshole? Eddie thought. That people were afraid of me? "I think maybe it wouldn't hurt," he said.

One of the girls stood up. She was thin and blonde, wearing battered jeans and a man's sport coat with nothing under it. She'd left the bottom button undone. When she stretched Eddie saw bare skin up to the bottom of her rib cage.

"Want to do something?" she said.

Eddie didn't remember her name. Not that it mattered. He thought about Lindsey, back at the hotel. She'd have been asleep for hours now. Sex was pretty much a dead issue between them these days. He was pretty sure she'd been sleeping around, and God knew he had too. Besides which he was still pissed off from that fight he couldn't quite remember.

"Sure," he said. "Let's go." He waved goodbye to the others. Anson had his eyes closed and didn't wave back. Eddie felt like apologizing to him. Then he decided it wasn't his fault if Anson couldn't score.

He took the girl upstairs in a freight elevator and let her into the spare room. Hendrix had crashed here while he was recording his last stuff, the album that would have been *First Rays of the New Rising Sun.* Now Jimi was dead and it was 1973 and it didn't look like that new sun was going to come up after all.

Hendrix's people were halfway through turning it into Studio C. They had the control room walled off and glassed in. It made Eddie feel like he was under observation. Enough hall light came in around the edges of the door that he could see the girl. "Why don't you take your coat off and stay a while?" he said.

The girl smiled and took the jacket off. She was skinny enough that Eddie could count her ribs. Nice breasts, though, with pale nipples that seemed to look up at him. Eddie put his hands on her waist and she reached up to put her arms around his neck. There was an ugly bruise inside her elbow. Eddie wondered what she'd been shooting. Not now, he told himself. Pay attention. He leaned over to kiss her. She opened her mouth wide before his even got there, like a baby bird expecting a worm.

He kissed her anyway. Her mouth tasted like cigarettes. She had an agile tongue and it did what it was supposed to do. His dick got hard. He tugged at her jeans and she pulled them off and lay down on the bare mattress. He took his clothes off. The room was cool and his heart was pumping hard. He was vibrating all over like a low E-string. He looked for something to put over them. He found an unzipped flower-print sleeping bag and got under it with her.

They kissed some more and Eddie touched her breasts and her tiny, firm ass. She was still dry. She wet one finger and stroked herself with it. Her eyes closed and her hips moved on the mattress. Eddie sat back and watched. She touched her left nipple with her other hand, tugging gently at it. After a little while she said, "Okay, let's make it."

He almost told her to go ahead without him. Instead he got on top of her and she guided him in. Once he was inside her everything was okay. It felt terrific. Sex, he thought. What a great idea. After a while he rolled onto his back and she stradled him. She didn't seem to weigh anything. She rode him until they both came and then got off and curled inside his arm.

I'm not myself, Eddie thought. The consciousness riding his body belonged to another time, another head. It was somebody that could get laid and enjoy it without getting tied up in guilt or love or the goddamn meaning of life. But it was somebody who couldn't play guitar worth a shit either. Sorry, pal, he thought. Wrong astral plane for the guitar. You backed off a little too far, got yourself a little too karma-free.

Eddie gave the girl a few minutes to fall asleep and then gently got his arm out from under her. She mumbled something and rubbed her head into the pillow. Eddie got up and put his clothes on. He had to stop for a second and remember what time of year it was. Late spring. They'd spend the summer mixing down the album, putting in the strings, recutting some of the vocals. It would be out in the fall.

He found a green herringbone sportcoat in the closet and went downstairs. The jacket made him feel more a part of things. He remembered having it since high school. It was good to be able to wear it again.

Everything on the lower level was shut down. He went through the darkened lobby, past the curving concrete walls and the blue-and-yellow cosmic mural that Jimi had hated so much. There was a guard at the door, a huge black man in black leather and chains and a motorcycle cap, a relic of the paranoia of Jimi's last days. He let Eddie out onto Eighth Street. "Y'all be careful now, Eddie," he said.

"Oh yeah," Eddie told him. He walked over to Sixth Avenue and stepped off the curb to look for a cab. The wind pulled at his hair and the ends of his coat. He didn't think he had anything in mind, but when a cab pulled up he got in and said, "Warwick Hotel."

It was a straight shot up Sixth Avenue. There turned out to be a lot of money in his wallet. "For expenses," Dick had said, courtesy of Epic Records. He paid off the cabbie with a twenty and went upstairs.

Lindsey was asleep, of course. Eddie got into the shower without making any noise and steamed himself for half an hour. Afterward he stared into the fogged mirror, trying to get used to the pale skin, the pouches of flesh on the sides of his waist, the swollen stomach. Not that tempting a package, he thought. Twenty-two years old and already coming apart.

He toweled himself dry and left the bathroom door open a crack so he could see. He put on clean clothes, bell-bottom jeans and an embroidered Indian cotton shirt. He felt like he was getting ready for a long trip. His brain recognized the psychedelic logic of what he was doing and went with the flow.

He sat on the edge of the bed and watched Lindsey sleep. For part of him it had been close to ten years since he'd seen her. She slept with her arms outside the covers, clamping them to her body. Eddie had hated her for it.

Whenever she turned in her sleep she took all the covers with her.

Her skin smelled warm and sweet. A strand of his dark wet hair fell across her cheek. He moved his hand down the bare skin of her arm, so lightly he could feel the goosebumps come up. "Unghh," she said, and jerked her arm away.

Eddie felt the anger come up out of his *muladhara* chakra. It seemed to live in the body, an autonomous creature that thrived on sugar and caffeine and never forgave anything. When Eddie moved into the body the monster came with it.

"Lindy," he said, "wake up. Come on." He touched her face and kissed her throat.

"Don't," she said. She pushed him away with both hands, not even opening her eyes. She rolled away from him, taking the covers with her and leaving her back exposed.

It was no good. Even if he did wake her up, she would come out of it in a lousy temper. Her moods were stronger than the thin barrier between waking and sleeping. She fell asleep easily and slept hard, her body tense the whole time like she didn't want the anger to get away. He shut off the light in the bathroom and let himself out into the hall.

Riding down in the elevator, he put both hands flat against the mahogany paneling. He almost expected them to go through. He had an awareness that he was tripping, though he couldn't remember what he was on. He knew he expected some kind of answer out of it. It's not music, he thought. It's not sex, or love, if there's a difference. So what is it?

He was waiting to hear the click. The best dope was the stuff that slotted him right into the universe. It transcended words and everything else. Suddenly he was a part of the all. Not like speed, which made him think he'd reasoned everything out, then turned his brain to mush. Pure, right-brained connectedness. He'd touched it before on acid and mushrooms, and lost it again when he came down. This time, though, this time it should have flipped the switch for good and all.

It wasn't happening. Instead he was getting detached, shedding his karma like dandruff.

He went through the small, muffled lobby of the War-wick and out onto Fifty-fourth Street. The night was clear and cool and dark. "Xaman," Eddie said, not knowing where the word came from. "Xaman, which way?"

He crossed Sixth Avenue, toward Seventh and then Broadway just beyond it. There would be cabs there, and he could head back downtown. Things would still be cooking there. Maybe even a jam at the Scene.

He stopped. Something glowed at the back of an alley. It looked like men back there. Eddie squinted. They were naked except for loincloths and feathers in their hair. The one in the middle had tanned Caucasian skin. The other two were Indians. Looking at the one in the middle was like looking at a scrawny version of himself.

He took a half step toward them, thinking, this is nuts. You're walking into an alley in New York City at five in the morning. Do you want to die?

He took another step. They seemed to get farther away instead of closer. He smelled garbage and old motor oil. He kept walking anyway. He couldn't see the walls on either side of him. Then the three men faded out completely.

He stopped and turned around. There was no more light from the street.

He started to run. He got about two steps before his feet weren't hitting the pavement anymore. Then he was falling.

He fought his way up through the bullets of colored light. It was harder this time. It took all he had. He lay naked in the dirt for almost an hour, eyes and mouth wide open, pushing air in and out of his lungs with slow, deliberate effort. Finally the pressure in his bowels drove him into the bushes. He mopped up after himself the best he could with a handful of leaves and stumbled back into the clearing.

He couldn't sleep. There didn't seem to be any reason to close his eyes. So he just lay there.

It was the heat of the sun that pulled him out of it. He smelled like something that had died. He got onto his hands and knees, tried to keep the blood from going to his head.

He didn't think he'd been there more than a few hours. It could have been days just as easily. It had been a catatonic episode, like he used to have at Timberlawn.

For the first time he was really scared. A little physical abuse was nothing, but he didn't want to be crazy again. He was starved and dehydrated and exhausted and he couldn't keep the tears from coming up in his eyes.

I have to stop this, he thought. I really have to stop.

When the helicopter came he was still cleaning up, standing in the high grass where his hammock had been, scrubbing himself with water from the odd-shaped pot and the remains of his T-shirt. He got into his jeans on the run.

The others were already headed for the Temple of the Inscriptions and the forest path just beside it. They crouched along the path where they could see back toward the ramadas. Eddie dropped down next to Chan Ma'ax and crossed his arms over his stomach. He'd run maybe fifty yards and it had cramped him up something fierce. "What's happening?" Eddie said. "Is it the government, or what?"

Chan Ma'ax shook his head. Of course he wouldn't know any more than Eddie did. Somebody coughed and spat. The Lacondones all sat with their arms around their knees, rocking a little. The helicopter got quieter, then louder again. Circling. Suddenly the noise echoed off the hills like gunfire.

"They're landing," Eddie said.

Most of them had their eyes shut. Chan Ma'ax looked at Eddie and then closed his eyes. Okay, Eddie thought. He did it too. He listened to the insects and pretended he wasn't afraid. It got to be like the moonlight, or the drug. He started to forget where he was.

Then he heard his name.

"Jesus," he said. He jumped up, held onto a tree when everything tilted sideways. It was Lindsey's voice. It was crazy. Just when he'd been thinking about her, had seen her last night in that hotel room. The voice came again and he started down the path, steadying himself with his left hand against the cool stone of the pyramid.

He walked out into the sunlight and Lindsey was there. So was Thomas. And Chan Zapata, and Oscar, the pilot from San Cristóbal. "Hello, Eddie," Thomas said.

Eddie could only nod. Lindsey stood in jeans and a sweatshirt, weight on one leg, pushing her hair back with one hand. She was five, six feet away. If he could make his feet move, he could go to her.

"Are you okay?" she said. Her eyes flicked back and forth, looking first in his right eye and then his left. About every third time they glanced down toward his mouth.

"Fine," Eddie said. "I'm fine." His legs went all wobbly and he staggered back to where he could sit on the steps. "Fine," he said. "I'm fine."

"Jesus," Lindsey said. "Can you guys carry him? We need to get him to a hospital."

"No," Eddie said. "Can't leave yet."

"What do you mean?" Lindsey said. She got close enough to touch him but didn't seem to know what to do next.

"Can't," Eddie said. "Not yet." He had to stretch his face to keep his eyes open. They were all looking at each other the way Dick and Gregg had looked at each other. Run, he told himself. Get away, get out of here.

He tried to stand up and fell in the dirt.

It was afternoon. They were in the sleeping ramada, Eddie and Lindsey and Chan Zapata. The other Lacondones were over in the godhouse, burning copal. It smelled like a cookout in the suburbs. Eddie was confused, dislocated, and the sky was full of clouds.

Thomas and Oscar came toward them out of the jungle. "What's going on?" Lindsey asked.

"There's a problem," Thomas said. Eddie couldn't get over the way Thomas looked. Big and capable. Grown up.

"I may have pushed it a little hard this morning," Oscar said. "It don't want to start up again."

Lindsey's stomach felt cold and hard, like she'd just swallowed a big piece of ice. "Oh God."

"It's not a big deal," Oscar said. He didn't sound all that convinced. "It's probably just a clogged fuel line. All I have to do is take it apart and clean it out and everything should be okay."

"The radio still works fine," Thomas said. "If worse comes to worst we can call for help." He looked at Oscar. "Of course we don't want to do that unless we pretty much have to."

"Because of that helicopter that . . . that crashed," Lindsey said.

Oscar nodded. "We probably be better off laying low here tonight anyway," he said. "I was just listening, on the radio, you know? They got copters and planes all over the place out there."

"We camouflaged the thing with branches and stuff," Thomas said. "If you hear anything, get under cover here and stay put."

"I think I can get it fixed by tomorrow morning," Oscar said. "Then we can get the hell out of here. Maybe to Villahermosa, if we have to."

"Okay," Lindsey said.

"Lindy," Eddie said.

"Yes, honey, I'm here," she said. She looked at him like he was a dog that had been hit by a car, like she wanted to help him but was afraid of hurting him worse. Or afraid of getting blood and drool all over herself. "Nobody's called me that for years."

"Do you remember . . . when we were in New York for *Sunsets?* Do you remember that?"

"Yeah, I guess, kind of."

"We were staying at the Warwick. We had this really

outrageous fight. I was at the studio late and I came back
to the hotel and tried to wake you up. Or maybe I didn't,
maybe I didn't come home at all."

"We used to fight a lot," she said.

"You don't remember? If I came back? And tried to
wake you up?"

"It's been a long time, Eddie," she said gently. It was a
talking-to-a-crazy-person voice. "Is it really important?"

Thomas stared at him and Oscar looked away.

"No," Eddie said. "Not really."

He stretched out on the mat. As he drifted on the edge
of sleep he felt Lindsey's tentative hand on his forehead.
A few seconds later it started to rain.

L INDSEY WATCHED EDDIE'S
eyes go out of focus. "Eddie?" she
said. It looked like he was doing a swan dive off the steps
of the pyramid. He pushed off with his legs and went face
first into the dirt.

Thomas ran to him and rolled him over. "He's out
cold," he said.

Lindsey just stood there looking. "What in God's
name is wrong with him?"

"You want a guess? I'd guess he took that goddamn
mushroom. If he did it's a miracle he's not in a coma."

A tiny old man in a nightshirt stepped out from beside
the pyramid. He was about as tall as her shoulder. Three
more Indians followed after him. Chan Zapata walked up
to within a couple of feet of the old man and said something to him. It sounded like he was choking on some of
the words, and the rhythm was different from Spanish.
She was pleased she could at least recognize Mayan, even
if she couldn't understand it.

The old man just nodded to Chan Zapata. They didn't

hug each other the way Mexicans did, or even shake hands. "Ask them what happened to Eddie," she said to Thomas.

Thomas was already getting up. He said something in Mayan to the old man, and Lindsey made out the name Chan Ma'ax in it. It surprised her. She couldn't believe this was the sorcerer everybody made such a big deal about. He looked to her like one of those dolls made out of an apple that dried into nothing but wrinkles. Except that he still had so much wild black hair.

After they talked a little Thomas said, "It's the mushrooms, all right. Goddammit. Chan Ma'ax says he warned Eddie but Eddie got into them anyway. He says we shouldn't move him yet, that he needs to stay here for a few days."

The old man still hadn't looked at her. It was like she wasn't really there or something. "Can we move him out of the dirt, anyway?" she asked.

Oscar and Thomas carried him to one of the huts with no walls and laid him out on a mat. Lindsey sat in the dirt next to him. He seemed really hot and his pulse was fast. She didn't know if she should put a blanket over him. The morning was already so hot.

Her feet hurt and she took her shoes off. She hadn't imagined this. No way could she have known Eddie would be so bad off. She'd put a lot of effort into not getting her hopes up, into telling herself that the guy in the picture might not be Eddie after all. It was only when Chan Zapata recognized him that she really started to believe. And from there, after all she'd been through, after getting so close, she'd thought it was going to be okay.

Some of it had to do with memories, she supposed. She'd let herself forget a lot of the really nasty stuff. Eddie shooting heroin for the hell of it, back in '75 or so, getting so far into it he was barely able to quit. The women, for God's sake. At least twice he'd let her find him with them when it had to be deliberate. It wasn't, after all, like he didn't know how to screw up, and screw up big time.

Thomas, walking by, put his hand on her neck, right where it met her shoulder. The tenderness of it was unexpected. She looked up.

"I brought you something to eat," he said. "It's like stew, I guess. You want to be careful, it's real spicy. Here's some water." He gave her a glass with Sylvester the Cat on it. The glass was chipped and most of the paint was worn away. The water inside looked a little yellowish.

"Is this okay to drink?"

"This far from anywhere it probably is. I put in some iodine tablets anyway, just to be on the safe side. That's where the color comes from. That pot over there is the safe stuff. Just eat slow and drink a lot between bites. Don't spit it out or act like you don't like it or it'll hurt their feelings, okay?"

"Okay," she said.

It was a little like black bean soup with little pieces of meat in it. It *was* hot. It took a minute or so for the charge to build up, and by then her mouth felt raw and swollen. It felt like the peppers had literally blistered her lips. The water smelled like band-aids when they were fresh out of the wrapper, a plastic, medicinal kind of smell. She could taste the iodine in it, even after she swallowed.

Thomas sat cross-legged a couple of feet away and ate from another bowl. They had to share the water glass. Lindsey cut the heat with four thick corn tortillas and two glasses of water. She refilled the glass from the big clay pot.

"He'll be okay," Thomas said suddenly. "Eddie. Just the fact that he was up and around and talking. He'll pull through."

"So what's the plan? Are we going back this afternoon?"

Thomas took a second to answer. "I guess so."

"Is anything wrong?"

"I don't know. I'm a little nervous about moving Eddie, I guess."

"Because of what Chan Ma'ax said? Come on, Thomas, you're not into all that mystical crap, are you?"

"Look who's talking. What about you and your astrology?"

"That's different. It's fun. I don't let it mess with my life." Thomas looked like he was about to laugh. "Well. Maybe I've used it for an excuse a time or two."

Oscar brought over a bowl and sat down. Thomas shifted away from her, no more than a half an inch, but enough for her to notice. Playing it cool in front of Oscar. She wanted Thomas not to be a problem, but she could already see that he was going to be.

After lunch Lindsey watched Oscar and Thomas walk off toward the helicopter. The stew had given her heartburn and she wished she had some Rolaids.

Chan Zapata came and sat against one of the support poles. He had been over with the other Indians, but off to one side. Lindsey got the feeling he'd screwed up by coming here. It wasn't something she could ask him about. Eddie was tied up in it somehow and she was tied up with Eddie.

Her canvas carry-on bag was by her leg. She'd put her copy of *Spanish Made Simple* in there to read on the bus. She opened it to Chapter 1. It seemed kind of futile now, with them so close to leaving. But she was tired of not knowing what everyone was saying. Even if they were only in Mexico for another couple of days she would learn what she could.

"This book," she read, "teaches the pronunciation of our Good Neighbors in Spanish America." She thought about her good neighbors that had almost shot her out of the sky that morning. Her good neighbors in Nicaragua that Reagan wanted to drive into the ocean. Her good neighbors in El Salvador with their death squads.

She went on to Chapter 2. *"Cuanto cuesta la camisa?"* she said quietly. *"Cuanto cuesta el vestido?"*

Thomas and Oscar came back with the rest of their bags. They said there was something wrong with the helicopter but Oscar thought he could fix it. They would have to stay overnight. Thomas didn't seem to mind, for all the hurry he'd been in before. Lindsey thought he was still in love with his ruin.

Eddie woke up asking her about something that had happened in New York fifteen years ago. She got him to drink some water. There was an awkward moment where Thomas looked at Eddie and she could see a lot of unfinished business there. Then he and Oscar went off to pile some palm fronds around Eddie's tent, to make it hard to see from the air.

A couple of hours later Oscar was back. His hands were greasy and he was rubbing them with a rag that smelled like gasoline. "You want some help with that?" he asked.

Lindsey was still reading the Spanish book. "I thought you had to work on the helicopter or something," she said.

Oscar smiled. "The fuel filter's out and soaking. Can't do nothing more for a while." He had obviously figured out there was something between her and Thomas. With her still married to Eddie that made her a slut and therefore available.

"Okay," she said, reluctantly. She did what she could to let him know she wasn't interested, like making too much room for him to sit down. He kept touching her knee or her hands. Between that and two hours of intensive Spanish her head started to hurt. Finally he left her alone.

Once during the afternoon the Indians jumped up and started running around. They threw lids on the pots with incense in them and ran for the cover of the trees. Then she heard it too, the low, throaty rattle of helicopters. She sat motionless under the thatched roof, hanging on to Eddie's hand. The copters flew straight overhead but didn't slow down or come back, though Lindsey stayed put for another half hour. She wondered if they were looking for Oscar, if the copter that had chased them really had crashed, if anyone had died in it. Don't think about it, she told herself. Don't even think about it.

* * *

There was more stew for dinner. Eddie was awake long enough to eat some beans and tortillas. Afterward Lindsey took him back to the tent and sat on the floor next to his bed, holding his hand.

"I went back," Eddie said.

"What?"

"I went back to New York," Eddie said. "When I ate the mushroom."

"Was that what all that stuff was about?"

"I saw you there. In the hotel. It was so fantastic." His eyes were damp with sincerity.

"Eddie," she said, "you're crazy."

He laughed. "At least you're not afraid to say it out loud. Like Dick and Gregg."

"Who?"

"It doesn't matter. What's important is the drug." His voice wasn't much more than a whisper. "There's got to be some way to synthesize it. It's the most fantastic trip you could imagine."

"It nearly killed you," Lindsey said.

"It fucks you up some," Eddie said, "but it's not that bad. It's worth it. I mean, can you imagine? Going back and reliving anything you wanted? To be able to make sense of yourself, of your own life, to have it all there for you?"

"There's a word for it," Lindsey said. "Ego tripping."

"No, man, it's not just some selfish thing. If you can understand yourself, I mean, really *understand* yourself, you can understand everything else. The whole universe. It's the first step."

"We'll talk about it later, okay? Right now just get some sleep."

Eddie closed his eyes. A little later a scratching noise outside the tent made Lindsey jump. It had gotten full dark while she wasn't paying attention.

Thomas stuck his head in. "Am I interrupting?"

"No, he's asleep."

"Come on, I want to show you something."

"I really shouldn't leave him . . ."

"He's fine," Thomas said. "He's not going anywhere."

The moon was only a couple of days away from being full. Lindsey was amazed at how bright everything was. "This way," Thomas said.

"Where are we going?"

"You'll see." Being back in Na Chan had changed him. He seemed like he belonged here. Seeing him like this, cheerful and relaxed and mysterious, made her start to like him again. He led her past the long, low temple and into a thicket of grass and small trees. "Over there's the ball court," he said.

She made out a long flat area with heaps of rock on either side. "Baseball or football?" she asked.

"Basketball. Only they couldn't use their hands. You've heard all this, right?"

"No."

"There's two versions of the story. One says the losing team got sacrificed. The other says it was the winners."

"I like it," Lindsey said. "It's sort of romantic, in a screwy way."

She heard moving water for a couple of minutes before she actually saw the river. It was twenty feet across, running parallel to the path, glittering like rhinestones in the moonlight.

"This way," Thomas said. "Be careful." He started backward down a steep slope. "It's okay," he said, when she held back. "I'll catch you if you slip."

She followed him down. The noise of the water was a lot louder now. When she got to the bottom she saw she was next to a waterfall. Little drops of light flew off the rocks like fireflies. All the words went out of her head. She turned slowly around in a full circle.

"Your mouth is open," Thomas said.

She put her hand in the water. "Can you . . . can you swim in it?" Thomas nodded. "Oh God . . ." She didn't stop to think about it. She peeled off her sweater and jeans and underpants and waded in. The water was perfectly cool and made her skin tingle. She rolled onto her back and then her stomach and swam to the sandy bottom. It was deep enough she could feel the pressure on her eardrums. She came back up and saw Thomas watching her from the bank.

"Well?" she said. "What are you waiting for?"

Thomas undressed and took his glasses off and dove in. She felt stoned and silly. She swam up to him and threw her arms around him and kissed him. He held onto her and his feet touched bottom. He wasn't smiling anymore. He kissed her hard and squeezed her until she thought she was going to faint. The next thing she knew she was half out of the water, on her back. He was kissing her and she felt the emptiness of the entire world between her legs.

Thomas pushed himself up on his arms. "I haven't got . . ."

"It's okay," she said. "I'm fine now. I was just, like, being extra careful before."

"Are you sure?"

"I'm sure, I'm sure, oh God, Thomas, please . . ."

He slipped inside her. She held him by his bare buttocks just to prolong the feeling. It was like getting back a piece of herself that was lost. She held his face and ran her tongue around the inside of his lips, hungry for his flesh. He rubbed her breasts until she felt like her veins were full of molten metal, pumping liquid heat into the middle of her body. The stubble of his beard scratched her lips and chin and his hips ground into her pelvis. The little pains made her crazy. She lunged against him, splashing up the water around them, pumping him hard until he went as stiff all over as a plastic mannequin, not even stopping then until the frenzy burned right through her and left her limp and heavy and turning cold.

Thomas got off her and lay on his side, out of breath. He looked puzzled without his glasses. She pushed his hair back off his forehead and kissed his chest and swam out in the middle of the pool. She could feel his stuff start to run out of her and she held her legs together to keep it in. Not yet, she thought. She lay face down and pretended there was no bottom down there and imagined forgetting to lift her head to breathe.

Eventually she swam back to the edge and rinsed the

mud and sand from her backside. She dragged Thomas out into waist-high water and washed him, too. He kissed her again, sweetly this time. Then they got out and put on their clothes. She reached out to steady herself on his shoulder while she tried to get her wet legs into her jeans. He put his hand on top of hers, and they held hands all the way back to the camp.

When she unzipped the door of the tent he edged away.

"Are you coming in?"

He shook his head.

"Where are you going to sleep?"

"Oscar's staying in the copter. I could stay with him. Or there's a hammock and mosquito net that Eddie had. It'll be okay."

"You could stay here."

He looked away, then down. "I'll be okay," was all he said.

She went over to hug him. His hands went around her but hardly touched her. "Good night," she said.

"Yeah." He was smiling when he walked away.

Oscar had some emergency rations in the helicopter, so there were powdered eggs for breakfast. Lindsey was relieved it wasn't stew again. Thomas offered some eggs to the Lacondones and it turned into a party. They ended up cooking all they had and nobody got enough, but they all sat around in the dirt and laughed anyway. Chan Zapata translated as much as he could into English for her.

It was a little strange being the only woman with so many men, but it didn't hurt her ego, either. She got a lot of attention.

After breakfast Oscar said, "I don't think we're going to get out of here today. Maybe tomorrow, though."

"You sure you don't want to call for help?" Thomas said.

"I can get it," Oscar said. "I don't want to tell anybody where we are unless I have to. You know?"

"It's okay with me," Thomas said. "It won't hurt to let things cool down some more."

Right then Lindsey got a weird feeling, almost a premonition. We're never going to get away from here, she thought.

"Eddie's better," she said. "I think he could travel now. I mean, as soon as we can."

"A little more rest won't hurt him," Thomas said.

"No," Lindsey said. "I guess not."

The rebels moved into the ruins just before sunset. Lindsey was on Chapter 8 of *Spanish Made Simple*, "In the Office of Mr. Adams."

She impressed herself with the way she handled it. She looked up and there were about twenty men in jeans and khakis, all of them with guns, standing in a circle at the edge of the jungle. There were a lot more behind them in the trees. She looked down at the book and then up again and said, *"Buenas tardes, señores. Mucho gusto en verles."*

They didn't seem too happy to find Americans there. They shouted questions at her in Spanish. She just shook her head and pointed at *Spanish Made Simple* and said, *"No hablo."*

The guns scared her absolutely shitless. Nobody had ever pointed one at her before. All she could think about was how little it would take to set one of them off. Just a twitch of the finger. Somebody might do it by accident, or just for the hell of it, because it was so easy.

I'm going to die, she thought. She didn't even know who these people were. Rebels, probably, but who could tell anymore?

Nobody has the right, she thought. Nobody has the right to make another human being feel this helpless. Her eyes heated up and she had to blink to keep from crying. I could kill any of them, she thought. I could kill anybody who made me feel this way.

The soldier nearest her gestured toward her feet with his gun barrel. *"Bájale,"* he said.

"I don't understand," she said, hoping it was true.

He grabbed her shoulder and pushed her to her knees. Christ, what now? Were they going to rape her first, here in front of everybody? Or just shoot her straightaway?

The soldier grabbed one arm and then the other and put them on top of her head. Then he shoved her over onto her stomach. She was shaking. She didn't want them to see her being afraid. She hated them too much for that.

She turned her head to one side. They were making all the Lacondones lie down, too. She could see Chan Ma'ax and the idiot was smiling. She didn't know if it made her feel better to see that or not.

"Lindsey?" Thomas said. He was somewhere in front of her but she was afraid to look up. "Lindsey, are you okay?"

"Yeah, they didn't—" Something hard poked her in the back. Her vocal cords froze solid. She could feel her death just inches away, at the other end of the barrel.

"Cállate," the soldier said.

"Okay," Lindsey said.

She heard people moving around but couldn't see what they were doing. She heard Thomas say, *"Cuidado, por favor. Está enfermo." Enfermo* meant sick. He was talking about Eddie.

One of the soldiers patted her down discreetly. He seemed afraid of offending her. He barely touched her buttocks and didn't even turn her on her back to finish the job. Then for about five minutes the soldiers just stood around waiting. Lindsey realized they didn't know what to do next. We must have surprised the hell out of them, she thought.

A woman's voice began to shout orders. The man guarding her whistled and gestured for her to stand. She got up and made to brush herself off. The soldier knocked her hand away with his rifle barrel. It really hurt but she was afraid to touch it. The soldier pantomimed putting his hands on his head. Lindsey linked her fingers behind her neck. She rubbed her wrist gently against the back of her skull.

The soldier stepped aside. They were all in a ragged

line now, facing a woman who sat on the steps of the pyramid. She had a crude wooden crutch next to her and one foot in bandages. The foot looked bad. The bandages had almost turned black with dirt and sweat. Lindsey could tell it was hurting her. The woman's face was stretched into tight lines and creases.

Carla, Lindsey thought. It's Carla. On the news back home they didn't have anything but sketches and a picture from when she was a teenager. Lindsey suddenly saw herself as being in the middle of history.

Thomas stood a few yards to her left. Eddie sat cross-legged next to him. He was alert enough, but looked like he could pass out any minute. Carla asked if any of them spoke Spanish.

Thomas nodded and said something Lindsey couldn't follow. He and Carla talked back and forth and then Carla nodded at Lindsey. Thomas turned to her and said, "You know who these people are, right?"

"Carla?" she said. Her voice came out a whisper.

"You got it. She says they don't want to hurt us, all that happy shit. But they have to keep us under guard until they decide what they're going to do with us."

"So we're hostages."

"It kind of looks that way."

"But . . . that's insane. We could end up in the middle of a war with the U.S."

"Carla says we already are. She says there's already American troops down here. She saw them in Usumacinta. She says they're hunting her."

"What about . . . ?" She looked at Oscar, then back at Thomas, not knowing how much she should say.

"The helicopter?" Oscar said. "They already found it. They took the fuel pump away. We're not going anywhere."

"So we're fucked, is what you're saying."

"Yeah," Thomas said. "We're fucked."

The Lacondones didn't seem to care if there were people pointing guns at them or not. They built a big fire at the edge of their sleeping hut and warmed up some more stew. Chan Zapata looked at the ring of guards around them and said, "They are outside in the cold. We are inside with the fire. Better to be inside, no?"

Lindsey nodded. Nobody had seriously hurt her, though her wrist and the middle of her back were still sore. She wasn't tied up. They'd been through her purse and her luggage but hadn't taken anything.

Still. She felt like the rug had been pulled out from under her. She couldn't understand why this was happening. She should be in an airport somewhere, waiting for a flight back to the States. Why wasn't she? It didn't make sense.

She was still awake after midnight. She had one of the rebels, a tiny, serious woman, walk her out to the latrine. It was just a couple of boards to sit on over a pit with some chemicals in it. Lindsey had a roll of toilet paper from her suitcase and she stashed it back in her shirt when she was done. As long as she had toilet paper there was still hope.

When she got back Thomas had his eyes open. "Can't sleep?" he whispered.

She shook her head. She looked at the guards but they didn't seem to care if she talked to him. It was colder than she thought it would be without the tent. She put on a sweater and huddled up with her arms around her folded legs, swiping at the mosquitos when they got too close.

"I'm sorry about all this," he said.

"It's *my* fault," Lindsey said. "I'm the one that dragged you here, remember?"

"You didn't exactly drag me."

After a couple of minutes she said, "What was your wife like?" Then she said, "You don't have to talk about this if you don't want to."

"I don't mind. I guess I'm pretty much over it by now." He shifted around to where he could lie with his head propped up on one hand. "She was crazy. Like certifiable. When I first met her she was devout Church of Christ. At the same time she drank like a fish. Vodka-and-anything. Lemonade, ice tea, anything. And she loved rock and roll. Especially glitter rock, like David Bowie and Mott the Hoople and all that."

"So what happened?"

"My fault, I guess. She quit going to church when we moved in together. I thought she wanted to, but she was doing it for me. And I guess she always resented that. Eventually it came out that she wanted me to convert. I just couldn't see it. It's like asking me to believe in the Easter Bunny, you know?"

"Not exactly. But keep going."

"She missed her old friends and I was always working. It ended up in a real mess. She started hanging around church again and seeing one of her old boyfriends, and they ended up in bed together. I mean, for Christ's sake. She ends up going back to church—a goddamned fundamentalist church, at that—to get laid. She was completely schizo and she could never admit it."

"So she ended up with the boyfriend?"

"Nothing's ever that simple. We had to go through the business where she broke up with him and we tried the marriage again, and went to counseling, and it took forever before we finally got out from under each other."

"What was her birthday?"

"You're not going to start that with me again, are you?"

"Come on, it's the middle of the night. Everybody's asleep. Indulge me a little. Who's going to know?"

"November 23rd."

"Sagittarius. Figures. You guys never had a chance. You're adjacent signs. But she was on the cusp with Scorpio. You guys had great sex, right?"

"Yeah."

She poked him in the stomach. "Don't sound so wistful. You're over it now, right?"

"Right." He didn't say anything for a while, and then he said, "When I met her, I really believed there was only one great love in anybody's life. You know?"

"I didn't know you were such a romantic."

"I got over it. When she was with that other guy I was at UT and there were a lot of women around. Prigogine was there too. He'd won the Nobel in '77 and there was a lot of heat generated just from working with him, even though we weren't in the same department or anything. And suddenly there were women interested in me. And suddenly it seemed like there were a lot of different women that could make me happy."

"And did they?"

"For a while. Look, I still believe in love and everything." There was a pause. Lindsey knew he was deciding how far he wanted to go with this, whether or not he was going to tell her that he loved her. She didn't want to hear it from him. Not now. She looked away.

"I mean," Thomas said, "there are people I love that I've loved for years. That I'll probably always love. But I can't see one man, one woman, together forever. Not anymore."

Eddie was sleeping on the other side of her from Thomas. She couldn't help but look over at him.

"You're not saying anything," Thomas said. "This is a little one-sided."

"I don't know what I believe anymore," Lindsey said. "I know things don't work out by themselves. Love especially. Relationships. Everything is so goddammed hard." There was a big black-and-white striped beach towel in her suitcase. She took it out and curled up under it like it was a blanket. "Sometimes I get tired just thinking about it."

"When you found out about Eddie, weren't you . . . I mean, weren't you seeing anybody or anything?"

"Not anybody special."

"You could just pack up and walk away."

"You don't understand. My life isn't like yours or Eddie's. It never was. I don't need to see my name in the papers to know I'm real. I have an ordinary little life. I manage a Kwik-Kopy in a strip center in the suburbs. I live day to day. I worry about the machines running out of toner. I have friends that I go out to eat with. Sometimes we go to clubs and things and sometimes I meet a man and sometimes I let him come home with me. About half the time it turns out they're already married. They're always just about to leave their wives but they never do."

"It sounds very sad."

"It's *not* sad. It's dull. There's worse things. I'd sure as hell rather be in good old boring San Diego right now." She yawned. "Listen, I'm going to try to get some sleep, okay?"

"Okay," Thomas said.

She turned her back to him and closed her eyes, pulling the towel over her face to keep out the bugs. It seemed to take forever for her mind to let go.

By morning the place had already started to change.

Work details moved through the brush between the big pyramid and the thing Thomas called the Temple. They were putting up tents and plastic tarps and setting up kitchens. There were kids and dogs and women in smocked dresses. A middle-aged guy in a cap and beard like Fidel Castro limped around giving directions. He seemed to be trying to keep as many of the little trees standing as he could, to keep the camp from being too visible.

They were down to three guards: two for the Lacondones and one for the four of them, a dark-skinned kid with dreadlocks that they called Righteous. It was obvious nobody was going anywhere.

There was no breakfast. Lindsey worked on her Spanish with Oscar through the morning, and by noon she was cranky and lightheaded. She stood up. Thomas was reading a spy novel from his suitcase and Oscar was drawing handguns in the back of *Spanish Made Simple*. The guard finally looked at her. She pointed at herself and then toward the latrine. Righteous shrugged.

Halfway across the clearing she looked back. Righteous was paying no attention to her. They're not going to shoot you, she told herself. Just don't run or panic or act like you're trying to get away.

She turned toward a bunch of teenaged kids chopping firewood with machetes. She kept looking for the man with the cap and the beard, but he didn't seem to be around. *"Hola,"* she said. *"Dónde está* Carla?" Fear dried her mouth and turned the words to mush.

"Mande?" one of the kids said. He was tall and skinny, with a mustache no darker than a smudge of dirt. A learner's mustache, she thought. He could practice stroking it and getting food caught in it and someday he would be a man.

"Carla," she said. *"Dónde está?"*

The kid shrugged and pointed farther back into the trees.

"Gracias," she said. She felt like an idiot. She would have done at least as well asking him in English and kept her dignity while she was at it.

She dragged her feet as she walked away, trying to be less feminine, conscious of their eyes on her. She would not look back at Righteous. If he saw her, he would see that she was talking to the other soldiers and not escaping. It would be okay.

There weren't that many tents. As for the rebel army, she figured there were somewhere between fifty and a hundred of them, counting wives and kids and babies. Enough to hold a few civilians hostage, maybe, but against a real army they wouldn't have a chance. She still hated their guns and their brutality, but mostly they seemed pathetic to her now.

The largest tent was right in front of her. Something was going on and the soldiers around it were all trying to see inside.

"Carla?" Lindsey asked one of them. "Carla *está aquí?"*

The soldier flapped his hands at her and rattled off something that she couldn't make out.

"We need food," she said. *"Comida,* understand? You can't just let us starve, for God's sake."

He was more interested in what was happening in the tent. Lindsey looked past him into the half-light and saw eight or ten people standing around a metal cot. One of them held up a bag of yellowish liquid with a tube coming out the bottom. Hospital, she thought, then the smell of blood hit her. She heard it dripping and spattering on the rocky floor. Her empty stomach heaved.

Her feet wouldn't move. She heard a rasping noise and then the sound of more blood hitting the ground. It was very quiet around the cot. Then there was yelling that sounded like swearing, and more yelling that sounded like orders. Somebody else moaned. There seemed to be as much fear in it as pain. One of the rebels watching turned and ran out. She looked maybe sixteen, over-weight in a squared-off sort of way. She pushed Lindsey aside and kept on running. The front of her khaki shirt was sprayed with bright red blood.

Lindsey started to back away. Everyone was moving around, and now the man with the cap and beard came out and stood blinking in the light. He was hyperventilating. He looked down at his left hand. There was a severed foot in it. The foot had been cut off just above the ankle. The skin hung in ragged flaps at the edges of the cut. There was a hole in the center of the foot, and the skin around it was dark and powdery-looking, like an old mushroom.

He started to hand it to one of the soldiers. The soldier stepped back, crossing himself. The man with the cap reached behind him in the tent and came out with a towel and wrapped the foot in the towel.

Lindsey ran. She ran all the way back to the hut and curled up in a ball.

"Are you okay?" Thomas asked her.

"Shut up," Lindsey said. Her voice sounded very calm and reasonable to her. "Just shut up and leave me alone for a while."

By the time they brought food Lindsey was able to eat a little of it. It was chicken soup and tortillas. Actually it was so thin that it was more like the idea of chicken soup.

It was just as well, since Oscar told her it was iguana anyway. "This part of Mexico, if you can't make out the shape of the chicken, it's iguana." Lindsey was beyond caring.

After the third try, Thomas gave up asking her what

had happened. She couldn't talk about it. Even if she wanted to.

She looked down at her feet and tried to imagine only having one of them. No more dancing. I cried because I had no shoes. She wasn't cheering herself up.

It would be worse for Carla. She had been able to lead an army, here in the heartland of macho bullshit, and now she was crippled. It made Lindsey feel crawly all over.

She gave the last of her soup to Eddie and lay down again. She couldn't stop crying. When Thomas tried to touch her face she slapped his hand away, as hard as she could. She wanted to be alone with it and knowing she couldn't be only made it worse.

Around sunset she found herself staring at a single green palm leaf hanging down from the roof. The sun gave it glowing red highlights and even the air around it seemed full of orange color. She was able to look at it and not think about anything. After that she could sit up and drink a little water.

"I just want to know if they hurt you," Thomas said. "I won't ask you anything else."

"No," Lindsey said. It was like she had been granted a vision. She felt different now, changed by it. Emptier, harder. "They didn't hurt me."

It was still dark when she woke up and noticed Eddie was gone. Righteous was off duty and the man who replaced him had fallen asleep. Lindsey knew right away what had happened, but still she walked out to the latrine and back to make sure he wasn't there.

She shook Thomas by the arm. He opened his eyes and didn't say anything, just looked at her. "Eddie's gone," she said.

"What?"

"The mushrooms. Dammit, Thomas, he's gone back to the mushrooms."

He licked his lips and rubbed his face. "How did he . . ."

"I don't *care* how he did it, we have to find him." She

went over to the other hut and woke up the old Indian. "Eddie," she said. "Where's Eddie? *Dónde está?*"

Chan Ma'ax sat up. Lindsey couldn't tell if he'd really been sleeping or not. Thomas offered him a hand but the old man ignored it and got up on his own. For the first time Lindsey noticed how old he really was.

"Tell him," she said to Thomas. "Tell him to take us to Eddie."

"I used to know where the mushrooms are," Thomas said. "I can probably . . ." The old man was already headed for the jungle.

Lindsey ran after him. Thomas caught up to her and shone a penlight on the trail in front of them. The old man didn't seem to need it.

They came up through a narrow wash and there was Eddie, lying naked in the dirt. He looked dead. Mosquitos swarmed around him in a cloud. His clothes were in a pile to one side and his hands were folded peacefully over his privates. A few yards beyond him were the mushrooms. There must have been forty or fifty of them, the biggest, ugliest mushrooms Lindsey had ever seen. Thomas moved the light over them and they gave off a waxy shine.

Eddie was still alive. He was sweating and his face was hot and red. Lindsey put her ear down over his heart. It was beating wildly. She looked up at Thomas. "What do we do? What can we do for him?"

Thomas shrugged. "Nothing."

"What?"

"There's no antidote. One of the summer kids pulled this when I was down here. Even Thorazine didn't do anything. There's nothing you can do except wait it out."

"Jesus. Oh Jesus."

"He came out of it before. Maybe he will again. We'll know in a couple hours."

She slapped Eddie hard across the mouth. "Damn you! You stupid shit!"

Thomas grabbed her hand before she could hit him again. "Come on," he said. "Help me get him back."

They tried each taking an arm but his bare feet dragged in the dirt. Finally Thomas took his shoulders and Lindsey took his feet. Chan Ma'ax carried his clothes.

The sky behind the Palace was turning pink by the time they got him to the hut. Lindsey covered him with the big towel. "He couldn't leave it alone," she said. "He just couldn't leave it alone."

"He was always like that." Thomas put his hand on Eddie's forehead. "The fever's breaking."

"That's good," Lindsey said. "Isn't it?"

Thomas pushed back one of Eddie's eyelids and felt at his neck for a pulse. "Shit."

"What's happening?"

"He's not waking up," Thomas said. "I think we've lost him."

W HEN EDDIE CAME OFF-
stage after the encore Hendrix was leaning against the cinderblock wall. He applauded Eddie softly, his massive rings clicking together. Eddie couldn't see anything but those enormous, powerful fingers. Then Hendrix shook his hand and said, "Yeah, man, that was like really groovy or something, you know?"

"Thanks," Eddie said, seventeen years old and knowing he should be scared shitless. But he was still cranked up to ten, remembering the way he'd got them up out of their seats, even though he was just the warmup and there was still the Soft Machine to go before Hendrix.

Besides which, Hendrix wasn't scary. Despite the black, acne-scarred skin, the Fu Manchu mustache, the heavy eyelids, those huge, huge hands. He seemed like a kid himself, full of manic good humor.

"I really love your playing, man," Hendrix said. When he talked the words all climbed on top of each other. "Listen, you should like stick around after we do the set, maybe you can come on with us and we can get into something real nice. Just some blues or something, 'Red House,' you know, something like that."

"That'd be great," Eddie said. Hendrix wore skintight pink satin pants and a cream silk shirt with balloon sleeves and six-inch cuffs. He had a scarf full of eyes around his neck and a leather vest and a medallion that looked like a flying saucer with rays coming out of it. He looked like he'd just stepped off a spaceship. That's what he said in his songs and Eddie believed them.

In a way it was like some kind of fantasy to be standing there talking to Hendrix and in a way it was the most natural thing in the world. This was where Eddie belonged. He felt more comfortable with Hendrix than he did with his own family, more than he had with anybody from high school. Which was why, when he turned sixteen, he'd dropped out and moved in with Stew and Stew's divorced mother, where he could play guitar all day.

A girl with ironed blonde hair to her waist put an arm around Hendrix and started chewing on his ear. "Jimi . . . c'mon."

"Yeah, right, brother, I got to go. Later, okay?"

"Sure," Eddie said.

Hendrix and the girl went out the fire door into the parking lot. A shot of cold air came in after them. The roadies for the Soft Machine started moving the big Hammond B-3 out from the wings. They had hair to their asses and long sideburns and weird jumpsuits. Eddie's band was making do with two of Stew's friends from St. Mark's in slacks and madras shirts, working for backstage passes. They wheeled out Eddie's Twin Reverb while he was putting his guitar in the case and wiping down the strings.

"Where's the groupies, man?"

"With Hendrix," Eddie said. "Where do you think?"

"You promised us sex and drugs, man. Let's get with it."

Eddie took his guitar back to the dressing room. The three guys from the Soft Machine were standing in the hallway, waiting to go on. The drummer wasn't wearing anything but a black bikini bathing suit and tennis shoes, with a long coat over his shoulders to keep him warm till he got onstage.

The dressing room was full of leftover hats and collars and shoes from *The Music Man*. It smelled like deodorant and cold cream and face powder. For some weird reason they'd booked the show into the State Fair Music Hall instead of the auditorium downtown and the place was overflowing. There hadn't been a major rock concert in Dallas for over two years, not since the Dylan tour in late '65. The pent-up energy in the audience was unbelievable.

In the back corner Mitchell and Redding, Hendrix's drummer and bass player, were passing a joint. Redding waved at Eddie when he came in. At least Eddie thought it was Redding. Both of them were pale, scrawny English guys with frizzy hair and paisley clothes and it was hard to tell which was which.

Stew was there too, sweaty and Edwardian in lace and black velvet, looking at himself in the makeup mirror that ran the length of the room. "What did Hendrix say to you, man?"

"He liked us," Eddie said. "Where'd you get the beer?"

Stew pointed to a green plastic trashcan full of ice. "He liked *you*, you mean."

"Us, man, us. Where's everybody else?"

"The girlfriends showed up."

"Oh." Eddie opened a bottle of Schlitz and sat down. "Hendrix said maybe I could come on and jam with him at the end of their set." He kept his voice down because he didn't know what Mitchell and Redding would think about it. He didn't want to piss them off and miss his chance.

"Jesus, are you serious?"

"I'm serious. That is a beautiful guy, man. I'm just telling you what he said, he may have been stoned or something."

"Did you see what he was wearing? I hope to hell he *is* stoned." Stew chugged the last of his beer and said, "You're too good, Eddie. You're going to blow the rest of us right out of the way."

"Hey, come on, Stewart. We got the best fucking band in the city. You guys are great." It sounded lame, no matter how much he meant it.

It was just that things were moving so fast. After four years of getting nowhere with fuck-ups and drunks and no-talents, he had a band that was actually willing to be successful. Suddenly there were gigs at the Studio Club and the Cellar and LuAnne's. Two more openers on the Hendrix tour and then out to San Francisco to cut a record at Wally Heider Studios for Epic. The contract was nailed to the wall at Stew's house.

"That's true for now, maybe," Stew said. "I don't know how long the rest of us are going to be able to keep up."

"Don't start that shit, man. I can't *sing*. I couldn't front a band if I wanted to."

"What if Hendrix wanted you to join?"

Eddie shook his head. "No way, man. He doesn't want another guitar player. And I don't want another band. We got to make some changes and all, but I don't want to change *you* guys."

Stew got another beer and came back. He drank about half of it and started picking at the label with his fingernails.

"What kind of changes?" he said, not looking at Eddie.

"More originals," Eddie said. "You know that as well as me. I want to be able to play two hours and not do any covers. Right now I'm not even sure we've got enough for the album."

"Yeah, okay. And?"

"And we need to change the name. The Other Side

really sucks. There's got to be five hundred bands called The Other Side. Besides, it doesn't mean anything."

"It has to mean something? Like Jefferson Airplane? Or the Strawberry Alarm Clock?"

"What do you think about Maya?"

"What, like the Indians?"

"That too, I guess, but it's like this Indian word. Indian from India. It means like the illusion of material things."

"Jesus fuck, Eddie, what are you reading *now?*"

Eddie shrugged. "Think about it, okay?"

"Yeah, I'll think about it." Stew stood up, shaking his head. "You're really weird, Eddie. It's a good thing you can play guitar, or you'd never get laid. Speaking of which, I'm going to go try to find some dope and something to fuck before these British assholes get it all squirreled away where I can't find any."

"You always were the sensitive type."

"There's a time and a place for everything, and this is the fucking time to celebrate." He went over and said something to Mitchell and Redding and then the three of them walked out together, laughing.

The Soft Machine started up. From where he was all Eddie could hear was the bass, droning a two-note pattern, over and over. He opened another beer.

Hendrix had left his guitars there in the dressing room. There were five of them, perfectly matched white Strats, strung upside down, with a peg for the strap on the short arm of the cutaway and the whammy bar so that it would dangle down over the bridge. Eddie touched the low E-string with one fingernail. It was like a steel hawser. He couldn't imagine the strength in Hendrix's hands, to play strings that heavy.

When he turned around his brother was standing in the doorway.

Eddie's first instinct was to look for another door. There wasn't one. Thomas came at him with his hand out. He had on a white Ban-Lon shirt and a blue blazer and loafers. Between that and the tortoise-shell glasses he looked about as unhip as anybody possibly could. "Hey Eddie," Thomas said. "Pretty shitty when a guy has to buy a ticket to see his own brother."

"What do you want?" He ignored the hand and Thomas put it away. Then Eddie felt like an asshole for doing it.

"Maybe I just wanted to check you out. That could have been me up there, if I hadn't quit playing drums."

Eddie shrugged. "That was a hell of a long time ago."

"Speaking of time, when was the last time you were by the house?"

"Couple weeks."

"Yeah. Like since Christmas. More like two months."

All the old helpless anger came back, like he'd never left home at all. "Don't give me that shit, man. They threw me out. If they wanted me around they shouldn't have done that." It wasn't that he hated his parents. It was just that he wished they would die in a car crash and get out of his life. They were like quicksand, pulling him down.

"They feel shitty about it. You know they do."

"So they drown themselves in TV. Last time I was over there the old man didn't even look up. Get to the point. What do you want with me?"

"I want you to come home. Tonight. Right now. Try to patch things up."

"No," Eddie said. "That was easy enough. Anything else?"

"Listen, you little shit, I'm trying to help you out, here. Even though you won't admit you need it. You're going to be eighteen next year, they're going to draft your ass and send it to Vietnam. You better start thinking about the future."

"The future meaning college, right, like you? I got a fucking record contract, you asshole! I got a future playing guitar. That's the only one I care about. We're going out to San Francisco next week, for Christ's sake."

"Yeah, we heard all about it. From Stew's mom. But a record contract isn't going to keep you out of the Army."

"Come on, man! I'll go to Canada, okay? Why can't

you leave it alone? You've been trying to bring me down all my life because you're jealous. You think everything's supposed to be easy for you because you're the oldest. Well fuck that, man. I worked for all this. I stayed alone back in our room and played guitar while you were out sneaking vodka with your asshole friends and coming home and puking all over the place. That's all you ever do is puke on everything. Well you're not going to puke on this, you understand? You're not going to ruin it for me."

"Jesus, Eddie, I think maybe you ought to see a doctor or something."

"You come in here with this line of shit, you fuck with my head, you do everything you can to bum me out, and you wonder why I get mad? Fuck off, Tommy. Just butt out and fuck off."

Thomas held up his hands. "Okay. I ought to kick your ass on my way out, but I'm not going to. First because I think you're really crazy and second because you're still my brother and maybe it's a kind of going-away present."

"Just get the fuck away from me." Eddie turned his back and looked at Hendrix's guitars. He focused on them like they were sacred relics. After a couple of seconds he heard the door close.

His hands shook. What the fuck was he doing hanging around by himself in the dressing room? I am not going to let this bring me down, he told himself. He drank the rest of his beer, just to give Thomas time enough to get out of his way.

In the hall the Soft Machine was a lot louder. The organ sounded like an animal being butchered. Eddie went out the fire door he'd seen Hendrix and the girl use earlier. They were probably in a limo in the parking lot. If they were through with what they were doing, maybe they'd take him in.

It was like he'd forgotten it was February outside. The air was so thick and cold it bruised his throat as it went down. There was a loading dock right outside the door

and he grabbed the metal railing around the edge of it.
The cold came up through his hands and made him
shake all over, like a wet dog. It sobered him up and let
something out of the back of his head.

Jesus, that thing said, this is really intense.

He wiped his face on the sleeves of his shirt, a hideous
black-with-blue-polka-dots number that he'd bought at
Penny's in Northpark. The richness and color of his
memories amazed him. He'd lost so many of them. Like
the business with Thomas. He'd forgotten it, or at least
pushed it aside.

Instead he remembered jamming with Hendrix on "Pe-
ter Gunn" and "Red House" and afterward smoking Mo-
roccan hash in the back of Hendrix's limo with the
blonde with the ironed hair. Hendrix had split and it was
just the two of them, Eddie badly stoned and more nervous than he had been on stage with Hendrix. And then
the girl casually unzipped his tight black corduroys and
gave him his first blow job, and it seemed to Eddie like
some kind of initiation, like getting his head shaved after
sailing across the equator. He was transformed by it,
knew that this, at last, was the Big Time, or at least the
outer edge of it. Thomas and his parents weren't connected to the Big Time and so they'd been written out of
the scene.

I don't belong here, he thought. Somehow I'm cheat-
ing my seventeen-year-old self out of this just by being
here, by taking his place, when he worked so hard for
this. It was turning out like both the other trips, stripping
his connections away from him, even the ones he wanted
to hang on to. And still there was no click.

He went down the steps to the asphalt parking lot,
staying in the darkness between streetlights. Let me out
of here, he thought. I'm ready to go back. He tried to
remember the floating feeling that had come over him at
the end of the last trip. He closed his eyes, tried to make
it real.

Nothing.

He kept walking. At the far edge of the lot he saw
something shining faintly and his throat went tight. It

was the three glowing men again. This is it, he thought, waiting for the pavement to dissolve under his feet.

Instead they just got closer. He could see details now, past the shimmering effect of the yellow-green light. The one in the middle, the white guy that looked like him, waved Eddie on. He made big gestures with his arm, like he was throwing something over his shoulder in slow motion.

Eddie started to run. It didn't seem to make any difference. They looked like some kind of 3-D projected image, a hologram. Only it was like he was projecting it himself and so he could never catch up to it.

His sneakers made weird, metallic echoes on the asphalt. It was a couple of seconds before he realized that he'd lost the streetlights again, that it was starting to happen like it had happened the last time. He started falling and he saw the bullets of light.

This time he couldn't stop.

He was falling hard, hard enough to make his heart hammer at the back of his throat and his eyes push up in their sockets. The end of the tunnel of light had turned the same yellow-green as the glowing men. There was a pressure like a soundless wind against his face and shoulders and chest, and the feeling of blood rushing to his head, his cheeks swelling and his ears wanting to pop. He stretched his hands out in front of him, as if they could somehow break his fall.

He'd read about life-after-death experiences. This was too similar. The headlong rush, the light ahead of him. Chan Ma'ax warned you, he thought. You kept kidding yourself you could handle it and now you're going to die.

He fell for a long time.

Eventually time itself didn't mean anything. He couldn't tell if his eyes were open or closed, what direction he was falling, where his hands were. And once he realized all of that he found out his eyes were closed after all.

He opened them to sunlight. He lay in a field of short grass, surrounded on all sides by limestone walls. Not the bleached, worn limestone of the ruins but smooth-finished limestone painted with warriors and gods and serpents.

Just like when Na Chan was new.

And then he saw the two men in feathered robes standing over him and knew, beyond question, where he was.

THREE

THOMAS WAS SITTING on top of the big pyramid when Faustino's man found him. He'd spent the early morning cleaning out the temples with a shovel he'd found inside. Somebody, probably Eddie, had already made a start at it. With a machete he could have cleared the plants off the roof and sides. He didn't see much chance of getting one, though.

Faustino sent Righteous, the dark-skinned kid with the knitted tricolor Rasta cap. The kid started climbing the high, narrow steps of the pyramid and gave up after the first dozen or so, leaning on his gun and breathing hard. *"Oye!"* he yelled when he got his wind back. *"Su hermano!"*

It was something about Eddie. He started down.

Faustino had been checking on Eddie for three days now. He had an old-fashioned leather medical bag with almost nothing inside. A stethoscope and a blood pressure gauge with a cracked dial. That was about it. Whatever drugs he'd had were used up long ago.

Thomas thought it was a waste of time. Eddie was gone, catatonic, like the other kid who'd screwed around with the mushrooms. Now there was news. The first thing, the obvious thing, that came into his head was that Eddie had died.

When he got within ten or fifteen steps he said, "Eddie?"

"*Sí,*" Righteous said. The kid was twitchy, moving to internalized rhythms. He left a pause after the "sí," like he wanted to add "señor" but wasn't sure of the politics of it. "He is awake," he said in Veracruz Spanish.

"Jesus Christ," Thomas said.

They had the flaps open, but the inside of the tent smelled sour and decayed to Thomas, mildewed. Eddie looked like somebody had let almost all the air out of him. Faustino was taking his blood pressure with the battered gauge and Lindsey was trying to talk to him in Spanish. She didn't really speak any, but she'd been trying to learn it out of a book. Thomas supposed he had to admire her for the attempt. Her clothes hung loose on her body and there were fatigue circles around her eyes. It didn't make her any less desirable.

"Hey, big brother," Eddie said.

Faustino made some notes on a piece of lined paper. It was almost filled with other writing and had turned brown along the folds. He put it and the stethoscope and blood pressure gauge back in his bag. "If he rests," he said in Spanish, "I think he'll be okay."

"*Gracias,*" Thomas said. Like with Righteous, formalities came hard. "*Muy amable.*"

On the one hand the rebels were feeding them and otherwise leaving them pretty much alone. On the other they *were* hostages of a sort. Even though Carla hadn't said anything to them about ransom demands. In fact, with the last-minute decision to come to Na Chan instead of Nahá, nobody knew where they were, not even Lindsey's parents or Shapiro back at the project. It could be weeks before anybody even thought to look for them.

Of course, if they were crazy, they could always try walking out through the jungle.

Faustino nodded and left. Thomas looked at Eddie, lying there with his feeble, self-satisfied smile, and thought about how all of this had been because of him. And in gratitude Eddie had gone and eaten more of the mushroom. "You're an idiot," Thomas said. "You know that?"

"Hey, man," Eddie said weakly. "Don't be pissed off at me."

"Why not? That shit's poison. Literally. It could kill you outright, not to mention frying your brain. And you're lying there grinning like you just won a goddamn marathon or something."

"Okay, man, take it easy. How long was I out, anyway?"

"Three days."

Thomas was relieved to see that Eddie could still be frightened. His eyes seemed to pull back into his head. "Three *days?*"

"They made you swallow sugar water," Lindsey said.

"Otherwise," Thomas said, "you would have dried up and blown away. You could have died from dehydration alone."

"I took it before, you know," Eddie said.

"Yeah," Thomas said. "We know."

"Twice before. It wasn't that bad."

"Bullshit," Thomas said. "I wish you could have seen yourself. You looked like death."

"Thomas," Lindsey said. "C'mon. Take it easy."

"I can't believe you're doing this to yourself," Thomas said. "I just can't believe it."

He shut up. Lindsey was looking at him like he should have done it earlier. Finally he couldn't stand it anymore and he asked, "What did you see?"

"First it was just stuff from my life. The last time it was high school, and you were there. Remember the Hendrix concert? My band was the warm-up?"

Thomas shrugged. "I guess."

"Then it got real weird and there were Mayans. Old Mayans. Back when this place was new and there was paint on all the temples and stuff."

It gave Thomas a chill. It was the kind of detail that somebody off the street wouldn't be likely to know.

Maybe Eddie'd read it somewhere. Most people thought
Mayan ruins had always been plain white stone, like they
were now. Most people didn't know they'd been painted
in all kinds of reds and yellows and purples.

"Last time," Lindsey said, "he hallucinated this whole
scene in New York, back in the seventies."

"It didn't feel like a hallucination, man," Eddie said.
"It felt like I was really there."

"Eddie, get real," Thomas said.

"I'm not bullshitting. The big guy there was named
Chilam Sotz'. Where would I come up with something
like that?" It was the right pronunciation, and a plausible
name for a Classic Mayan priest. Thomas had no idea
where he got it.

"They were playing ball," Eddie went on. "It was different from what you said in your book. There were a lot
more players. Some could use their hands and some
couldn't. They had all kinds of different costumes. Some
of them were naked. I watched for about an hour and
then I went into the city."

"What was it like?" Thomas asked. "I mean, were you
a ghost? Could other people see you? Were you just plain
old Eddie Yates, only naked? What?"

"I was one of them, man. I was in one of their bodies,
anyway. Except he had real light skin. Not as light as
mine, but light for them. And he had facial hair, a fuzzy
kind of beard, like a fifteen-year-old's or something. But
he dressed like them and they didn't seem freaked out by
him—me—or anything. I don't know what happened to
the guy's mind while I was in there."

"What about the city?" Lindsey said. "What did you
do in the city?"

"I walked around for a while. Everything was colored.
I never knew that. The temples were all painted and so
were all the statues and those column things . . ."

"Stela," Thomas said.

"Yeah. It was amazing. And then this guy came and
took me to one of the temples. It was one of that bunch
over on the hillside, the one that faces back this way."

"The Foliated Cross."

"Whatever. They didn't have names for them. The Chilam Sotz' guy was there. He kept asking me questions."

"Could you understand him?" Lindsey asked.

"Yeah. It was different from Lacondon, but not that much. Like Mexican Spanish and Spanish Spanish. I couldn't tell him what he wanted to know. He kept asking about Muh-*Shee*-Kuns or something."

"Christ," Thomas said.

"What?"

"It's what the Aztecs called themselves. It's spelled the same as 'Mexicans.' The Aztecs—Mexícans—were just starting to be heard of down here at the end of the Classic period."

"So," Eddie said. "You're starting to believe me."

"How can I believe you?" Thomas said. "I mean, how *can* I?" He couldn't look at Eddie's face. "Go on. Then what happened?"

"That was it. I was really tired and I just crashed out. It felt like I was out for a long time, and then I woke up here." He yawned. "I felt kind of like I do now. Really wasted." He smiled contentedly. "I really better get some more sleep."

Thomas saw that Lindsey had followed him outside.

"You don't believe him," she said.

"Of course not. You want me to believe those mushrooms are magic?"

"What it is," Lindsey said, "is you're willing to believe in vague spiritual stuff, like God or destiny or karma or something, but you won't believe in a mechanism you don't understand."

"Like astrology."

"For example. How are you going to explain all those details Eddie came up with? Maybe there really is a 'rational' explanation for what happened." She put quote marks around "rational" with her fingers.

"I looked for one," Thomas said. "I tried. I talked to all these 'psychophysicists' and all these other New Age science types. This one guy tried to convince me that memory is passed on genetically. He said we have all these 'silent genes' that we don't know what they do. The right kind of drug could turn them on and open up completely new neural pathways. They think now that maybe that's what acid flashbacks are, some kind of weird mental skill that we used to need when we were living in caves or something, that got called up by the LSD."

"But you don't buy it."

Thomas shrugged. "This other guy tells me the entire universe is just a hologram. There aren't any physical objects, just interference patterns. Then he says memory is holographic, and we all have the entire universe in our brains, past and future. Because any piece of a hologram has the whole picture in it, just in less detail. Whoever took the drug would start off with like a central image out of this holographic library, something out of the actual past, like a stage set. Then they would be acting out a little hallucinated play inside that set, all inside their own heads."

"Doesn't that kind of thing turn you on at all?" Lindsey said. "I mean, I don't really understand it but it sounds trippy as hell."

"The thing is, what's the difference between that and Jung's 'racial memory' or any other wild idea that you can't prove? Maybe Eddie has called up some kind of racial memory of the ancient Mayans. But what happens if you don't have any Mayan ancestors?"

"Maybe you go crazy. Like that kid you keep talking about."

"It's fun to sit around and think about, but it's not going to get Eddie out of his coma if he eats any more of that mushroom."

"You know what I think? I think you're jealous. I think you want to take it yourself. You wish you had the nerve to try it."

"Not me. I'm not crazy, whatever you think. I just want you to keep him from doing it again." He wondered if it was true, if that really was all he wanted.

"I'm not sure I can make him do anything."

"You have to try. Aside from what the alkaloids are

doing to his mind, that shit is full of cumulative toxin. Toxin. That means poison."

"My God," Lindsey said. "You can really be an arrogant prick sometimes." She turned around and went back into the tent.

Thomas got a towel and headed for the swimming hole. He wanted to save something before the whole morning went sour. He stripped and dove in from the bank and the cool water soaked the anger right out of him.

He couldn't help thinking about the night he and Lindsey had made love there. Since then she'd been distant again and left him feeling like a lovesick teenager. There was no question in his mind that the argument they'd just had wasn't about Eddie. They could have been talking about horse racing. They were knocking sparks off each other out of pure sexual tension.

Then there were the memories of the place itself, the year he'd spent here in '73–'74. He was all-but-dissertation and there were two first-year graduate women that were both interested in him. He'd ended up having both of them, Gail fairly openly, Ann on the sly. It amazed him he'd actually gotten any research done.

For all the intensity he'd felt at the time, there were only a few disjointed details left. Gail was tall and blonde and wore pale, flavored lipstick. He couldn't remember what it had tasted like. Ann bathed twice a day but never wore perfume or deodorant or makeup. She had hair the color of walnut hulls and the intensity of her pleasure depended on the amount of effort involved in it. They had coupled in the dead leaves on the jungle floor and standing up inside a half-excavated temple. He remembered her breasts had been small, nearly flat, but he couldn't see them in his mind, or remember the way her skin had smelled, or the feeling of her tongue darting into his mouth.

What would it be like to relive all that? The way Eddie said he had? Thomas just wished he'd been paying more attention at the time. Memorized everything. The wealth of specific data would connect him to the emotions again, more strongly than any memory of the emotions themselves ever could.

And then, Thomas thought, there was the rest of it. Seeing the city come alive again. Really seeing it, really believing he was there. How much would something like that be worth? What would he give up for it?

He swam a few laps, four strokes over and four strokes back. After a while the water started to feel clammy and he got out and put his clothes on. He didn't want to go back to camp. If he saw Lindsey they'd argue again, and there was nothing else for him to do but work on the temples. Now that he was away from it, he could see how futile it was to try and clean them up by himself.

He threw tiny pebbles into the water. The turbulence made them dance, two steps to the right, up for a second, then spinning off sideways and down. Waterfalls were very big in chaos theory, of which Prigogine's work and Thomas' own work were just a part. According to classical physics the patterns should be predictable, because everything that went into them was quantifiable. Volume of water, depth of streambed, angle of gradient, everything. But the patterns were like living organisms, influenced by their own histories and their reactions to each other, and they could never be nailed down.

What does this tell us? he thought.

He got his feet under him and was just standing up when he saw the hand.

It was blackened and waxy-looking, one of the fingers split halfway down the nail and caked with dried blood. The arm it was attached to was covered in olive-drab fabric. Thomas couldn't see anything past the elbow because of the thick bushes along the riverbank.

He looked both ways and climbed up for a closer look.

The rest of the body leaned against a tree like it was asleep, dressed in military fatigues, the head tilted back at about thirty degrees. The left hand lay on the chest and right under it was more dried blood. An M16 was just out of reach behind the head. The name PORTER was stenciled in black over the left shirt pocket.

The man had an inbred, hillbilly face—thick lips, broken nose, heavy ridge of bone over the eyes. Even closed the eyes looked small and were too close together. There were smudges of dirt and grease all over the face. Flies crawled on one cheek where it had been scraped raw and had just started to scab over.

He was Northamerican, Thomas was sure of it. Carla had said there were U.S. soldiers here, that they'd chased her out of Usumacinta, and Thomas had thought it was just a paranoid fantasy.

All his unresolved feelings about Vietnam came back to him. Here he'd always wondered what it would have been like to be over there, in the midst of death and all-out horror, to have been changed like everybody he knew who'd been through it. And now war was closing in on him, like the ghost of Vietnam come to haunt him.

He looked at Porter again. What was the body doing here, anyway? Why hadn't they said anything about it? Carla would freak if she knew there were U.S. soldiers inside her perimeter.

Actually, once he thought it through, it wasn't that hard to understand. One of Carla's soldiers hearing something moving in the jungle and shooting, Porter crawling away wounded, the rebels not finding his body and assuming it was an animal or even just the wind. Porter heading for the river and dying before he could make it.

Then he saw that the man's chest was still moving, jerking up and down in convulsive rhythm.

I don't want this, Thomas thought. Anything I do is going to be wrong. He took one step backward and then another. He's going to be dead in a couple of hours no matter what. Then Carla's people can find him by the smell.

A twig snapped under Thomas' boot and Porter opened his eyes. The man blinked and moved his mouth but nothing came out.

I'm not doing this, Thomas thought as he knelt down next to him.

"American?" the soldier whispered.

"Yeah," Thomas said. "Porter? That your name?"

The man ducked his head half an inch. "Need a doctor. Not one of the spics. White doctor."

"Okay," Thomas lied. "Just relax. I'll get somebody. You're okay now."

"Gun," Porter said.

Thomas pretended to look around. "I don't see one. Don't worry about it. You'll be okay here."

Porter shut his eyes and Thomas stood up. On the far side of the tree, where Porter couldn't see him, he bent and snatched up the M16 without slowing down.

Spics, he thought.

The gun felt good in his hands. It was like putting on a really well-made suit for the first time. He remembered the toy guns he'd had as a kid, the sense of completion they gave him when he held them. He carried the gun as far as the base of the falls and then realized what he was doing. The rebels would shoot him if he took it into camp.

He put it under some bushes and covered it with dead brown leaves. Even if Porter woke up again he wouldn't be able to find it. Thomas told himself he was just protecting Porter by hiding the gun, but it didn't work. Just knowing where it was gave him a tremendous sense of power.

Things were starting to look up.

The camp was empty during the day. Most of the soldiers were on patrol or hunting. A fat, middle-aged man with thinning hair and a mustache sat on the steps of the Palace, cleaning his rifle. His name was Gonzáles. He'd told Thomas once that he didn't hold with the nommes de guerre the others used, thought they were stupid and childish. Probably because they all referred to him as Gordo. Fat Man.

He stared at Thomas suspiciously. "Where you been, eh?" he asked in sloppy Spanish. There was a distant gunshot. Somebody shooting at a monkey, most likely, but Thomas thought of Porter and the bloodstains on his chest. He could feel the guilt shining out through his eyes.

"Swimming," Thomas said.

"You have a nice swim?" Gonzáles said. "While the rest of us have to work?" Thomas didn't say anything. There was another shot and Thomas' shoulders curled involuntarily. He couldn't get used to the sound.

"Where's Carla?" he asked. If the U.S. forces were closing in, he had a right to know. Maybe he would even tell her about Porter, get it off his conscience.

"Over talking to the brujo," Gonzáles said. "I guess she finding out how we gonna win the war with no food and no soldiers."

Oscar lay in a hammock under the nearest ramada, reading one of Lindsey's paperbacks. He'd folded the cover all the way around so he could hold it in one hand and leave the other one behind his head. "Hey," he said as Thomas went by.

"Hey," Thomas said.

"What's up?"

"Nothing," Thomas said, and kept walking.

Chan Ma'ax and Chan Zapata sat cross-legged on mats under the other ramada, the godhouse. Carla had both her legs out in front of her, the left one propped up on a knapsack, keeping the bandaged stump out of the dirt. Thomas stood by one of the support poles, waiting for permission before he went in.

Chan Ma'ax looked up at him. *"Hola,* Tomás," he said in Spanish. "We are talking about the end of the world."

"Soon now," Thomas said. "No? Twenty-five years." The long-count calendar was due to run out on Christmas Eve, 2011.

"But already," the old man said, "things . . . come apart. Even though it is not yet the end of the . . . the big circle. I'm sorry. My Spanish is not best. What I say is Carla and her people are here to help things come apart."

"When things get bad enough," Carla said, "maybe it's time for them to end."

"Ah, *sí,* I don't say you are bad, what you do. It is

time." He wiped the dirt in front of him smooth with his hand. "Take away what is there, build again. But you have to be careful what you take to the new world. You have to bring the old ways and the new ways . . . together." He clasped his hands together like a Christian praying.

"I understand you, old man," Carla said. "But the old ways are for old times. We're building something new. We'll leave the old ways to the foreigners and the capitalists."

Chan Ma'ax said, "Not those old ways. You think Northamericans—*cómo se dice?*—'United Fruit Company.' I mean more old than that. The kind of old ways where you know that all things have roots that go into the ground. The roots, they all grow together. When you cut down a mahogany tree, a star falls out of the sky. You understand?"

Thomas would have figured Carla to sneer at that kind of mysticism, but she seemed almost hypnotized by it. "What about this place?" she said. "They cut down the forest to build these temples."

"It was time to build temples. Then it was not time and they all go."

Thomas squatted next to Carla. "Where?" he asked Chan Ma'ax.

"La selva," the old man said. "Back to the forest. To put roots into the ground again."

"How?" Thomas said. "What made them decide it was time?"

Chan Ma'ax smiled.

"Was there fighting?" Thomas asked. He was about to say the name Haawo' and Chan Zapata seemed to know it. He put his hand on Thomas' arm and shook his head.

"He's not going to talk about it," Chan Zapata said.

Thomas could see it was true. "Why not? What difference does it make? If he doesn't tell me, or tell somebody, his knowledge is just going to die with him. Then what good is it?"

They sat that way for ten or fifteen seconds. Thomas stared at the old man, the frustration chewing him up inside. Goddammit, this was important. If he could get some kind of folklore or tradition to back up his dissipative structure model, he could actually *prove* something. The old academic fervor made his palms sweat.

The old man turned his head toward Chan Zapata but kept looking at Thomas. He whispered something Thomas couldn't hear, then got up and walked away.

"Well?" Thomas said. "What did he say?"

Chan Zapata looked embarrassed. "He said, ask your brother. Ask Eddie."

"What did he mean?" Carla said.

"Nothing," Thomas said. "Maybe he was making a joke." He wondered sometimes how the old man had lived so long.

"They say your brother takes the mushrooms," Carla said.

Thomas changed the subject. "Listen," he said. "What about those Northamerican soldiers. How close are they?"

"Why do you want to know?"

"I just wanted to find out if we're about to get caught in a war, here."

"You will be safe," Carla said.

It was not, Thomas decided, his day for answers.

"Calm the fuck down, will you?" Oscar said.

Thomas couldn't hold still. Everything that had happened in the last two weeks—the takeover at the project, sex with Lindsey, the rebels, now the soldier with the gun —all seemed to line up, like an arrow pointing at something he couldn't quite make out. Each new twist had pumped him higher, and now he was nearly manic.

The problem was he liked it. He'd never felt so lucid, so aware, so full of energy. He'd been hibernating for years, pissing away his life. Now he was really alive. "Let's take a walk," Thomas said. "Okay?"

"Where to?"

"Like in the direction of the helicopter."

Oscar squinted at him. "What are you up to, man?"

"I just want to talk."

Oscar got reluctantly out of the hammock and Thomas led the way across the stubble of cleared trees. "You find some speed somewhere or something?" Oscar said.

"It's not speed," Thomas said.

"Carla finds me with that aircraft, I don't know what she'll do. I think the whore would love to torture my ass. If she thought it would do any good. Like if she could torture the skill out of me and into somebody else so they could fly that thing."

Thomas cut around into the trees to avoid the rebel tents. "You didn't tell them I could fly?"

"Fuck no. I'm not doing shit for those assholes. They been giving me ideology sessions about twice a day. A lot of threats and promises. They know better than to lay a hand on me. If they fuck me up I won't be able to fly at all."

"Listen," Thomas said.

"Yeah?"

"Something's happening. I found something this afternoon."

"Quit fucking around, man. What did you find?"

"A soldier. By the river."

"U.S. soldier?" Thomas nodded. "Dead?"

"Nearly."

"Leave him to it, then."

Just ahead was the clearing where the crippled helicopter lay under a net and a layer of brush and palm fronds. "Think for a second," Thomas said. "What's he doing here? How many more of them are there? Are we about to get overrun? What'll Carla do if she finds him?"

"I don't even know why you're asking me all this shit."

"I think maybe we should hide him someplace. Try and keep him alive, find out some things. Like where Marsalis really is. Like does he know we're here and what does he plan to do about it."

"Where are you talking about hiding him?"

"I was thinking about maybe in the helicopter," Thomas said.

"Are you nuts?"

"I can't just leave him out there to die. If he was already dead I wouldn't care. But he's a human being, for Christ's sake. Even if he is one of Marsalis' goons."

Oscar shook his head. "Do we have to put him in the helicopter?"

"They don't watch it anymore. They know it's not going anywhere. Nobody's allowed inside. We could hide him there for days. There's even a first-aid kit in there, right?"

"Maybe. Unless they found where I hid it. What happens if they catch us?"

"What if they do? We're just trying to help one of our own."

"One of *your* own, you mean. I'm not too crazy about you gringo motherfuckers being down here in the first place. And neither are they. Don't kid yourself. Piss these compañeros off and they'll beat you to death. And don't expect Carla to save you. They're just peasants, man, and they're not that thrilled about a woman giving them orders. She puts too tight a leash on them and she's gone, too. We're not talking noble causes and political ideals and shit. We're talking a lot of hungry, pissed off, desperate people. Don't ever think you got a handle on what they're going to do."

"Are you going to help or not?" Thomas said.

"I got to think. When you talking about moving him?"

"It's got to be tonight. That trail over there goes right to the river. The moon's still nearly full. We could get him here in ten, maybe fifteen minutes. We can make a stretcher out of a blanket or something."

"There's a stretcher in the aircraft." Oscar held up his hand. "*If* I decide to do it."

"Yeah, okay. About that first-aid kit . . ."

"What, you want it now?"

"Just some stuff. Enough to keep him alive until tonight."

It was about one in the afternoon. Thomas' stomach hurt from nerves and hunger. The rebels only fed them twice a day, in the morning and again around sunset. Thomas still wasn't used to it.

The path came out just north of the falls. Thomas found his way back to Porter's body and when he got there he thought he was too late. Porter looked white as steamed fish meat and the wound in his stomach had started to smell. But when Thomas touched the man's arm he could feel the muscles spasm.

He brought river water in a tin folding cup. "Drink," he said. He tilted the cup until water ran down Porter's chin. Finally Porter's tongue broke through his scabbed lips and he licked at the water. Thomas fed him half a cup and then splashed the rest where the shirt was stuck to Porter's stomach with dried blood.

He peeled the shirt back and Porter's right leg jerked reflexively. Thomas wanted to run away. I don't know how to deal with this, he thought. The wound was a thumbnail-sized crater just under the rib cage and opposite the heart.

Thomas opened the brown plastic bottle of peroxide that Oscar had given him. All the medicine in the kit was primitive. Thomas poured the peroxide into the wound. His hands moved in tiny, awkward jerks, the way a child's would. Porter worked his eyebrows in mild surprise as the peroxide foamed up thick and white. Thomas kept pouring more on until the bottle was empty. He daubed the hole dry with a wad of gauze and then squirted some Betadyne into it. He smeared it around with one finger and then wiped the finger on his pants.

Porter sat through all of it without moving, his eyes barely tracking what Thomas did. This is ridiculous, Thomas thought. He was probably doing more harm than good. If the stomach or the intestines were torn up he shouldn't even have given him water. Thomas taped gauze over the bullet hole and stood up.

Porter's arm hung out in plain view. Thomas moved it against the man's side and pulled a tree limb next to it for camouflage.

A fly was already poking at a carmel-colored smear of Betadyne at the edge of the bandage. Hopeless, Thomas thought. A chunk of dried mucus had formed in the corner of Porter's right eye and Thomas resisted the urge to brush it away. Porter seemed even worse off than he had two hours before.

"Guh," Porter said. "Guh." Then his face wrinkled up like he was going to scream and Thomas got out the needle. He pinched up some loose skin on Porter's arm and poked the needle in, holding it by the shaft like a dart. He pushed down the plunger. Oscar had been amazed that the morphine was still in the kit. If the rebels had found the morphine, though, they would have taken everything else with it.

He left about half the morphine in the syringe and put the plastic cap over the needle. His hands shook. He stuffed everything into one of Porter's pockets and stood up to go.

The sound of voices dropped him back to his knees.

"You okay?" he heard Lindsey say.

"Yeah." Eddie's voice.

"Be careful."

Thomas watched them climb down the slope. Once they both had their backs turned Thomas faded deeper into the forest. He kept his feet on the rocks so he wouldn't make any noise.

He knew even then he could have said something. He had as much business there as they did. But seeing them together gave him a knotted-up feeling inside and he wanted to watch what happened next.

Eddie sat down at the bottom of the cliff. "Let me rest a minute," he said. The water reflected his voice cleanly, making him sound closer than he was. Lindsey walked up to the edge of the pool and started to unbutton her shirt.

It was like watching an accident. Thomas could not look away. She turned to drop her shirt and Thomas saw ragged spots of sunlight touch her small, soft breasts. The sun was almost straight overhead. She took off her jeans and hopped for a second on one leg. There was a pretense of shyness in the way she stood with her back to Eddie but Thomas didn't believe in it. She skimmed off her underpants and dove in the water.

She splashed for a few seconds and then rolled over on her back. Her nipples were tight from the coolness of the water. From this distance she was streamlined, perfect, like a picture in a magazine. "Come on," she said to Eddie. "It feels wonderful."

Eddie waded into the pool. He was wearing cutoffs and a T-shirt and no shoes. With his spikey hair he looked like a little kid. After a minute he took off the shirt but left the shorts on.

Good for you, Thomas thought. Then he thought, listen to me. What am I doing here, anyway? I should get out now, before this really turns ugly.

Eddie sat in the shallow water, leaning back until it came up under his chin. Lindsey swam over and pulled him into the middle of the pool. Eddie was painfully thin and Thomas could see him shivering from the chill.

After a while they got out. There was a little scrap of beach there. It was inevitable and horrible, like a rerun of some badly made movie on TV. Thomas knew what was going to happen and it made him a little sick. But it didn't seem real enough to get up and walk away from.

Eddie stood in the sand while Lindsey knelt and peeled his shorts down to his feet. His erection looked like an obscene practical joke, a dildo hung on a lab skeleton. Lindsey took it in her mouth.

Thomas sat down in the leaves. He made a little noise doing it but it hardly mattered in the circumstances. He paid careful attention to everything he saw. It was, after all, not the sort of thing most men got to watch. His blood felt very, very cold, but other than that he was focused and alert.

Lindsey held on to Eddie's hands and pulled him toward her as she lay back in the sand. Neither of them said anything, for which Thomas was grateful. Eddie dropped to one knee. He planted his elbows on either side of her rib cage and kissed her on the mouth. She kissed him back and then she pulled his head away and moved it down to her chest. He took one nipple in his teeth and pulled on it, stretching the loose skin of her breast into an isoceles triangle. When Thomas had made love to her in Mexico City, just a week ago, she had moved his head to the same breast, the left one.

Toward the end Lindsey seemed to forget where she was. She thrashed her head from side to side and her breathing was very loud. Thomas got up and walked away, back toward the helicopter and the camp.

Thomas climbed the Temple of the Inscriptions, thinking he would work until supper. He went up on the collapsed roof, pulling out fallen slabs, using the handle of the shovel as a lever. So he was outside, where he could see, when Lindsey and Eddie came back into camp. They were holding hands. He watched them go into Eddie's tent and then he bent over the shovel again.

Around four o'clock, after the rain, Chan Zapata came to help him. He was stripped down to his loincloth and had, miraculously, a machete.

"They let you keep that?" Thomas asked.

"Lacondones don't make trouble. They like to get drunk, and sometimes they argue with each other, but they don't make trouble." Thomas couldn't tell if he was being sarcastic or not. "All the world knows this."

The next time Thomas looked down, Carla was watching. Somehow she'd gotten a folding aluminum lounge chair with red and yellow and green plastic webbing. The contrast with her khaki shirt and black beret and rifle was more strange than it was funny.

After a while she sent Gonzáles, the fat man with the mustache, up to where they were working. She hadn't let him bring his rifle and Thomas had seen him argue with her about it. When he finally got to the top of the pyramid he was sweating and angry.

"Carla says to help you," he told Thomas. "You stupid *gabacho cabrón*. What are you trying to do up here?"

Thomas let Gonzáles hold the smaller pieces of the arch in place while he and Chan Zapata set the capstones. It was easy work, but Gonzáles never stopped complaining. When Thomas said they were finished, he spat and shook his head and hurried back down to the ground.

There was a long hour of twilight between the time the sun went into the trees and the time it actually set behind El Chichón. Thomas sat with Chan Zapata, swatting mosquitos. They watched the rebels come back into camp, a few of them with food.

"Beautiful, no?" Chan Zapata said, holding both hands out to the jungle.

Thomas nodded. To hell with her, he thought. He could manage all right on his own.

Every night there were one or two more for supper. The Lacondones ate in the godhouse, and in the other ramada it was Thomas and Lindsey and Oscar, plus Carla and Faustino and a self-important little man named Ramos. Tonight there were six other rebels as well. Thomas understood it was some kind of reward for good hunting or bravery or political correctness.

Eddie had gone to eat with the Lacondones. Either he'd told Lindsey she wasn't welcome or she'd decided for herself to face Thomas without him. She sat next to Thomas but kept her distance.

"There is much news today," Ramos announced in Spanish. "It has been found out that your country secretly sold arms to Iran. It was part of a very complicated trade to get hostages out of Beirut. Your President is greatly embarrassed. How does this make you feel?"

Thomas shrugged. It didn't seem any worse than the usual government lying and meddling. "I try to stay out of politics."

"I'm sorry," Ramos said, "but that isn't really a choice for you anymore. Politics has arrived in your life. Here we are, no?"

They all sat on mats and ate with their fingers. There was a big pot of roasted bird meat, maybe some kind of wild duck, and tortillas. The hard work had left Thomas hungry, but being next to Lindsey had made his stomach close up. Every time he looked at her he saw her with her eyes closed, her hair whipping back and forth.

"What about us?" Oscar asked. "What's it going to take for you to let *us* go?"

"We've told you," Ramos said. "You're not hostages. It's just necessary for us to keep you here for a few more days."

"Right," Oscar said.

"Of course, if you wanted to cooperate in the matter of the helicopter we could all be out of here that much sooner."

"Kiss my ass," Oscar said.

Ramos got very flushed and it looked like he was going to reach over and slap Oscar, if not shoot him. Carla stared somewhere between the two of them, her eyes dark and very Indian-looking. She was afraid, Thomas realized. He remembered what Oscar had said about how fragile her control was. She wasn't going to stand up to Ramos. If there was trouble Thomas didn't know where it would stop.

"Can I have a tortilla?" Lindsey said.

Ramos looked at her and then back at Oscar. He handed her the green plastic plate of tortillas and the tension broke.

Thomas ate what he could. Ramos and Carla talked about the Iran arms deal and what it meant. The conversation was stiff and sounded like they'd rehearsed it. They disagreed on almost everything. Carla thought it would make the U.S. back off a little from Central America and Ramos thought it would make things worse. The argument ended up, as usual, in Nicaragua. Ramos had a long list of statistics to prove how the Sandinistas were responsible for the only economic growth in the region. Carla thought the revolution had been betrayed. It was pretty dry stuff, altogether.

Thomas thought about what it would do to them to know about the wounded soldier. He kept trying to get Oscar to look at him. Finally they locked eyes and after a couple of seconds Oscar nodded yes, he would do it.

Thomas began to get scared.

* * *

After dinner, when the rebels had all wandered off, Thomas changed into a black long-sleeved shirt from his suitcase. He tossed Oscar a navy blue sweater.

"Hey, great, man," Oscar said. "We going to put black shit under our eyes, too, like real commandos?"

Thomas said, "Let's get it over with. We can get it done and get back before anybody notices." Just talking about it being over made him feel better.

"Whatever," Oscar said. "Don't forget this was your idea, man."

They took towels and a flashlight down to the river like they were going to wash up. Nobody seemed to care. Once they were out of sight of the camp they cut back to the helicopter and got the stretcher. Every pop and rustle in the forest sent Thomas' pulse off in another direction.

Thomas timed them as they walked from the helicopter to the falls. Eight minutes. A loaded stretcher couldn't do worse than double it. Half an hour from now, he told himself, everything is going to be fine.

Oscar set the stretcher down next to the body and unrolled it. Thomas masked the flashlight with his fingers before he turned it on.

"Jesus," Oscar said.

Thomas fumbled with Porter's wrist. Porter jerked it away before he could find a pulse. "He's alive, anyway," Thomas said.

"Water," Porter said.

Thomas took the folding cup down to the pool. He stood where Eddie and Lindsey had been going at it. He squatted down to scoop out the water. He thought he could see the faint impression of Lindsey's ass still in the sand.

The moonlight seemed bright as day. Everything was intense. He felt like there was a freight train inside him, driving him on.

Instead of taking the water straight back to Porter he went to the bush where he'd left the M16. Just to see if it was still there. He set the water and flashlight down and felt around in the leaves with both hands. His fingers touched hard plastic.

He must have known what he was going to do. Once he had the gun in his hands he couldn't leave it behind. It was a bad idea whose time had come. He slung the strap over his shoulder and took the water to Porter.

Oscar looked up and saw the gun. "What the fuck are you doing? Where did you get that?"

Thomas knelt and tried to feed Porter the water. "It's his," he said.

"Are you crazy? Get rid of it."

"No," Thomas said. Porter could barely swallow. Most of the water ran down his face and neck.

"All you're going to do is get us both shot."

"If they find us," Thomas said, "carrying this guy on a stretcher in the jungle in the middle of the night, they're going to start shooting anyway. This could buy us some time, keep their heads down so they don't recognize us."

"Fucking guns," Oscar said. "You're just another cowboy, like all the others."

They stared at each other in the moonlight. Thomas thought about how much he hated Oscar right then. He couldn't imagine not hating him. The hatred, like everything else, was vivid as lightning. He could taste it in the back of his throat.

"Let's do it," Oscar said. "Just get it over with."

"Okay," Thomas said. He took Porter's shoulders and Oscar took his feet and they lifted him onto the stretcher. The gun slipped off Thomas' shoulder and rasped in the dirt as he struggled with the dying man's weight. Porter sagged in the middle as they carried him and Thomas imagined he could hear the wound tearing open.

He slung the rifle again and grabbed the handles of the stretcher. Oscar turned his back and picked up his end. "Go," he said, and Thomas straightened up.

The weight was worse than he'd imagined. His muscles burned from the long afternoon of work, from not enough food. He thought about not being able to eat at dinner and that made him think about Lindsey. He got a little crazy then and didn't care what happened to him.

They made a lot of noise getting down to the river-bank. Then Oscar missed the end of the path and they had to back up and look for it. Once they found it and got into the trees the darkness was absolute.

"I have to have the flashlight," Oscar said.

"Yeah, okay," Thomas said.

They set Porter down. Oscar tucked the flashlight in his armpit and they started off again, following the circle of yellow light. Thomas wondered how far away some-body could see it. He had nothing to do but go where the stretcher pulled him and it gave him too much time to think.

The worst was that he kept tripping over rocks and branches in the path. Not badly enough to go down, but every time it happened it sent a jolt up through his aching arms and legs and made his glasses bounce. He couldn't see his watch. It was just as well. He knew the hands wouldn't even seem to be moving.

He thought about what he was going to do when he got out of this. Go back to the States, to start with. He might have been able to put up with Espinosa before, but Carla and Ramos had soured him on petty tyranny. He'd lost his taste for it. If he could get something—anything —out of Chan Ma'ax he could write a new grant pro-posal and take it back to UT in Austin. Where there were winters and it even snowed sometimes. Where they had Tex-Mex food, tamales and ground beef tacos like they didn't have on this side of the border. Magazines. Warner Brothers cartoons every Saturday morning that he could watch in his air-conditioned bedroom from his queen-sized bed.

They must have gotten onto the wrong path. It couldn't possibly be taking this long. He couldn't feel his hands anymore. He kept watching for something to tell him they were almost there, but all the trees looked the same.

And then they swung a little to the left and Thomas could see the moon again. The jungle thinned out to nothing and Thomas stopped, nearly jerking the handles away from Oscar. "The light," he hissed. They had to put the stretcher down so Oscar could shut off the flashlight and put it back in his belt.

There was the helicopter, just ahead. Thomas flexed his hands. They felt like they were full of knives.

"I'm going to check it out," Oscar said.

"Okay." Thomas didn't offer the M16 and Oscar didn't ask for it. Thomas crouched by the stretcher and listened to Oscar's footsteps crashing away. He didn't check to see if Porter was still alive because he didn't want to know. It wouldn't make any difference at this point anyway.

Something metal squeaked and groaned. Thomas waited for the sound of gunfire. Instead he heard Oscar running back. Oscar took his end of the stretcher and didn't say anything.

Thomas put the gun next to Porter and they carried him into the clearing. The cargo door was open. Oscar rested his handles on the edge of the door and climbed in. Together they wrestled Porter onto the cabin floor. Thomas got in and shut the door and picked up the M16 again. He wanted a drink about as badly as he'd ever wanted anything. Maybe the Lacondones had something. Soon, he told himself. Soon.

"You give him all the morphine?" Oscar said.

"Half," Thomas said. "The rest's in his shirt."

Oscar turned the flashlight on and held it by the end with the bulb. His fingers glowed red in the light. He fished the needle out with his other hand and held it in front of Porter's open eyes. "Hey, hombre," Oscar said. "Wake up." Lit from underneath, Oscar's face looked demonic, his long hair a mass of writhing shadows.

"Doctor?" Porter said.

"Not yet. We'll get you one. But we got this needle here, make you feel a lot better." Porter closed his eyes. "Hey, man, you got to talk a little first. Understand?" Porter opened his eyes again and seemed to move his head. "Good," Oscar said. "Now. Are you with Marsalis?"

". . . salis," Porter said.

"For Christ's sake," Thomas said.

"Wait outside if you want," Oscar said. "Fuck, go back to camp if you want. We brought him this far, I want to hear the fucker talk."

Thomas stayed where he was.

"Scared," Porter said.

"What?" Oscar said.

"'M scared," Porter said. "I'm gonna die. Aren't I?"

"Oh, man," Thomas said. "This is not right."

"This was your idea," Oscar told him. "Live with it." He looked back at Porter. "You're gonna be fine. Let's talk about Marsalis."

"What . . . you know about Marsalis?" Porter mumbled.

"We're supposed to hook up with him. Resupply. You're in a Huey, okay?" Oscar showed the light around the walls a little. "But we can't find where he's bivouacked at."

"South," Porter said. There was a gargling noise down in his chest. "South of Usumacinta. 'Bout twenty miles."

"Where's Usumacinta?" Thomas asked.

"About forty miles north and west of here," Oscar said. "Too goddamn close."

"Commies in some ruins," Porter said. His lucid moment was over. "Blow them to shit."

That was it. It put Thomas over the top. It was like seeing Death in front of him with a scythe and an hourglass and a shit-eating grin. The brain chemicals he'd been churning out all day turned to adrenaline. He swung open the cargo door and was halfway out when a beam of light stabbed toward him from the jungle.

He pulled his foot back in and slammed the door and scrambled over the pedestal to the pilot's seat.

"What the fuck?" Oscar said.

"Rebels, man, they're outside," Thomas said.

"What are you doing?"

"I'm running away!" Thomas said. "Are you coming or not?"

"What about this guy?"

"Fuck him," Thomas said. He sprung the door and jumped out into the night. He was on the other side of the helicopter from the rebels and there was at least a chance they hadn't seen him. He sprinted for the jungle. The guns started to pop behind him before he quite made it. The leaves next to him danced in a wind he couldn't feel. Bullets, he thought. It's bullets making them do that.

He held the M16 to his chest with both hands and dove into the underbrush. His glasses came halfway off and he pushed them frantically back up on his nose. When he looked back he counted four guns flashing yellow in the darkness. He pointed the M16 over their heads and pulled the trigger. It didn't move. Safety, he thought. Most of his brain had shut down with the first shots. He found a switch just above his thumb and pushed it one way and then the other until he felt it click twice. This time the gun made a high-pitched rattle and bucked and pulled up and to the right. The muzzle flash lit up the trees around him.

He rolled a little more and then got up and ran to his left, deeper into the trees. Somewhere in there he'd banged his left knee and it hurt something fierce. Yes, shit, they were coming after him. At least he gave Oscar a chance to get out of there. The asshole, why didn't he run?

He gave them another short burst. He remembered reading somewhere that the muzzle would overheat if he fired it too long. He didn't know how long that was. He didn't even know, for Christ's sake, how many rounds were left in the clip.

He dodged right again. You can't keep this up, he thought. His feet did a little dance of nerves without his conscious control. Do something. Come on, come on.

He thought of Lindsey again, Eddie putting it to her there in the dirt. He thought about Ramos saying how does this make you feel? Porter saying blow them to shit.

He turned his back on the camp and ran due north into the jungle.

THESE WERE THE LOW-
lands, parched and drab gray-
green. The trees had been cut back from the road so
many times they had grown in on themselves in a kind of
vegetable despair, gnarled and thick and low.

Carmichael was an hour south of Usumacinta in a
rented Volkswagen Safari. There was a hand-drawn map
on the seat next to him. The road was paved, more or
less, but he hadn't seen another car since he'd left town.

It was not helping his nerves.

For the last week he'd been trying to put together a
story on Marsalis without actually having to confront
him. He interviewed everybody in Usumacinta who'd
done business with Marsalis' men, at the market and the
garage and the liquor store. He talked to the two semipro
hookers who worked at the laundry by day, politely de-
clining their offers, though it had been a long time for
him.

He put together his map with an *X* where he was
pretty sure they'd set up camp. He had an estimate of
troop strength and the idea they were going to be here for
a while. And he confirmed what he already suspected
about their mission. They were after Carla.

He called L.A. every day for more background on
Marsalis. He found out Marsalis was a member of something called the Church Universal and Triumphant, out
of Malibu, as well as the Council for World Freedom and
the World Anti-Communist League. He was divorced,
with two kids in Montessori schools. There wasn't much
else to tell.

Then, in the last two days, the Iran arms deal had
broken and Pam had been keeping him current. Now
there, Carmichael had to admit, was a hell of a story.
What really got to him was that it looked like the U.S.
had turned a big profit on it and nobody knew where the

money had gone. It was a sign of the times that after everything Reagan had done—from making war on Granada to escalating the arms race to supporting terrorism in Nicaragua—it was a bungled business deal that finally turned the public against him. And even then it might not have happened if the economy had been doing better.

Whatever the reason, Carmichael knew he was not going to blow Iran off the front page with a lot of second-hand crap. At two o'clock that morning he'd realized he was putting off what he had to do because he was afraid. Once he looked at it that way, he didn't really have a choice.

Up ahead he saw a discoloration on the asphalt and took his foot off the gas. He coasted up to the tracks and recognized the jeep treads he'd seen in town. They came from a dirt road that led off toward the west. He checked his map and everything about it looked right.

The highway went on perfectly straight and flat for miles in either direction. The jungle grew within three feet of the tarmac. He was not going to be able to hide the car.

His muscles cramped with the same fear he'd felt when he hid in the closet in Usumacinta, waiting to get bayoneted or worse. He drove a few yards past the turnoff and left the car with two wheels on the road. He opened up the engine and yanked loose one end of the cable that went from the distributor to the rotor. Car trouble, see? Everything that could connect him to *Rolling Stone* was back in his hotel room.

His mouth was very dry. He took the canteen and the camera and just one extra roll of film. A real tourist wouldn't be carrying more than that.

He stopped for a second where the dirt road met the highway. The sun burned down on him from an empty sky. He could smell the dust and the bitter leaves of the roadside bushes. The insects sounded like tiny electric motors.

He started walking.

He kept close to the side of the road. With a little warning he could shove his way into the underbrush, though it would cost him some blood. He wished he'd worn long pants instead of hiking shorts.

Sooner or later, he told himself, there would have to be some kind of trail leading away from the road. After nearly a mile, he found one. He crouched and looked at the bootprints in the soft ground. The grooves in the sole were clear enough that they might mean something to an expert. He went ahead and took a picture because he didn't know how much else he would be able to get.

When he looked up there was a gun barrel pointed at his face.

"Jesus," he said. "You scared me. I'm really glad to see you guys. You're Amer—"

"Shut up."

There were three of them. The one holding the gun had dirty blond hair to his shoulders, tied back with a headband. He had a couple of days' worth of reddish-yellow beard, an olive-drab T-shirt, and blue jeans that had faded almost to white. One of the knees had been patched with a piece of bandana. He might have been the one that had spotted Carmichael in Usumacinta the week before.

The second man looked to be in his forties, caucasian, brown hair, khaki workclothes. The third was black and in his twenties, in camo pants and a hunter's bright orange vest. Two of them had bullpups, the streamlined infantry rifles he'd seen in town, and the older white guy had an M16.

"Lessee that camera," the blond said.

Carmichael handed it over. His legs were starting to hurt from the cramped squatting position. It was all he could do to keep them from shaking. "I didn't mean anything," he said. "My car—"

"I said shut up." The blond dropped the camera in the dirt and pushed the lens through the body with his heel. It made a sound like a beercan full of broken glass. Then he said, "Okay, stand up. Gene, pat him down."

The older white guy slapped at Carmichael's pockets, not bothering to be gentle or very thorough. He found the film can and handed it to the blond, who said, "Watch him." Gene brought his M16 up level and the blond tucked his bullpup under his arm. He pulled the unexposed film out of the cannister in a long, silvery ribbon. "Nope," he said, holding it up to the sun. "Nothing on here." They all laughed. "Always wanted to do that," he said. "Where's this car of yours?"

"Back on the highway."

The blond dropped the film in the dirt and Gene handed him Carmichael's wallet and pocket notebook. He looked through the blank notebook first and gave it back. Then he opened the wallet and looked at Carmichael's driver's license. "John Carmichael. Mind if I call you John? You got any dope in that car, John?"

"What?"

"Got any pot, Johnny? You know, grass? Smoke?" He pantomimed inhaling off a roach, making a loud sucking noise.

"Sorry," Carmichael said. His dope was back in the hotel too.

"I bet." He handed Carmichael the wallet. "Let's go."

They had to walk single file on the narrow trail. The black man went first, then Carmichael and the blond. Gene lagged well behind. The trees never got more than six or eight feet high, leaving Carmichael in blinding sunlight. The trail was clear enough, though, and he eventually got into his cross-country rhythm. If they were going to shoot him it wasn't going to be right away.

The trail ended in a base camp that was obviously still in progress. There were piles of burning brush around the edges of the clearing, and soot-stained men still working with machetes and chainsaws. In the largest open area were four military-green helicopters. As far as Carmichael could tell they were the same kind of Hueys the U.S. had used in Vietnam.

The rest of the camp was made up of long GI barracks tents, with tatami on the floor and the side flaps rolled all the way up to the roof. Inside were folding tables and chairs and cots. There were five tents, with about twenty men in each, reading or cleaning weapons or drinking coffee. That came out to about twice the number Carmichael had estimated. Some of them must have come in on the helicopters. They all stared as he went by, and some of them whistled and cheered.

At the far end of the clearing was a four-man tent, side walls in place but the front flap open. The floor was plywood and Carmichael could see a wooden table and armchair inside.

The black man went in first. Carmichael heard low voices for a while, then the man came out again. "Colonel says bring him in."

The blond motioned to Carmichael with his rifle barrel and followed him into the tent. Over his shoulder Carmichael watched the other two wander away.

The inside of the tent was compulsively neat. There was a map cabinet with long, flat drawers and a Mr. Coffee on an upended wooden crate. On the back wall were three framed prints, evenly spaced, at Carmichael's eye level. They were each about the size of a hardcover book and done in the gaudy, luminescent style that Carmichael associated with Indian religious paintings, like in the *Bhagavad Gita*. The face on the left was the traditional Jesus: light suntan, curly hair, doe eyes, and a full beard. Carmichael didn't recognize the face on the right. A European with swept-back hair and a pointy mustache.

The picture in the middle was some kind of allegory. The top half was a series of brightly colored concentric circles, with white rays coming out of the middle. The bottom was a landscape, with a figure in white robes apparently consumed by purple flames, then rising up in a cylinder of white light. Scary shit to see in a military office, Carmichael thought.

Marsalis himself sat up straight in his chair, both arms comfortably on the desk in front of him. His skin was deep black and he had a small, neatly trimmed mustache. His hair had been straightened and was cut short and parted on the side. He wore neatly pressed khakis without insignia, but the cap on the hatrack had two eagles on it. The desk was empty except for a stack of greenbar computer printouts in one corner and a complex emerald crystal that was holding them down.

"Carmichael," Marsalis said. "What a pleasant coincidence. I've been hoping to meet you ever since I heard you were down in our neck of the woods. I enjoyed your story on Count Basie last year, by the way. Though I'm afraid I have trouble with your more political pieces."

Uh oh, Carmichael thought. "My car broke down," he said. "On the highway."

"In fact," Marsalis went on, "word has it you just scored quite a coup. An interview with Carla herself."

"Where did you hear that?" Carmichael said.

"Oh come on, John, don't be naive. Now I know it's too much to expect you to actually have the tapes *on* you. But if you'll tell me where they are, I can send somebody after them."

Pretending ignorance seemed like a waste of time. "The story's finished and turned in. I already reused the tape. Sorry."

"Really?" Marsalis said. "That seems odd. I'd think you would have wanted it maybe for a souvenir." Carmichael shrugged. "Well, that's a problem. It's going to make things a lot more difficult."

"What do you mean?"

"Well, if you haven't got the tapes, we'll have to just get you to reconstruct the interview from memory."

"Um, my memory was never that good."

Marsalis smiled. "You might be surprised. It's amazing what people can remember."

"What are you going to do," Carmichael asked. "Torture me?" The words came out a little too high-pitched for bravado.

"Billy?" Marsalis said to the blond. "Put John somewhere you can keep an eye on him for a few hours. Let him think things out."

"My editor knows where I am," Carmichael said. "They know you're here. If anything happens to me, they'll know where to look."

"That pretty much shoots your car trouble story, doesn't it, John? Not that anybody was really buying it anyway. As for *Rolling Stone,* you'll forgive me if I'm not exactly shaking in my shoes. Billy?"

"Let's go," Billy said.

If anything, Carmichael thought, it would be drugs. Torture just had to be messy and unreliable. Not an eighties kind of thing to do to somebody.

He sat on a cot in a two-man tent. Billy was under a tree outside with *El Libro Sentimental,* a digest-sized Mexican love comic printed in foul-smelling brown ink. It was two o'clock, almost time for the afternoon rain. The sky had started to cloud over and there was enough wind to gently rattle the sides of the tent.

Billy looked at the clouds and put the comic aside. He leaned his bullpup against the tree and stood up. "Om," he said, putting his palms together at his forehead, drawing out the word until it hummed.

What the hell? Carmichael thought.

"Ma, Hum," Billy said, moving his steepled hands to his throat and the center of his chest. He sounded a little like the insects in the trees. "Vazra," he said, and made a quick downward gesture with his fingers, like a piano player hitting a chord. It was a strangely delicate gesture for somebody that meaty, sunburned, and tough-looking. "Guru," he said, turning his palms up, "Padme," a figure eight with index fingers touching thumbs against his stomach, "Sidhe," like two OK signs, palms out, "Hum," bringing the heels of his hands together.

He went through the whole thing again, over and over, until the rain started. Then he brought the gun and the comic into the tent.

"What was that about?" Carmichael asked him.

"The mudras, you mean?" Billy said. "Sealing my light. There's that kind of vibe you get right before the storm moves in, you know? Gives me the willies."

He seemed friendly enough when there wasn't anybody else around to impress. "Is it okay if I talk to you?" Carmichael said. "I mean, it wouldn't get you in trouble."

"Fuck no," Billy said. "Colonel would probably like it. We going to talk about Carla?"

"No," Carmichael said. "Not Carla."

"Whatever. You'll be talking about her later, anyway." Billy laughed and Carmichael felt his stomach tense.

"What's the story with you guys, anyway? What are those pictures Marsalis has up in his tent? The first one is Jesus, right, but who's the other guy?"

"St. Germain."

"You mean . . . wait a minute. Are you talking about that guy that *Dracula* is supposed to be based on?"

"Yeah, but that was a lot of superstitious shit. St. Germain is one of the ascended masters."

"Ascended masters."

"Yeah, the Great White Brotherhood. You know? I mean, not 'white' like some fascist shit, 'white' as in 'white light.' "

Carmichael sat for a second, letting it sink in. "You guys are all into this?"

"More or less. When the Colonel talks it all makes a lot of sense. I mean, it's all just about tapping your potential, is what it comes down to. The mystical shit, it's just like a crutch or something."

"Does this have anything to do with that church? What was it, the Church Universal and Triumphant or something?"

"Yeah, Marsalis used to be with them. They kicked him out. Didn't like his politics. But he says you don't need to be part of a church. You can do it for yourself."

"How'd you get into it?"

Billy leaned back and put his arms behind his head. "Most of us was in the Nam together. It was a pretty heavy scene, but it was cool in some ways, too. I mean, once you got away from the fact we were letting the gooks beat the shit out of us and people were getting killed and everything. But that's just karma, you know? Being over there really changed a lot of people's heads. People were turning on, getting away from material shit, trying to change themselves, thinking about what the point of it all was, you know? Not just in the Nam, but back in the world, too. And then it got to be the seventies, and it looked like everybody got tired of it."

"Most people, yeah," Carmichael said. "Everybody wanted a BMW and a VCR."

"Yeah, really. All those initials, man, got to have 'em. But what the Colonel says is, it's not over. It's just gone underground. People realized they couldn't change the world, so they started trying to change themselves. Like, did you see that rock on the Colonel's desk?"

"Yeah. It looked like some kind of emerald."

"It's made of a bunch of crummy emeralds dissolved in acid, and then like recrystallized into one big matrix. Transformed, see? Keeping the essence and making it into something better. I mean, look at you guys at the *Stone*. You're real slick these days, but you still got principles and shit. Hey, man, I admire that. I mean, there's all these networks now of guys that think the way we do."

Carmichael wasn't sure he wanted to be part of that "we." "You guys are a network?" he asked.

"Yeah. Yeah, we are. See, what the Colonel says is, America has got a special destiny. The Brotherhood, the ascended masters, they're watching over us, and our job is to bring on the Aquarian Age. And that's what it's really all about down here. Communism, let's face it, man, is a very unhip, unenlightened way to live. We got to keep America free or we're going to miss the fucking boat."

"The boat?"

"We're talking the end of the Piscean Age here, my friend," Billy said. "Twenty thirteen. Either you got your shit together and you transcend, or you go back to the trenches for another two thousand years."

"You're talking literal transcendence?" Carmichael asked. Billy narrowed his eyes. "What I'm saying, you're really going to get carried away to some other place?"

"Yeah, the cosmic dustoff, man. Nirvana. They'll probably come for us in UFOs. I don't know if I actually believe that part of it, but man, the Colonel makes it sound real convincing. There's all kinds of evidence. The

Mayas, you know, they believe the same thing. End of the world, early twenty-hundreds. Egyptians got the same thing, the same calendar and everything. That's because you can trace both of them right back to Atlantis. That's a fact, man."

"That's, uh, really heavy," Carmichael said.

"You better believe it. It's happening. Listen, are you sure you don't got any dope? It's scarce as a mother-fucker down here."

Carmichael shook his head.

After a while the rain slacked off and Billy went back outside. Carmichael watched him go through some more mudras and then fold up his legs and start a yoga breathing exercise.

Carmichael took the little spiral notebook out of his back pocket and scrawled out some notes. They would probably end up taking it away, but what the hell. Just the act of writing things down helped him hold on to them.

He filled up five pages and then lay back with his head on one fist. Something about the tropics, he thought. Some kind of pollen or pheromone, or maybe just the endless heat. It seemed to stun the higher brain functions. The craziest things started to sound reasonable. Jim Jones in Guyana, or the Aztecs with their bloodless Flower Wars and bloody human sacrifices. For that matter, what about the fundamentalists in the Southern U.S., and all the kooks in Florida and California? Crazy from the heat, all of them.

They came for him in the late afternoon. By that point Carmichael was too scared to even be able to talk. Billy took hold of his left arm and a young latino had his right. Gene brought up the rear again. They weren't rough or even pushy, just businesslike.

They took him to Marsalis' tent and sat him down in a metal folding chair. Before his eyes even got adjusted he felt a needle go into his bicep. He tried to jerk away but Billy still had hold of his arm.

The man with the needle was tall and skinny, probably

in his mid-fifties. He wore a cream-colored safari suit. His hair was mostly white and had receded halfway back across his skull. He had a thick white mustache that overhung his lower lip and was stained yellow from nicotine. His eyes were deep in their sockets and, Carmichael thought, a little cruel.

The needle came out and Billy let him go. Carmichael rubbed his arm. "Pentothal?" he said.

The man in the safari suit said, "Hell no. Pentothal's not worth a good goddamn. People can tell you any damn thing in the world and not even know what they're saying. Same with scopolamine. Gives you delusions, makes you paranoid." He put the syringe in a plastic box and propped one hip on the edge of Marsalis' desk.

"Yeah?" Carmichael said. He felt a little lightheaded, but he was sure it was psychosomatic. There hadn't been time for anything to happen yet.

"Besides," Marsalis said, "all that shit is very unhip. Isn't that right, Rich?" Marsalis was nearly lost in the shadows behind his desk. Carmichael could just make out the emerald matrix in his hand.

"Very," said the man in the safari suit. "You ever hear of MDMA?"

"That's 'Ecstasy,' right?" Carmichael said.

"That's right. A.k.a. 'Adam.' One of those new designer drugs. See, you can change the structure of an illegal drug just enough that the law doesn't specifically cover it anymore. Like this synthetic Demerol they were making down in Florida. Cheap as hell because it was legal. Only it was eating the substantia nigra and giving folks Parkinsonism. They got lucky with MDMA, though. Interesting stuff. You could say that MDMA is to LSD what a mild chablis is to rotgut whiskey."

"What you just got," Marsalis said, "isn't exactly Ecstasy either, though. I don't really like the idea of synthetic drugs."

"Right," Carmichael said, thinking, you'll hold somebody at gunpoint and shoot them up with truth serum, but it has to be the right *kind* of truth serum. Marsalis was the type of guy who would be sure to use honey instead of refined sugar when he staked somebody out over an anthill.

"It's what they call an endogenous equivalent," Rich said. "It's a hydroxylated serotonin that the body naturally produces. MDMA just mimics the effects artificially."

"That's good to know," Carmichael said. Actually he didn't feel bad at all. He could tell his adrenaline was a little up, but that was to be expected. Other than that he was starting to feel like he was going to come through this all right. "Where do you get the money for stuff like that?"

"Some things you don't need money for," Rich said. "The company I work for is very interested in testing this kind of thing."

Something about the way he said "company" made it sound like it was capitalized. CIA, Carmichael thought. Of course. "Like those LSD experiments you did in the sixties."

"Score one for the reporter," Rich said.

Marsalis said, "Money isn't that big a problem anyway."

"But it's illegal for you guys to be down here. Congress specifically said no more money for counterinsurgency in Latin America."

"Now, John," Marsalis said. "You're being naive again. Money doesn't always have to come through Congress."

Holy shit, Carmichael thought. "The money from the Iran arms deal," he said. "They gave it to you."

His eyes had adjusted now. He could see Marsalis look at Rich and see the two of them smiling at each other. "That's pretty clever," Marsalis said. "Rich, you should make a note of that. 'Promotes insight.' Actually, son, we had to split the money with the Contras. Congress shut their water off, too. And we had a little operation back in December that we had to finish paying for."

December. Carmichael felt another piece fit into place. "Acuario. You guys killed Acuario."

"Not us personally," Rich said. "Though it probably

would have been a hell of a lot cheaper if we'd done it ourselves. Not to mention what a pain in the ass our hired help turned out to be."

"Who was that?"

"Just a certain disaffected member of the guardia. Who ended up getting more out of it than we planned."

"Venceremos," Carmichael said.

"You know, Rich," Marsalis said, "we may have underestimated this guy. I hope it doesn't get to be a problem, him knowing all this stuff."

Carmichael shook his head. "Oh no, no problem." He felt a deep desire to help them, to protect them. "I mean, it's all just politics, right? You guys were just doing the best you could in the circumstances."

Rich and Marsalis were smiling at each other again. Carmichael had another insight. It was the drug making him feel this way. But he couldn't see anything wrong with it. Why in the world shouldn't people get along with one another?

"Yeah," Rich said. "You got that right. Of course, Venceremos didn't pull the trigger. He got one of his boys to do that. But he kept the biggest chunk of the money. You really have to appreciate the irony here. I mean, even if Venceremos wins, we end up owning him. He's tainted meat. His buddies'd turn on him in a second if they knew. Ain't that a hoot?"

"Are you feeling okay?" Marsalis asked.

"Yeah," Carmichael said, nodding. "I feel fine. Really."

"That's good," Marsalis said. "Because you could really help us out if you wanted to."

"I'd like to," Carmichael said. "If I can. Really."

"Do you feel like talking about Carla?"

"Sure," Carmichael said. "What do you want to know?"

It was the middle of the night when he woke up. At first he thought he'd dreamed it. But his left arm was a little sore and his head hurt and he knew it had all really happened.

I didn't know that much, he told himself. It wasn't like I had any state secrets to give away.

It didn't help.

He sat up and looked out the front of the tent. There was a new guard outside, a big white man with a full beard and a leather jacket. He shifted around a little, as if to let Carmichael know he was paying attention.

Carmichael was covered with sweat. The night breeze felt chill and sticky on his skin. The moon was up and there were muted bird and insect noises coming out of the jungle. Some anonymous soldier coughed in the darkness.

Carmichael felt lousy. Betrayed and traitorous at the same time. Not your fault, he told himself. Not your fault.

He went over everything that he'd said. Finally he got to the part where Marsalis had talked about the Iran money, about Acuario and Venceremos.

His pulse lurched into high gear. He had the story of the decade, and no way to get it back to L.A. I'd kill, he thought, for a telephone right now.

And then he thought, would you? Would you really? And knew it was a question he was going to have to answer. Soon.

L INDSEY WAS SITTING in the tent with Eddie when she heard the shots. She knew right away something was wrong. It was the first time there had actually been gunfire at night, and there was a lot of it. She put *Spanish Made Simple* face down on the silver floor of the tent and went outside.

It was coming from over by the helicopter. A half dozen campfires lit the night around her and in their light she could see heads turned toward the shooting. Some of the rebels took their guns and ran off to see what was happening.

Lindsey went back into the tent. Her stomach hurt from the tension. Eddie was still asleep and she was careful not to wake him up. The air was hot and sticky with smoke from the fires but she was suddenly cold. She put on a flannel shirt and felt the nervous sweat break under her arms.

They came for her half an hour later. There were four of them. Gordo, the fat man, and three others she had seen but didn't know by name. They just walked into the tent and ordered her outside. Eddie managed to sleep through the whole thing.

"Qué pasa?" she asked, once they were outside, but they didn't answer except to tell her to keep moving. The rebels were back at their fires now, drinking coffee and acting like nothing had happened. Then it wasn't the Americans, Lindsey thought. No rescue tonight.

They took her to Carla's tent. Carla sat on a creaking wood and canvas cot, her foot propped up on a pillow. The place smelled of sweat and spoiled meat. Lindsey's first thought was that the amputated foot had gotten infected, that Carla was right on the edge of delirium. Her eyes were dull and stared blankly over Lindsey's shoulder.

Faustino was there, and Ramos. They looked like a latino Mutt and Jeff with their beards and uniform khaki and jeans. Faustino was tall and stoop-shouldered, Ramos short and energetic, with his arms folded across his big chest. They were both obviously tired and scared, but Ramos looked impatient, too. That and angry about something. The fourth person in the tent was a little girl, maybe ten or eleven, in bare feet and the filthiest white dress Lindsey had ever seen.

Carla mumbled something, the words slurred and very quiet. The little girl looked at Lindsey and said, "She say, where he get the gun?"

"What?"

"The gun. Where he get the gun."

"What gun? Who are you talking about?"

"You friend Tomás. He shooting at people with the gun."

"Thomas? You're out of your mind."

It took another ten minutes for her to get the story out of them. Thomas was gone, had disappeared into the jungle with an automatic weapon. He'd left Oscar behind in the helicopter with a dying U.S. soldier.

Lindsey couldn't believe it. Thomas would never do something like that. She listened to the bits and pieces of the story literally with her mouth open. Then she started flashing back to the look on Thomas' face when she and Eddie came back from the falls. Had he figured out what they'd done? Had he split because of her?

It must have been obvious even to Ramos that this was the first she'd heard of it. Still they kept after her for an hour or more, asking the same questions over and over, and Lindsey had to fight to make herself understood through the little girl's wretched English.

Finally they let her go. She went back to the tent long enough to get her suitcase and a blanket. She took them out to the ramada and curled up there, just in case Thomas came back. Gordo and the other three stayed with her the whole time, ending up cross-legged in the dirt to watch her as she tried to sleep.

Oscar was gone, of course. They were probably working him over with rubber hoses somewhere back in the jungle. She was lying in the strange empty space where Thomas would have been. That left only Chan Zapata, still in exile from the Lacondones for the crime of having not been invited. He lay awake on the other side of the ramada, twenty feet away. He hadn't said anything all night. He seemed to be pulling further back into himself by the minute.

This place is making him crazy, she thought. Just like the rest of us.

She didn't get much sleep. For a while she looked up every time she heard somebody move around, hoping it was Thomas. She drifted off sometime after midnight, then woke up to the sound of a baby crying.

The sound wrenched at her heart. She got up and followed it to a smoldering campfire a hundred yards into the trees. The mother was exhausted, sleeping right through it. Lindsey picked the baby up and held it against her.

"Shhhh," she said. The baby made a questioning sound, then hid her face in Lindsey's shirt.

She was not much more than a year old. She was dressed in a tiny shift, with no underwear, let alone diapers. Already trained to go in the dirt, like an animal, Lindsey thought. Who could let their child come to a place like this, constantly on the run, never knowing when she could be hurt, or killed, or left without anybody to take care of her?

But then, Lindsey thought, she was hardly in a position to talk about thoughtless parents. She'd just made love to both Thomas and Eddie without any kind of protection. And right in the middle of her cycle, too. She'd been off the pill since February. It wasn't like her to take chances. It seemed like half the women she knew had had an abortion because of that kind of sloppiness, and she'd always been careful, always promised herself it wouldn't happen to her. She had to wonder if her subconscious was pushing her toward a decision her conscious mind refused to make.

She was thirty-two. If she was going to have kids, it was time. She'd felt the pull, seeing her friends with their babies, holding them herself. It was the way they smelled that did it. It sent her hormones crazy, gave her wave after wave of mindless longing.

Even this baby, dirty, smoky, with her bean breath and her filthy dress, still had that smell to her.

If I got pregnant, Lindsey thought. If it happened. What would the kid be like? She counted the months and came up with Aries. Impulsive, sexy, dynamic. She could handle that. She tried to turn in on herself, to feel what was going on inside her. She couldn't tell any difference. She was tired, scared, and hungry. How else was she supposed to feel?

The baby was asleep. Lindsey put her back with her

mother and went back to the ramada. It was almost light by the time her exhaustion caught up with her, and then she had intense, anxious dreams about Thomas and her parents and a boyfriend she hadn't seen in years.

She woke to the sound of scraping, chopping, and hammering. Oscar knelt beside her, one eye half-closed and red around the edges, his lips split and swollen. It was nine-thirty.

She sat up, hugging the blanket. "Are you okay?" she asked him.

"Oh yeah," Oscar said. "Never better."

All around them Carla's people were clearing off the ruins, digging out blocks of stone and levering them back where they belonged. The women and teenagers cleaned out the last of the saplings between the Temple of the Inscriptions and the Palace, chopping out the stumps and roots and smoothing the ground over again. Carla herself sat in the middle of the new clearing in her aluminum-and-plastic lounge chair, supervising. Chan Ma'ax crouched next to her, making diagrams in the dirt with a stick.

Oscar said, "Did he tell you he was going to pull this?"

"You mean Thomas? No. The first I heard of it was last night. Who is this soldier they were talking about?"

"His name's Porter. He's some gringo Thomas found by the falls. Apparently he's with Marsalis."

The mention of the falls gave Lindsey a moment of panic. No, she thought. He couldn't have seen us. It would just be too much. She got up and washed her face and brushed her teeth at the clay pot in the corner. It was nearly empty, she noticed absently. She would have to fill it. She looked up and saw Chan Zapata on top of the big pyramid, commanding his own work crew.

"This is crazy," Lindsey said. "What are they doing screwing around with these ruins if the Americans are that close?"

"You think you're unhappy about it," Oscar said, "you should see Ramos. He's ready to bust his fucking gut. The shit is hitting the fan everywhere else but here."

"What do you mean?"

"The revolution. It's really happening. They had the radio on while they were working me over and everybody kept stopping to listen. They had to airlift all the Northamericans out of Acapulco. The rebels own Piedras Negras and Taxco and there's serious shit coming down in Mérida and Juárez and Cuernavaca. Cuernavaca, man! That's like only an hour from Mexico City!"

"I know," Lindsey said. "We were just there." She thought about the guardia captain that had taken over Thomas' project. He was the one, Thomas said, that convinced him to come find Eddie. He had seemed all right. She wondered what was happening to him, if he was even still alive. It was weird, knowing that he could be dead because of the war. It made the whole thing personal.

"You know who Venceremos is?" Oscar asked her.

"I must have heard the name," Lindsey said.

"It used to be everybody talked about Carla like she was the revolution, all by herself. Now this Venceremos guy is hogging the spotlight. He's head of the FPML, which is like an umbrella group, okay? Like the Sandinistas in Nicaragua. Well, this guy Ramos is in Venceremos' pocket. And Venceremos thinks Carla should be kicking ass, not hiding out. Even if it means taking some two-bit town like Usumacinta, just to get the rebel flag flying somewhere in Chiapas."

"What about the U.S. soldiers?"

"I don't think Venceremos or Ramos, either one, takes them seriously."

"But they *are* real, right?"

"This guy Porter was real. He's a bad motherfucker, I'll tell you."

"So what does this mean for us?"

"I don't know," Oscar said. His voice got very quiet. "We could be in deep shit. If Carla doesn't stop fucking around, there's liable to be a takeover. She's really asking for it with all this mystical crap. There's a real macho backlash building up around here." Lindsey thought that was almost funny, coming from Oscar. Then he said, "If

Ramos does get in, he might just kill us to get us out of the way."

"Come on, Oscar, you're starting to get me spooked."

"Am I? Am I scaring you? Well, it's about fucking time, because I been scared since these assholes first showed up. I been shaking in my fucking shoes since Thomas pulled that shit last night. And this morning? This morning I am scared to death."

Breakfast was cold beans and cold corn tortillas. The tortillas were tough enough she could have resoled her shoes with them. She didn't have much of an appetite anyway.

Oscar, for all his being afraid, curled up in the sunlight and went to sleep. Lindsey took the clay pot down to the river and rinsed it and filled it up again. The water seemed warmer than it had, but she wasn't even sure of her own perceptions anymore. Two of the rebels followed her, but neither of them offered to carry the pot. When she got back to the ramada she dumped in a half dozen of the iodine pills, the way Thomas had taught her.

Later she went to Eddie's tent. Her guards sat outside to wait. Eddie was playing guitar. There was something about his eyes she didn't like. They didn't move enough. They focused on something and then they just stayed there. She didn't recognize what Eddie was playing. It sounded kind of aimless anyway, chords played one note at a time, Eddie listening like he was trying to hear something in them. Finally he stopped picking with his right hand and looked at her. His left hand kept moving up and down the neck, squeaking on the strings. He didn't seem to notice it.

"Lindy," he said.

"Hi, Eddie. You okay?"

"Sure. I feel good." He didn't look good, and he didn't smile when he said it.

"Do you really, Eddie? You look . . . tired."

"I'm fine."

"When was the last time you had anything to eat?"

"I don't know. Last night, I guess. I'm not really very hungry anymore."

It was some kind of long-term effect of the drug, she thought. She needed to get him to a real hospital. "Are you strong enough to walk? To run, even, if you had to?"

"Why should I have to?"

"There could be trouble. The rebels are starting to squabble and stuff. And the U.S. Army is getting real close. There could be fighting here, like any time now."

"That's not trouble for us."

"Eddie, if they start lobbing artillery shells in here, it doesn't matter which side you're on. And Carla may be the only one that even cares about keeping us alive."

"There's Chan Ma'ax."

"Chan Ma'ax can't do anything against guns, Eddie! Get real!"

"This *place* isn't real," Eddie said. "It's sacred. It's more important than any of this political stuff. If you could just get into the feeling of the place, just feel the spirit, none of this would touch you."

"Eddie . . ." She knelt in front of him and laid her arms across his legs. "Eddie, I'm really scared for you." This close she could see how bloodshot his eyes were. His hair stuck out oddly and his skin seemed yellowish. He hadn't looked this bad since he came out of the coma.

He set the guitar aside and said, "Don't be scared." He put his arms around her.

She turned her face up and kissed him. His breath was a little stale and his stubble poked her like needles, but his mouth knew hers like nobody else's ever had. "I love you," she said.

His arms tightened around her. She let herself melt against him. He held her for a while, long enough that she could feel him getting uncomfortable. Finally she let him pull away.

"I've been working on a song all morning," he said. His stare was so intense it was hard to look into. "A new one. It's about you. Do you want to hear it?"

She nodded. Her throat had tightened up on her and she didn't think she could speak. He picked up the guitar and played a couple of introductory chords. She recognized it immediately. "There are places I'll remember," he sang. She felt the tears starting in her eyes. He sang all the way through Lennon's "In My Life," screwing up the words a couple of times. The tears broke and ran down her face.

Finally he finished. He put the guitar down and worked his fingers a little and smiled shyly. "Did you like it?" he asked.

She couldn't look at him. "It's beautiful," she said. Eddie nodded, pleased. "Listen," she said. "I have to go. I'll be back later, okay?"

"Okay," Eddie said.

She found his hands and held them for a second and then stood up. She had to find her way out by touch. Everything had blurred and turned to water.

She sat down with her Spanish-English dictionary and wrote out a list of phrases in Spanish. Where are the North American soldiers? Please don't shoot, I am not a soldier. He is my husband. He is my friend. Please don't harm him.

Then she wrote down a list of other words, words she wanted to be able to recognize if she heard them. Kill. Trial. Execution, traitor, spy.

She knew as she did it that it was an act of sheerest desperation. But Eddie was in no shape to help her. Thomas was gone. That left only Oscar and Chan Zapata that spoke any English, and she couldn't count on their being around if there was trouble. That left it up to her.

It was not, she was surprised to find, the worst feeling she'd ever had.

The rain came at one-thirty. Carla let the workers off and Chan Zapata ran over to where Lindsey sat under the ramada. The work seemed good for him. It sweated out the aguardiente puffiness he'd brought back from San Cristóbal and it took his mind off the way the other Lacondones were treating him. Standing there, flushed and breathing hard, dotted with rain, he looked fit and terribly young.

As always the rain started suddenly and fell hard. It hit the thatched roof with hundreds of tiny slapping noises. Chan Zapata dipped a glass of water out of the clay pot and made a face. "Tastes funny," he said.

"I just filled it this morning," Lindsey said. "It tasted okay to me."

"Like . . . like burned matches."

He handed Lindsey the Sylvester glass and she sniffed at it. This time she noticed it too, a very faint sulfur smell behind the iodine. She remembered how warm the creek water had felt. She wondered if it meant anything.

Chan Zapata sat across from her on the mat. "There's going to be trouble," he said.

"No kidding," Lindsey said.

"This morning Carla tells Gordo, the fat guy, to work on the templos and he says no. Right in front of everybody. He takes his gun and goes off into the selva. Everybody complaining about the work and she don't say nothing. She can't keep doing this."

"But your father is helping her. Telling her what to do."

"Chan Ma'ax always playing a game. Not the same game all the time, but always playing some kind. Maybe she thinks she and him playing the same game. But . . . not true."

The rain was like another jungle, a jungle of water, that had grown up around them. Oscar slept on in the corner; otherwise they were alone. Lindsey could barely see the outline of the godhouse a few yards away. "What does he want?" she asked. "What's he trying to do?"

"I don't know," Chan Zapata said. "They don't talk to me anymore. But I think it is about Eddie. Eddie and *los hongos.* The mushrooms."

Gordo walked into camp just as the rain ended. He had a big smile on his face. Dangling out of his left hand was the most beautiful bird Lindsey had ever seen.

It was the size of a small parrot. Most of its neck and part of one wing had been shot off. It was neon green.

When the sun broke through for a second the green seemed almost turquoise, with a metallic sheen underneath. It had a crested head and a red stomach and its tail feathers must have been a foot and a half long.

"Quetzal," Chan Zapata whispered.

"My God." Lindsey caught herself whispering too. "I didn't know there still were any."

Chan Zapata shook his head. "Not so many. I saw two before now. When I was a kid. Not for years. I can't believe the son of a bitch kill it."

Gordo was talking in a loud voice about eating the bird. Lindsey couldn't tell if he meant it for supper or if he was planning to cook it and eat it on the spot. The rest of the rebels came out of their tents and shelters and stood at the edge of the clearing, just looking at him.

The shouting woke Oscar up. He stood next to Lindsey, combing his long hair back with both hands. "Jesus," he said. "Would you look at that."

Then Chan Ma'ax walked up to the fat man and simply took the bird out of his hands. It took a couple of seconds for Gordo to realize what had happened and by that time Chan Ma'ax had already walked away, stroking the dead bird's feathers and talking to it softly. *"Oye,"* Gordo said, *"qué haces?"* He didn't say it loud enough that he was committed to anything, that it was a real challenge with his honor on the line. Chan Ma'ax just kept on walking.

The old man took the bird under the roof of the godhouse. He held it loosely in one hand while he looked through his vinyl mesh shopping bag with the other. He finally came up with a pair of white shoelaces, still in their plastic wrapper. He made a sling for the bird, running the shoelaces under the wings and tying the ends together. Then he hung it on one of the roof supports, facing the rebel tents.

The bird swayed there at an odd angle, chest out and wings dangling, like it was trying to push itself straight up into the air. The head had tipped over to one side and the lifeless eyes glittered blackly.

Gordo was still asking what was going on. His friends

had him now, taking him by the arms, trying to turn him around. He started cursing the *"Indios."* Lindsey was so pleased with herself for being able to follow him that it took her a second to realize that things were coming apart. Gordo saw Carla sitting inside the godhouse and he started yelling at her.

"Uh oh," Oscar said.

"What's the deal?" Lindsey said. "He's asking if she's an Indian now too, is that it?"

"You got it," Oscar said. "I don't think he's going to get real far with that. Most of us are at least part Indian. Carla should be able to shut this down."

But she wasn't. Faustino went over to her, rubbing his beard nervously, and she said something quiet to him. Faustino shook his head. Carla argued with him and finally he stepped out from under the shelter of the godhouse and said in a loud voice, *"Volvemos a trabajar."*

"I don't believe it," Oscar said.

"She's sending them back to work?" Lindsey asked. "Isn't that like begging for trouble?"

"No shit," Oscar said.

Gordo grabbed the shovel out of the hands of the man next to him and threw it on the ground. *"No!"* he shouted. *"Ya basta! No más!"* He started shouting for Ramos. There was a lot more that Lindsey didn't catch.

"This is weird," Oscar said. "He's calling Ramos out about something. Says Ramos owes him. Says he doesn't have to take this shit. Says what about Mexico City." Oscar shook his head. "I don't know what the deal is."

Lindsey wasn't clear on what happened next. Gordo had his rifle up. Maybe he was going to take a shot at Carla, though it didn't really look that way to Lindsey. Nobody reached for him. Everybody between Carla and Gordo either started running or hit the dirt. Lindsey crouched behind the corner post of the ramada, unable to look away.

Gordo was close enough that she could have hit him with a rock. She could see the sweat on his lip, just above the big mustache. She could see his hands on the rifle, shaking with anger.

And then Ramos stepped in front of him and shot him in the head.

It was close range, maybe eight or ten feet. Ramos had one of those military .45 automatics, dark and square and efficient-looking. The bullet took Gordo on the left side of his nose, just under the eye. It went clear through his head. When it came out the back it took a handful of red and yellow meat with it. Gordo spun around and fell on his face. As he went down his rifle fired a burst into the dirt, inches away from Ramos' feet. Ramos didn't even flinch.

Lindsey felt her stomach drop, like it had fallen right out of her body. She thought it meant she was going to be sick but nothing else happened. She just felt cold and empty inside.

It was quiet except for the insects. A couple of flies had found the hole in the back of Gordo's head and were crawling around the edges of it. Ramos put his pistol back in its holster and slowly everyone got up again, slapping the dust off their pants. Somebody laughed, a little hysterically. It didn't catch on.

"OK," Faustino said. *"Andamos!"* People started to shuffle their feet. Nobody actually took a step toward the temples.

Ramos held up his hand like a traffic cop and they all stopped again. He shouted something at Faustino that Lindsey didn't get.

"What'd he say?"

"He wants a committee meeting," Oscar told her.

"What does that mean?"

"It means," Oscar said, "he's ready to make his move."

Nobody touched the body. They just left it lying in the dirt. Lindsey could see it perfectly from where she sat, fifteen feet up on one of the ledges of the Temple of the Inscriptions. The only dead person she'd ever seen before was her grandmother, lying in a coffin. She'd never seen anybody die before. Let alone anybody murdered. It was a lot of firsts for one day. She didn't know if she could take many more.

Ramos had set up his meeting with due concern for the drama of the moment. Chan Ma'ax, Lindsey, Oscar, Faustino, and Carla sat in a row on stage right, with a discreet guard at either end. On stage left was a line of rebels in their jeans and khakis, standing at attention. Ramos' loyal inner circle, Oscar said. They'd been there when Ramos questioned him about Porter, and most of them had eaten with Ramos at the ramada at one time or another.

Ramos himself stood on the lowest landing of the steps, level with Lindsey but farther forward. He had a classic stance, legs spread wide, fist either in the air or pounding against his left hand. Carla's entire army, numbering maybe eighty men, women, and children, sat at his feet.

Lindsey's legs dangled over the ledge. She kicked them up and down, impatient with the seriousness of it all. Oscar sat on her right, Chan Ma'ax on her left. Chan Ma'ax seemed like a child, amused with himself, leaning back with his arms stuck out straight behind him. He watched the birds or the clouds, anything but Ramos' theatrics.

Lindsey wondered if the speeches were going to go on all night. She'd heard stories about rallies like this, the endless ideological arguments, the power struggles, the concern for appearances. They'd been at it for a couple of hours already and the sun was halfway down, the long shadows reaching across the clearing.

"So what's he saying?" she asked Oscar.

"He says Carla's fucking up. He says they have to get out of the mountains and link up with the FPML. He says *tercerismo* isn't working."

"What isn't working?"

"Tercerismo. That's prime revolutionary jargon, man. The old way is the *montoneros,* the Prolonged War method. Like in Cuba. Live in the hills, attack and retreat. The new way is to work out of the cities, strikes, marches, all that. Proletarian revolution. Tercerismo is the 'Third Way.' Very hip slang from Nicaragua. Supposed to combine both kinds of fighting, build up to a 'spontaneous' uprising of the population. Carla was really into all that, always trying for the new synthesis and like that. Very modern, very hip. Ramos is your basic hardline Marxist."

"So if Ramos takes over . . . and this FP whatever—"

"FPML."

"—FPML wins, they're going communist. Russian advisers and the whole nine yards."

"Socialist, actually, but yeah. That's probably it."

"Reagan won't put up with it."

"I wouldn't think so."

"So there'll be war. Like big time."

"That's what it looks like."

"And if Carla got in?"

Oscar shrugged. "Who's to say? It would be up to Reagan, I guess. The U.S. had their chance with Nicaragua, and those guys were more Marxist than Carla. The Sandinistas asked the U.S. for help and the U.S. told them to fuck themselves. So the next day they asked the Russians. That was when the hammer and sickle went up on the flagpole. What else were they going to do? But Carla would play ball with the U.S. if she got a chance."

He looked over to his right, where Carla was sitting. Lindsey looked too. Carla's eyes were glazed over and her back slumped. Oscar shook his head. "The old Carla would have. I don't know if she's got the stuff anymore."

"I thought you didn't like her," Lindsey said.

Oscar shrugged. "It wasn't me wanted this revolution. I didn't need it. I was okay before, you know? But if it's gonna happen, better Carla than some asshole like Ramos or Venceremos."

Ramos got to the end of a thought and there was some applause, a few shouts, one or two cheers. Carla struggled to stand up and Faustino helped her onto her crutch. Her voice was not very strong, but all the stone around her gave her some natural amplification.

"Compañeros," she said.

Oscar translated as she talked. She talked about the betrayal of the Nicaraguan revolution, the loss of ideals in Cuba. "She says each country must make its own revolution." Oscar kept his voice low, just above a whisper. "Each of us must find our own revolution inside ourselves. Our country must lose what each of us as people must lose. The lust for material things. The hatred and jealousy we feel for our brothers. The chains that are put upon us by those who are stronger than we are."

That much went over pretty well. They were all listening. "For countries and for people, you can never forget where you came from. This is what makes us brave, makes us able to fight those who outnumber us and have better weapons and more money. It is what will make *la república* able to stand up to the United States and the Soviet Union both, make her free to be whatever we want to make of her." This time she actually got some grudging applause.

"Este lugar," Carla said, and Lindsey could feel the way the words went through the crowd, making them tense up and lean away from her. Carla must not have noticed because she kept on talking. "She says this place is where we come from," Oscar translated. "There is knowledge and wisdom here that we have to have. We need what is here in this place for us."

People in the crowd were talking now, quietly, but the noise was building and they were starting to shift around.

" 'There is magic here,' " Oscar said, making a disgusted face.

At the same time somebody in the crowd stood up and shouted, *"Mierda!"*

It all fell apart in seconds. Thirty different people were on their feet, yelling and waving their arms. Carla tried to go on talking but it was no good. Faustino had been standing off to one side, and now he took her arm and made her sit down.

Finally Ramos settled them down. He didn't let them get completely quiet. He just stood with both his hands up until he had their attention, and then he took their anger and started using it.

"He's telling them they have the power," Oscar said. "He says they have to decide. If they want to let Carla lead them and keep them here playing with rocks—" Lindsey could barely hear him over the shouting of the crowd. "—or if they want to march to victory and bring de la Madrid to his knees." The boos and denials turned to cheers. A lot of them, Lindsey noticed, came from the armed men on the other ledge of the pyramid.

Lindsey didn't need Oscar to translate Ramos' next line. "And who," he shouted in Spanish, "will lead you?"

They obediently started chanting, "Ra-mos." They were all on their feet by now. It went on and on. Lindsey pulled up her legs and hugged her knees. "Are they going to kill her?" she asked.

"I doubt it," Oscar said. He had to shout to be heard over the mob. "She's too good a symbol. She's Acuario's wife. They can't kill the wife of their number one martyr."

Faustino stood up next to Ramos and put his hand on Ramos' shoulder. He looked resigned. He held out his hands to the crowd and started talking.

"He says Carla accepts their decision. Without bitterness, he says. Brothers in the common struggle."

Carla hadn't said a word to him since she sat down. "Et tu, Faustino?" Lindsey said.

"He must have seen this a hundred times, in nasty little camps like this all over this half of the world. Once you start a revolution, where's it going to stop? Once you convince some farmer he doesn't have to take shit from the government, how much shit is he going to take from you? You learn to go with the flow. The revolution is more important than the individual, right? Now he says she's going to give up her rank and fight beside her soldiers."

"She's only got one leg," Lindsey said. "How's she going to fight anybody?"

"This is just the bullshit phase. The expected thing is that she takes five or ten people and goes to start her own *tendencia,* her own splinter group."

"And thus is history made," Lindsey said.

Oscar shrugged at her and pointed at his ear. There was so much noise he couldn't hear her any longer. Ramos was leading them in cheers now. *"Viva la república! Viva la libertad!"*

Suddenly the cheering tapered off. Five or six people were looking up and then all of them were staring up into the sky. And there, right overhead and a couple of hundred feet up, was an olive-drab U.S. Army helicopter.

In the sudden silence it dipped and turned and flew away toward the north.

E DDIE CRAWLED OUT of the tent and tried to throw up. There wasn't really anything in his stomach. A guard watched him without interest from the steps of the pyramid. The sun had just cleared the tops of the trees and the ground was still cool with dew. Eddie felt the individual blades of grass itching against the bare skin of his wrists and knees.

He made it back to the water jug and rinsed his mouth a couple of times. The water brought him around, made him feel a little stronger. He found a patch of sunlight and lay down on his back. The big pyramid looked golden in the morning light. Beyond it a thin plume of smoke rose out of El Chichón, the dead volcano.

Something about the pyramid looked different and it took him a minute to realize what had happened. They'd been working on it. He turned his head and saw that the block-long, forty-foot-high row of steps in front of the Palace had been cleaned and straightened too. Both temples looked younger, stronger, and seeing them threw Eddie's time sense into even worse confusion.

He was in bad enough shape to start with. In fact, he was pretty sure he was dying. The thought of eating or drinking made him sick to his stomach. The only thing he could think about putting in his mouth was the mushroom. He pictured himself eating just a little sliver of it and saw all his pain fade away.

Don't start, he told himself.

There had been some kind of big deal going on here yesterday afternoon. Eddie had heard the shouting and applause but he hadn't felt up to getting out of bed to see what was happening. Now the entire area was deserted. Even the Lacondones were gone.

It occurred to him that they might simply have packed up and gone home in the night. Why not? The rebels would hardly have noticed. And Chan Ma'ax didn't owe Eddie any explanations. He'd made that clear enough.

The sun gradually warmed him, even if it didn't help the cobwebs in his brain. He sat up and got into a half-lotus and did some yoga breathing. Finally he felt strong enough to try walking around a little.

He got up and stretched, wondering where Lindsey was. She hadn't spent either of the last two nights with him. He'd barely seen her since they'd made love down by the river. Even his memories of the sex had blurred. The only things he could remember with any conviction were the mushroom trips.

He decided to look for her by the river. If he took it easy and stopped to rest he could make it that far. The rebel who was supposed to be guarding him had gone to sleep. Eddie decided not to bother with shoes and walked off in his T-shirt and cutoffs and bare feet.

He saw an iguana on the far end of the Palace steps and stalked it for a while. It was a real beauty, three feet if you counted the tail, and the same dusty white as the temple's limestone blocks. It had long spines on its back that wobbled when it moved. Whenever it turned its head Eddie would move a couple of steps closer. Then it would turn back and stare at him with black, lizard eyes.

First the temples were restored. Now he was playing tag with a dinosaur. What next? Eddie wondered.

He'd gotten within six feet when there was a gunshot and the iguana bolted. It came from the ball court, off to

Eddie's left. He moved toward the sound, staying in the shadow of the Palace's north wall.

Ramos was there, and Faustino, and Carla leaning on her crutch. They were lined up with four other soldiers in khaki and jeans. Directly in front of them was a man on his knees and another man lying on his stomach in the dirt. Facing them across the clearing were another dozen soldiers, poor paisanos with ragged clothes and rope belts and cheap canvas shoes. Only a couple of them had the shiny new assault rifles like the officers did. The rest had shotguns and .22s.

Somebody had been working here, too. The worst of the weeds and brush had been cleared out between the collapsed stone grandstands. At the edge of the ball court they'd made a hole. It was the size and shape of a shallow grave.

Ramos stood in front of the kneeling man, a .45 automatic in one hand and a red plastic notebook in the other. ". . . of this tribunal," he read out of the book, "that you are guilty of the crime of desertion, for which the sentence is death. Do you have anything to say?"

The kneeling man's hands were pressed against his crotch. His arms shook and they made the front of his shirt vibrate with them. Ramos put the gun against the man's head. He paused for an agonizing second and then he fired, jerking the gun back as he pulled the trigger, like it was a toy pistol. The sound got to Eddie a fraction of a second after the image, out of synch, and echoed off the stone wall of the Palace. Blood dribbled off the dead man's face and for a horrible moment it looked like he was going to stand up, but it was just some kind of muscle spasm that straightened his back and sent him falling over into the fresh-cut weeds.

Ramos put his gun away in a holster with a flap on it and buttoned the flap. "Tell everyone what you have seen today," he said to his ragged audience. "You and you, put the bodies in the ground." Two men came forward and clumsily stretched the first corpse on its back. The one at the end where the head was wouldn't touch the dead man's skin. He grabbed a handful of shirt and carried him that way.

Eddie turned away. He would have to cross the ball court if he wanted to go to the river and it wasn't worth it. He wondered if Ramos was conscious of the irony, if he knew that Mayans had made their human sacrifices in the same place, maybe even for the same reasons. Making that all-important equation of political power and the power over life and death.

It was obvious enough that Ramos was running things now. It was his hand on the gun. It was Carla's eyes staring at the ground in silence. Eddie knew this was bad news, though he wasn't sure how bad or what it meant specifically.

He walked slowly back the way he came. His eyes and lungs burned and he could hear his pulse beating in his ears. He thought about going back to sleep but his muscles were wound up tight. Maybe just from the fear of sleeping and not being able to wake up again.

Instead of going back to the tent he circled around through the scrawny trees at the north end of the clearing. He felt physically and mentally down, the way he would coming off a long acid trip.

If you take the mushrooms again, he told himself, you will die.

He heard digging up ahead. He found Chan Ma'ax and half the Lacondones working in a trench. Ma'ax García was there, and Nuxi', with a palm leaf tied around his head. They were all stripped down to their loincloths. Eddie was relieved to see them. The trench was over ten feet long, growing at both ends. Chan Ma'ax stood in the middle, leaning on an army entrenching tool.

"Tal in wilech," he said to Chan Ma'ax.

"Everybody look," the old man said in Mayan. He had his wrist cocked at an angle that made him look like a clown, or a crazy man. "Kukulcán comes back from the east, just like they always said."

"Kukulcán?" Eddie said.

"Careful," Chan Ma'ax said. "They put you to work too."

There were two soldiers looking on. They sat with their backs against trees, smoking, and they didn't seem interested in Eddie at all. He was apparently not covered by their orders. Eddie squatted Mayan-style at the edge of the trench. "What was that Kukulcán business about?"

"You know," Chan Ma'ax said. "The Aztecs, they call him Quetzalcoatl. The snake with feathers. A white man who comes out of the west to save us. But he gets drunk and screws his sister and has to leave in disgrace. He sails off to the east, saying he will come back someday. And here you are."

"I can't even save myself," Eddie said. "What are you doing here?"

"Digging holes," Chan Ma'ax said. "So the soldiers can hide when the Northamericans come."

"Have you seen Lindsey? Or Thomas?"

The old man shook his head. "Probably working somewhere. Everything is different now. Ramos is boss man now. Not much longer till the end."

"I thought it was another twenty-five years." Eddie was trying to kid him around but it wasn't working.

Chan Ma'ax licked his thumb and rubbed a cut on the knuckle of his left hand. "Even the end has to start somewhere."

"*Ándale,*" said one of the guards. Chan Ma'ax looked at Eddie for another long second and then bent over and started shoveling dirt out of the hole.

What was the point, Eddie wondered, in being t'o'ohil if you still had to take orders from some kid with a machine gun? He grabbed at handfuls of leaves as he walked back toward the clearing, crushing them up until his fingers hurt.

Everything was coming apart. Including his body. He was so weak. He sat down in the path. A sharp rock dug into his hip. The pain was comfortable, reassuring, told him he was still alive. He lay down on his stomach, pressing himself into the rocks and dirt and decaying leaves. He could hardly feel anything. He rubbed the palm of his left hand against a slab of limestone, back and forth, over and over, until he felt the stone turn slick with blood.

He rolled onto his back. His feet were moving, like they were tapping out the beat to some inaudible song. He had to let them go or his leg muscles would cramp. The stubble on his face itched and his scalp hurt where he'd slept with his hair matted wrong. He wanted to eat meat, to get drunk, to fuck Lindsey. He touched the crotch of his cutoffs. His penis was soft. Malnutrition, probably, or just another side effect of the drug.

He felt a long, slow scream building up in his lungs, but when he opened his mouth nothing came out.

He didn't remember coming to the mushroom grove. Here he was anyway. He sat down in front of the plants. Really, he should at least say goodbye to Lindsey. She'd said she still loved him and all. But then he'd tried to find her and she wasn't around. He didn't have that much to say to her anyway. Just goodbye.

He broke off a thumb-sized piece of mushroom and ate it. Then he ate another. His left hand had stopped bleeding. He slapped it gently against his leg, punctuating the rhythm of his jiggling feet. He ate one more little piece, just for luck.

Okay, he thought. That should do it.

He lay back on his elbows and waited, and a few minutes later the ground began to move under him.

He lay in a hammock strung between the walls of a stone room. Most of the front wall was open to the sky. He could see clouds and sunlight and the tops of trees.

He swung his legs over the edge of the hammock. He was dizzy for a second and then it passed. He put his feet in the sandals that were lying there and stood up.

Across the three-sided room was a man in a jaguar skin and bright green quetzal feathers. His hair had been shaved in front and then tied in a topknot to show off his long, sloping forehead. He stared at Eddie with tired eyes. "You're awake," he said.

"Yes."

"You've been sleeping for three days. Your arms and legs moved, like an animal's."

Eddie nodded. He remembered being carried here, but not much else. He walked carefully to the open wall of the temple and held onto the lintel overhead for balance.

He was in a cluster of smaller temples east of the big pyramid. Two flights of steps led down to a paved avenue below him. His temple, and the one next to it, were built out of the side of a mountain. He could see the entire south end of the city. There were two temples across from him, set on low pyramids. Their steep roofs were carved and painted with historical scenes, and above them were the elaborate brickwork grids of their roof combs. In the middle distance he could see the ruler's palace with its tower, and beyond it the great pyramid.

To the west the trees started again, orchards of ramón and chicosapote. Between the trees were the family compounds, thatched wooden huts on dirt platforms, all facing a central square. The largest compounds belonged to the nobles, and they were ones closest to the temples. Some of them had burned to the ground, the ashes still smoking. Thousands of peasant huts and milpas and orchards stretched out beyond them to the horizon.

It was early afternoon and the harsh sunlight washed out the brilliant reds and yellows of the temples. If Eddie squinted his eyes they looked like they had no color at all. It reminded him of something but he couldn't think what.

The army was camped in the main square, between the ruler's palace and the great pyramid. Most of them were sleeping. The worst of the wounded were being bandaged and fed. It all seemed strange and familiar at the same time. Eddie couldn't say why the army was there, in the middle of the city with their weapons, but it seemed right that they were.

"Do you remember anything?" the feathered man asked him. "Do you remember me?"

"Chilam . . ." Eddie said, and then shook his head. "I don't know."

"Chilam Sotz'," the man said. "I am chief priest. Do you even know your own name?"

"Eddie," he said. "I think my name is Eddie." It sounded wrong even as he said it.

"That's not a proper name," Chilam Sotz' said.

Every time Eddie tried to concentrate he lost what he'd been thinking. All he could remember was a little old man who looked like a monkey. "There is another name . . . Kukulcán. You could call me that."

"Do you know how you got here?"

"No."

"Some soldiers found you walking in the city. You were dressed like a true person, but your skin was so pale they thought you were a ghost. So they brought you to me. I am to learn if you are a ghost or not."

"Have you decided?" Eddie asked.

"Yes. You are not a ghost. If you were a ghost, you would not speak Mam so badly."

"Why are . . . why are the soldiers out there?"

"Because of the war."

"What war?"

"We are fighting with our own people."

Eddie felt dizzy again. "Your own people."

"I don't know what to tell you about this," Chilam Sotz' said. "I don't know what it is that you don't know."

"Tell me everything. Tell me about the people you're fighting against."

"They are young, mostly. Peasants. They say there are too many priests. That's one thing. Too many nobles, too many temples. They say the world is out of balance. They say the gods have turned their backs to us. This is why the crops have been bad for so many years, why the animals are so hard to find." Chilam Sotz' leaned his head against the wall behind him. He was old, Eddie realized. Maybe twice Eddie's age. Old and very tired.

"They have a new religion," Chilam Sotz' went on. "They have these funny ideas about time. Everybody knows time goes in a circle, but they think time can't take care of itself. They think we have to leave the cities and go back to the jungle, forget everything we know. So that

when the cycle ends everything will be the way it was
when it started. Men like animals, living in the dirt."

"I saw it," Eddie said suddenly.

"What?"

"The end of the cycle." It surprised him as much as it
did Chilam Sotz'. "What they say is true. The temples
will be grown over with jungle. The people will live in
huts by themselves. They won't have any priests. They
won't remember the names of the gods. They won't even
remember the Long Count."

"So," Chilam Sotz' said.

"I'm sorry. I make it sound like this city—all this
beauty—like it's all for nothing. But other people will
remember you. People with skin the color of ghosts. Like
mine, but even lighter."

"It doesn't matter," Chilam Sotz' said. "There is no
meaning in the great cycle. It exists, that's all. You can't
worry too much about your place in it. You can go crazy
if you do." He got up and straightened his feathered
headdress. "If you're strong enough we should go see the
ruler. He wanted me to tell him when you woke up."

"Why not?" Eddie said.

The air in the plaza smelled of smoke and sweating
soldiers and dust broiling in the sun. The soldiers wore
loincloths and woven headbands. The only weapons Eddie saw were spears, some of them with obsidian points,
some just sharpened and hardened in a fire. They all
shifted away from Eddie when he walked by, afraid of his
pale skin.

The plaza was paved with limestone blocks. Eddie felt
the heat coming up through his sandals. At the north
end, well away from the soldiers, he saw a few merchants
and traders still trying to do business. They had their
mats laid out and covered with pots and feathers, ear-
spools and rings and necklaces, seashells and occasional
pieces of jade. Nobody was buying.

The temples towered over all of them, defying the jungle, defying time itself. High up on the Temple of the
Inscriptions two lords consulted a priest. The lords wore

fur boots and short capes and knee britches of cloth painted with stylized glyphs. They wore elaborate hats made from the heads of deer. The animals seemed to be craning their necks to look up at something. The priest had jaguar boots like Chilam Sotz', and a headdress with peacock feathers. They all wore ear-spools and necklaces of jade.

There were low-relief sculptures everywhere, on the roofs of the temples, on the sides of the stairs, on stone tablets taller than Eddie, standing upright in the square. Eddie stopped in front of one of the tablets. The glyphs, like rows of fat, curled bugs, were painted in shades of red and brown. They surrounded the figure of a nobleman with red skin and green feathers and black and yellow furs.

"This way," Chilam Sotz' said. He climbed the steps of the Palace. Two guards at the top of the steps nodded to him and stood aside to let him in. Eddie followed him across a narrow room with a high, vaulted ceiling and then into a grassy courtyard. The tower rose up out of the southwest corner. There were men up in the highest level, one in each of the four windows, staring out into the distance.

They went up a short flight of steps and into another set of rooms. There was more stucco relief on the walls, pictures of past rulers. Eddie stopped to look at one of them. The man was in profile, as always, to show the long forehead that bulged smoothly into the hatchet nose. His headdress was full of seabirds and fish. His right hand held what looked like a sword, except it had branches coming off it like a tree.

"Pacal," Chilam Sotz' said. "He made this into the greatest city in the empire. There hasn't been a ruler like him since." Eddie saw two more guards coming toward them. Chilam Sotz' made a small noise in his throat. "Until now, of course." The guards bowed to Chilam Sotz' and looked at Eddie with suspicion.

"Where is the ruler?" Chilam Sotz' asked them.

"The steambaths, lord."

Chilam Sotz' nodded and took Eddie to the back of the

palace. Most of the rooms he passed were empty, or were full of material goods, pots and furs and rolls of dyed fabric. There didn't seem to be any state business going on, no laws being written, no verdicts handed down, no ambassadors being entertained.

The door to the baths was closed with a woven mat. Inside there didn't seem to be any air at all. The walls were glazed, like pottery. Naked male servants carried in dishes of glowing coals from the cooking hut. They dumped them into stone troughs and poured water over them, sending up clouds of steam and the stink of wet ashes. Sweat came out all over Eddie's body.

The ruler sat on a stone bench, naked except for jewelry and quetzal feathers braided in his hair. He was tall and his face was smooth and nicely proportioned. He would have been handsome except for his huge stomach and chest. His eyes were small and had a look of cheerful dissipation. A short, thick-waisted woman, also naked, stroked his chest, ears, and neck with another handful of feathers. Water had beaded up on her skin, on her small, squarish breasts, on the dark tangle of hair between her thighs. Another woman crouched between the ruler's legs, his half-inflated penis in her mouth.

Chilam Sotz' dropped to his knees, crossed his arms over his chest, touched his head to the floor. Eddie awkwardly copied him. "The stranger, lord," Chilam Sotz' said, sitting back on his haunches. "He says his name is Kukulcán."

Eddie stayed bent over a little longer. The air was cooler close to the floor and it also made it easier for him to breathe if he didn't look at the naked women. When he sat up he said, *"Utz-in puksiqual."* My heart is good. Sweat ran off his hands as he held them out, palms up.

The ruler nodded distractedly. Chilam Sotz' said, "He has had a vision, while he slept. He has seen the great cities in ruins at the end of the cycle."

"What's the matter with his skin?" the ruler said. "Is he a Mexican?"

"No, lord. The Mexicans have small noses and no foreheads."

"Maybe he's sick." The ruler picked up a bowl and slurped at it. Eddie could smell the chocolate and it made his stomach growl. "Are you sick?" the ruler asked him.

"No, lord," Eddie said.

The ruler looked at Chilam Sotz'. "Well, then. He doesn't seem very fearsome. What should we do with him?"

"We should ask him more questions, lord. His vision may be very important. If it is a true dream—"

"I don't care about dreams," the ruler said. "But you can do with him what you want."

"Lord, if it is true that the great cities will be empty at the end of the cycle, then maybe we should listen to—"

"By the end of the cycle you and I will be dirt." The ruler opened his eyes wide, as if he'd caught himself going to sleep. "Take your Mexican and go away. Don't talk to me anymore about the end of the cycle."

"Yes, lord." Chilam Sotz' bowed again and so did Eddie, and they backed out into the hallway.

Chilam Sotz' took Eddie to the cooking hut to eat. It was behind the Palace and on a low dirt platform, oblong and rounded at the ends, like peasant huts. Smoke leaked out between the wall slats and through the dried brown thatch of the roof.

Eddie sat on a mat between the cookfires. There were three male cooks, and women and children grinding corn and cutting vegetables wherever there was room. All of them seemed agonizingly conscious of Chilam Sotz' and Eddie. Every couple of minutes a servant ran out with a dish of coals for the steambath.

"Do you want meat?" Chilam Sotz' asked. Eddie shook his head. "Good. There isn't much meat these days." He gave Eddie beans and tortillas and strips of fried squash and a lumpy bowl of manioc.

He watched Eddie eat for a while and then he asked, "What did you think of the ruler?"

Eddie stared at him. The question didn't make sense. Rulers were like the great cycle. They weren't something to have an opinion about. "It looked like he wasn't really listening to you," he said finally.

"No," Chilam Sotz' said, "he wasn't. He's afraid of hearing that he could be wrong. He's afraid of a lot of things. More every day. He was brought up to eat well and father little rulers and remember all the religious days. He doesn't know how to deal with trouble like we have now. There wasn't anybody to teach him about it."

Eddie looked around. Everyone was pretending not to have heard the blasphemy. "I don't understand why he wanted to talk to me," Eddie said. "If he's afraid of what I had to say."

"He wanted to see if you were dangerous," Chilam Sotz' said. "If he thought you were he would have had you killed."

"Oh," Eddie said.

"It's the only thing he really knows how to do. He has a wall of priests and nobles between him and the real world. If something gets through that wall and scares him, he has it killed."

"You think the ruler is wrong," Eddie said quietly. "You agree with the others. The ones that want to leave the city."

"I am chief priest. The chief priest owes his life to the ruler."

"Whatever you say. These people. The 'others' you were talking about. Do they have a name for this new religion?"

"They don't call it a religion. They call themselves a clan."

"A clan?" Eddie said. The word made him uneasy.

"Yes. They call themselves after the Raccoon. The Haawo'."

Eddie had been awake for a long time now. Long enough to watch the last of the light fade and feel the heat of the day start to let up. Chilam Sotz' snored quietly in a hammock on the other side of the temple, apparently immune to the mosquitos that were driving Eddie crazy.

The food had helped, that and a long nap during the afternoon rain, while Chilam Sotz' went off to do something he didn't want to talk about. Eddie felt stronger, his brain a little clearer. He felt like pieces of his personality were slowly seeping back from some other place.

He went outside and sat at the top of the steps, looking out at the night. Torches around the plaza shot off flames in long, rattling streamers as the wind whipped between the buildings. There were only a few guards. Most of the soldiers had gone to sleep wherever they'd been sitting.

The wind moaned and a torch across the way flickered out. For a second Eddie thought he saw somebody moving in the darkness at the edge of the palace. Shadows, he told himself.

There were shadows in his head, too. The little monkey man. The city in ruins. A woman with yellow-brown hair.

Eddie looked around and his heart jumped in fear. There was a man walking toward him from the side of the temple.

He was naked except for a loincloth. He moved like he didn't want to put his weight behind it, like he had broken pieces of obsidian underfoot. Instead of a spear he had a bow and a handful of arrows. Eddie blinked. None of the city soldiers had bows and arrows. Where had they come from?

"You are Kukulcán?" the man asked.

Eddie was still too shaken up to answer. A voice from behind him said, "Yes. He's the one."

It was Chilam Sotz', wrapped in his jaguar cloak. The wind pulled at his feathers and made the jaguar's tail dance around. "Go with this man," he said. "He'll take you out of the city."

"He's one of the others," Eddie said. "The Haawo'."

"Yes."

"You're helping them."

"I believe the vision you told me was true. No one can change the future. All anyone can do is try to be part of it. The ruler is finished. The city is finished. Even the gods, if they exist, are finished. Go with this man."

"Thank you," Eddie said. He had a strange impulse to take Chilam Sotz' right hand with his own right hand. He didn't know why. "You are a hach winik."

Chilam Sotz' smiled. There was some bitterness in it. "Go now," he said.

The Haawo' led the way around the back of the temple and into the forest. The moon was just less than full and there was enough light to see by.

"Where are we going?" Eddie whispered.

"Quiet," the man said. "Walk quietly."

Eddie could see the path if he didn't look too hard for it. The Haawo' was moving so fast Eddie had to keep breaking into a run to keep up. He wasn't used to running in sandals and they felt like they were about to come off.

They came out into the open near the top of the hill. Eddie could see the city laid out below him, flickering in the torchlight. In the second he spent looking at it his sandal slipped on a mossy rock. His feet went out from under him and he went down. A chunk of limestone clattered down the hill.

Somebody shouted in the distance. "That way," the Haawo' said, pointing. "Run." Eddie scrambled to his feet and ran into the trees again. For a little while he heard the other man behind him and then there were more shouts and he was running alone. He heard spears clattering together and more shouting. Two screams. One of them stopped in the middle and then there were a lot of running feet, all coming toward him.

Eddie knew that his clumsiness had just killed a man. He couldn't seem to take it seriously. This wasn't his fight. He hadn't asked to be taken out of the city. All he wanted was to keep himself alive.

He got off the path, running in the wide spaces between the trees. He slowed down for a thicket of palms and felt a hand on his arm. He choked, nearly shouted, and then a dirty hand covered his mouth. "Quiet," the voice said, and Eddie nodded.

The hands let him go and he turned around. There

were three of them, all young, dressed in loincloths. Their foreheads were shaved, but they let their hair fall loose on the sides instead of pulling it back in topknots.

One of them pointed the way and started off. The other two got on either side of Eddie and pushed him gently to get him moving. They pushed him again whenever he slowed down or missed a step. They weren't being all that gentle and Eddie worried about what that might mean.

Finally they came to a milpa. What few stalks of corn there were had been bent double to protect them from the rains. The ears were small and badly formed. Beyond the cornfield was a compound of five or six huts. Eddie could smell the smoke from the cookhouse fires.

They brought him in through the central square. Women in long white peasant robes squatted in the dirt, holding their naked children. They all stared as the men hustled him by.

"Can I get something to eat?" Eddie asked. "Some water, maybe?"

"Not yet," one of the men said. "You have to talk to the t'o'ohil."

All of the huts were on dirt platforms a couple of feet off the ground. It was enough to keep them from flooding during the rainy season. They all looked like the cooking hut back in the city: thatched roofs, a vertical row of sticks for walls. Eddie was exhausted and couldn't get his breath. It hurt his calf muscles to climb up onto the platform of the t'o'ohil's hut.

One of the Haawo' warriors pushed him through the door. There were half a dozen fires inside, burning in clay pots. The air was full of the pine smell of burning copal.

On the far side of the clay pots was a tiny, wrinkled old man who looked like a monkey.

"Hello, Eddie," Chan Ma'ax said.

T HOMAS SPENT THE FIRST
night in a tree.

He'd been running for two hours, telling himself Carla's people wouldn't try to track him until morning, if at all. He told himself a lot of things. He told himself the big jungle predators had pretty much died out, that the few that were left would run from the noise he made.

He was definitely making enough noise.

Mostly he kept telling himself he was going to be okay, over and over, like a mantra. He had a gun, after all. Between the various homesteading Indians and the lumber and oil companies there were roads everywhere. He was bound to find one sooner or later.

The tree he found looked like some kind of oak. He slung the M16 and jumped up to grab the lowest branch. He hadn't tried to climb a tree in years. The bark ripped at the skin inside his wrists and it was all he could do to swing his legs up and over the branch. He hung there, upside down, the blood running to his head, losing the feeling in his hands, and then desperately clambered up into the tree, tearing out the pocket of his shirt in the process.

He finally settled in a thick cluster of limbs, his feet on one, ass on another, folded arms and head on a third. He even slept a little, for ten or fifteen minutes at a stretch, dreaming that he was still awake and staring out into the dark. He woke up at sunrise, shivering, his clothes drenched with dew. A column of tiny black ants had detoured across one knee. He stood up and slapped and brushed at them with his right hand, holding on with his left. His clothes were so wet that his hands came away beaded with water.

His muscles ached and every inch of bare skin was covered with mosquito bites. He didn't even have a canteen. He considered the idea of going back. To what? he thought. A firing squad? He wasn't even sure he could find the way.

He ended up chewing on his shirt for the moisture.

Early in the afternoon he found a grove of wild orange trees. Their skins were mostly green and yellow, not the bright dyed orange Thomas was used to seeing in the grocery. The insides were sweet enough, though, and he ate what he could and bundled up another five or six in his shirt.

Half a mile farther on he found the ruins of a stone house. He had no idea how old the place was. There was no roof left, but the beams were still in place. There was a layer of dirt over the stone floor and a few weeds and small trees growing up through it. Thomas kicked the plants down and scuffed the floor smooth with his boots. The sky was clouding up for the daily rainstorm. He gathered up enough leaves and branches to get half a roof onto the existing timbers. By then it had started to rain.

With a few branches in front of the door he felt reasonably secure. His roof leaked a little, but the back corner stayed dry. He closed his eyes and told himself it was okay to sleep. It didn't happen.

He kept wondering who'd lived in the cabin, and what had become of them. They'd left nothing behind except the ruined house and the orange trees. If they'd built a road it was gone now. At least the Mayans had left *something* of themselves, art and writing and pottery and bones.

But then the Mayans had been an entire civilization. Whoever had lived here hadn't been more than a single family. Maybe just one person. And how much, Thomas thought, does anybody really leave behind?

By the time the rain stopped he was asleep.

He spent the second night there, and slept well enough, all things considered. He could have stayed another day or two if he'd been willing to live on oranges. So far he hadn't seen another living creature. He'd heard birds and monkeys in the trees, but they'd stayed out of sight.

The sun came up behind the house. Thomas tried to fix

its position in his mind relative to El Chichón, which he could still see in the distance. He'd been headed west the day before. If he turned a little toward the north he should hit Usumacinta. From there he could find some way to get hold of Marsalis, warn him that there were civilian hostages at Na Chan, keep him from starting an attack.

He slung his M16 over one shoulder and a new shirtful of oranges over the other. By nine o'clock he'd picked up a trail, and by ten the trail had crossed a logging road.

One of Marsalis' patrols picked him up before noon.

He was replaying music in his brain, Motown, Talking Heads, anything with a good steady beat to keep his feet moving. Suddenly he was on his face in the dirt and his glasses were gone. He felt the M16 being jerked away from him and a knee in the middle of his back. He turned his head sideways to look.

He couldn't focus that well without his glasses, but it looked like his gun was sailing through the air. It was caught by a kid in baggy fatigue pants and an olive-drab T-shirt. Then a huge open hand, black at the fingers and lighter at the palm, pushed his face into the roadway.

At first the only thing Thomas could think of was to wonder if he'd been singing out loud and making an idiot out of himself. He was so exhausted he couldn't remember.

He stared up through the fingers at the blur of a round, sweating African face. "You just lie there a minute, honey," the man said. The M16 sailed through the air again. They were tossing it around like a baseball in the infield.

"Where'd this hairball get a M16?" somebody said.

"This is Porter's gun," somebody else said. "Got his notches in the stock from Nam."

"Those his gook notches?"

"Fuckin' A."

"Is that gooks killed or gooks fucked?"

"Killed, stupid. Them other notches he cuts in his dick."

"Porter would."

"Hey, Jamie."

The man with his knee in Thomas' back said, "What?"

"You think this hairball killed Porter? Let's cut his balls off."

"Well, honey?" Jamie said. "What'd you do with Porter?"

"Rebels shot him," Thomas said. It was hard to talk with the pressure on his face.

"What rebels?"

"Carla."

There were wolf whistles and cheers. "I can't wait to fuck that bitch," somebody said. "I been saving my hard-on for months."

"Is he dead, honey?"

"Not yet. Still alive when I left."

"Left where? Left when?"

"Night before last. Rebels are at Na Chan. In the ruins."

"And where was you headed with Porter's gun?"

"Looking for you guys. You're with Marsalis, right?"

"He ain't lying," Jamie said. "At least about Na Chan." He took his hand away from Thomas' face. "What y'all think we ought to do with him?"

"Cut his balls off!"

"Shoot him!"

"Fuck him!"

"Gang bang him and then shoot him!"

"Shoot him first!"

Thomas waited them out. Finally the pressure on his back went away. He sat up in the road and brushed the pebbles and sand off his chest and the left side of his face. His glasses were right there in front of him. He got his shirt loose from the oranges and cleaned the glasses off. They seemed to be okay. He put them on and hung the shirt over his shoulders.

There were five men in the patrol. None of them wore anything like a normal military uniform. Jamie had an M16, but the others all had weird-looking green plastic rifles. What they looked like, Thomas thought, was a gang of survivalists playing at life after the bomb.

Jamie got out a walkie-talkie the size of a bar of soap and said, "Tell the colonel we got somebody here escaped from Carla's camp. Some honky from the States." The reply sounded like pure static to Thomas, but Jamie said, "Okay, that's a roger." He put the receiver back on his belt. "All right, ladies, fall out."

The patrol sat down along one side of the road. Somebody lit a joint and passed it. The man next to Thomas took his turn and said, "Wanna hit?"

"Thanks," Thomas said. It burned his throat and made his stomach lurch but he felt calmer right away. When it came around again he took another, then a third. The last hit stoned him. His stomach felt like an open wound.

"You guys got anything to eat?" he asked. A hefty white guy at the end passed him a Kit Kat and a canteen. Thomas started to drink and then hesitated at the smell. "What's in here?"

"Kool-Aid," the guy on the end said. "Black cherry. Covers the taste of the goddamn iodine. Made with real sugar, too, none of that NutraSweet shit."

Thomas drank it with the candy. He felt ten years old. The caffeine in the chocolate and all that sugar hit him like a dose of speed.

About ten minutes later a jeep came up the road and stopped a few yards short of where Thomas was sitting. A cloud of dust hovered over the back of the jeep for a second and then slowly settled. A cartoon insignia on the side said FIGHTING 666TH. The driver was a beefy blond with shoulder-length hair in a headband and a few days' growth of beard. Next to him was an elegant-looking black man in khakis and a dress cap with two eagles over the bill. Marsalis, Thomas thought. There was a civilian in the backseat, a kid with dark-blond razor-cut hair and a mustache. He had the kind of pampered good looks and thin, muscular body that Thomas associated with California, with the record promo people that used to follow Eddie around.

As soon as the jeep stopped the patrol got back on its feet. Not to stand at attention or salute, just to make an automatic, almost unconscious gesture of respect.

"This the man?" Marsalis asked.

"Yessir," Jamie said. "Just came strolling down the road. Had Porter's gun with him. Says the rebels shot Porter pretty bad, but he may still be alive."

Marsalis looked at Thomas. "What's your name?"

"Thomas Yates."

"Really? The Yates who wrote *Lords of the Forest?*"

"Yeah, that's right," Thomas said, surprised.

"Never read it. Always meant to, though. Billy, why don't you get in back with Carmichael? I'll drive for a while."

"Yessir," the blond said. He got out and Marsalis slid over behind the wheel.

"Hop in," Marsalis said.

Thomas got in. He wished now he hadn't had the marijuana. His head was puffy and his tongue was thick and he couldn't think straight. Marsalis carefully turned the jeep around and then waved to the patrol, like they were his kids that he'd just dropped off at a shopping mall. He worked his way slowly up through the gears, but within five minutes they had built up a punishing speed. The worst of the bumps practically threw Thomas out of his seat.

Marsalis hooked his thumb over his shoulder. "That there is John Carmichael. He's a reporter for *Rolling Stone.*" Thomas glanced back at Carmichael. Carmichael nodded and looked away.

What's the deal? Thomas wondered. Was Marsalis actually letting *Rolling Stone* write about what he was doing? Carmichael wasn't taking any notes and he didn't have a camera or recorder with him. Something else was going on here, but Thomas couldn't figure it out yet. Billy, sitting next to Carmichael, seemed to be enjoying the ride, slapping his left hand cheerfully against the side of the jeep.

"How many of you people does Carla have up there, anyway?" Marsalis asked.

"Two other Northamericans," Thomas said. "Plus about a dozen Indians." He wasn't sure he wanted to mention Oscar or the helicopter just yet.

"I didn't think there were any gringos left in this neck of the woods."

"We were looking for my brother. He . . . kind of went native, I guess you'd say. He was living with a tribe of Lacondones, up at Lake Nahá. They went to Na Chan on some kind of pilgrimage and Eddie went along."

"We?"

"Me and . . . Eddie's wife. My sister-in-law."

"Which Lacondones was he with? North or south?"

"North," Thomas said. "He was there about three years."

"No shit. Those are pretty hip guys." Marsalis looked over to check Thomas' reaction. "I didn't just blunder down here, my friend. I've been doing my research. We learned some hard lessons in Nam, those of us that lived through it."

Thomas heard the staccato rumbling of a helicopter and turned to look behind him. A Huey dove toward them out of the sky. Thomas' empty stomach turned cold at the image from a war he'd never fought in. He wanted to crawl under the seat. The copter came over them low enough that the wash from the rotor hit Thomas like a physical blow.

Marsalis didn't even look up. He waved his hand casually and the copter wagged its tail back at him. Then it was gone.

"Where are you taking me?" Thomas asked.

"Back to camp. Got to decide what to do with you and the boy wonder back there. We got a show tonight, and I don't want to have to be riding herd on you two."

"A show?"

Marsalis looked over at Thomas and smiled. "We're going to go up there and kick Carla's ass."

Thomas was stunned. "What about Lindsey and Eddie?" he said, finally. "What about the Lacondones? What about the ruins, for Christ's sake! You can't just go in there and start shooting up those temples!"

"Don't talk to me about the temples," Marsalis said. "It was Carla that decided she wanted to hide out there. If any of her precious heritage gets wiped out, it's on her head. As for civilians, that's Carla's lookout too. The U.S. has got in the habit of rolling over and playing dead every time some crackpot takes a hostage or two. Well, that kind of crap just isn't going to cut it anymore. It just endangers more lives, and costs more lives, in the long run."

"You've got to be kidding," Thomas said. "I can't believe I'm hearing this."

Marsalis settled back, letting his left arm hang out the side, steering the swaying, bouncing jeep with his right wrist. "I promise you I'm not. People just don't seem to be able to take the long view of things anymore. They just don't think things through. Hell, they don't think at all. The guys in my outfit, well, we like to think of ourselves as philosophers as well as soldiers. Right, Billy?"

"That's right, sir."

"This is insane," Thomas said. "These are innocent civilian lives you're talking about. Not to mention your own man Porter up there, too. You have to protect them—"

"My friend," Marsalis said, "I don't have to do a damned thing." He sounded more bored than angry. "If I get too tired of your whining, I can pull over right here and take you out of the car and blow your brains out. If Carmichael doesn't like it he can go too. This is Latin America. *Aquí, cada día se desaparecen,* you dig?"

Thomas understood. People disappeared here every day.

Just as they pulled into camp the road seemed to rise up in front of the jeep. Marsalis hit the brakes. All four tires went off the ground at once. The jeep bounced hard and the engine died. Marsalis wrenched the wheel to keep them from coasting into a tree.

"What the hell was that?" Billy said.

"Temblor," Marsalis said. "Earth tremor." He ground the starter and the jeep's engine caught. "It happens around here." They were barely rolling again before an aftershock came through and shook the jeep gently from side to side.

Thomas was frozen in his seat. All he could think about was Mexico City, the smell of smoke and concrete dust.

Marsalis parked in the middle of camp. Thomas stared straight ahead of him at four freshly painted, reconditioned helicopters. There were three UH-1's and a lean, heavily armed Cobra gunship. The Cobra and two of the UH-1's were staked down against the wind, one rotor lashed to the rear of the fuselage. The third Huey was the one that had buzzed them on the road. The crew was unloading supplies through the cargo doors. The tremor had split one of the crates open and Thomas could see the metal ammunition boxes inside.

"Billy?" Marsalis said. "Put these two somewhere till I can figure out what to do with them."

"Yessir."

"Could I maybe get something to eat?" Thomas asked. "It's been a couple days."

"And feed him. Anything else?"

"I wish you'd reconsider," Thomas said. "Sir. About the civilians."

Marsalis shook his head in disgust. "Take them away. And Carmichael, you might want to think twice about shooting your mouth off to Dr. Yates, here."

Carmichael still didn't say anything.

A couple of the long barracks tents were leaning at odd angles, but otherwise the quake didn't seem to have done much. Billy took them to a two-man tent and sat down in the grass outside where he could watch them. Thomas and Carmichael sat across from each other on two cots. Thomas watched Billy call a latino kid over and say something, pointing to Thomas. Ordering me lunch, Thomas hoped. The kid was about the same age as the correos that Carla's people used.

"What was that business about not talking to me?" Thomas asked.

"I found out some stuff yesterday that's pretty hot.

Marsalis is right, you know. If I talk to you, it'll just get you into worse trouble than you're already in."

"I'm not sure that's possible," Thomas said. He'd thought at first that Carmichael was some poor little rich kid, out looking for political kicks. Now he got the feeling that Carmichael was in this pretty deep. "I'll take my chances," Thomas said, "if you want to let me in on it."

"Your funeral," Carmichael said. "I'm not going to pretend I haven't been dying to tell somebody. The more people that know about this the better the chance of it finally getting out. How long were you up there with Carla?"

Thomas had to think about it. "Just a week, I guess. Seems more like a couple of months."

"Then you haven't heard about the Iran arms deal."

"The what?"

Carmichael told him a story of government shady deals and ineptitude that was worse than Watergate. They were interrupted when the latino kid brought Thomas a plate of hot dogs and Boston beans. Hot dogs. Thomas could hardly believe it. The kid also brought cold beers for both of them. It all tasted so good it took the edge off Carmichael's story.

"Nobody else knows about this?" Thomas asked.

"I don't think there's even that many people in the government that know. Maybe they even kept Reagan out of it, though I doubt it. He's so in love with his Contras they would have had to tell him. Anyway. This revolution is really picking up steam, and a story like this could put them over the top. Did you hear they took over in Cuernavaca?"

"No," Thomas said.

"Burned some Northamerican outfit to the ground. Supposed to be some genetic engineering project or something."

"Jesus," Thomas said.

"What's the matter?"

"I used to work there," Thomas said. "Night before last, I was trying to decide if I wanted to go back there or not, if I got out of this. Now I guess I don't have a choice."

"I'm sorry," Carmichael said.

"It's stupid, you know. There was stuff in that project that could have saved lives. If they weren't so afraid of foreigners and technology. Stuff that could have made their revolution work."

"Maybe they'll come back to it."

"Yeah," Thomas said. "Maybe."

"Anyway," Carmichael said. "You can see why I was a little nervous about telling you this stuff. God knows what they're going to do to me. Put me under a Mexican prison somewhere, most likely. You too, now."

Thomas leaned a little closer to make sure Billy wouldn't hear. "Well," he said. "I take it this means you want out of here."

"You don't know," Carmichael said, "what I would do to get out of here."

Thomas felt nervous suddenly. As long as he didn't say anything he wasn't committed. "I can fly a helicopter," he said.

"No shit?"

"I learned on a Huey like the ones out there."

"What, was this in Vietnam or something?"

"No, it was . . . a private deal. Here in Mexico. But if something happens, if we get a chance—"

"It's nice to think about," Carmichael said. "But I can't see them giving us one."

"You never know. Just be ready if it happens."

The rain came before Thomas finished eating. It felt good to be dry and not be hungry or thirsty. To have a place to lie down and somebody to talk to. You would think it would be enough, he thought, just to feel this good.

Carmichael went to the door of the tent. "You want to get out of the rain?" he said to Billy.

Thomas could see Billy sitting under the tree. He was soaked. He smiled at Carmichael and said, "What rain?"

Carmichael shrugged and sat down again. He started

talking about interviewing Carla, about the air attack where she got hurt, about meeting Raul Venceremos. Then Thomas told him about Carla losing the foot, about the mystical kind of trip she'd gotten caught up in since.

"Man," Carmichael said, "that really sucks. I don't know if she's going to be able to do much with only one good leg."

Thomas stared at him. "Are you out of your mind? Once Marsalis is through with her, there won't be *anything* left." He heard somebody coming and sat back guiltily.

Marsalis' voice came from outside. "Okay, you guys can fall out now."

Thomas followed Carmichael into the last of the rain. The sun was already breaking through and there were just odd drops that hit Thomas every few seconds, seemingly from nowhere. Standing next to Marsalis was a guy in mirrorshades and polished motorcycle boots. He looked to be in his early thirties. His black hair was cut short and combed with hair oil. He had a thin smile and a handgun in a holster with a flap.

"This is Captain Fowler," Marsalis said. "The one on the left is Carmichael. That's Yates, with the glasses."

"Where you want me to take them?" Fowler said.

"Veracruz. Have them both detained. Official Secrets Act. You know the drill."

"I haven't done anything," Thomas said, terrified.

"I'm afraid you were alone with Carmichael for over an hour. There's no telling what he might have spilled to you."

"You set this up," Thomas said. "The whole thing. Bringing Carmichael along in the jeep. Leaving us alone in that tent. To give you an excuse to lock me up."

"Now, now," Marsalis said. "Let's not be paranoid."

"I trusted you," Thomas said. "I came to you for help. And you're just going to go ahead anyway, and if you kill a few innocent civilians, well, that's just too bad."

"Billy, will you escort these two to Captain Fowler's helicopter?"

"Yessir. You want me to go along?"

"No, I'll need you here. I don't imagine either of these two will give Captain Fowler any trouble. Do you?"

"No sir," Billy said. "I don't guess so."

Thomas could see that talking wasn't going to do anything else for him. He walked through the wet grass to the helicopters.

"You," Fowler said to Carmichael. "The reporter. You want to ride up front, get the bird's-eye view?"

Carmichael looked at Thomas. "No, that's okay," he said. "I get airsick."

Fowler shook his head. "Jesus, get in back, then. And don't puke on anything."

Thomas went automatically toward the far side of the helicopter, to get in the left seat. "Whoa there, fella," Fowler said. "You take this side. I like to fly from the left." Thomas nodded and got in.

Fowler put on his radiophones and started his pre-flights. "You know something about helicopters?" he asked.

"Just ridden in them a couple times," Thomas said innocently.

"Most people would try to get in on the right, see, like it was a car. I got used to flying this seat in Nam. I'd rather be able to see the ground than have a few extra instruments."

Thomas nodded as if it didn't mean anything to him. Fowler was talking about the fact that the instrument panel on the left side of a Huey was chopped to let the copilot see out the foot-level port. Play dumb, Thomas told himself.

Thomas strapped himself in. He looked around the cockpit as if it was all strange and wonderful. Fowler's gun was there, just to his left, in easy reach.

He didn't want to think about it. But there it was. He had to have the gun.

Thomas knew the rules of the game, even if he'd never played it before. If he did manage to take the gun away he had to be willing to use it. Otherwise there was no point. Could he do that? Point it, pull the trigger, kill somebody? Shooting Fowler in the leg wouldn't be enough. If the chance came everything had to be ready in his mind, the decisions already made.

"Just be careful not to touch anything," Fowler said, cranking the engine. "And don't get any bright ideas. This isn't TV. You can't just get on the radio and have somebody talk you down. You'd crash this thing in a hot second."

Thomas nodded. It would be easier if he could see Fowler as some kind of villain. Instead Fowler was just an ordinary soldier, doing his job. Even Marsalis, for all his crazed ideas, didn't have the stink of evil about him. Neither did Billy or Jamie or any of the others. It was the danger, Thomas thought, of knowing the enemy too well.

Fowler pushed on the cyclic as they lifted, dragging them forward and up at the same time. He took them low over the clearing and then swooped through a one-eighty, doubling back over the road as he climbed. Then he glanced back at Carmichael. "Whoa, sorry about that, fella."

Thomas turned to look. Carmichael was bent double in his seat, mouth slack, one eye half-closed. There was an open toolbox at his feet.

They were really into it now. It was happening. Thomas felt a second of the same kind of hatred he'd had for Oscar when they were carrying the body. Hatred because they'd both taken him at his word, forced his hand, not given him room to get scared and change his mind.

Something shiny moved by his right leg, between the edge of the seat and the door. It was a crescent wrench. Carmichael was sitting up again, holding his head.

How much longer could he put it off? They were headed north and west, almost directly away from Na Chan. Every minute took them farther in the wrong direction.

He let his right hand drift down until it touched the cool metal of the wrench.

Fowler kept swiveling his head, looking constantly in all directions. Vietnam reflexes, Thomas supposed. He made himself think about Lindsey and Eddie and Chan

Ma'ax. They would die if he didn't get them out of there. That bastard Marsalis . . .

He waited until Fowler's head was turned completely to the left. Now! he thought, and tried to bring the wrench around, but suddenly it weighed a hundred pounds and he couldn't lift it.

I can't do this, he thought. He shut his eyes. If he looked in the back he would see Carmichael, waiting. Carmichael who'd done his part, already taken his risks.

I'm going to count to ten, he thought. It was the way he used to get himself out of bed on cold mornings. One. Two. He opened his eyes.

Three. His right hand came up with the wrench in it. Chrome, gleaming. Four.

Fowler turned, saw the wrench. "What the hell?"

Thomas lunged at him. The wrench bounced feebly off Fowler's headset, knocking the mirrored sunglasses partway off. The helicopter lurched into a sideways dive as Fowler's hands came off the controls. Thomas could barely move, held in by the straps on his seat. He switched the wrench to his left hand and swung again, grabbing the cyclic and pulling it back to neutral with his right. Fowler's glasses hung by one stem now.

Fowler blinked, stunned but not unconscious. Blood trickled out of a cut on his forehead. Thomas got his seatbelts off. He felt like he was drugged or dreaming. Fowler's hand twitched at the flap on his holster. Thomas hit him in the wrist with the wrench.

Before he could pull the gun out himself Carmichael was there. "Watch the controls, for God's sake!" Carmichael shouted. "I've got the gun!"

Thomas spun in his seat. They'd been falling longer than he realized. The tops of the trees were rushing up at them. He dropped the wrench and pulled the collective up with his left hand, adding throttle as he pulled. He forgot to compensate for the extra torque and the nose started to swing around.

"Are you sure you know what you're doing?" Carmichael shouted.

"Shut up!" Thomas shouted back. He should have

taken Oscar up on his offer to fly the Huey out of San Cristóbal. It had been years. The machine seemed cumbersome and underpowered compared to the project's sleek little Robinson. He finally got them leveled off and started looking for a place to set down.

He risked a quick glance at Fowler. Carmichael was holding a .38 revolver against the man's head. Fowler kept blinking. Thomas couldn't stand to look at it. "If you have to shoot," Thomas said, "make sure it doesn't go through the instruments." He said it to convince Fowler how bloodthirsty they were. In fact he doubted if Fowler could even hear him.

They'd been following a dirt road. Thomas picked it up again and spotted a deserted crossroads that was big enough to set down in. He landed the Huey as cautiously as he knew how and still bounced a little on the skids.

"Get him out," he said. The vibration of the levers kept Carmichael from seeing how badly his hands were shaking. He was so pumped up he could hardly stay in the seat.

Carmichael worked the left-hand door open, then crawled around to where he could shove Fowler out with his foot. Fowler tumbled out into the dirt and lay on his side, still blinking.

"I think there's something wrong with him," Carmichael said.

"Shut the door," Thomas said.

Carmichael shut the door and strapped himself in Fowler's seat.

Thomas lifted them off again. "He's alive," he said. "That's all he gets." He looked back to make sure Fowler was still lying in the road and not hanging on the skids. Then he waited until they were another mile or so away before he turned them back toward the southeast. He was not taking any chances.

After a couple of minutes Thomas gave Carmichael a headset and showed him how to work the footswitch for the intercom.

"Where are you going?" Carmichael said.

"Na Chan."

"Listen. I have to get this story turned in. It can't wait."

"And I have to try to get those people out of Na Chan."

"Do you really think they'll let you just come in and take them?"

"I have to try," Thomas said. "And that means I can't risk dropping you off. If somebody spots this helicopter they might decide to just shoot me down." He looked at Carmichael. "I'm sorry. This is life and death."

Carmichael still had the gun in his hand. Thomas looked at the gun and back at Carmichael.

"Just yesterday," Carmichael said, "I was thinking I would kill to get this story filed." He took the bullets out of the gun and threw it in the back. "I guess I was wrong."

FOUR

LINDSEY SPENT THE NIGHT under the ramada again, though she was sure now that Thomas wouldn't be back. He was probably dead. She couldn't manage to feel much of anything.

Ramos started the new regime at dawn. He put everybody to work except Eddie, who was obviously too sick to bother with. Dying, Lindsey thought. It was one more thing she couldn't stand to think about.

She and Oscar and the Lacondones were issued entrenching tools, little shovels with blades that folded down so they could be used like picks. Ramos' first priority was making the ruins defensible, which meant trenches around the perimeters.

By ten o'clock her hands looked like raw steak. She stank and her clothes were covered with mud. Ramos hadn't even let her cut her fingernails and so she'd broken at least half of them, a couple right down to the quick. At first she'd thought the little shovels were cute. Now she hated them with a passion second only to the hatred she felt for Ramos. Her head ached from the constant shocks of the entrenching tool hitting rock.

By noon she couldn't do any more. She crawled out of the hole and sat under a tree and used all the strength she had left to keep from crying. It was just a matter of principle.

There were four others in the trench with her, two boys and two girls, all of them around sixteen. The kid guarding them was maybe twenty, but he had the jeans and khaki shirt of seniority. His name was Rigoberto.

"You can't work no more?" he asked her in English.

"No," she said. She showed him her hands.

"You know where la cocina is? You know, comida and everything?"

"The kitchen," she said. "Yes."

"There is woman name Graciela. Una vieja. You say, is okay you work for her. Okay?"

"Okay," she said. "Thank you." Now she was really close to crying. The pain of getting up kept her from feeling the full impact of his kindness.

The old woman had her take food and water around to the workers. The food was orange slices and fried strips of bananalike plátano. She carried everything in recycled, industrial-sized tin cans. No one seemed to be watching her too closely. She timed it so that when the rain came she was close to Eddie's tent. She made a break for it and crawled inside.

Eddie was gone. She tried at first to tell herself that he was down at the swimming hole or with the Lacondones, but she knew better. He had taken the mushroom again. She sat and listened to the rain. Even if she found him in time, she thought, even if she slapped the damned stuff out of his hands, it wouldn't do any good. Even sex hadn't been able to call him back. He was lost.

That's it, Eddie, she thought. You've done it to me one too many times.

It suddenly came to her that everything she'd ever done had been because of a man. From going on the road with Eddie at seventeen to not being able to keep that kitten last year because she was dating a guy with allergies. From the way she dressed and wore her hair to keeping Budweiser in her refrigerator back in San Diego. To being here in the middle of Nowhere, Mexico, because of Eddie again. It was simple and obvious, but she'd never put it in exactly those terms before. The realization actually made her cheeks hot with shame.

The only thing I ever wanted for myself, she thought, was to have a kid.

And then she thought, be careful what you wish for. Because it could be happening, right now.

It was about an hour after the rain that they heard the helicopter.

She was at the northern edge of the ruins. There was only a single trench there. Everybody expected the attack to come out of the west, where there was level ground, but Ramos wasn't taking any chances. All day there had been this sense of doom and when they heard the helicopter everybody stopped what they were doing and looked at each other and then looked up at the sky.

Lindsey flashed on her ninth birthday, October 24, 1962. It was just two days since the President had told Castro to get rid of his Soviet missiles. Everybody thought there was going to be war. She remembered being at school, out on the red dirt playground, looking up and seeing the biggest plane she'd ever seen. There just weren't that many planes over Athens, Texas in 1962, let alone anything that size. She'd just stood there, too afraid even to run, burning with the injustice of being only nine years old and about to die.

She was no more ready now than she had been when she was nine.

It was just one helicopter, coming in low and slow from the north. My life has prepared me for this, Lindsey thought. From the Cuban missile crisis to the Vietnam War on TV, she had been taught that death came out of the sky and there was nowhere to run to get away.

When she saw the white flag hanging out the window it was almost an anticlimax. It was Thomas, she realized. Who else could it be? He'd come to get her out. She dropped the cans and ran toward the clearing where the helicopter was setting down.

* * *

Ramos and Faustino and another ten or so rebels were already there. All of them but Ramos had their guns pointed at the cabin of the helicopter, waiting for the men inside to come out. Ramos didn't carry a rifle anymore, just the pistol he'd used to shoot Gordo through the head.

Lindsey saw Oscar in the shadow of the ramada. Near him was a middle-aged woman in a striped dress. She had two kids, both of them less than three years old. Each had hold of one of her hands. She watched the helicopter with tired patience and no curiosity.

Thomas got out of the right side of the helicopter. He had both hands up about shoulder-high. He started talking in Spanish. "I have news," is what he said. "I have to see Carla."

Ramos answered him. Lindsey got the gist of it. He said that Carla had stepped down. He now found himself, apparently to his own surprise, thrust into the position of leadership.

Lindsey took a couple of steps toward Thomas. He looked over at her and it was obvious from his face that he knew about her and Eddie. That stopped her, and she kept her distance, waiting on the edge of the growing crowd.

Oscar came over to stand next to her. For a second she was afraid he would do something stupid like put his arm around her. He had gotten used to translating for her, which was in its own way a relationship. One where she was dependent and he had all the cards.

But she had underestimated him. All he wanted to know was if she was okay. She showed him her hands. "Except for these," she said. "You all right?"

"I guess. That soldier, Porter? He died last night. Ramos was trying to make him talk. Tried a little too hard, I guess."

"I'm sorry," Lindsey said. "I never even saw him."

"He was a piece of shit," Oscar said. "That doesn't make me like Ramos any better."

Another man got out of the helicopter. He was very

good-looking, in a soap-opera kind of way. Blond hair over his ears, mustache, hiking shorts and boots that looked childish in the jungle, a gray Mickey Mouse T-shirt that only made it worse. He couldn't have been more than twenty-five.

"*Teniente* Ramos," the man said, with a certain nervousness. "*Cómo va?*"

Teniente, Lindsey thought, meant lieutenant. She wasn't sure how high Ramos had promoted himself, but he obviously didn't like being called by his former rank. He nodded, his head moving maybe a quarter of an inch, and said, "*El estimado Señor* Carmichael."

"Faustino," Carmichael said. He put his hand out and Faustino took it, a little reluctantly, Lindsey thought.

Then Thomas and Ramos got into it. Lindsey heard her own name, and Eddie's, but couldn't make much out of the rest. "Thomas says Marsalis is attacking in a few hours," Oscar said. "Sometime after dark." Lindsey nodded, suddenly lightheaded. "He wants to get us out of here. I get the idea the pretty boy is some kind of journalist. Interviewed Carla a couple weeks ago. Thomas says if we all get out it'll do the revolution more good than keeping us here."

"What's Ramos saying?"

"About what you'd expect. Impossible. Can't be done. He says Thomas should fly the helicopter against Marsalis. Which Thomas says he won't do." Oscar smiled at her without humor. "It's what we used to call in Texas a Mexican standoff."

Ramos turned and looked through the crowd. He stopped when he got to Lindsey. "You," he said in Spanish. "Come here."

"Maybe he's going to make a deal," Lindsey said.

"I fucking doubt it," Oscar said. He followed along behind as the rebels got out of her way. They looked less like soldiers than prisoners on a road gang. A lot of them were stripped to the waist and wore sweaty bandanas around their heads or necks. There were a lot of bad vibes going around. It must have had a little to do with the look on Ramos' face. He looked scared as much as anything, like he was operating on nerve and instinct rather than brains. Meanwhile everybody else was moving away from him, leaving five or six feet of open space between him and Thomas.

She stood in front of Ramos. He made a stirring motion in the air with his index finger. He wanted her to turn around.

She turned around. It was very quiet. She could hear the wind in the leaves across the clearing. Ramos put both hands on her shoulders, pushing her to her knees.

She let it happen. There were men with guns all around. Ramos took his right hand away. His left hand stayed on her shoulder. She heard a snap, then the sound of metal moving against leather. She felt the barrel of his gun against her ear.

Ramos was talking again. She couldn't hear him. There was a noise like running water inside her head. She kept seeing Gordo's face as the bullet hit. She looked at Thomas, waiting for him to explain what Ramos was saying. He wouldn't meet her eyes. She looked at Oscar. When she turned her head it pushed the barrel of the gun into her skin.

"He says," Oscar said, "that . . . that if Thomas doesn't fly the helicopter, he will kill you."

She had never been able to imagine herself dying. If she was dead, whose eyes would she see it through? When she tried to picture it, it turned into a movie. The camera slowly pulling away. But she knew movies weren't real.

If she could have imagined it she might have been more afraid. Instead she was just angry. She was tired of being treated like what she thought and what she felt weren't important. She reached up and put her hand around the barrel of the gun. Her hand was weak and shaking, but that could have been anger as much as fear.

She pushed the gun away.

Ramos was too startled to react. She stood up. "Tell him," she said to Thomas. She was shaking all over, even her shoulders were shaking. "You tell him. Tell him no."

Her voice was high and trembling, like a quiet scream. The tears she'd been holding back all day ran down her face. "If he's going to shoot me he can just go ahead and do it. But he's not using me. I won't be used. You tell him that!" She wanted to slap Thomas across the face to make sure he'd heard her.

"Mande?" Ramos said behind her. *"Qué dice?"*

"Tell him," she said, and walked away. Oscar stood aside for her. She didn't care if Ramos shot her or not. She really didn't. She was not going to be humiliated anymore because of men's games. They could kill her, but she was by God not going to play anymore.

She was halfway to Carla's tent when she realized she wasn't dead.

No one had even followed her. They couldn't, she thought. She'd gone off in a direction perpendicular to their universe. She was giddy with relief. I must have turned invisible, she thought. Simply disappeared from their world.

She went into Carla's tent. She wasn't sure exactly what had brought her there but when she actually saw Carla something came loose inside her. She sat on the edge of the cot and felt blindly for Carla's hand.

She started to laugh and cry, taking turns, no more than a few seconds of each at a time. She was free for the first time in her life. And in a few hours Marsalis would arrive and she would die anyway. Carla shifted on the cot, sitting up, and slowly took Lindsey in her arms. Lindsey put her forehead against Carla's neck and closed her eyes and let herself be comforted.

Finally she sat up, got out her handkerchief and wiped her face and blew her nose. She held on to Carla's right hand with her left.

Carla had changed. It wasn't the amputation that had been killing her, Lindsey realized. It was the pressure of being in command. Now that it was off her she looked rested, stronger. She almost seemed to glow. But then everything was glowing. The air was full of smells and the touch of the earth, even through her shoes and the floor of the tent, felt vibrant and alive.

"Thomas *regressa*," Lindsey said. Her accent was bad and she wasn't sure she'd used the right ending on the verb. She would take it slow and Carla would understand.

"*Está solo?*"

"No," Lindsey said. "*Con journalista.*" Carla shook her head. What was the word? "*Periodista.*"

"Ah," Carla said. "*El chico de* Rolling Stone? *Muy guapo?*"

Lindsey shrugged. She pointed at Carla. "*Y tu,*" she said. "*Estás mejor?*"

Carla nodded. "*Si, me siente mucho mejor. Anoche, me dormí toda la noche.*" She pantomimed sleep with a hand on her cheek and closed eyes. "*La primera vez en . . . muchas semanas.*" The first time in weeks.

Lindsey nodded. The emotional upheaval and the awkward conversation had tired her. She wondered if she should mention Marsalis, the coming attack. Would it do any good? Before she could make up her mind she heard voices outside.

Thomas came in, followed by Ramos and a couple of other rebels. Thomas looked at Lindsey and then looked away again. "We have to talk," he said to Carla in Spanish.

"*Claro,*" Carla said. Lindsey squeezed Carla's hand and went to stand on the other side of the tent. Ramos rattled off a string of Spanish at Carla and she waved at him to be quiet.

Thomas started a complicated explanation. While he talked, Oscar, then Faustino and Carmichael came in as well. Between them there was barely room to move around. Thomas had his back to her, but she could see Carla's face. Lindsey watched her go through five or six emotions, fighting the whole time to keep them from showing.

"What is it?" she asked Oscar. "What's going on?"

"This guy Carmichael, he just found out Venceremos killed Carla's husband." Oscar said it like it wasn't much of a surprise to him, like he'd been more or less expecting it. "Acuario. Maybe you heard of him. He used to run this whole movement. The CIA paid Venceremos to do it, back in December in Mexico City."

"Oh my God." Everything was still very intense. Her brain was going at high speed. "That business with Gordo yesterday. You remember? He said something about Ramos owed him. He said Mexico City."

"Of course," Oscar said. "Of course. That's the way it always works here. The money stays at the top and the shit runs right down to the bottom. The CIA hires Venceremos. Venceremos passes the buck to Ramos. Ramos gets the fat man to pull the trigger."

Even whispered, Ramos heard his name. The look on his face was something Lindsey would take to her grave. It was fear and hatred melted down into a seamless, feral whole. He was counting corpses in his mind.

Oscar took a step toward Carla. Ramos moved his right hand down over his gun. Lindsey was suffocating. There wasn't enough air for all the people in that one dim, musty tent. She couldn't get enough into her lungs to yell. All she could do was choke out the name "Faustino!" and a warning she dimly remembered from the San Diego streets. *"Cuidado!"*

Faustino followed her eyes. Oscar ducked and turned instinctively, his eyes wide. The gun was just coming out of the holster. Lindsey looked at the mouth of the gun that had been against her head just minutes before. How could one hand hold something so enormous?

Faustino got both hands on Ramos' arm, pulling it down. Something exploded. Lindsey had shut her eyes without meaning to. When she opened them she thought she would see blood running down the front of her shirt. Instead there was a hole in the canvas at her feet and three men were dragging Ramos to the ground.

They held Ramos down while Oscar explained about Gordo. Before he finished Faustino had the pistol in his own hand and was holding it to Ramos' temple. He had a handful of Ramos' hair and was pushing the man's face into the tent floor. Lindsey was glad she didn't have to see his eyes.

She sat down on a crate near the door. She felt like she was about to pass out.

Carla wouldn't let them shoot him. She sent them for rope and they tied Ramos up until he couldn't move at all: hands and feet and great loops of rope around his chest and legs. She wouldn't even let them rough him up while they did it. Then she ordered all the rebels out except Faustino.

Faustino stood on the left side of the tent. Thomas and Carmichael were by Carla's cot. Oscar crouched down and translated quietly.

"Faustino wants to know is she going to lead them again. She says maybe. Faustino says no more mystical bullshit. She says no, no more. Thomas says Marsalis is coming in just a few hours, will she let us go. She says no. She wants Thomas to fly the copter, just to observe, to give them positions. Thomas says no."

Thomas turned around. "What about you, Oscar? I won't do it, but you could. If you wanted."

"They been after me for days about this," Oscar said.

"That was different," Thomas said. "Back then there was still some hope of getting out of here."

"Then why don't you do it?"

"It's personal," Thomas said. "That's all."

"So what's she offering?" Oscar said. "If I do this, will they let me go?" There was some more talk in Spanish and then Oscar said, "In other words, maybe. If they decide they don't need me anymore."

"It's the best deal you're going to get," Thomas said. "She's not going to just let us go. Not all of us, anyway. She still thinks she can hide behind us. I tried to tell her but she won't listen. She just won't believe that Marsalis would let anything happen to us."

"Shit," Oscar said. He stood up and took a couple of nervous steps, turning his back to all of them. He put his hands in his pockets and kicked at a seam in the floor. Thomas, apparently, was willing to let the silence just go on. Finally Oscar turned around. "Fuck it, man, if I stay here I'm just gonna get killed anyway. I got a better chance in the air."

He looked at Lindsey, like he wanted her to tell him it was okay. She didn't say anything. It wasn't her decision to make. "Yeah, okay," he said. "If they give me my helicopter back, I'll do it." He looked at Thomas. "That leaves yours in case something happens. In case you get a chance to split."

"That's right," Thomas said. "That means look out for yourself. Don't worry about us."

Carla and Faustino got excited and there was a lot of talking back and forth. Lindsey got a word or two here and there, not enough to understand it all but enough that she didn't feel completely helpless.

Nobody is completely helpless, she thought. This is what I learned today.

Carla got up and leaned on her crutch. Lindsey stood up too. Oscar hugged Thomas and then stopped in front of her. "Maybe I'll see you again," he said.

Lindsey hugged him. "So long, Oscar. Thanks."

"Yeah," Oscar said. "Carmichael? You want to come?"

"You serious?"

"Why not? It's a crapshoot, man, but I'd say your odds were better with me than stuck here in the shooting."

"Hell yes. Put me on the next anything out of here." He came over to shake Lindsey's hand. "Nice meeting you, I guess. Such as it was. You have a lot of guts, lady."

Lindsey nodded and looked at her feet. Carmichael shook Thomas' hand and then left with Oscar and Faustino.

Maybe I should go with them, Lindsey thought. But her feet didn't move and then the moment was past and everything was quiet again. She could hear the whine of the cicadas and, far off, a parrot screaming.

"You okay?" Thomas asked her. There was a flatness to his voice that said he was concerned, but only to a point.

"Yeah," she said. "I'm okay."

"Where's Eddie?" He said it in a way that wasn't quite bitter. Like he was making a real effort not to be.

"Guess," she said.

"The mushrooms."

"You got it."

"Christ, of all the stupid . . ." He left it hanging. "Carla wants us out of the way. She's going to round up the Lacondones and put us in the safest place she can find."

"Safe? What's going to be safe from rockets and helicopters and artillery?"

"Well," Thomas said, "Carla thought maybe the Temple of the Inscriptions."

Lindsey sat just outside the door of the temple, looking down the stone terraces of the pyramid. Thomas was sitting in the doorway behind her. Inside, Chan Ma'ax and the other old men had broken out their last cigars with great formality. The room was full of their sour smoke. Two of Carla's men had brought Eddie from the mushroom grove. Now he lay in the middle of the floor like a corpse, his arms folded over his chest.

Down in the clearing a couple of soldiers dismantled the machine gun from Thomas' helicopter and carried it off at a run. "That's the deal Faustino made with Oscar," Thomas said. "He takes the machine gun and two soldiers with him. Faustino says it's for self-defense. I think everybody knows there's going to be some shooting."

"Are they going to be okay?" Lindsey asked.

"Who the hell knows?"

A few minutes later they heard the engine of Oscar's helicopter crank and start to turn. After another minute or so it rose slowly out of the underbrush. "Yeah!" Thomas whispered, making a fist and holding it chest high. "All right!"

"If they couldn't fix Oscar's they could always take that one," Lindsey said, nodding to the helicopter in the clearing. "Or were you going to change your mind after all?"

"I don't know," Thomas said. She'd expected sarcasm or anger, but instead he was very quiet. "I may have killed somebody today," he said. "Hitting him in the head with a wrench."

"Jesus."

"That's how I got away from Marsalis." He was quiet again for a few seconds. "It was different than you would think. It was clumsy and nasty and scary as hell. But the worst thing was that part of me liked it." He toyed with the laces of his tennis shoes. "Whenever I'm not thinking about anything else I keep seeing that guy's face. So I don't know if I'm really up for any more heroics today."

She didn't notice Chan Zapata standing behind them until he said, "Tomás. My father wants to talk to you."

Lindsey turned around. They were both there in their dirty white robes, Chan Zapata tall and smooth-faced and earnest, Chan Ma'ax withered and vaguely malevolent, like some kind of cosmic bag lady. "My father wants me translate for you. Make sure you understand."

Thomas scooted out of the doorway and Lindsey made room for him next to her. They all sat in a row in the afternoon sunlight. There were only two rebels around that she could see, sitting in the cargo doors of the helicopter, making sure that Thomas didn't just get in it and fly it away again.

"My father says your brother supposed to come back. But he doesn't come back. My father says somebody has to go and get him."

"Go get him?" Thomas said. So far Chan Ma'ax hadn't said anything himself. Lindsey was starting to wonder if this was all some weird plot on Chan Zapata's part. Then Chan Ma'ax held out his hand. In his palm was something brownish and wrinkled, like a piece of marshmallow that had fallen in the dirt.

It looked so harmless. It was hard for Lindsey to imagine that the act of a second or two, of putting that little piece of fungus into her mouth, chewing and swallowing, could change her life beyond hope of rescue. It was like looking down at a pit viper in an open-topped cage.

She could tell that Thomas felt it too, from the look on his face. "First of all," he said, his voice straining, "why should I be able to come back when Eddie can't?"

Chan Ma'ax mumbled something and Chan Zapata

said, "You are strong and Eddie is weak. You hold on very strong to what you think is real. Eddie, he can't do that now."

"I thought it wasn't any good if you took it away from where it grows. From the other mushrooms."

Chan Zapata answered without checking with his father. "This is sacred place again. Made finished again. It has power here."

"This is crazy. How can *me* taking the drug help Eddie? It doesn't make any sense." Lindsey could hear in his voice how badly he wanted to be talked into doing it.

Chan Ma'ax looked at Thomas. "Not crazy," he said in English.

Chan Zapata said, "You know it makes sense. You know what kind of sense it makes. The only thing wrong is *I* should be the one to take it."

"Go ahead," Thomas said. He pushed Chan Ma'ax's open hand toward Chan Zapata. "Be my guest."

"No," Chan Ma'ax said. He closed his fist, brought the hand around until it was in front of Thomas and then opened it again.

"Why not?" Lindsey said. "Chan Zapata, why won't he let you take it?"

"He says there is other plans for me. He says is not for me. He won't tell me any more."

"Thomas?" Lindsey said. "You're not really thinking about doing this, are you? Tell me you're not thinking about it."

"Why not?" Thomas said.

"Because it's poison. Remember saying that? Look what it did to Eddie. Nobody else can fly that helicopter, and you can't fly it if you're tripping. It's our only hope of getting out of here."

Thomas shook his head. "That helicopter's no good to us now. There's no way in hell we could take it without getting shot to pieces. It's not going to happen."

"You don't believe that crap about bringing Eddie back, do you?"

"Who was it giving me shit for not believing in a mechanism I didn't understand? Remember?"

"Even if it wasn't addictive, even if it wasn't going to make you sick or crazy or maybe even kill you, this is just not the time. Eddie needs a doctor."

"The doctors didn't help that kid on the dig twelve years ago," Thomas said. "Maybe this won't help Eddie. But anything is worth a try. I'll be okay. It's true what Chan Zapata said. Eddie's out of it. Mentally and physically. But I'm in good shape. I can handle taking it once. And what if I could see the stuff he was telling me about? Na Chan in its prime."

"Even if you did it would be a *hallucination*. It wouldn't be real. Not like Marsalis is real, not like guns and bullets and bombs are real."

"I can't do anything about the guns and bullets and bombs. What if it is just a hallucination? Just to *believe* you were walking around back then. Do you know how many times I've dreamed about it?"

"That's all it would be. Another dream. Meanwhile this place gets turned into a war zone all around you."

"Maybe . . ." Thomas said, "maybe I don't want to see that."

Chan Ma'ax had just been sitting there all this time, holding out the piece of mushroom. Thomas took it from him and walked away across the broad, flat top of the pyramid. He went right to the edge and stared at the forest.

Lindsey followed him. The closest trees were only a few feet away, on the slope behind the pyramid. She could look straight out into their upper branches. From a distance they looked like stacks of dark green cumulus clouds, but up close they were random, chaotic, shadowy and frightening.

"You're just like Eddie," she said.

"What do you mean?"

"You've got your lab and your computer and your grant money but all you really want is to find the secret of life." The sun was getting very low and a light breeze puffed up out of the north. "Well, guess what? There's no secret. You live and work and you have kids or don't have kids and then you die. That's all."

Thomas shook his head. "No. The work has to mean something. You have to be able to find your place in things, to know that it means something. You have to connect with other people. What about love, for God's sake?"

He was walking on the edge of all the unsaid things they still had between them. This seemed like a really lousy time to bring them up. "What about it?" she said. "For men love is wanting to get laid. For women love is wanting to have somebody's kids. The rest is ego and power games and kidding yourself. That's no secret of life."

Thomas shook his head. "Not a secret like that. Just a feeling. Like when you're really stoned sometimes and everything seems to make sense. That kind of answer. Seeing the pattern. That's what Prigogine's stuff is all about. Order out of chaos. Finding the pattern. That's what's important."

"What does any of that have to do with eating a poisonous mushroom?"

"Everything," Thomas said. He rolled the piece of mushroom between the ends of his fingers. Reddish sunlight glinted off his glasses. He put the mushroom in his mouth and ate it.

"Well," Lindsey said. "I guess that's it, then."

"Lindsey . . ."

"Have a really great trip," she said. She crossed her arms and leaned back against the stone wall of the temple. "Don't forget to send me a postcard."

"Lindsey, please, it's just something I have to do."

"Look, I don't care, all right? I don't want to hear about it."

He stood there a while longer and then he walked past her, back to Chan Ma'ax and the rest of the Indians and his comatose brother.

The temple was a long, narrow rectangle of limestone blocks, taking up most of the top of the pyramid. It was walled off into three rooms. The middle one was in the best shape, with the stone floor cleaned smooth and the roof completely rebuilt. That was where the Lacondones were.

Lindsey sat outside, as far away from them as she could get, her back to the long drop-off and the face of the Snake God below. She watched Thomas and Chan Zapata as they carried Eddie into the empty chamber nearest her. Thomas looked at her once or twice but she turned away and wouldn't meet his eyes. They went back into the middle room.

It was getting dark. The wind blew her hair around and brought her the smell of flowers out of the jungle. She wondered if it always had to be like this, that her feelings could only be this intense under some kind of dire threat.

A few minutes later Thomas and Chan Zapata came out again. Thomas was wearing a Mayan robe and smiling half heartedly, turning his head sideways and blinking like there was something in his eye. They went into the room where Eddie was and only Chan Zapata came out again.

It was completely dark now, quieter than it had been in days. The insects, she realized. She couldn't hear the insects anymore.

She got up, started back toward the safety of the temple. A noise came out of the sky. It sounded like somebody trying to suck up the last bit of milkshake through a straw, only louder. She knew what it was. She'd grown up hearing it on the evening news. Incoming mortar fire. She looked up but she couldn't see anything. The noise faded. She kept waiting for her heart to start beating again. A second later there was a flash over by the ball court and a quiet thump, like somebody flattening an empty beercan. The pyramid shook under her feet.

It had started.

EDDIE STARED AT CHAN
Ma'ax. The old man came from
the end of the cycle, from the time where the city lay in
ruins. The only thing was, he was younger than Eddie
remembered him, by ten or fifteen years. And he didn't
look exactly like the other Chan Ma'ax. He was taller,
with a broader nose. But Eddie recognized him just the
same.

"Your name *is* Eddie, yes?" Chan Ma'ax said. "Chilam
Sotz' said that is what you first called yourself."

"Then you don't know me," Eddie said.

"Not yet," Chan Ma'ax said. "But I will. I will meet
you in the other time."

"I know you," Eddie said. "Your name is Chan Ma'ax.
Isn't it?"

"Yes. This is the body of my ancestor, but right now,
inside, it is me. Chan Ma'ax. Eddie, you must go back
there."

"Back?"

"Back where you came from. Back to the other time."
Eddie shook his head. "Sit down and listen to me," Chan
Ma'ax said. Eddie sat cross-legged on the dirt floor. "You
ate a mushroom. You are having a dream. It is called
hach pixan, the true dream. In the other time you are
asleep right now. Your mind has come here and is walking around in a body from this time. You are dreaming,
but you are seeing true things, you understand?"

"And you're dreaming too," Eddie said.

"Yes, I'm dreaming too. But now you must stop
dreaming and do the work that you have to do."

"I don't know what you mean."

"You have work you must do, back in the other time.
You will know it when you see it."

"Even if I would know it, I don't know how to get
there."

"That's because you are ts'ul, a foreigner. You don't understand time." The old man dropped more knots of copal onto the coals. The incense melted and bubbled and sent out clouds of sour smoke. The straight, thin-walled pots seemed both odd and familiar at the same time.

"Everything is in circles," Chan Ma'ax said. "You see?" He drew three circles in the dust with his fingers. There were two small ones, one above the other, and one larger. He touched the upper small circle and said, "Names." He touched the lower one and said, "Numbers. Thirteen numbers and twenty names. Makes 260 days. Look. One Imix." He made a dot on each of the circles. "That could be the name for a day. Then the next day is 2 Ik." He moved clockwise around the circles and made another dot on each. "Then the next day is 3 Akbal. The names are always in the same order, you see? All the way to 13 Ben, and then you have no more numbers. So you start the numbers over but keep going with the names. So this time through, the numbers go with different names."

"Slow down," Eddie said. "I don't understand."

"Because there are more names than numbers. They keep coming up in different combinations. One Ix, 2 Men, 3 Cib. All the way to 7 Ahau, and then you've used up all the names. So you keep going with the numbers but you start the names again. Eight Imix, 9 Ix, and so on. You understand?"

"I guess. But what does this have to do with finding my way back to the other time?"

"Everything. Pay attention. You have the two little wheels here. These are the ritual days. Then you have the days of the sun. That's the big circle. That's like your calendar. Eighteen months of twenty days each. Then the five unlucky days of Uayeb. Makes 365 days."

"Why do you have both kinds?"

"You put the ritual days together with the days of the sun. That gives you many more kinds of days. That way each kind of day only comes every fifty-two years of the sun. That means if today is 12 Ix 19 Yaxkin, it will be fifty-two years before there is another 12 Ix 19 Yaxkin."

"Why can't you just tell me what year it is *really?* What year is it the way they count years in the other time?"

"That tells you nothing. Every day is different, every day is special. Every day is like a person. You see, you don't even know what day it is." He wiped out the drawings with the side of his hand and smiled. "I know. That's why I'm t'o'ohil. If you are a borracho like Nuxi' or you are ts'ul, you never know what day it is. Soon, in the other time, no one will even know the names of the days."

"Why is that so important?"

"Because if two days have the same name, they are the same. You have to know this to know if a day is going to be good or bad. You have to know which gods to pray to, and when. You have to be able to know where you are when you move between the days."

"Between the days?" Eddie said. "You mean like I did?"

"Yes. If the days have the same name, you can move between them in the hach pixan." Chan Ma'ax touched the skin below his right eye with his right index finger. "It is known."

Eddie rubbed his forehead. The smoke and the weight of the new ideas made his head hurt. Memories of the other time were coming back to him. "What is it you want from me?" he asked. "You were the one who showed me the mushrooms. You wanted me to do this. Why?"

"I can't know this for sure. Because for me, in the other time, I have not met you yet. I haven't shown you the mushrooms. But you are here, so I must show them to you. Isn't this enough reason?"

"No," Eddie said.

"Then I will say this. Some people the mushroom calls. It can bring them from across the world. If it has work for them. Maybe it brought you here to teach you something."

"Look, Chan Ma'ax, this is getting a little hard for me to believe . . ."

"Think about it. What have you learned?"

Eddie looked into the fire. He could remember taking the mushroom before, barely. He remembered pieces of another life. "Not . . . learned, exactly." There was something Chan Ma'ax had said to him once. "More like, I don't know, like saying goodbye. To parts of myself. To things I thought were important."

"Saying goodbye to the parts of you that were Eddie. Making yourself open to the parts of you that are someone else."

Eddie shivered. "Kukulcán," he said.

Chan Ma'ax nodded. "My people call him Akyantho. The god of foreigners. The god with pale skin, like a dead man."

"I'm not a god," Eddie said.

"No," Chan Ma'ax said. "You are *xiw*. You take the place of a god. You must give up yourself."

"What do you mean?" Eddie said. "Are you talking about sacrifice? Are you going to put me on an altar and cut me open?"

"Not like that. Be calm. You must give up the rest of the part of you that is Eddie. You must stop being who you think you are and be who you must be."

Eddie shook his head. "How did I get into this? I'm just an ordinary person. I'm like anybody else. You make it sound like I have this great . . . purpose or something."

"You wanted to know where you belong in the world, no?"

Eddie shrugged.

"The world is all of us. We all have a place. We all have things we must do. The purpose of the world is to move through the cycles and become better. To become new again. You have a part of this that is yours. You come from the time of the *xu'tan*. The end of the world."

"Is this another joke?" Eddie said. "When you say the end of the world, you mean, everybody dies?"

"The end of the cycle. Not the little circles like I drew before, but the great cycle. There were four worlds before this one. This is the fifth. Kukulcán was there when it was made. He gave it movement."

"What's going to happen?"

"Some people will die. The ones who can't change. Like me. Maybe like you too. I don't know you yet. The first world was the world of giants. They were killed by jaguars. The second world had people in it but most of them were killed by a big wind. The ones who lived were turned into monkeys. Then there was a new world with different people in it, and most of them were killed off by a rain of fire. The ones who lived became birds. The people of the fourth world died in a flood. The ones who lived turned into fish."

"And this time? What happens this time?"

"It was born in movement," Chan Ma'ax said. "It will die the same way." He held his hands out, palms down, and rocked them up and down. "The earth itself will move."

"Cabracan," Eddie said.

"Ah," Chan Ma'ax said. "You know the story."

"You told it to me."

Chan Ma'ax nodded. "I will have to remember that. Yes, Cabracan will wake up. He will shake the mountains and his brother Kisin will come and take the dead away. And you will take the living down from the mountains and into the cities. Then you will take the ones who are left into the new world."

"It doesn't sound like me. It's hard for me to picture this."

"Not Eddie. Kukulcán. Listen. To live through the rain of fire you must become a bird and fly away. To live through the flood you have to become like the fish. That is the lesson. To live through the xu'tan, the end of the world, you have to change."

"Change into what?"

"I don't know. Maybe something that never was before. Something that can live in the new world. The new world will want new kinds of things and new kinds of people. Maybe it will be a world with *computadoras* and mahogany too. A world with no *evangelistas* and no *bombas atómicas.* Who can say? In the stories Kukulcán tried to turn people away from war and human sacrifice. In this world he was cast out. Maybe in the new one it will be different."

One of the Haawo' whistled at the door and came in. He knelt in front of Chan Ma'ax and showed him a handful of arrows. "We have four hundred, t'o'ohil."

Chan Ma'ax held one up where Eddie could see it. It wasn't terribly straight and had ragged chicken feathers tied on with string. "They put the ends in the fire to make them hard, you see? I don't let them have arrowheads because the white men would find them back in the other time and go crazy."

Eddie said, "You showed them how to make bows and arrows?"

"Of course. I want them to win, you see?" He handed the arrow back. "Very good. Remember to take your time. Use them wisely."

The Haawo' said, "We are ready, t'o'ohil."

"Kukulcán," Chan Ma'ax said. "You have one more lesson. Go with these men now and do . . . do what seems right to you. Then you must find a way to go back where you came from."

"Come," said the Haawo'. "It's time."

Eddie stopped in the doorway. Chan Ma'ax nodded to him and said, *"Ki'iba' a wilik."* It was the Lacondon goodnight. It meant "be careful what you see."

The night was full of bonfires. There was one in the middle of the packed earth between the huts, and others in the distance, flickering between the trees.

Eddie and the Haawo' warrior walked out of the hut and stopped. The Haawo' held both his hands up in the air and shouted, "Kukulcán!"

There must have been close to one hundred men there, standing in a half-circle on the far side of the fire. They started to echo the name "Kukulcán" over and over, until it sounded like a forest full of birds. Most of them had bows and they held them in the air and shook them.

The man took Eddie to the edge of the fire. He dipped

his fingers in the ashes and carefully painted a raccoon mask around Eddie's eyes. "Now you are Haawo' too," the man said.

He tugged at Eddie's robe and Eddie took it off. Now he was dressed like the others, in just a loincloth. Two and three at a time they began to run off into the forest.

The man offered Eddie a bow and five arrows. The bow looked familiar. Somebody Eddie knew made toy bows like this, with the same feather ornaments and carved designs. He sold them to foreigners and used the money to get drunk. It must have happened, Eddie thought, in the other time. These bows were full-sized and strung with milky-yellow gut.

Eddie shook his head. "No," he said. "Thank you. You keep them."

"Come," the man said. Eddie trotted after him, back toward Na Chan.

The jungle was full of Haawo'. Their running feet made a low, throbbing noise that came from everywhere at once. Somebody started singing and the others joined in. Eddie couldn't understand all the words but it seemed to be about Hunahpu and Xbalanque. And Kukulcán.

Instead of following the hills above the city they circled around to the west. Eventually they broke out of the forest and crossed the packed-dirt streets toward the plaza. The moonlight had washed the reds and yellows from the temples and the torches had burned low.

The city seemed deserted except for two sentries, watching the road from a temple on the west side of the square. Eddie saw them die. Two arrows missed for every one that hit, but three or four hit each of them and it was enough.

A middle-aged man that had been leading them whistled sharply. The Haawo' stopped and formed up into a ragged line that stretched all the way across one side of the plaza. They stuck their arrows into the ground between the paving stones, hundreds at a time. The sound was like a hard rain. Most of them had been carrying their bows over their shoulders and now they took them off and nocked arrows on the strings.

The ruler's army had just realized something was happening. They were struggling to their feet, reaching for spears, trying to run for cover.

They never had a chance. The first volley of arrows was frenzied but effective. At that close range even the crude arrows of the Haawo' were accurate enough. Some of the Haawo' jumped up and down with excitement and joy. There was a lot of shouting. The middle-aged leader yelled at them to take their time, to aim carefully, not to waste their arrows.

The second volley was controlled and twice as deadly. There wasn't even time for the ruler's men to fight back. They died where they lay and they died with their arms cocked back to throw their spears. They died charging blindly into a wall of arrows and, finally, they died running away. They didn't get to throw many spears, and the ones they threw didn't hit anyone. The Haawo' that didn't have bows took the spears and threw them back, adding to the bloodbath.

In ten minutes the square was empty except for the dead and the wounded.

There were a lot of wounded. They lay crying or screaming or staring in horror at their own blood and at the feathered sticks that were growing out of their bodies. The headless arrows didn't penetrate far and it was shock and pain that had brought most of them down. The Haawo' moved through the square, cutting throats with obsidian knives.

"Eddie?"

He turned around. It was the middle-aged leader, smiling and leaning on his bow. He looked almost familiar, the way Chan Ma'ax had.

"The t'o'ohil told me about you," he said. "He says one day I will know you better. In the other time, you know? My name is Nuxi'."

Eddie tried to picture him as an old man. There was a resemblance, of a sort. "You're dreaming this, too," Eddie said.

He waved at the Haawo' around them. "Many of us

are dreaming this. The others come from a time before yours and mine and Chan Ma'ax's. None come from after us. We are the last."

"What about the dead?" Eddie asked. "Are they real? Or are they just dreaming that they're dead?"

Nuxi' laughed and kicked the head of a corpse that lay at his feet. The dead man's throat had been cut and the head rolled in a half-circle, the man's long black hair smearing the pool of blood underneath into curving lines. Eddie could see a ragged clump of yellowish neck muscle, clotted with dust.

"A very hach pixan this one dreams, no?" Nuxi' said. "I would say he is pretty much dead."

The savagery of it made Eddie look away. "If I die here, what happens to me?"

"I guess you'll dream you're dead."

"A real dream? A hach pixan?"

Nuxi' laughed again. "Only a ts'ul would ask that." He pulled his bow over his head and started back toward the forest. "I will see you," he said. "But when I do you won't remember me yet."

Eddie walked aimlessly through the square. He was remembering something called a Vietnam. He didn't know exactly what the word meant, but it brought images of a jungle clearing like this one, littered with the dead and dying and people howling in pain. A Vietnam was something he'd tried to stop once, and now here he was, in the middle of something else that seemed just like it.

Everything in circles, Chan Ma'ax had said. Everything happening over and over again.

But Chan Ma'ax had also said that things had to change. That Eddie had to change. It had to start somewhere. It could start here.

Eddie ran for the Palace.

The ruler's guards lay in pools of blood on the steps. Eddie sprinted past them, wincing at a stitch in his side. He ran through smoky, flickering hallways to the courtyard. There were fires in some of the rooms; they'd put the torch to all of the ruler's wealth that would burn.

Just as Eddie realized he didn't know where he was going, he heard a high-pitched, almost-feminine scream. He followed it through another long hallway and into the ruler's sleeping chamber.

An ornate hammock filled most of the room. There were brightly painted potshards all over the floor, and in the middle of them five Haawo' had the ruler stretched out on his back. Four of them were holding his arms and legs. A fifth was drawing a thin line of blood across the ruler's groin. The ruler was screaming and weeping. The Haawo' with the knife seemed more embarrassed and afraid than anything else.

"Let him go," Eddie said.

The man with the knife stopped, looked up at Eddie.

"Kukulcán," he said. The ruler was still screaming and the man kicked him, almost gently. "Shut up," he said.

"You don't need to kill him," Eddie said. "It's over."

"He has debts," the man said. "Let him pay them."

"Why?" Eddie said. "If what you want is to leave the cities, then go. The cities will die without you. The priests and the nobles won't have anybody to grow food for them or hunt for them or make their clothes. Isn't that enough?"

One of the others said, "Then maybe it's better for them to die now."

"What you have to do," Eddie said, "is make new things." He didn't really have the words to say what he wanted. "Think about new things. Live your own lives. Don't think about the old things anymore. They will take care of themselves." It seemed like a mistake he had made himself, in other places.

"Let him go," the man with the knife said. They did, standing up and away from the ruler. The ruler crawled off into a corner and held his knees against his chest. His eyes were wide and staring but he was obviously not seeing anything.

The man with the knife crossed his arms and bowed to

Eddie. "Kukulcán," he said. He laid the knife at Eddie's feet.

"Tell the others," Eddie said. "Tell them to stop the killing, to go back to the forest. Tell them . . . Kukulcán told you this." They all bowed this time. "Go now," Eddie said.

They left him alone with the ruler. He deserves to die, Eddie thought, if anyone does. He picked up the obsidian knife, just to get the heft of it. I could kill him myself, Eddie thought. But there was no passion in him for the act. Death was easy. It was living that was hard.

He went back out and stood at the top of the Palace steps. His orders were being passed along. He saw the Haawo' putting down their knives. Some of them were high on the adrenaline rush of killing and had to be pulled away from it. Most of them looked relieved to have a reason to stop.

Eddie felt the power in himself. He had changed things. Stopped the sacrifices. Just like Kukulcán.

Maybe he *was* Kukulcán.

There was a little of his old self still lingering. He let it go.

He was Kukulcán. He had been here when this world was made. Chan Ma'ax said he would be there when it ended. He could shape the new world, turn it away from killing.

If he could only find the way to get back to it.

CARMICHAEL HELPED OS-car strip the leaves and branches off his helicopter. Every couple of minutes Oscar would look back toward the camp, waiting for Faustino to show up with the fuel pump. Carmichael didn't try to start any conversations. Now that he had the time, he was having second thoughts.

He'd known Oscar less than an hour. The guy was old enough that he had a potbelly and lines under the eyes, but he was still trying to come off like a macho kid. Carmichael had problems with the whole rock star getup of shoulder-length hair and mirrorshades and five o'clock shadow. In L.A. he would have been dismissed as a real flake. Carmichael tried to give him the benefit of the doubt. Standards were different down here.

That didn't excuse the helicopter. At least the one they'd hijacked from Marsalis had smelled of fresh paint and WD40 inside. Oscar's was peeling and layered with grime. The armor on the seats was so worn that the fibers showed through. The seat belts were brittle and the weatherstripping was cracked and crumbling.

"Pass me that toolbox when I get up, will you?" Oscar said. He climbed on top, right up under the mast that supported the rotors. Carmichael handed him the tools. Oscar had the engine cowling open by the time Faustino got back. He had the fuel pump with him, wrapped in oily rags.

Oscar looked it over and nodded and went to work. It took him about ten minutes to get everything put back together. He crawled down, wiped his hands, and then held one black-smeared hand out to Faustino. "I need the key," he said in Spanish.

"Why?"

"I have to see if it's going to run."

Carmichael watched Faustino think it through. He was trying to decide if Oscar was going to make a break for it. Finally he said, "All right." He could have unslung his rifle, to make the obvious point, but he didn't. Carmichael thought that showed a certain amount of class.

Oscar took the key and sat in the right-hand seat. "Get clear," he shouted, and Faustino and Carmichael backed away. He started flipping switches. After a few seconds he cranked the engine and it caught the first time. He let it run, the rotors slowly picking up speed and the turbine climbing in pitch, and then he switched it off again.

"Okay?" Faustino shouted.

Oscar gave him a thumbs-up, but stayed looking at the instruments for another minute or so. Thinking about his chances, Carmichael figured.

Finally Oscar got out and shut the door. Two young rebels came running up with the M60 machine gun from Marsalis' helicopter. They bolted it to a platform just outside the cargo door while Oscar looked on. He didn't seem happy about it.

"These two compañeros will go with you," Faustino said.

"*Claro,*" Oscar said.

"If you try to escape with the helicopter they'll kill you. They understand that they will die when the helicopter crashes. They're very brave and this doesn't bother them. You understand what I'm saying to you here?"

"Yes," Oscar said.

"Okay," Faustino said. "Good luck." He didn't offer to shake hands. But then, Carmichael thought, Oscar's hands were still very dirty.

Faustino walked away. Carmichael said, "So now there's soldiers coming too."

"Yeah," Oscar said. "That was the deal."

"I guess I didn't quite understand. I had the idea we were just going to call in a couple positions and then get out of here."

"Nothing's that easy."

"So now, even if Carla decides she's through with you, you still have to come back here and drop those guys off."

"Stay here, then," Oscar shrugged. "Maybe you'll be in just the right place when I bring 'em back and you can catch a ride with me then. But if they get shot up or fall out of the aircraft, then brother, I'm out of here."

They looked at each other for a couple of seconds. He's scared too, Carmichael realized. The thought didn't exactly cheer him up. "All right," Carmichael said. "I'm in."

"Let's do it," Oscar said.

* * *

As they came up over the treetops the land unfolded for Carmichael. In the long rays of the setting sun all the colors were rich and intense. The plain to the west was a solid yellow-green, dotted with darker green clumps of trees. The forest itself was the darkest green of all, streaked with shadows and reaching up into the deep blue of the sky. They climbed to the east, over the silver flash of the river, and then turned south. The crater of El Chichón, twenty miles away, was straight ahead.

Carmichael could hear Oscar talking to the rebels. The external channel was turned down to no more than a whisper in Carmichael's headphones. He had one fierce moment of longing to be away from there, headed home and away from danger.

Don't start, he told himself. Don't even think about it.

The left side cargo door, just behind Carmichael, was locked open so the rebels could get to the machine gun. The inside of the helicopter was like a wind tunnel. When Carmichael looked back, the rebels were leaning out the open door like a couple of kids in the back of a pickup truck.

Carmichael's headphones clicked. "I'm going to take us around for a look," Oscar said in English. "There shouldn't be any trouble. Not at first, anyway. In this light they won't be able to tell the difference between us and one of their own. They ain't gonna shoot their own people."

Carmichael found the footswitch for the intercom. "What do you mean 'at first'? When *is* there going to be trouble?"

"When we start shooting, I imagine."

"I thought we were just scouts."

"You see those two kids in the back? They used to be in the guardia. They know how to work an M60. They're not up here just to keep me honest. I thought you understood. The only question is how long they're going to be able to hold themselves back before they start shooting."

"What happens then?"

"We just have to make the best of it, man."

They banked into a long turn toward the west. At first Carmichael tried to lean away as the floor tilted under him. It only seemed to make it worse. He saw Oscar sitting straight up in his seat and made himself do the same.

"What about you?" Carmichael asked him. "Thomas said you used to live in Texas. Doesn't it . . . I mean, don't you feel a little weird about this?"

"Listen, man, I got nothing against you guys, one to one, you know? But don't ask me to feel sorry for those motherfuckers down there. I don't want them here, they got no business here."

They leveled out over the western plain. The forest here had been slashed and burned for farming years before, and when the soil went dead the farmers moved on. It had grown back as grassland. Given another hundred years it would be jungle again.

Na Chan was almost directly behind them as they flew into the sunset. It was hard to see details in the twilight. The first Carmichael saw of Marsalis' army was a flash off to his right, through Oscar's window. Oscar banked them around to the north in time for Carmichael to see fire and smoke erupting from the ruins.

"Mortars," Oscar said. "That's it, then." He radioed something back to Carla. His voice in the phones sounded like he was a long way away. Another mortar opened up within a hundred yards of the first.

Oscar said, "You speak Spanish, right?"

"Yeah."

"Those vaqueros back there don't have no headphones. I need you to go back and tell them not to shoot till I say so. Make them understand. If they start going nuts they'll get us all killed."

"You mean . . . just get up and walk back there?" He pictured himself sliding out the open cargo door.

"That's the idea," Oscar said. "Think you can handle it?"

Carmichael took off his headset and hung it up above him. He unbuckled his harness. Oscar looked over at

him, the last of the sunset glaring off his mirrorshades.
Then he took the glasses off and put them in his pocket.
He winked at Carmichael and looked away again.

The macho, Carmichael decided, was not just a pose.

He stood up, bracing himself on the back of his seat,
and stepped carefully over the pedestal control panel between the seats. He found handholds in the exposed
framework of the ceiling. It was hard to make his fingers
let go so he could move from one to the other.

The sun was no more than a line on the horizon. The
rush of damp night air brought involuntary tears to his
eyes. He leaned over the nearest of the rebels, who was
sitting in one of the green canvas passenger seats, taking
belts of ammunition out of their boxes. The other man
was already facing out, the grips of the machine gun in
his hands.

"You need to wait," he shouted at the nearer man.
"You guys shouldn't shoot yet, okay? Not till Oscar says
it's okay."

"Okay," the man said. He was so thin his hollow chest
seemed to pull his shoulders down into a slump. He wore
a dirty white T-shirt and jeans and running shoes. He
was trying to grow a mustache and not getting very far. He
didn't seem to be paying attention to Carmichael at
all.

"It's very important," Carmichael said. "They don't
know who we are yet, understand? So we have to keep it
like that."

"*Sí,*" the man said. He passed a belt of ammo to the
gunner, who poked and prodded it into the open gate of
the gun with little slaps of his fingers.

"You need to tell *him,* okay?"

Finally the man turned to the gunner and passed the
message along. At least he seemed to. The wind tore most
of his words away. The gunner looked at Carmichael and
then back at the other rebel and nodded.

Carmichael could feel their disdain. He wanted to be
back in his seat but he didn't want the rebels to see him
being afraid. So he stood there, hanging on and looking
out to where the dark blue of the sky met the blackness of

the land. The moon was already up, a little better than half full. There were more flashes from the mortars. He couldn't hear them over the roar of the air from the open door.

Oscar looked over his shoulder and shouted, "Okay back there?"

Carmichael nodded and made his way up to the front. He stood behind the seats, one hand on each. Oscar reached up with his left hand and pulled the headphones down around his neck. "I'm going to take us in over the mortars," he shouted. "Just for a look-see. Tell your boys to pay attention, but no shooting. Next time it'll be for real."

"I don't know the word for mortar," Carmichael said.

"Mortero."

He took the message back to them. Walking was a little easier this time. The gunner had the ammo belt locked into his weapon and was tracking the barrel through figure eights, puffing out his cheeks with sound effects Carmichael couldn't hear. He looked up when Carmichael finished shouting at him.

"No voy a tirar," he said. I'm not going to shoot. He smiled. His face was very round, the eyes close together, his sideburns extending out into his cheeks from the bottoms of his ears.

Carmichael sat down next to the thin one. "What do they call you?" Carmichael asked him.

"El Hambre." The Hunger. The name suited him.

"John," Carmichael said, pointing to himself. "And the man with the gun?"

"He calls himself Cantinflas," El Hambre said, clearly disappointed that anybody would name themselves after a comedian when there was a serious revolution to be fought.

They had circled all the way around and were coming in over the mortar emplacements from the north. Carmichael sat up on the edge of his seat. He saw twenty or so U.S. soldiers lying prone in the high grass. There were two mortars. The rest of them had the bullpup infantry rifles. Carmichael couldn't see if any of the rifles were set up to launch grenades. He tried not to think about what a grenade would do to the inside of the helicopter.

The men were looking up, and a couple of them waved. Carmichael started to wave back and then pulled his arm down. On the next pass the kid with the joke name would be opening up on them with an M60 machine gun.

Carmichael's nerve broke. He got up and started for the front of the ship. He was cold and sweating at the same time and his bladder burned with the need to piss away his fear. "Listen," he said to Oscar.

Oscar had his headset on again and didn't hear him. He looked up and said, "We're turning around. Tell them to get the mortars. The mortars first, understand?"

"I—" Carmichael said. The floor tilted under him and the helicopter came around. He staggered, reset his feet.

"This is it," Oscar said. "Get ready."

Carmichael didn't know what to say. He couldn't think. He walked back to the rear of the helicopter. It seemed to take forever and still it was over too soon. He told Cantinflas to take out the mortars first. El Hambre opened more ammo boxes and laid the belts out flat on the floor. Carmichael stood a couple of feet back from the open doorway, watching with sick dread.

Ten years from now, he thought, what am I going to wish I'd done?

If I'm alive ten years from now, he told himself, I'm not going to care.

They came in lower this time and Cantinflas opened up with the M60. The orange tracers seemed huge in the darkness and the first burst arced into the dirt a hundred yards away from the mortars. Cantinflas let out some kind of war cry and stood up in the doorway, jerking the handles of the gun around and firing again. Carmichael saw bodies twitch like puppets as the bullets tore into them.

He closed his eyes. He remembered lying in the leaves and dirt while the government planes roared overhead, knowing he was going to die. No, he thought. Wrong image. It put him too close to the men on the ground. Think about Marsalis, he told himself. Think about Rich, his CIA pal. Think of the way they squeezed what they wanted out of you and threw you away.

It didn't help. He was starting to shake. It wasn't fear, or at least not fear alone. It was an overwhelming sense of wrongness. He climbed back to the front of the helicopter, hand over hand. The rotors sucked the cordite from the machine gun into the cabin, choking him. He crawled into the left-hand seat and strapped himself in. He put on the headset to help block the sound of the gun.

Oscar's voice came over the intercom. "You all right?"

"Yeah."

There was a new sound now, a smaller sound, a ticking, like gravel hitting a windshield. Suddenly Oscar grabbed the lever next to his left hand, pulling and twisting it in the same motion, and they shot up into the air. Then the nose of the helicopter went down and Carmichael felt a rush of vertigo.

"What was that?" Carmichael asked. "That ticking sound?"

Oscar looked at him like he was an idiot. "As the vets up at Bell used to say . . . we're taking some hits, old buddy."

"Jesus Christ," Carmichael whispered.

"Those little bullets don't look like much," Oscar said, "but they got a hell of a muzzle velocity."

The noise had stopped. Carmichael hoped it was because they were out of range. "Do we go back to the camp now, or what?" he asked.

"Somehow," Oscar said, "I get the feeling your heart isn't in this."

"I'm a feature writer," Carmichael said. "I got no business here."

"You mean you interview rock stars, and shit like that?"

"That was supposed to be the idea."

"You know Linda Ronstadt?"

"Only the big shots get the Linda Ronstadt interviews. That's why I'm down here. This whole story—Carla, Marsalis, the CIA—that's my ticket to the big time. To get to where they'll let me interview somebody like Ronstadt. Or Dylan, or whoever."

"Good luck."

"Yeah. Thanks. Just get me out of this alive, okay? I can handle the rest."

A white-hot flare sizzled into life a few hundred feet away. Carmichael was blinded for a second. When he could see again the jungle looked like a model train layout, the trees pale and spindly, their shadows wobbling as the flare drifted down toward them.

Two more mortars opened up from the north side of the ruins. Ground troops were running across the plain now, heads down, rifles held out in front of them. Something moved in Carmichael's peripheral vision and he turned his head to the left.

There was a helicopter coming up on them fast out of the east.

"Oscar, there's—"

He let his foot off the intercom switch and Oscar's voice cut in, "—see it."

The machine gun opened up in the back. Carmichael's hands tightened on the armrest of his seat. Oscar yanked the controls and suddenly they were in free fall. Carmichael's heart lurched and his stomach tried to crawl out of his mouth. It didn't help when he told himself that Oscar knew what he was doing. It was a cellular panic, beyond his conscious control.

He could see Oscar's feet pumping on the rudder pedals, making the tail of the helicopter wag like a dog's. The turbine howled with a tortured metal sound and a light flashed amber on the pedestal control panel. In his mind Carmichael could see the helicopter shaking itself to pieces, see himself flying through the air, arms over his head, his clothes billowing out around him.

The ground rushed up at them in the harsh light of the flare. Marsalis' soldiers were swarming like insects, seemed to be crawling right out of the earth. Sometimes there was a burst of flame from one of their rifles. Sometimes one of them fell down from invisible enemy fire. There didn't seem to be any pattern to the fighting, just frenzied individuals and random death and dismemberment. Then Oscar swung around and they were climbing again. The M60 rattled steadily behind them.

And then the other helicopter was back.

It came up fast, again from the left. They were going after Cantinflas, Carmichael realized. He could hear the pounding of the other engine, even over the noise of the machine gun and their own machine. His heart seemed to be trying to keep time with it. There were frantic voices in Carmichael's headphones, speaking English, but not loud enough for him to make sense of them.

The other copter had four machine guns, two on each side, operated from a joystick in the cockpit. Carmichael watched the barrels come to life, twitching and spitting tracers. The tracers seemed to sail toward him with impossible slowness. He stomped on the floor switch, yelling Oscar's name into the intercom.

Oscar swung the stick to the right and forward. Carmichael's vision tunneled and he tasted bile at the back of his throat. The cockpit was suddenly suffocating him, despite the buffeting wind. His head throbbed and his chest felt hot and tight. The other helicopter danced and blurred in the frame of his window.

And then, finally, Cantinflas was shooting back.

Carmichael felt like he was reaching out physically with the stream of bullets. Despair washed over him as they missed, as if it was his own body falling uselessly into the void. And then another volley spun out and he felt himself rising up in his seat, whispering "please, please." And then he felt the glowing orange pieces of himself cross the front of the helicopter, felt the release as the enemy windshield exploded under him, felt all-consuming joy as the rotor tilted and the U.S. helicopter dove headlong for the ground.

He fell back into his seat, exhausted, trembling all over. For three or four seconds he had glimpsed a different existence, an existence without questions. The lives of the men in the other helicopter, his countrymen, had not mattered. Truth and justice were irrelevant. Carmichael's life had been on the line and he had won.

He saw then what had always escaped him before: how people could go to war, could physically carry out the act. It was like a different order of consciousness. It had been intense and primal and he knew already that it had changed him. It had been a surrender as intense as sex, as powerful as drugs, and just as much a denial of self. He had become his hatred and he had seen his hatred take effect.

They were back over the ruins now. Oscar waved his left fist in the air and shouted in triumph. In the trenches below, Carmichael saw the muzzle flashes of the rebel FALs, a continuous sparkling, like a line of Christmas tree lights. West of the trenches was no man's land, an empty plain dotted with dead U.S. soldiers. Beyond that was a wave front where Marsalis' attack had stalled.

Marsalis' people were definitely using grenade launchers now. Between the grenades and the mortars, the rebels were taking a pounding. Some of them crawled out of the trenches and scurried back into the cover of the ruins. Carmichael could see the sense of it, the potential hiding places, the possibilities for ambush. Marsalis would have to knock the ruins to the ground to get them out.

But then Marsalis seemed to be willing to do just that.

Carmichael was just turning back in his seat when the second helicopter came out of nowhere.

They never had a chance.

The second helicopter was the Cobra gunship, armed with M60s and rockets and mini-guns. It was impossibly thin and streamlined, like a Huey smashed flat from the sides. Before Carmichael had a chance to be really afraid, it was over.

The Plexiglas windscreen spiderwebed and something thudded into the roof. Oscar jerked back in obvious pain. There was a crunch and the engine died. It sounded like a long, fading scream. A red light on the pedestal flashed and an alarm hooted.

Carmichael looked at Oscar. He was still moving. His right hand was on the stick and he reached out with his left and shoved the lever next to his seat all the way down.

They were gliding smoothly, not plummeting the way Carmichael had thought they would be. "Don't touch anything," Oscar said in the headphones. His voice sounded pinched. "We got autorotation."

Carmichael knew the word. It meant the rotors were turning from the upward pressure of the air as they fell. "Are you okay?" Carmichael asked.

Oscar didn't answer. He was staring down between his feet as the ground came up at them. He pulled back on the stick and the nose of the helicopter came up. At the last moment he jerked up with his left hand. The machine hesitated for a fraction of a second and then skidded to a stop on the grassy plain. Oscar slumped back in his seat and closed his eyes.

Carmichael got out of his harness and crawled over to look at Oscar. There was a dark stain around his collarbone on the left side. His color was bad and he was barely breathing.

Carmichael glanced up to see Cantinflas struggling to get the machine gun loose from its mount. Through the open doorway he saw El Hambre running for the rebel trenches. Suddenly the little man stuck his stomach out like a sprinter stretching for the tape. His arms went up and his knees turned in. There was a line of red circles, darker in the center, from his waist to his right shoulder. He staggered for another couple of steps and fell in the grass, twitching.

The hull was ticking again from Northamerican bullets. Carmichael fought with Oscar's harness. The seat began to move under him and he looked up to see Cantinflas doing something to the frame that held it up. Then the entire seat tilted straight back and Cantinflas pulled Oscar out onto the cabin floor.

"Can you get him?" Cantinflas said.

"*Creo que sí,*" Carmichael said.

"Good. Then I'll get the machine gun."

Carmichael got out of the helicopter. The deck was a few inches higher than his knees. He leaned in and grabbed Oscar by the collar and dragged him to the edge of the door. His legs felt cold where they were exposed below the body of the machine. He danced nervously from one foot to the other.

The Cobra was still circling up above them somewhere. The rebels were shooting at it but the Cobra didn't seem to care. Carmichael expected to be taken out by a rocket at any second.

"Come on, come on," he said. He turned Oscar onto his stomach and kept pulling. It got easier as Oscar's blood began to wet the floor.

Overhead the flare sputtered out and everything went dark. Oscar made a whining noise that faded in and out, like part of it was going too high for human hearing. Carmichael knelt and pulled Oscar into a clumsy fireman's carry, his shoulder jutting into Oscar's stomach.

He sprinted for the trench.

He knew they were shooting at him. He was moving so slowly. He had plenty of time to see El Hambre getting hit and going down, over and over in his mind.

Finally the trench was there. Carmichael jumped in. The extra weight made him hit hard, going to his knees, and Oscar slipped down into his arms. The bottom of the trench was still muddy from the rain that afternoon. Carmichael eased Oscar's dead weight down into the mud.

There was a sharp explosion up in the sky. Carmichael looked up and saw flames coming out of the Cobra. The rebels had hit it with something. "Gotcha, you son of a bitch," Carmichael whispered. The Cobra wheeled off, trailing smoke. He waited for it to blow up, but it didn't happen. That was okay. That made two of their helicopters down, not to mention the one that Thomas had stolen. They only had one left and they'd have to be cautious with it.

Another flare went off. A harsh shadow appeared on the back wall of the trench, moving up and down ever so slightly. That and leftover airsickness made Carmichael think seriously for a while about throwing up. It took him a minute or two to fight it down.

His perceptions were sharp and clear, but his brain

couldn't seem to make anything out of them. The dirt around Carmichael was burned black in a jagged pattern, like a child's drawing of the sun. Grenade, Carmichael thought. The mud under his feet was red with blood. He saw an arm, stiff and shiny as a mannequin's. The stump was blackened gristle, the kind of flaky carbon that came off the bottom of an oven.

He looked in the other direction and saw somebody crawling toward him. The face was painted in shades of blood and dirt, one eye closed and clogged with mud. Carmichael couldn't see if the man's legs were still there or not. He didn't want to know. The man was starting to crawl over Oscar and Carmichael had to push him away.

"*Cálmase,*" Carmichael said. "Be cool, now." He tugged Oscar out from under the crawling man and got him sitting up against one wall. A mortar shell hit a dozen yards away and Carmichael grabbed his knees and ducked. Chunks of dirt and limestone pounded down on him.

Something was burning his hand. He opened his eyes and saw a jagged piece of metal, shaped like a tiny lightning bolt, just lying on the web of his right thumb. Shrapnel, still hot from the explosion. He shook it off and sucked the burn until the first bright pain of it went away.

The crawling man lay with his face in the mud. Carmichael rolled him onto his side, brushing the dirt away from his mouth. He gasped when Carmichael moved him and that seemed to start him breathing again.

I can't take this, Carmichael thought.

He crawled out the back side of the trench, got Oscar under the arms, and dragged him up out of the hole. He smelled burned meat, then a second later realized why. That's all any of us are, he thought. Meat.

He got Oscar over his shoulder and ran for the cover of the forest. Something tripped him up a few feet away from the first of the trees. He went down on all fours, Oscar's head thudding into the dirt. He got up again and kept running. Something was wrong with his right foot. He ran until he couldn't hear bullets hitting around him

anymore. Then he put Oscar down and turned his foot up
to look at it.

A bullet had knocked the heel off his hiking boot. The
foot underneath was tender and probably bruised, but the
skin wasn't even broken. It seemed like a joke. Carmichael was afraid if he started laughing he wouldn't be
able to stop.

There were limestone blocks the size of end tables on
all sides, but nothing big enough to hide behind. He
would have to keep moving. For the moment Carmichael
couldn't seem to get up. The leaves overhead turned the
light of the flare to an aquarium green. It was a peaceful
light and he leaned back against one of the limestone
blocks and got his breath.

The rebels must have pulled back from the trenches.
Only the crawling man and the dead were left there. In
any case Carla was losing. The helicopter Thomas stole
from Marsalis was still in the clearing. With a little luck
it hadn't been hurt. The rebels were in no position to stop
him. They were taking too much of a beating. He and
Thomas could get out of there, with as many of the other
civilians as they could carry.

It was a happy enough thought to get him back on his
feet. Just ahead the path curved around a low hill. On top
of it was a three-foot-high wall, the beginning of a restored temple. The big pyramid, and the helicopter,
would be in that direction. He hoisted Oscar and took
two steps and then saw a gun barrel gleaming in the eerie
green light. He stopped and braced his legs, balancing
Oscar with one arm and holding the other over his head.
"Don't shoot!" he called out in Spanish. "Carla knows
me, okay? Don't for God's sake shoot me now!"

A second later a round face looked over the wall. Cantinflas. He was grinning. "John! Hello, John!" he said in
English. He held up the M60 with one hand and an
ammo belt with the other. Very brave, Faustino had said.
His death would not bother him.

Carmichael didn't know whether to feel sorry for him
or not. He put his hands down and started moving again.

He fell into a shambling trot, limping on his bruised right foot. The mortar shells were really coming down now. The path curved back in the opposite direction and Carmichael came out of the trees into the central square. There was a long, low temple in front of him with some kind of tower coming out of the middle. Beyond it was the helicopter and the big pyramid.

He ran for the shelter of the temple. It was farther than it had looked. His foot hurt and his lungs wouldn't inflate. Oscar weighed a thousand pounds. He made the last few yards on sheer willpower. He leaned Oscar against the wall of the temple and lay face down in the dirt.

The ground shook from mortar shells. The gunfire built up to climaxes that ended with mortar explosions, a rhythm like ocean waves crashing on the rocks. Carmichael wanted, unbelievably, to go to sleep, right there in the middle of the noise and smoke and death.

He stared across the clearing. He could see the two Mayan huts at the base of the pyramid. One of them was burning. The ground between Carmichael and the pyramid was cratered, smoky, desolate as the moon. There were rebel tents on all sides of him that were collapsed or shredded or burnt.

There was somebody moving in the undamaged Mayan hut. Thomas, he hoped. He waved one hand, but the only answer he got was another mortar shell. He crawled over to the temple wall and lay there as they fell, over and over. It was relentless, spiteful, crazed. They were blasting the city into gravel.

He tried to count the seconds between explosions. He couldn't concentrate enough to manage it. They were going off every time he breathed and for a few panicked instants it seemed like the two things were connected. He tried to hold his breath. There was no air in his lungs for him to hold.

When it finally stopped it took him a long time to realize it. He'd pulled back into a part of himself that touched the outside world as little as possible.

His eyes were open. There was a tree in front of him,

and his back was against the temple wall. His right leg made a small whispering noise as it moved in the dirt, kicking out in a slow, unconscious reflex. There was no other sound. No mortars, no gunfire, no insects, no helicopters.

He stood up. He had to grab for the tree as his legs tried to fold under him. No good, he told them. He staggered over to Oscar and felt the man's neck for a pulse.

There wasn't one.

"No," he said.

He tried the wrist, held his palm against Oscar's nose to feel the air move as he breathed. Nothing.

He ripped Oscar's shirt off. A dark purple bruise covered his stomach and chest. Internal bleeding. No doubt made worse by being slung over Carmichael's back.

"Goddammit!" Carmichael shouted. "It's not fair!" He'd nearly killed himself to save the son of a bitch's life and now the son of a bitch was dead anyway. What was the fucking point?

He slapped Oscar across the face. "Goddamn you!" he screamed. He swung again and missed and fell on his knees in the dirt. "Goddamn you!" he said. "Goddamn you!"

And then there was a new noise. Voices. Not a human sound, but human voices making it. The voices of Marsalis' soldiers, making their final charge. It was high and hollow, a hundred wolf howls, the notes beating against each other like reverberating feedback.

It was the most terrifying thing Carmichael had ever heard. It sounded like a single mythic monster, screaming for his blood. He backed away from Oscar's body, still on his knees, and slowly turned around. He heard Cantinflas' machine gun start up. Against the howling voices it was a thin and hopeless sound.

He could hear their footsteps now. They literally shook the earth. The pounding seemed to come from all around him, shaking dirt and rocks loose from the temple and bringing them down around Carmichael's head and shoulders.

And then he realized. It wasn't just the soldiers.

The tree in front of him split in half with a sound like thunder, showering him with splinters. The ground humped up in front of him and knocked him over. He got up again and started running toward the pyramid, toward the helicopter, knowing he was too late.

Not just the soldiers. The earth itself. The earth itself was rising up against them.

THOMAS WALKED through the burning city. His brain felt hard and glittering, like some kind of gemstone. There was too much to take in but he tried to absorb what he could. There had been some kind of battle and now it was over. There were bodies in the central courtyard, flames rising up out of the Palace and the Temple of the Inscriptions.

Eddie was standing on the steps of the Palace.

It didn't look quite like Eddie; his skin was redder, his nose longer and his forehead flatter. But Thomas knew it was Eddie just the same.

He climbed the steps toward him. "Eddie?" he said. "Eddie, is that you?"

"Kukulcán," Eddie said. "My name is Kukulcán." He was speaking Mayan with an accent Thomas had never heard before.

"Eddie," Thomas said. "You're freaking, man. Come on, snap out of it." He stopped on the step below Eddie's and reached out one hand. Eddie grabbed his wrist and pushed him back.

"Go away," Eddie said.

"What's this shit around your eyes?" Thomas said. It looked like he'd been rubbing ashes on his face or something. "And speak English, for Christ's sake."

"English," Eddie said.

"Attaboy. Me Thomas, you Eddie, okay?"

"Thomas?"

"Your brother."

"Yes," Eddie said, in halting English. "I think I know you. What are you doing here?"

"Same as you. Chan Ma'ax gave me a piece of mushroom, told me to come and get you."

"Get me?" Eddie said.

Thomas was feeling a little nervous. The night was oddly bright from the flames and the flickering made everything look like it was just a projection and not solid at all. He turned around and looked at the dead men on the steps.

"It's happening right now, isn't it?" he said. "The collapse. Right in front of me. I'm actually standing here, watching the collapse of Classic Mayan civilization."

"It was the kids that did it," Eddie said. "They got tired of war. Tired of priests and nobles getting rich while the peasants starved and died for them."

"Like the sixties," Thomas said. "Kids against the world." He picked up an arrow from the steps. "Amazing," he said. "I always wondered if they could have had these."

"Chan Ma'ax gave them to the Haawo'. To the rebels."

"Chan Ma'ax?" Thomas said. "He's here?" He shook his head. "Of course he's here. He's been taking the mushroom for years."

"He's bringing on xu'tan. The end of the world. It starts here. It ends in three *baktuns*. In twelve hundred years."

Thomas looked him over and shook his head. "Eddie, you're in bad shape. We need to get you out of here."

"I don't know how. Chan Ma'ax wants me to go back, too. But I can't."

"How did you do it before?"

"I don't know. It just happened."

Thomas blinked, and then brought his hands up to his face. "It's funny," he said. "I just realized. This body I'm in . . . I don't need glasses. It's the first time I've been able to see clearly in twenty years." His face felt different, longer, narrower.

He climbed to the top of the steps and touched the stucco relief panel on the front wall of the Palace. The stonework was sharp and precise, but the paint had already started to fade. "Wouldn't you know it," he said. "I get to really see again and it's the end of the world. Christ, to have been here a hundred years ago, before the fighting and the burning. Can we go inside?"

"The ruler's soldiers may still be hiding in there. I don't know if it's safe."

"Yeah," Thomas said. "I guess not. This is just so fucking amazing. It's classic Prigogine. The society got too far from equilibrium and bang, now there's a new order. Makes you wonder what would have happened if we hadn't all gotten sidetracked in the seventies. If we'd kept pushing, really changed the world."

"It's not too late," Eddie said.

"Are you kidding? Ronald Reagan is President. They're trying to get evolution out of the textbooks and women back in the home, barefoot and pregnant. You can't even buy *Rolling Stone* in North Carolina anymore. They're starving black people and polluting the air and water. They're running up the national debt to build more missiles and start wars in Central America."

Eddie shook his head. He didn't seem to recognize much of what Thomas was saying. "All those old ideas," Eddie said. "They don't have much time left. People hold on to them because they're afraid. But the ideas are dying just the same. You have to . . . you have to make sure you're in the right place when they go."

"Come on," Thomas said. "You look like you're about to pass out. I'm getting you out of here."

Beyond the Temple of the Inscriptions was a set of steps, leading up the hillside. The trees had been cut back to make a wide, smooth path. There were smaller temples on either side, just big enough for a single priest to sit inside and burn copal.

Thomas stopped to look at them. "So now I know what happened to the Mayans. And I can't prove a word of it."

"What does it matter?" Eddie said. "As long as you know?"

"Yeah," Thomas said. "Easy for you to say. You've never tried to get tenure."

The path narrowed. The light of the city was gone now and the moon was almost on the horizon. There was a short flight of steps up and then a longer one down, ending in a narrow ravine. There were stone benches and pots of water and incense at the near end.

"No, Thomas," Eddie said, staring at the rows of red-capped mushrooms. "It won't work. You're crazy."

It had just been an impulse, but there was a certain logic to it. Thomas went over to the mushrooms and broke off two pieces. He took them over to where Eddie sat on a carved bench. "Eat this," he said.

"If this is a dream," Eddie said, "then this is only going to make us have a dream inside a dream."

"Cut the mystical shit and eat the goddamned mushroom," Thomas said. "Or I'll hit you in the face."

Eddie ate. Thomas ate his own piece and sat down next to Eddie. "I can't believe you'd call *me* crazy," Thomas said. "You're the craziest son of a bitch I've ever known. Sometimes I can't believe you're my brother."

"You came to get me," Eddie said. "That's really an amazing thing for you to do. I didn't think . . . I didn't think you'd do something like that for me."

"Yeah, well," Thomas said. "I'm here, aren't I?"

"It's like I don't even know you anymore. We never . . . never even really got a chance to talk. I don't know who you are now, what you've been doing."

"I've been in Cuernavaca the last two years," Thomas told him. "There was this project there doing all kinds of appropriate technologies. All ecologically sound, you know, solar cells, efficient sail power, all that kind of stuff."

Eddie nodded. "That's good, Thomas. That's really good."

"It was starting to be. What really sucks is, I had finally made up my mind to stick it out there. You know, really committed to something. For like the first time in my entire life. And then the revolution came along and took it away."

"It's a good thing to do," Eddie said. "Whether you do it there or someplace else."

"I guess so," Thomas said. "With what I know now I could go back to Austin, where I know they've got money for it. Set one up there, maybe take it overseas if the world ever settles down."

"Sure," Eddie said.

Thomas felt a sudden surge of warmth. He put one arm around Eddie's neck. "You're going to be okay," he said.

"I don't know," Eddie said. "I feel really strange. I can't tell you how strange I feel."

"Can you remember anything?" Thomas asked. "Do you remember the ruins? Carla? Oscar?" He waited a second and then said, "Lindsey?"

The last name made Eddie flinch. "Those are Eddie's memories."

"I got news," Thomas said. "You're Eddie."

"Kukulcán," Eddie said. "I am Kukulcán."

Thomas gave up. A few seconds later he noticed he wasn't seeing solid objects anymore, just dots of light. "Let's walk," he said.

Thomas sat up, blinking. His vision was blurred again. He walked across the stone room and got his glasses out of his clothes.

He remembered coming out of the forest with Eddie, the trees sparkling and dancing like they were under a strobe light, flickering too fast for the eye to follow. They had climbed the pyramid and gone back into the stone room where, for a second, Thomas had been afraid they would find their bodies still lying there, tripped out on the mushroom. But the room had been empty.

He remembered sitting down to catch his breath. Eddie had put a robe on over his loincloth and stretched out next to him. Now Thomas didn't know if it had really happened or if he'd dreamed it.

He was still in his Mayan robe. He didn't remember

putting it on, but he must have. There were his clothes, piled neatly in the corner. He got dressed. Eddie had fallen asleep again.

Or, Thomas thought, it never really happened. And he's still in his coma.

He knelt next to Eddie and touched his shoulder. Eddie opened his eyes. "Thomas," Eddie said.

"Yeah," Thomas said. "Listen, do you remember what just happened? Me coming to get you and everything?"

"Happened?" Eddie said. He was in a bad way. He looked like the Wild Man of Borneo. The war had started outside and that wasn't helping. Eddie winced painfully at every sound. Thomas didn't feel that bad himself. A little hollow and shaky, like he'd been up all night, but he was so charged with energy that it hardly mattered.

"Do you know what I'm talking about?" Thomas said. "Can you even understand what I'm saying to you?" Eddie just shook his head.

Thomas grabbed him under one arm and led him outside. The helicopter was still there, at least, and looked okay. Most of the shells had been hitting north and east, toward the Palace, though one had caught the ramada where he and Lindsey had slept. It had collapsed and the damp thatch was smoldering. There were lights in the godhouse next to it and Thomas heard the squawk of a radio. It could have been Oscar's voice; Thomas wasn't sure.

It did him good to see Lindsey's face when he walked in with Eddie. She was sitting in a corner with Chan Zapata and she looked up and saw them standing in the doorway. Her mouth came open and she couldn't finish what she'd been about to say.

"Hi," Thomas said. He had his arm around Eddie's waist. Eddie was conscious, but very weak. He stared at Chan Ma'ax and Chan Ma'ax looked back and nodded. The rest of the Mayans, Nuxi' and Ma'ax García and the rest, didn't seem to care. They all sat against the walls with their knees up and stared into empty space.

"My God," Lindsey said. "I saw you take it. I saw you put it in your mouth and chew it up and swallow it."

"I took it," Thomas said.

"Didn't it . . . didn't it do anything?"

"It did everything," Thomas said. "It was like Eddie said. I saw Na Chan at the end of the Classic period. It was as real as . . . anything. I found Eddie, like Chan Ma'ax told me to. I brought him back." He glanced away. "I don't know. That's what it felt like. But Eddie's too far gone to tell me if it happened for him the same as it did for me."

Lindsey stood up. She would go to Eddie first, Thomas thought. But instead she came up close to him and stood there with her arms crossed. "You seem different somehow," she said.

"It's not exactly normal around here." Her hair was stiff and clumped together, and there were bruise-colored crescents under her eyes. She smelled like sweat and smoke. There were streaks of dirt on her neck. Thomas wanted to put his arms around her and hold her as close as he could. He brought up the image of her and Eddie together, by the river, Lindsey's head thrashing from side to side. It helped him keep his distance.

"And Eddie's back," she said. "I can't believe it."

"Don't," Thomas said. "He's completely batshit. But he's able to walk around. That alone seems pretty miraculous. Maybe he'll get better."

"But you don't think he will."

"No."

"Why didn't it hurt you?"

"I don't know. Maybe Eddie and I have got some enzyme that protects us, and I've got more of it than he does. Maybe it's some great mystical thing, like Chan Ma'ax was saying. But then it doesn't really make any difference. Have you looked outside lately?"

Lindsey shuddered. "Yes."

"I mean at the helicopter. There's nobody left to guard it. You and me and Eddie could try to get out of here."

"Are you up to it? I mean, after taking the mushroom and everything?" She touched his cheek with the ends of her fingers. "Do you think you could fly it?"

He pushed her hand away. "I'm fine," he said, knowing he was overreacting. She'd just touched him, that was all. She hadn't meant anything by it. "I'm taking Eddie down there and I'm going to see what I can do. Once you hear the rotors start turning, you've got a couple of minutes to make up your mind. If I can get it to that point, where the machine's actually started up, then I'm leaving. You can either stay here or come with us. Whatever you want."

He could see the words hurting her. He told himself he didn't care. "No," she said. "I want to come."

Eddie hadn't been paying any attention to the conversation. Now he worked himself free from Thomas' arm and went to crouch by Chan Zapata. Thomas followed along, in case he decided to pass out.

"—the reason your father didn't want you to come here," Eddie was saying in Mayan. "He was trying to save you. He didn't want you to become xiw. You know what that is? That's what happened to me. It changes you too much. Once you start, you're no good for anything else."

"Better that than to be nothing," Chan Zapata said.

"You are more than you think. You will be the next t'o'ohil. The last one. It's very important. The new world will have to remember what went on before. You have to remember for them. You understand?"

"C'mon, Eddie," Thomas said. "Chan Zapata, I'm going to try to get us out of here. Round up everybody who wants to try it with me. When you hear the helicopter start up, bring them down. Okay?"

Chan Zapata looked at his father. "I don't know if they will come."

"Yeah," Thomas said. "I kind of figured it would be like that. Do what you can."

He grabbed Eddie and steered him toward the door.

He stashed Eddie in the shadows at the bottom of the pyramid and sprinted for the helicopter. The Northamericans had put up a flare, lighting the place up like a stage. He crawled in the copilot door and bent low over the seat. The flare sputtered out and the world went dark. He reached over to the right side of the pedestal and felt along the edge.

The key was gone.

"Shit," Thomas whispered. If Ramos had it, he'd never get it back. He didn't even know where they'd taken Ramos off to.

He crawled back out of the helicopter and inched around to where he could see into the godhouse. Faustino sat at the radio. He had his cap off and he kept running his hands through what little hair he had left. Carla sat a few feet away. She had her crutch by her left hand and a rifle by her right. She looked like she'd been crying.

The rest of the noncombatants were huddled in the godhouse with them. There were two middle-aged women and a dozen children under the age of eight or nine. The older ones, Thomas assumed, were out fighting somewhere, or running messages. Or dead.

The women and kids were bandaging the wounded that had already straggled back from the lines. They had three soldiers laid out on mats. One of them must have been burned in an explosion; his entire face and the left side of his body were purple. Another one kept trying to sit up and watch while they worked on a hole in his stomach. He was making high groaning noises that turned up at the end, like questions. One of the women kept pulling him down by the shoulders.

Two of the camp's mongrel dogs paced back and forth around the perimeter of the open hut, whining at every new explosion or rattle of gunfire. One of them stopped and looked toward the helicopter and barked.

What the hell, Thomas thought. He stepped out into the open. Then he saw that the dog was actually barking at Eddie, who'd wandered over from the pyramid. Eddie took something down that had been hanging from the rafters of the hut. It was a bird, Thomas realized, a quetzal. Eddie began stripping off handfuls of electric green feathers. The dogs crowded him, jumping up to try to get at the bird.

Thomas came up behind him. "Eddie?" he said. "What

do you think you're doing?" When Eddie didn't answer he tried again. "Eddie?"

Eddie turned around slowly. He had the eyes of a stranger. "Kukulcán," he said.

"Don't start that shit with me again. I need you with enough brain cells to help me get out of here."

Carla watched them without much interest. Thomas moved a little closer to her. He could tell from the smell of it that the man with the stomach wound was in real trouble. "What's happening out there?" he asked Carla in Spanish.

Another artillery shell hit, not far from them. Thomas jerked his head around instinctively to make sure the helicopter was still all right.

"You can see for yourself," Carla said.

"There was never a chance," Faustino said. "They are abandoning the trenches, falling back into the ruins. We can hold out here for a few hours, hiding in the old buildings."

"You should be glad," Carla said, "that I got them fixed up." She seemed to be making a joke, but Faustino was not amused.

"Why don't you let us go?" Thomas said. "We're no good to you anymore. We were never any good to you."

"It's not you anymore," Faustino said. "It's the helicopter. With the helicopter you could save the lives of our soldiers."

"No, I couldn't," Thomas said. "I could put off their dying for a little while. That's all. And in the meantime Lindsey and the others would die also. For no reason."

"He's right," Carla said. "Give him the key, Faustino. It's over. They don't need to die with us."

Faustino took the ignition key for the helicopter out of his pocket. It was about the size of a padlock key. He looked at it for a few seconds and then tossed it in the dirt at Thomas' feet.

"Please forgive the poor manners of my friend Faustino," Carla said gently. "I'm afraid none of us is having a very good day."

Thomas picked up the key. He felt, for the first time in days, a tingle of hope. He might actually live through this.

Faustino would not look at him. There was nothing Thomas could do, nothing he could say. This was not his fight. He had the privilege of simply walking out. Or he could piss his life away, and Lindsey's and Eddie's and Chan Zapata's too, in a completely meaningless gesture that no one would ever know about. It wasn't much of a choice.

He turned around to go start the helicopter. Chan Ma'ax and Eddie stood in his way. Eddie had worked the quetzal feathers into his robe and tied a string of them around his head. If he'd been self-conscious at all he would have seemed ridiculous, with his clumsy short haircut and skeletal face and outsized robe. But he didn't even seem aware of how he looked.

Out in the darkness the dogs were savaging what was left of the bird. "Let's go," Thomas said.

Eddie ignored him. He was staring at Carla. "Call your people here," he said in halting Spanish. Eddie's Spanish was now full of strange consonants and glottal stops. Like Chan Ma'ax's.

"Please," Faustino said. "Take your crazy brother and go."

"You have to stop the shooting," Eddie said. He ignored Faustino and sat on his heels in front of Carla. "You can't fight them with the same kind of weapons they use. You have to fight them with your ideas."

"Without guns," Carla said, "the ideas have no force."

"No," Eddie said. "With guns, all ideas are the same."

"If we die for the revolution," Faustino said, "we die as heroes. This gringo madman would have us all die as cowards. Carla, listen to me. This mysticism is your great weakness. It's no shame to be afraid to die. But you can't let it rule you."

Carla wasn't paying attention to Faustino either. She was looking at Eddie. "What are you saying?" she asked him. "What is it you want me to do?"

"Throw away your weapons," Eddie said. "Go to the enemy and take his weapons away from him."

"If they have guns and we don't," Carla said, explaining it slowly, like she was talking to a child, "they will shoot us. We will all die."

"Some of the enemy soldiers won't want to shoot," Eddie said. "It's hard to make yourself want to kill somebody when you can see that they don't have any weapons. Some of them will do it anyway. Some of you will die. But your victory will be greater."

Chan Ma'ax had been standing there all this time, staring at the ground. Now he leaned toward Eddie and said something that Thomas couldn't make out.

"What did he say?" Carla asked.

"He said, 'You will have help,'" Eddie said. "He means the earth. The earth will help you."

"I still don't understand you."

"When you go against the gods, it is like trying to swim upstream in a strong river. When you go with the gods, everything is easy. The gods means the earth." His hands outlined a sphere in the air. "Everything together."

"Nature," Thomas said.

"Yes, nay-chur. My brother Thomas understands. That's what he's doing now, trying to learn how to go with the gods. Your weapons won't help you. They only make you sink under the water."

"Carla?" Faustino said. Thomas looked around. Ten or fifteen rebel soldiers crouched in the darkness outside the hut. Thomas saw Righteous there, in his knit Rasta cap, and the small, fierce woman they called La Pequeña. Some of them were bleeding. All of them were blackened by dirt and smoke and gunpowder, their eyes supernaturally white in contrast.

Eddie saw them too. "Will you call the others?" he said.

Carla stared at Eddie. Thomas knew she was searching for some reason to go against her better judgment and believe him. Finally she looked away. "No," she said.

Eddie nodded. He walked past Chan Ma'ax and toward the soldiers. Thomas suddenly noticed how quiet it was. The shelling had stopped. The Palace was little more than smoking rubble, and there were bodies strewn around the clearing. But it was over, at least for now, and the helicopter was still intact.

Then he heard the war-cry of Marsalis' army. It made him want to crawl away somewhere and shake with fear. Carla and Faustino were looking at each other with no hope left in their faces. Eddie didn't even seem to have heard. He's completely out of it, Thomas thought. He's just going to wander off. He didn't even say goodbye.

And then he saw what Eddie was doing. Eddie went up to one of the soldiers and gently took the rifle out of the woman's hands. He took hold of it by the barrel and brought it up over his head, like he was going to throw it away or smash it against the ground.

"I told you no!" Faustino said. The eerie howling of Marsalis' men was clearly pushing him over the edge. Thomas felt about the same. Faustino scrambled to his feet, shouting, "Give her back the gun! Give it back or I swear I'll shoot you down!"

Faustino was already reaching for his rifle. Thomas didn't take time to think. He threw a body block and he and Faustino hit the dirt together, sliding across the godhouse floor. Thomas came out on top, straddling Faustino's chest, pinning the man's shoulders with his knees. "Leave him alone," Thomas said. "He can't hurt you. He's just crazy, that's all."

He looked up. Lindsey and Chan Zapata stood at the bottom of the pyramid. Lindsey had her suitcase with her. She was staring at Eddie, but he was oblivious.

"Get in the helicopter!" Thomas shouted at them. "Get Eddie and get in—"

The ground bucked underneath him. He looked up in time to see the poles of the godhouse going in four separate directions. Then he was buried in rotting palm fronds.

* * *

Thomas' nose filled with moldy dust. He sneezed and fought his way clear. The ground tilted and buckled and shook. Below the pounding and cracking of the earth he could hear the massive stone blocks of the Temple of the Inscriptions shifting against each other, a horrible, ominous, grating sound.

And then, just for an instant, everything hung suspended. He saw Chan Ma'ax standing at the edge of the forest. The other Lacondones were moving into the trees, almost out of sight. Chan Ma'ax was staring at Thomas, his expression completely neutral. Thomas tried to find a message there and failed. Then the old man turned his back and followed the others into the forest and they were gone.

The ground under Thomas fell away. One of the support poles from the godhouse jabbed him in the side as he hit. He rolled clear of the leaves and broken branches and got up on his hands and knees.

Eddie was still standing. He moved through the soldiers, helping them up, gently taking their guns away. He carried the guns over and threw them in a pile in one of the shell craters. The rebels were all too stunned to argue with him.

Chan Zapata helped Lindsey get up. She was in good enough shape to brush at her clothes and hair. Carla and Faustino had dug themselves out of the collapsed godhouse and were helping the ones who were still buried.

The noise from Marsalis' soldiers had stopped.

Thomas made it all the way up onto his feet. Lindsey and Chan Zapata ran over to him. "We didn't hear the helicopter," Lindsey said. "We got worried."

"The others?" Thomas asked, no longer sure if he'd really seen them there in the jungle or not.

Chan Zapata looked around. "They were with us when we came down. I don't know where they went. It doesn't matter, anyway. They won't come. Nuxi' said they will find their own way." He shook his head. "I will be t'o'ohil with no clan."

"I can't make them come with us," Thomas said. "I don't know if I can get us out in the helicopter or not."

"I know," Chan Zapata said. "I think maybe we should save ourselves."

Thomas glanced to his right. "Oh shit," he said. Eddie had a hundred-yard head start, leading his ragged column of soldiers back toward the front. Thomas ran after him, with Lindsey right behind.

There were bodies all around. Most of them were rebels who'd crawled back from the trenches to die. Some were wives and kids and parents who hadn't gotten away from the shelling. Thomas made himself look away.

"Eddie!" he shouted. Eddie ignored him until Thomas grabbed him by the shoulders and turned him around. "We have to get to the helicopter!" he shouted. "We can't wait around here anymore!"

"You go," Eddie said in English. The rebels had stopped where they were. They all watched Eddie, waiting for him to give them another signal.

"Stop acting like an idiot," Thomas said. "We didn't come all this way to leave you here to die."

"We're all going to die, sooner or later."

"You're crazy. You couldn't cross the street by yourself, you're so fucked up."

"Listen to him," Lindsey said. "Come with us. Let us help you."

Eddie touched Lindsey's hair. "I think maybe I am crazy," he said. For a second he almost seemed like the old Eddie. His eyes were more alert than they had been in days. "Maybe I'm even going to die tonight. But that's my right. I've got the right to live this out the way it looks to me."

"We can get you doctors," Lindsey said. "There has to be something they can do."

"You know there isn't," Eddie said. "Tell her, Thomas. It's a waste of time. I'm not going to let you take me. I'll fight you. It could take a long time to get me on that helicopter. And you don't have the time to waste." Suddenly he put his arms around Thomas, one hand on the back of Thomas' neck. "You take care of yourself," he said. Then he stepped around Thomas and walked away. The rebels closed in behind him.

"Thomas?" Lindsey said. "Do something!"

Thomas didn't answer her. It had begun to snow.

The snowflakes were tiny and granular and warm to the touch. Thomas held out his hand. Within a couple of seconds the palm had turned gray. Thomas looked at the sky. There weren't any clouds, but the stars were dimmer than they should have been. They were winking on and off. The air stank of sulfur, reminding him of the chemistry labs at UT. His eyes burned and the back of his throat felt so dry it was hard to breathe.

El Chichón. He turned toward the volcano and saw lights flashing all around the crater. Thick clouds of ash boiled straight up into the sky. A stream of glowing brown lava inched its way down the mountainside. Thomas pointed wordlessly and Lindsey followed his finger.

"Oh my God," she said.

"Run," Thomas said. He could see the top of the volcano vibrating, feel the vibration under his feet. He took Lindsey's hand and dragged her toward the helicopter.

"What about Eddie?" she screamed.

"There's no time!" Thomas yelled back. "He made his choice! I'm making mine! You want to stay here and die with him?"

They ran. The ground around them was turning gray. Thomas felt the ash on his face and neck, like a heavy coat of talcum powder. He gave his handkerchief to Lindsey and gestured to her to tie it over her mouth and nose. Then they ran again.

Chan Zapata was waiting at the helicopter. So was Carmichael.

Thomas blinked tears and ashes out of his eyes. There was blood all over Carmichael's shirt and face. "I'm okay," Carmichael said. "It's not my blood."

"Oscar . . . ?" Thomas asked.

"Dead. The copter's trashed."

"Ah, Christ," Thomas said.

"What happened?" Lindsey said.

"The Cobra—the big gunship—blew us out of the sky. Oscar got shot up bad. He got us onto the ground, but that was all."

"Christ," Thomas said again. Later, when he had time, he was going to have to deal with this. If it hadn't been for Thomas, Oscar wouldn't have been here at all, wouldn't have had to die.

"It's not fair," Lindsey said. She sounded bewildered. "He was my friend."

"We got one of theirs, though," Carmichael said. He was smiling strangely. "And the rebels got the Cobra while it was trying to finish us off. So they're down to one."

"Who cares?" Lindsey said.

"We do," Thomas said. "It gives us a chance to make it out of here. Let's take it."

"What is this stuff?" Carmichael said. "What's going on?"

"Volcanic ash," Thomas said. "El Chichón just woke up. The whole thing could blow any second. Now get in the goddamned helicopter."

Thomas looked behind him and found Faustino huddled in the shelter of the pyramid. "Where's Carla?" Thomas shouted.

Faustino pointed to the west. Thomas saw her limping off toward Eddie's ragged collection of soldiers.

"One last chance," Thomas said. "You want to come?"

Faustino shook his head.

Thomas just stood there for a few precious seconds, knowing there was nothing else he could do. It would be cruel even to wish him luck. He turned and ran for the helicopter.

Thomas fumbled the key into the ignition lock and turned it to the right. He ran through the checklist as fast as he could. Seat belts fastened, control frictions off, cyclic centered, collective down, AC circuit breakers in. He started to sweat. Carmichael, in the left seat, stared at him. Wondering, probably, what was taking so long.

Battery. Fuel switches. Throttle to engine idle. He checked the voltmeter. At 24 volts he pulled the trigger on the collective and heard the blessed sound of the engine cranking. The rotors started to turn, showering the windscreen with a fresh coating of ash.

Now was when he'd find out if they could still fly. The ash could be clogging the air intakes. The shaking from the mortars and the earthquakes could have torn loose any number of delicate systems. There could be shrapnel in the engine.

Thomas watched the RPM climb. At 40 percent he let off the trigger. The turbine kept running, self-sustaining now. He finished the rest of the checklist and shoved it back in the map case. He throttled up to 6,000 RPM and eased up on the collective. He'd worry about the fuel and the course and the radio once they were in the air.

The ground lurched. He felt his side of the helicopter go down. A crack opened up in the earth between the skids and shot out across the clearing. Steam poured out of the crack. The helicopter was tilting slowly to the left. Fifteen degrees was all it would take. The helicopter would turn over and the rotors would beat themselves to death in the dirt.

Thomas yanked up on the collective. They lifted, the torque pulling the nose to the right despite Thomas pumping the left pedal. The tailboom was swinging toward the wreckage of the burning ramada. He pumped the rudder again and pushed them forward and up with the cyclic.

The ground fell away.

Hot, wet air from the volcano swirled around them, making the rotors lose their grip. Thomas fought the controls, getting the wind behind him and straining for more altitude. The hull began to make ticking noises.

"We're getting shot at," Carmichael said into the intercom. His voice had a forced calm that grated on Thomas' nerves. Thomas shook his head and pointed to the front of the fuselage. Rocks the size of the end of his thumb were falling out of the sky.

Thomas switched on the radio and scanned through the frequencies. There was nothing in English. Marsalis was not broadcasting. Thomas wondered what that meant.

A chatter of static went through the phones and then a shrill voice cut in: "—*el Distrito Federal, temblores los más fuertes en memoria. Y también en Chiapas y Yucatán* —" There was another static burst and Thomas switched the radio off.

"What was that?" Carmichael said. "I couldn't make it out."

"Mexico City," Thomas said. "It's happening all over. Earthquakes." Xu'tan, he thought, though he didn't say it out loud. The end of the world. Just like Eddie had said.

The wind shifted and Thomas turned toward the west. The battlefield opened out in front of them.

Ashes covered the ground. The trees had dropped their leaves, shriveled, and turned into gnarled black skeletons. There were bodies everywhere, bas-relief sculptures in shades of gray. El Chichón lit the night in flickering pulses of light that made shadows leap and fade. Even inside the cockpit the smell of sulfur was overpowering.

The two armies still moved out on the plain. Thomas saw Eddie and twenty or thirty others moving slowly toward the west, leaning into the wind like travelers lost in a blizzard. Carla was in the middle, surrounded and protected by the others. They all had scraps of cloth over their noses and mouths.

Thomas dropped as low as he dared and circled around in front of them. A storm of ash blew up from the rotors. Finally Eddie looked up. Thomas was sure Eddie could see into the lighted cockpit, could see him there. Eddie pulled the handkerchief down from his mouth long enough to show Thomas that he was smiling. The quetzal feathers in his headband blew back from his face like strands of long green hair. He flashed Thomas a peace sign and pulled up the handkerchief and kept walking.

Thomas eased up to two hundred feet. He saw one of the rebels stop and pick up one of the futuristic plastic rifles from a wounded U.S. soldier. He turned it over in his hands and then threw it away. He bent over and helped the soldier to his feet. Then the two of them fell back into line.

So long, Eddie, Thomas thought. Good luck, bro.

Up ahead the ground was split open in a hundred places, some of the cracks ten or fifteen feet across and so deep that Thomas couldn't see the bottom of them. The Fighting 666th had been devastated. Bits and pieces stuck up into the air where the earth hadn't completely swallowed them: the fender of a jeep, an arm, the stock of a rifle.

The rest of the army had collapsed. Thomas saw the muzzle flash of an occasional gunshot, but most of the survivors wandered aimlessly along the edges of the cracks. The rest just sat in the falling ash and stared at the spectacle of El Chichón.

It was like the volcano had done no more than finish the job that Carla and Marsalis had started. The gray, shattered plain was the image of every battlefield in history, all in one.

Thomas felt something inside him let go. It was the end of the obscure guilt he'd carried around for twenty years, that had started back in high school, watching the nightly body counts from Vietnam. It was stupid, he knew, to regret not having gone to a war he knew was wrong, a war where he would almost certainly have been wounded if not killed. But there it was.

He'd grown up, like every male of his generation and all the generations before him, with the idea that war was how a man tested himself. It was where he found out what he was made of. Now he saw that people were the same as the tiniest of subatomic particles. The force it took to measure them was stronger than they were. They couldn't be measured that way without changing them into something completely different than they were before.

And of course he'd seen it all too late. He would carry this vision of ash and smoke and fire with him for the rest of his life. Along with the face of the pilot, Fowler, lying there in the crossroads. Blinking.

Thomas climbed higher and banked toward the north. He saw the last of the U.S. helicopters in the distance, flying away from them. It was headed northeast, toward Veracruz. Running away, Thomas thought. Who could blame them?

"Look," Carmichael said, pointing down. "It's Marsalis."

Sure enough, Thomas thought, pulling the cyclic back into a hover. Marsalis and Billy stood together in the falling ash, turning now to look up at Thomas. Marsalis waved both arms over his head, not realizing that the hovering helicopter no longer belonged to him. Thomas answered him by edging up on the collective and taking them up another fifty feet. Marsalis was shouting something.

Thomas let them begin to drift away. Billy pulled at Marsalis' arm, trying to calm him. Thomas was still watching them when something knocked him forward into his harness.

An instant later he heard an explosion that seemed to tear the very air to pieces. His head rang and he felt like his eardrums had been shredded. It was a full second before he realized that the sound had come from El Chichón.

He pushed in the left rudder and they came around to the south. They were just in time to see a huge ball of burning ash and gases, yellow at the center and red at the edges, come hurtling down the slope of the volcano.

The entire top of the mountain was gone.

Thomas couldn't believe what he was seeing. He turned in his seat. Chan Zapata leaned forward, staring in awe. The fireball was reflected in the darkened window next to his head. Lindsey hadn't even noticed. She lay back with her eyes closed, exhausted.

"Get us out of here," Carmichael said. "Now."

"Yeah," Thomas said. "I guess so." He spun them back around and put the nose down and cranked the throttle all the way open.

He looked down as they began to climb. Marsalis and Billy were motionless, staring east across the burned-out plain. They watched the dust cloud rising from Eddie's weaponless army as it moved slowly, inexorably toward them.

Then the figures shrank away to nothing. Thomas flew on into the darkness, toward the coast and the remains of his world.

L INDSEY STARED AT THE ceiling for a long time without moving. Finally she lifted her left hand over her face and looked at her watch. Two o'clock. From the light seeping in around the door she knew it was afternoon.

Around midnight Thomas had landed the helicopter in a field outside Villahermosa. He made them walk more than a mile down the highway before letting them rest. The smell of the asphalt and the roar of the passing cars seemed like something out of a dream.

Thomas left them sitting behind a billboard and walked on to find a phone. He came back for them an hour later in a taxi and took them to the Hotel Villahermosa Viva, a U.S.-style motel on the highway. Carmichael paid for the rooms, telling them it was all going on his expense account.

The place was luxurious in a uniquely Mexican style. The ceilings were high, the furniture was massive, there was a wet bar and a refrigerator in each room. The huge plate-glass windows opened on a view of a brick wall. The carpet was deep pile shag and had a large water stain next to the door. The air conditioner worked, but made groaning noises.

None of that mattered to Lindsey. There was hot water, lots of hot water. Afterward she and Thomas crawled into separate double beds and fell asleep.

She was still exhausted, but she didn't think she could sleep anymore. Thomas lay across the room with one arm over his face, breathing raggedly. Lindsey sat up in bed and felt her stomach turn over. Her temples seemed to pinch in against her brain. She staggered into the bathroom and let her stomach heave, though there was nothing in it. When it was over she washed her face and brushed her teeth and started back toward the bed.

Thomas was sitting up. "You okay?"

"Yeah," she said. "I'm fine. It's just . . ."

"Morning sickness," Thomas said.

Lindsey nodded.

"Jesus Christ," Thomas said. "You're pregnant."

"Maybe," Lindsey said. "Maybe it's just . . . everything I've been through." Or, she thought, maybe it's just wishful thinking.

"How long has this been going on?"

"It just started," she said. "I mean, I should be getting my period this week. If I'm going to. But I don't think I am."

"Isn't this a little early to be getting sick?"

"Kind of," Lindsey said. "I knew somebody once started throwing up the day after she conceived." She sat on the edge of the bed, facing him. "I would just as soon you hadn't found out."

Thomas said, "I would have found out sooner or later. Wouldn't I?"

They hadn't talked yet about what came next. Lindsey just let the silence hang.

Thomas sat back, rubbed at his eyes, put his glasses on. "Who's the father?" he said.

She could have lied to him. But she didn't want it that way. "You or Eddie," she said. "I don't know which."

"Christ," he said.

"It's not like I'm laying this off on you, okay? It's my

kid. I'm going to raise it. You don't have to have any part of it."

"If it's my kid, I *am* part of it. Me and Eddie are the same blood type and everything else. There's probably not a test in the world that could tell which of us it is."

"You'll just have to find some way to live with it."

"Are you even giving me that chance? *Am* I going to live with you? Are you coming back to Austin with me?"

She licked her lips. "Not . . . just yet."

"Is that how it's going to be? After everything we've been through, you're just going back to San Diego and be a welfare mother?"

Lindsey shook her head. "I don't know how to explain it to you. I *have* changed. I can take care of myself." She'd proved to herself that she could learn on her own. They had those little Macintosh computers at work that she'd always been afraid of. Now she saw how she could teach herself to do something with them. Something that would take her out of the rut she'd been in for the last ten years.

And more than that. Chan Ma'ax believed the old world was ending and a new one was about to start. Eddie and Thomas both had talked about it. Lindsey wanted in on that new world. She could sense the shape of it as surely as she could feel the child already starting to grow inside her. There were things she had to learn so that if she did go to Thomas it would be on her own terms.

"You have to let me do this," she said.

Thomas nodded. He'd pulled back into himself and his eyes had gotten very distant. She knew it was because of the way she'd hurt him. After a while he got out of bed and put his clothes on, keeping his back to her. "We should get started," he said. "We've still got a long way to go."

Chan Zapata caught a bus headed for San Cristóbal. Everybody promised to write. It was easier to just go ahead and say it, whether they believed it or not.

They managed to get on the 9:35 flight to Mexico City

that night. The airline also found Lindsey a 3 A.M. connection to LAX. Thomas would have to wait until seven for the regular flight to Houston.

They were only an hour late getting in to Mexico City. The airport was worse than it had been two weeks before. There were two- and three-hour waits to get into the bars and restaurants. Lindsey sat with the luggage in an orange chair with a ripped vinyl cushion. Carmichael went off to call his editor. Thomas found a vending machine and bought them paper cups of coffee. The coffee was dark and hot but didn't taste like anything at all.

Carmichael came back a half hour later. "More earthquakes," he said. "Argentina and New Zealand. They had some more shocks on the San Andreas Fault, too," he told Lindsey. "You want to think twice about going back out there."

In fact the idea of setting foot in California was starting to scare the hell out of her. Every time she even thought about earthquakes it was like it was all happening to her again. Her stomach churned and she started to sweat. "I have to go, at least for a little while," she said. "My parents are there, my apartment . . . there's stuff I have to take care of."

"If you believe the Mayans, we've still got twenty-five years," Thomas said. "I mean, there's always been earthquakes in Mexico and California. Maybe it's nothing."

"You don't believe that," Carmichael said.

"No," Thomas said. "It's going to get worse. Slowly, steadily worse. In twenty years . . . well, I think we need to all start looking for some solid ground."

"They've been watching the wire services up there," Carmichael said. "There's at least two different reports of a quote refugee army endquote headed toward Villahermosa. There's hundreds of them, supposedly. Rebels, peasants, U.S. soldiers. They say there's a woman on crutches and a Northamerican in a litter, dressed out in feathers and Mayan robes."

"Eddie," Lindsey said.

"Well," Thomas said. "At least he's still alive."

"I knew he was," Lindsey said. "I could feel it."

"I'm going to stay on here," Carmichael said. "Just for another day or so. Just to see how it comes out."

"You keep saying that," Lindsey said.

"Yeah, well," Carmichael said. "Things keep coming up."

They put Carmichael in a cab and waved goodbye. Then Thomas walked Lindsey to her gate. "Don't go," Thomas said. "Come back to Austin with me."

"And do what?"

"Start over. I'm going to sell the university a project like we had in Cuernavaca. We can get Shapiro and Geisler and everybody together again. It'll work."

"Maybe it will," she said. "But not for me, not just yet. Oh, Thomas, it's not like I don't care. I do. I just need some time first. Maybe in a few weeks. I've been through too much to just go off with another man right now."

"I wish—"

Lindsey touched his mouth with one finger. "No wishes, Thomas. This is the real world. Look, I found you before. I can find you again."

A voice called her flight in Spanish. She hugged him and picked up her suitcase. Then she leaned up and kissed Thomas one last time and ran to get in line for her plane.

AUTHOR'S NOTE

DETAILS OF THE PROJECT in Cuernavaca were taken from *Bioshelters, Ocean Arks, City Farming* by Nancy Jack Todd and John Todd (Sierra Club Books, 1984). Descriptions of the Lacondon Indians came from *The Last Lords of Palenque* by Victor Perera and Robert D. Bruce (Little, Brown, 1982). I used *The World of the Ancient Maya* by John S. Henderson (Cornell, 1981) as my principal reference on the Classic Maya. For an overview of "new age" science and philosophy (including the work of Ilya Prigogine), I recommend *The Aquarian Conspiracy* by Marilyn Ferguson (Tarcher, 1979). A more detailed study of dissipative structures is available in *Order Out of Chaos* by Ilya Prigogine and Isabelle Stengers (Bantam, 1984).

ABOUT THE AUTHOR

Lewis Shiner's short fiction has appeared in *Omni, The Fiction Magazine, Twilight Zone,* and many other markets. His work has been reprinted in *The Year's Best SF, Mirrorshades, In the Field of Fire,* and other anthologies. His previous novel, *Frontera,* was nominated for both the Nebula and Philip K. Dick awards. He lives in Austin, Texas.

SPECTRA SPECIAL EDITIONS

Bantam Spectra Special Editions spotlight some of Spectra's finest authors in their top form. Authors found on this list all have received high critical praise and many have won some of science fiction and fantasy's highest honors. Don't miss them!

☐ **Out on Blue Six** (27763-4 • $4.50/ $5.50 in Canada) by Ian McDonald. On the run in a society where the state determines one's position in life, Metheny Ard takes charge of her fate, turning from model citizen to active rebel.

☐ **The Nexus** (27345-2 • $4.50/ $5.50 in Canada) by Mike McQuay. The tale of an autistic girl who can literally work miracles and the reporter who brings her story to the world.

☐ **Phases of Gravity** (27764-2 • $4.50/ $5.50 in Canada) by Dan Simmons. An ex-astronaut goes on a personal odyssey to centers of power all over the earth in search of an elusive—but powerful—fate he senses awaiting him.

Buy **Out on Blue Six, The Nexus** and **Phases of Gravity** wherever Bantam Spectra books are sold, or use this page for ordering: